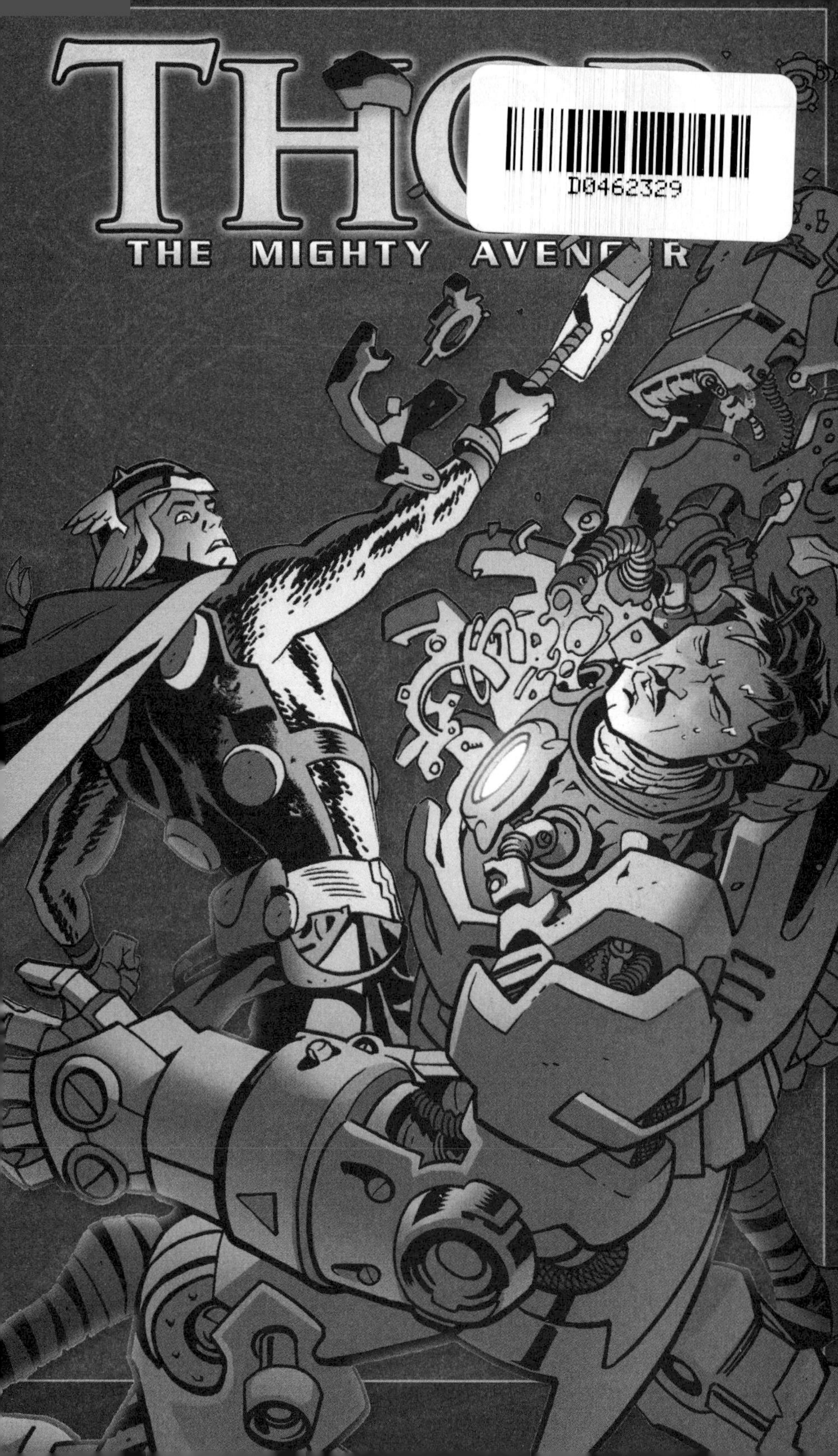
TH
THE MIGHTY AVEN

THOR
THE MIGHTY AVENGER

Writer
ROGER LANGRIDGE

Artist
CHRIS SAMNEE

Colorist **MATTHEW WILSON**

Letterers **VC'S CHRIS ELIOPOULOS (ISSUE #5)
& RUS WOOTON (ISSUES #6-8)**

Cover Artists **CHRIS SAMNEE & MATTHEW WILSON**

Assistant Editor **MICHAEL HORWITZ**

Editors **NATHAN COSBY & SANA AMANAT**

Journey Into Mystery #85-86 (1962)

Writers **STAN LEE & LARRY LIEBER**

Penciler **JACK KIRBY**

Inker **DICK AYERS**

Collection Editor **CORY LEVINE**
Editorial Assistants **JAMES EMMETT & JOE HOCHSTEIN**
Assistant Editors **MATT MASDEU, ALEX STARBUCK
& NELSON RIBEIRO**
Editors, Special Projects **JENNIFER GRÜNWALD
& MARK D. BEAZLEY**
Masterworks Editor **CORY SEDLMEIER**
Senior Editor, Special Projects **JEFF YOUNGQUIST**
Senior Vice President of Sales **DAVID GABRIEL**
Book Design **ARLENE SO**

Editor in Chief **AXEL ALONSO**
Chief Creative Officer **JOE QUESADA**
Publisher **DAN BUCKLEY**
Executive Producer **ALAN FINE**

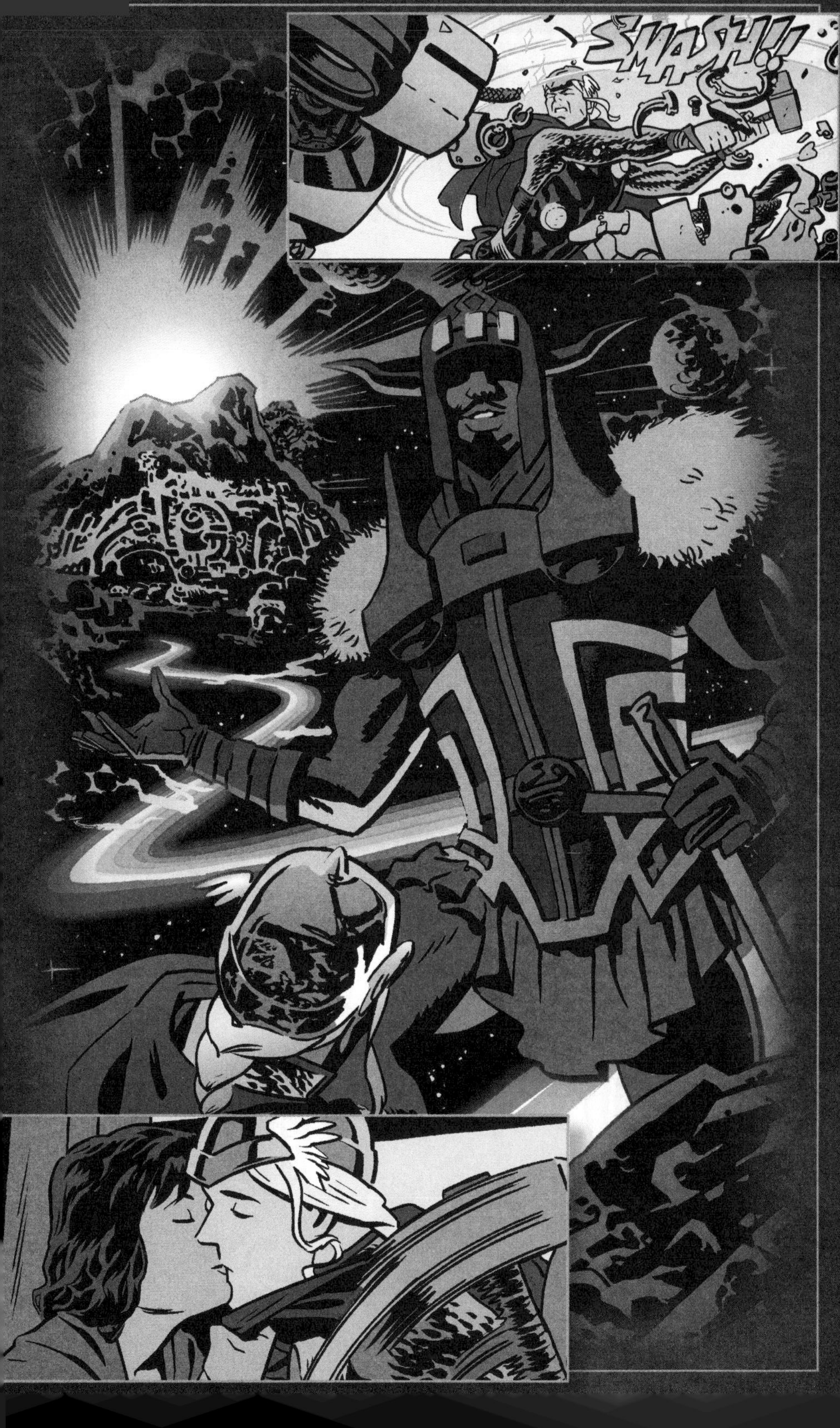
SMASH!!

THOR THE MIGHTY AVENGER #5

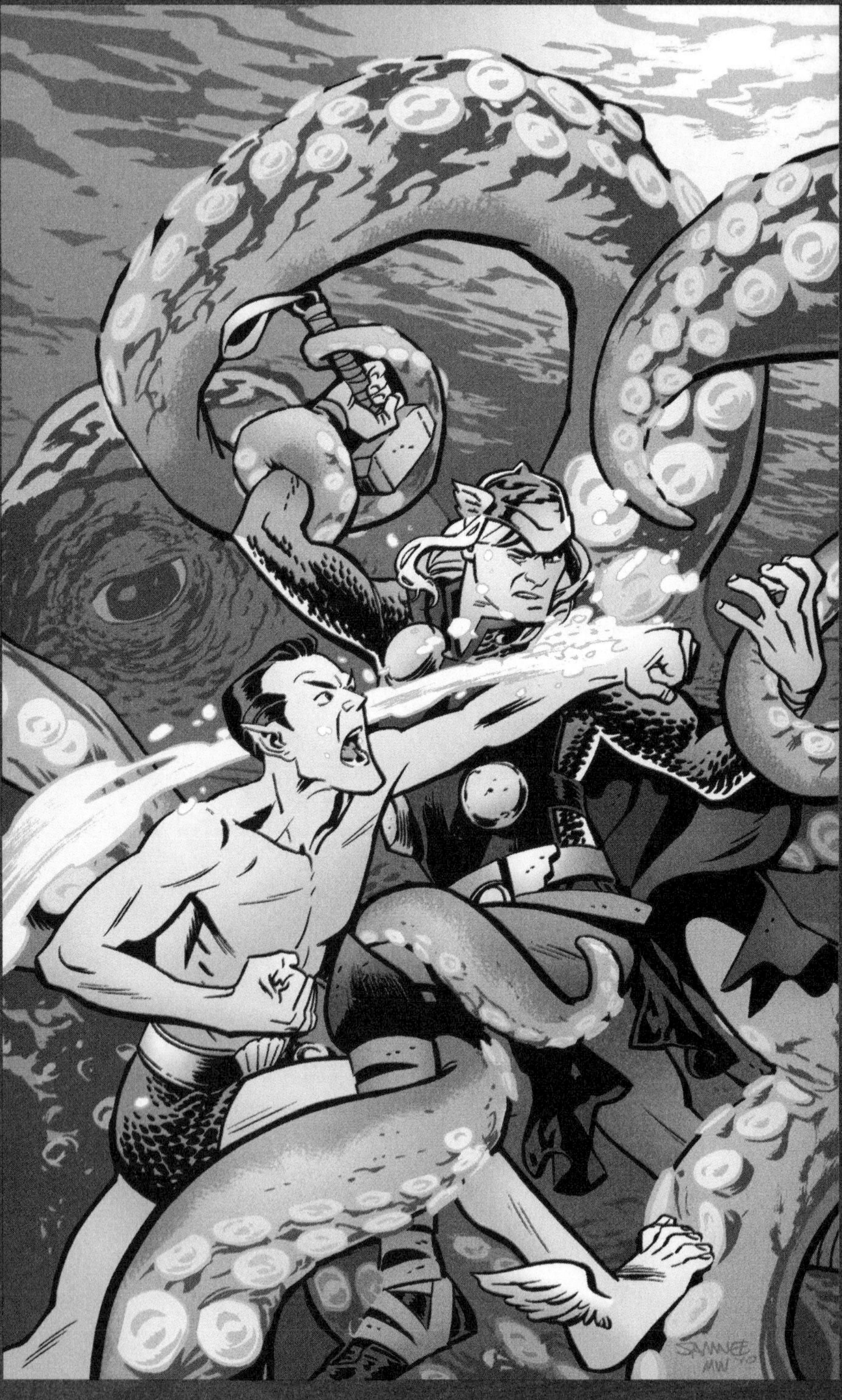

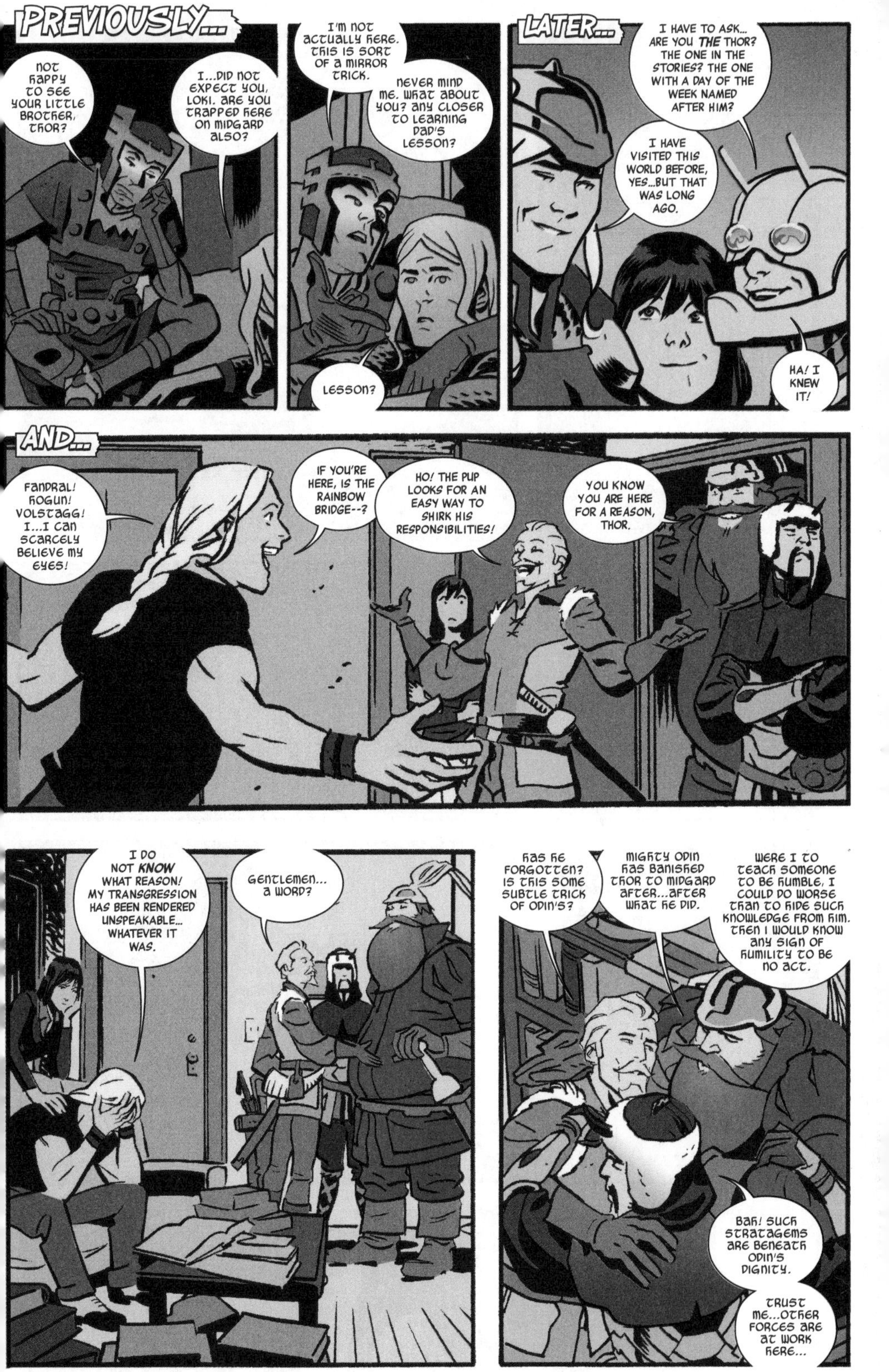
PREVIOUSLY...
NOT HAPPY TO SEE YOUR LITTLE BROTHER, THOR?
I...DID NOT EXPECT YOU, LOKI. ARE YOU TRAPPED HERE ON MIDGARD ALSO?
I'M NOT ACTUALLY HERE. THIS IS SORT OF A MIRROR TRICK.
NEVER MIND ME. WHAT ABOUT YOU? ANY CLOSER TO LEARNING DAD'S LESSON?
LESSON?
LATER...
I HAVE TO ASK... ARE YOU THE THOR? THE ONE IN THE STORIES? THE ONE WITH A DAY OF THE WEEK NAMED AFTER HIM?
I HAVE VISITED THIS WORLD BEFORE, YES...BUT THAT WAS LONG AGO.
HA! I KNEW IT!
AND...
FANDRAL! HOGUN! VOLSTAGG! I...I CAN SCARCELY BELIEVE MY EYES!
IF YOU'RE HERE, IS THE RAINBOW BRIDGE--?
HO! THE PUP LOOKS FOR AN EASY WAY TO SHIRK HIS RESPONSIBILITIES!
YOU KNOW YOU ARE HERE FOR A REASON, THOR.
I DO NOT KNOW WHAT REASON! MY TRANSGRESSION HAS BEEN RENDERED UNSPEAKABLE... WHATEVER IT WAS.
GENTLEMEN... A WORD?
HAS HE FORGOTTEN? IS THIS SOME SUBTLE TRICK OF ODIN'S?
MIGHTY ODIN HAS BANISHED THOR TO MIDGARD AFTER...AFTER WHAT HE DID.
WERE I TO TEACH SOMEONE TO BE HUMBLE, I COULD DO WORSE THAN TO HIDE SUCH KNOWLEDGE FROM HIM. THEN I WOULD KNOW ANY SIGN OF HUMILITY TO BE NO ACT.
BAH! SUCH STRATAGEMS ARE BENEATH ODIN'S DIGNITY.
TRUST ME...OTHER FORCES ARE AT WORK HERE...

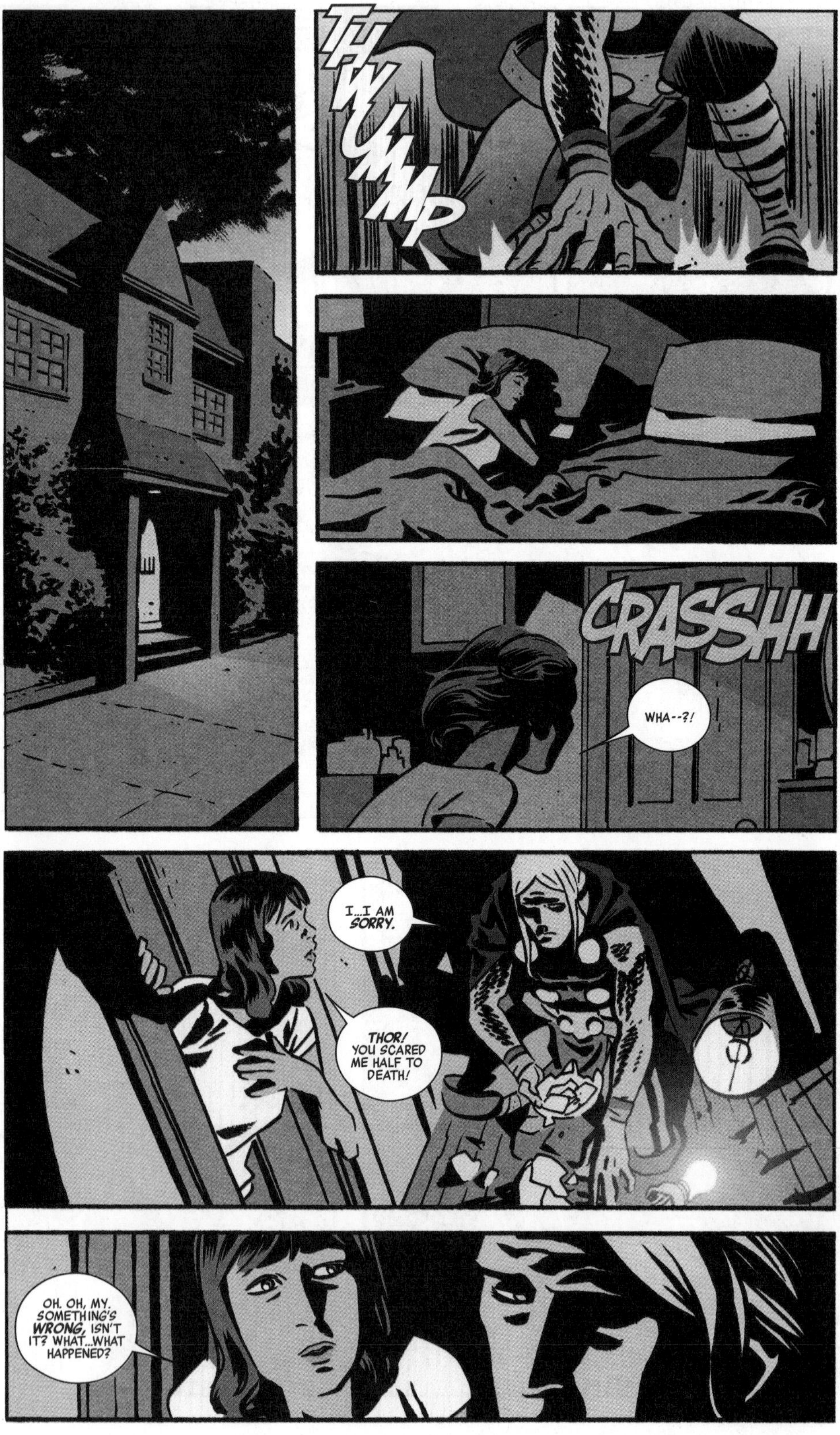
THWUMMP
CRASSHH
WHA--?!
I...I AM SORRY.
THOR! YOU SCARED ME HALF TO DEATH!
OH. OH, MY. SOMETHING'S WRONG, ISN'T IT? WHAT...WHAT HAPPENED?

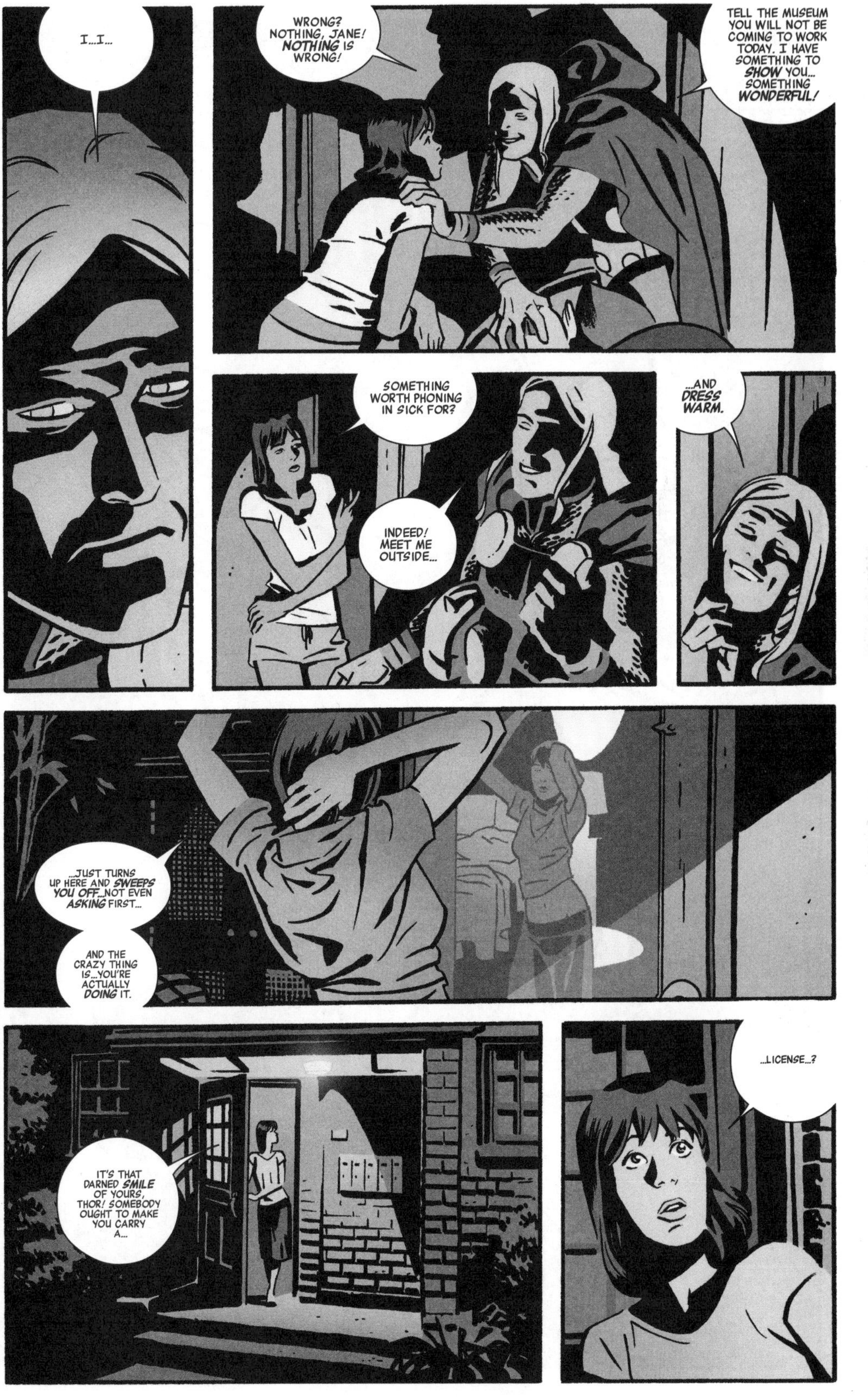
I...I...
WRONG? NOTHING, JANE! NOTHING IS WRONG!
TELL THE MUSEUM YOU WILL NOT BE COMING TO WORK TODAY. I HAVE SOMETHING TO SHOW YOU... SOMETHING WONDERFUL!
SOMETHING WORTH PHONING IN SICK FOR?
INDEED! MEET ME OUTSIDE...
...AND DRESS WARM.
...JUST TURNS UP HERE AND SWEEPS YOU OFF...NOT EVEN ASKING FIRST...
AND THE CRAZY THING IS...YOU'RE ACTUALLY DOING IT.
IT'S THAT DARNED SMILE OF YOURS, THOR! SOMEBODY OUGHT TO MAKE YOU CARRY A...
...LICENSE...?

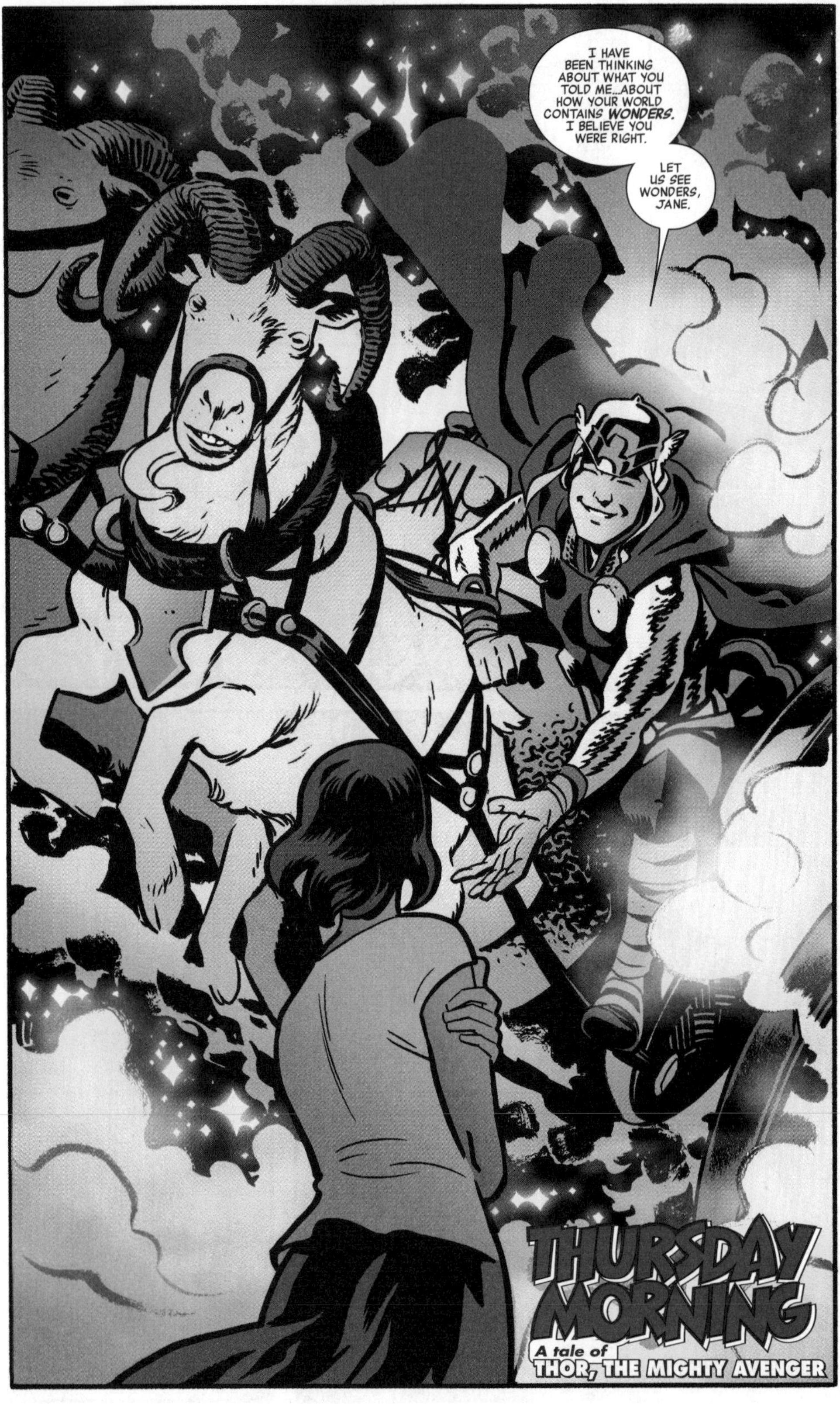
I HAVE BEEN THINKING ABOUT WHAT YOU TOLD ME...ABOUT HOW YOUR WORLD CONTAINS WONDERS. I BELIEVE YOU WERE RIGHT.
LET US SEE WONDERS, JANE.
THURSDAY MORNING
A tale of
THOR, THE MIGHTY AVENGER

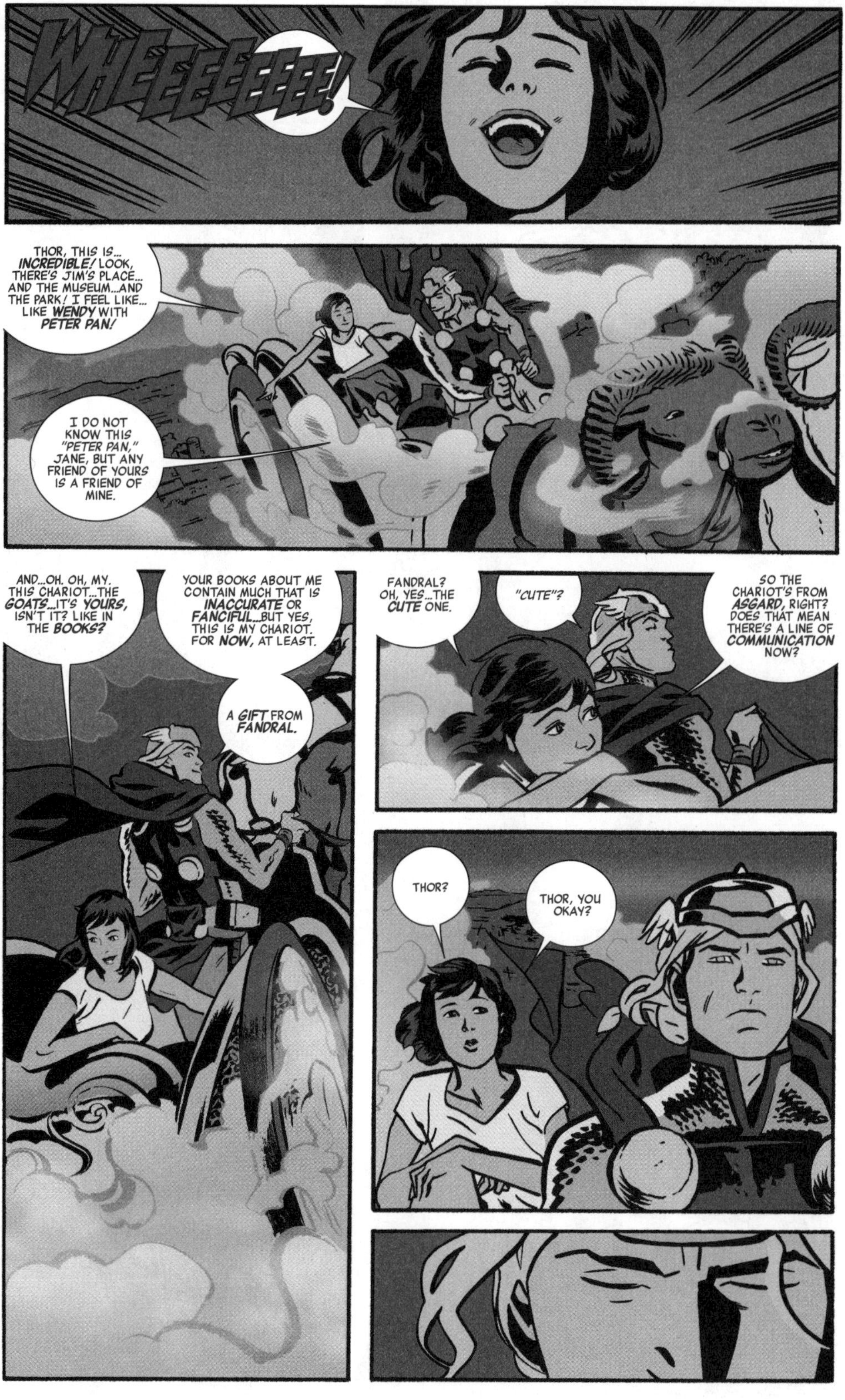
WHEEEEEEEE!
THOR, THIS IS... INCREDIBLE! LOOK, THERE'S JIM'S PLACE... AND THE MUSEUM...AND THE PARK! I FEEL LIKE... LIKE WENDY WITH PETER PAN!
I DO NOT KNOW THIS "PETER PAN," JANE, BUT ANY FRIEND OF YOURS IS A FRIEND OF MINE.
AND...OH. OH, MY. THIS CHARIOT...THE GOATS...IT'S YOURS, ISN'T IT? LIKE IN THE BOOKS?
YOUR BOOKS ABOUT ME CONTAIN MUCH THAT IS INACCURATE OR FANCIFUL...BUT YES, THIS IS MY CHARIOT. FOR NOW, AT LEAST.
A GIFT FROM FANDRAL.
FANDRAL? OH, YES...THE CUTE ONE.
"CUTE"?
SO THE CHARIOT'S FROM ASGARD, RIGHT? DOES THAT MEAN THERE'S A LINE OF COMMUNICATION NOW?
THOR?
THOR, YOU OKAY?

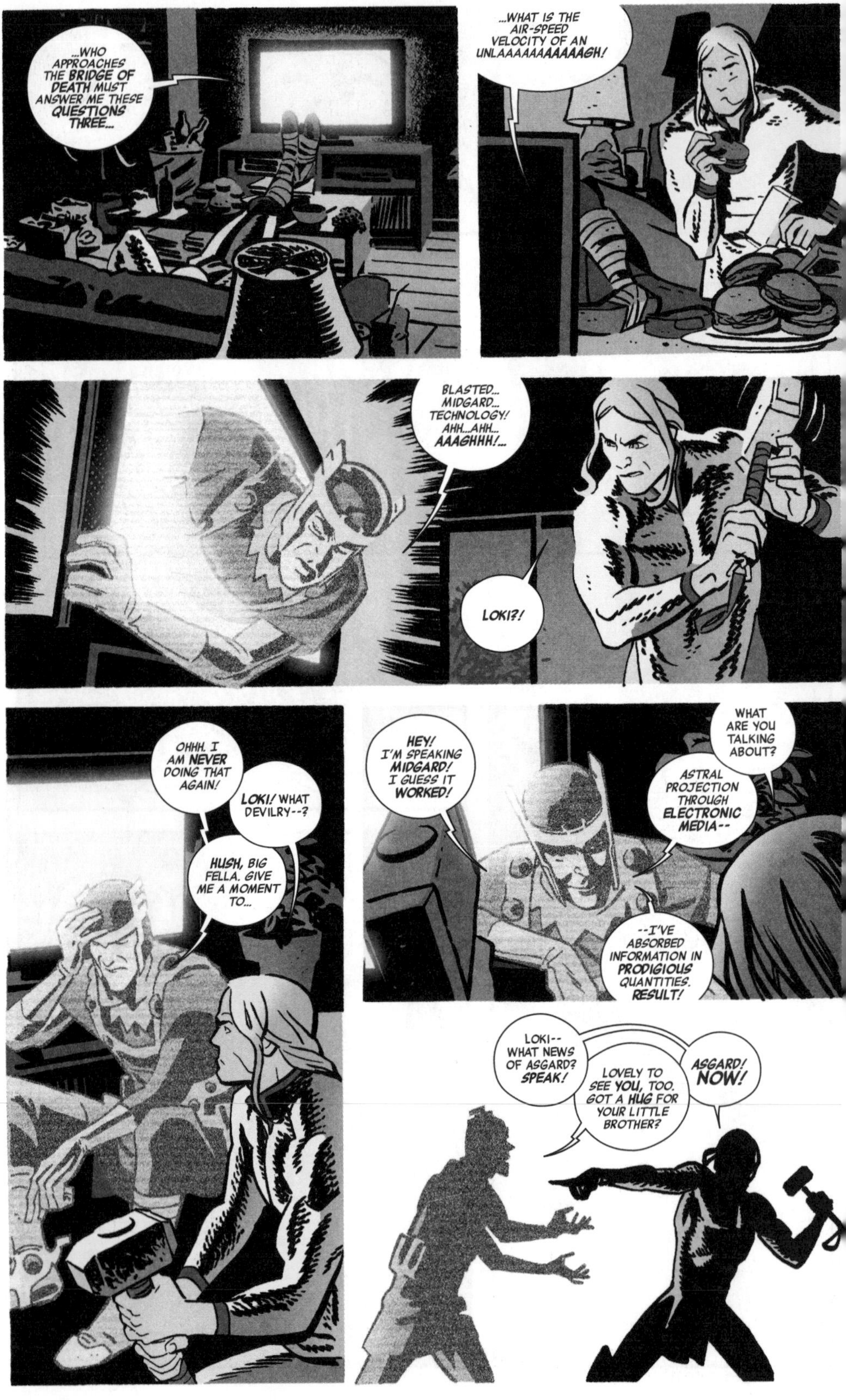
...WHO APPROACHES THE BRIDGE OF DEATH MUST ANSWER ME THESE QUESTIONS THREE...
...WHAT IS THE AIR-SPEED VELOCITY OF AN UNLAAAAAAAAAAAAGH!
BLASTED... MIDGARD... TECHNOLOGY! AHH...AHH... AAAGHHH!...
LOKI?!
OHHH. I AM NEVER DOING THAT AGAIN!
LOKI! WHAT DEVILRY--?
HUSH, BIG FELLA. GIVE ME A MOMENT TO...
HEY! I'M SPEAKING MIDGARD! I GUESS IT WORKED!
WHAT ARE YOU TALKING ABOUT?
ASTRAL PROJECTION THROUGH ELECTRONIC MEDIA--
--I'VE ABSORBED INFORMATION IN PRODIGIOUS QUANTITIES. RESULT!
LOKI-- WHAT NEWS OF ASGARD? SPEAK!
LOVELY TO SEE YOU, TOO. GOT A HUG FOR YOUR LITTLE BROTHER?
ASGARD! NOW!

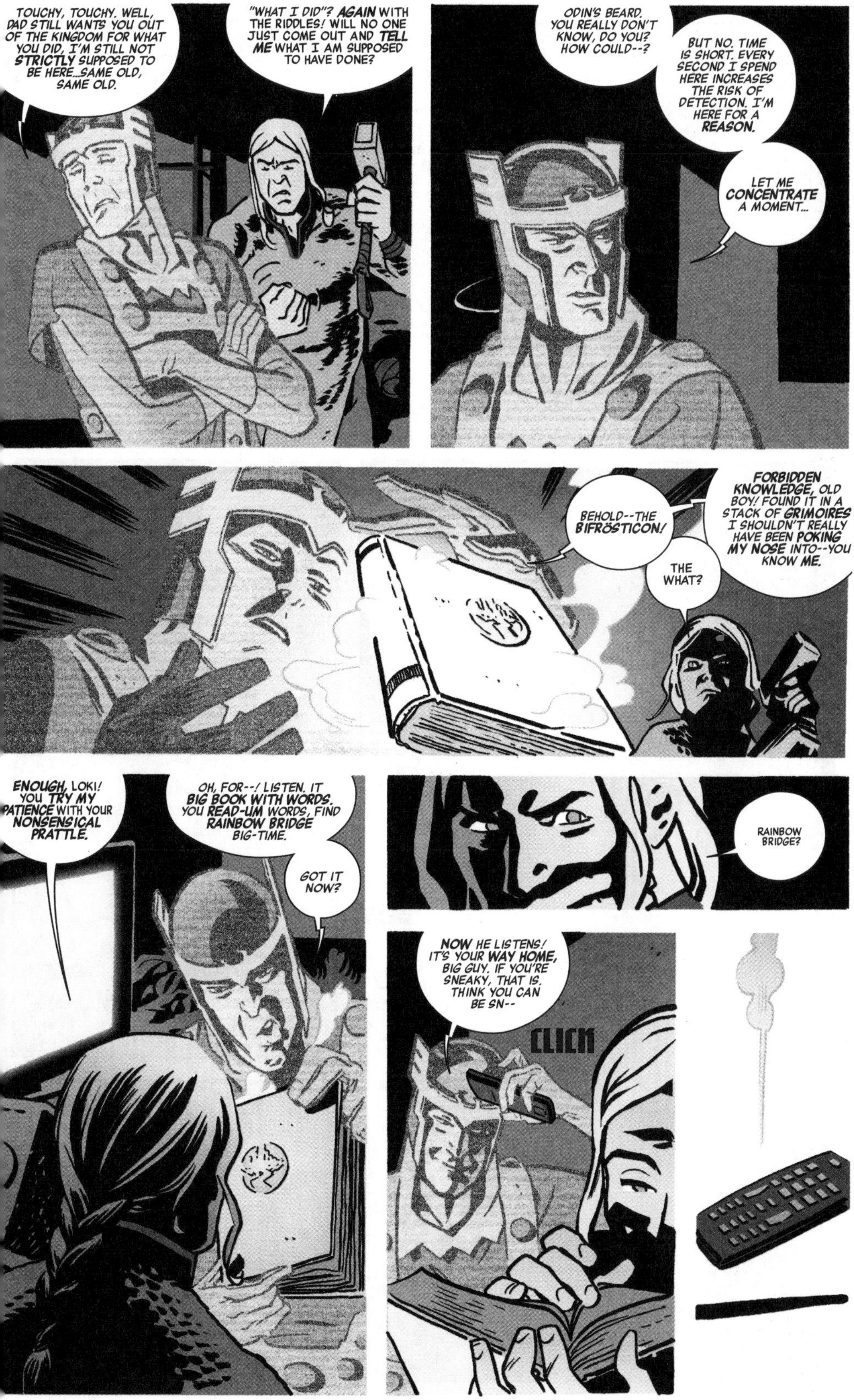
TOUCHY, TOUCHY. WELL, DAD STILL WANTS YOU OUT OF THE KINGDOM FOR WHAT YOU DID, I'M STILL NOT STRICTLY SUPPOSED TO BE HERE...SAME OLD, SAME OLD.
"WHAT I DID"? AGAIN WITH THE RIDDLES! WILL NO ONE JUST COME OUT AND TELL ME WHAT I AM SUPPOSED TO HAVE DONE?
ODIN'S BEARD. YOU REALLY DON'T KNOW, DO YOU? HOW COULD--?
BUT NO. TIME IS SHORT. EVERY SECOND I SPEND HERE INCREASES THE RISK OF DETECTION. I'M HERE FOR A REASON.
LET ME CONCENTRATE A MOMENT...
BEHOLD--THE BIFRÖSTICON!
THE WHAT?
FORBIDDEN KNOWLEDGE, OLD BOY! FOUND IT IN A STACK OF GRIMOIRES I SHOULDN'T REALLY HAVE BEEN POKING MY NOSE INTO--YOU KNOW ME.
ENOUGH, LOKI! YOU TRY MY PATIENCE WITH YOUR NONSENSICAL PRATTLE.
OH, FOR--! LISTEN. IT BIG BOOK WITH WORDS. YOU READ-UM WORDS, FIND RAINBOW BRIDGE BIG-TIME.
GOT IT NOW?
RAINBOW BRIDGE?
NOW HE LISTENS! IT'S YOUR WAY HOME, BIG GUY. IF YOU'RE SNEAKY, THAT IS. THINK YOU CAN BE SN--
CLICK

THOR!

HMM?

YOU *SPACED OUT* ON ME THERE. I WOULDN'T MIND, BUT YOU'RE THE *DESIGNATED DRIVER.*

I APOLOGIZE. I PROMISED YOU *WONDERS,* DID I NOT?

THEN LET US BEGIN...

...HERE!

OH!

IN *ASGARD* WE HAVE A TREE CALLED *YGGDRASIL.* IT IS SAID TO CONTAIN *ENTIRE* WORLDS.

THESE SEQUOIAS CONTAIN *ECHOES* OF THAT GREAT TREE. I CANNOT SHOW YOU YGGDRASIL...

...AND YET I AM CONFIDENT THAT THESE *EARTHLY* TREES WILL NOT *DISAPPOINT.*

THEY'RE...THEY'RE *MAGNIFICENT.*

YES, THEY ARE. ONE OF THE BIGGEST LIVING ORGANISMS ON EARTH.

WOULD YOU LIKE TO SEE A *BIGGER* ONE?

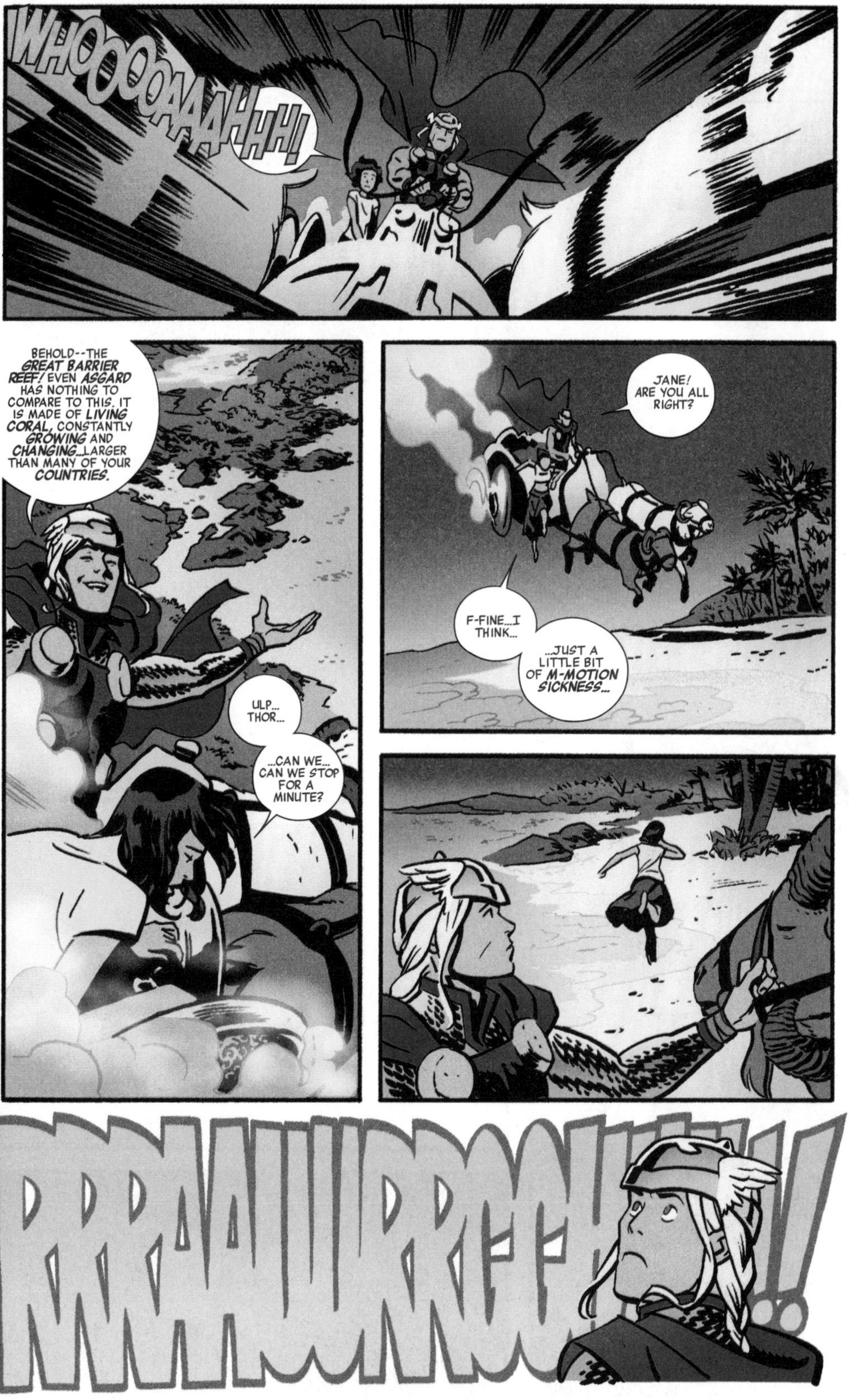
WHOOOOAAAHHH!
BEHOLD--THE GREAT BARRIER REEF! EVEN ASGARD HAS NOTHING TO COMPARE TO THIS. IT IS MADE OF LIVING CORAL, CONSTANTLY GROWING AND CHANGING...LARGER THAN MANY OF YOUR COUNTRIES.
ULP... THOR...
...CAN WE... CAN WE STOP FOR A MINUTE?
JANE! ARE YOU ALL RIGHT?
F-FINE...I THINK...
...JUST A LITTLE BIT OF M-MOTION SICKNESS...
RRRAAUURRGGHH!!

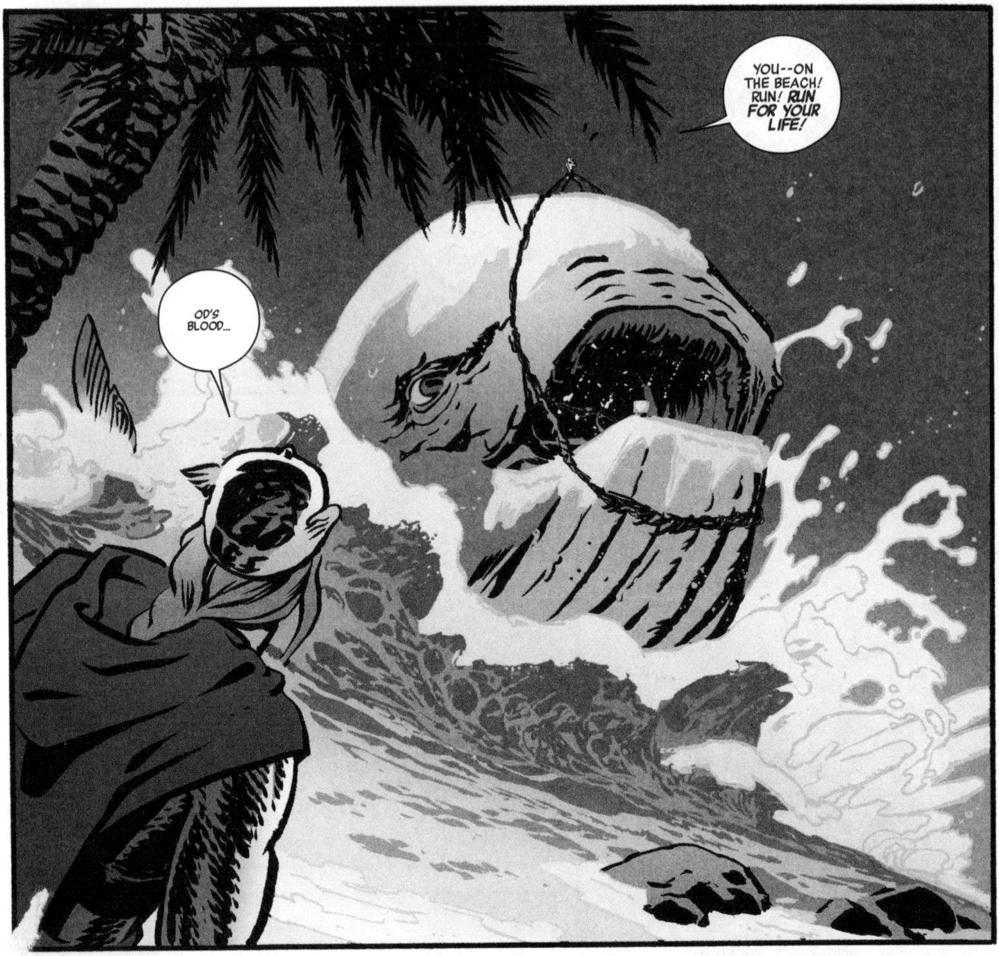
YOU--ON THE BEACH! RUN! RUN FOR YOUR LIFE!
OD'S BLOOD...

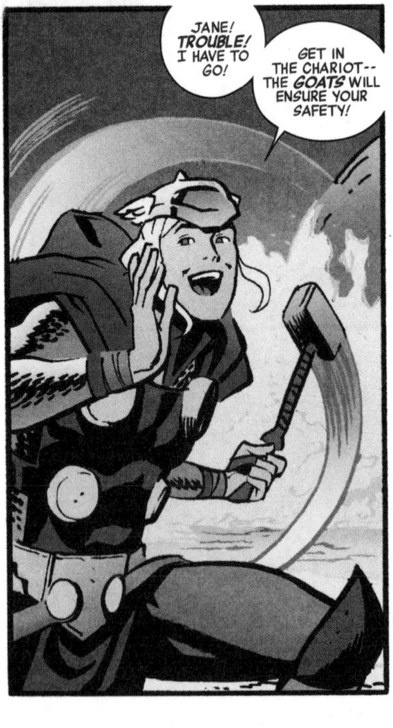
JANE! TROUBLE! I HAVE TO GO!
GET IN THE CHARIOT-- THE GOATS WILL ENSURE YOUR SAFETY!

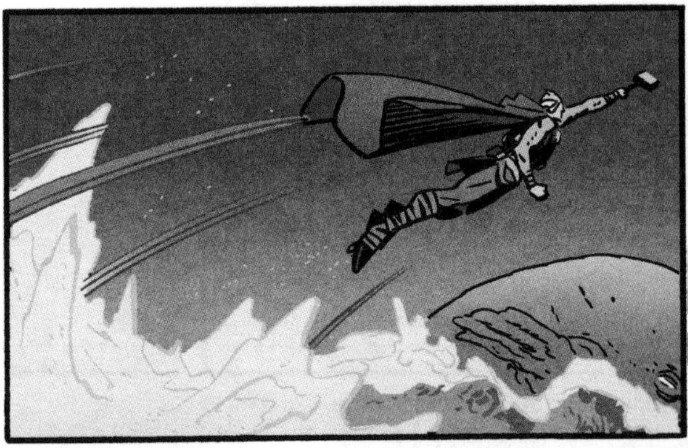

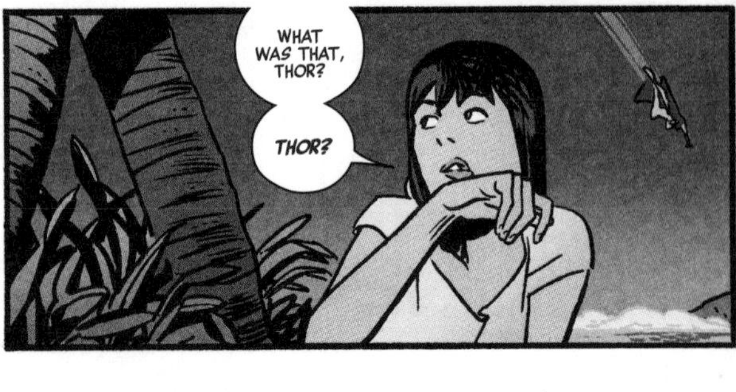
WHAT WAS THAT, THOR?
THOR?

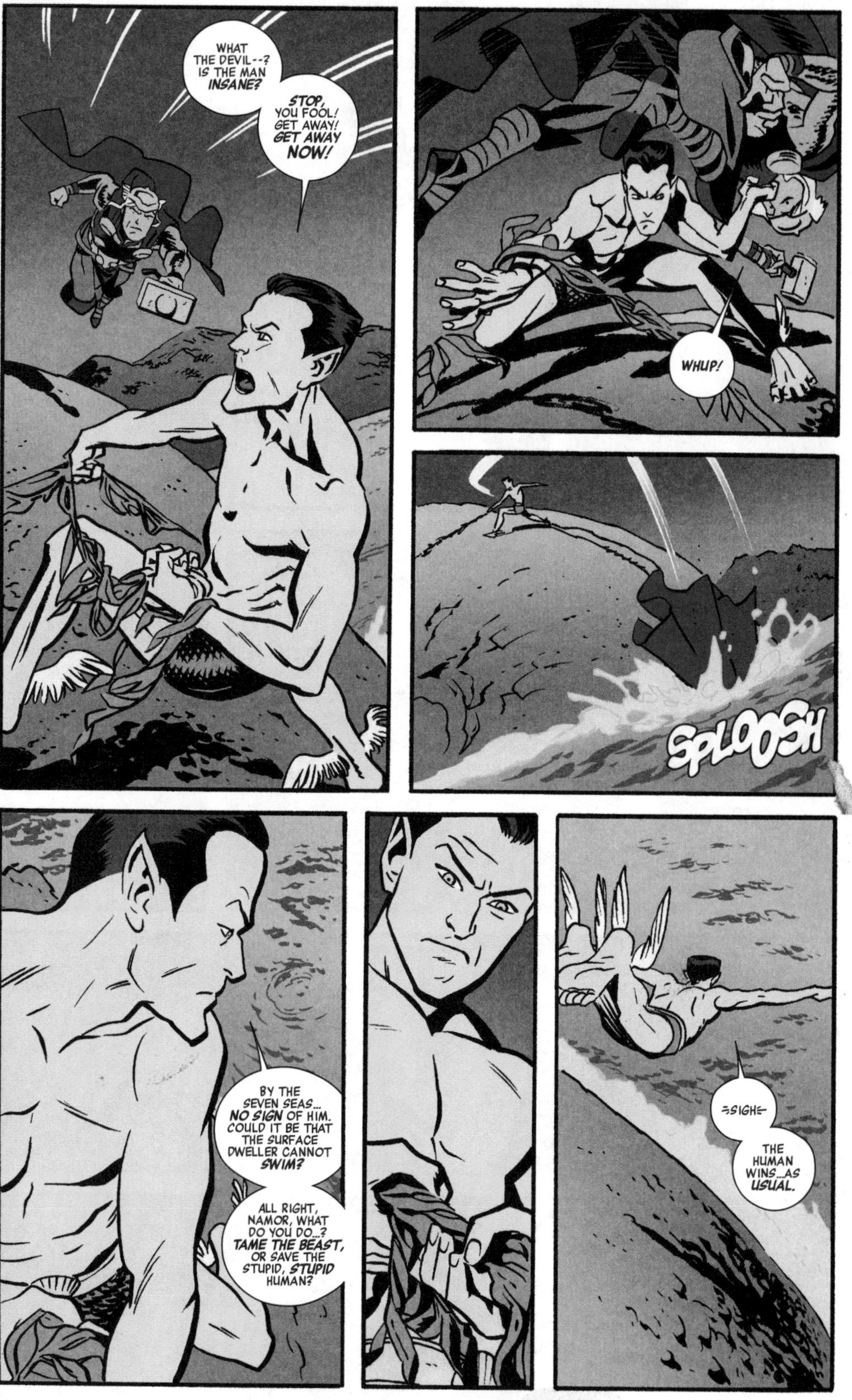

WHAT THE DEVIL--? IS THE MAN INSANE?
STOP, YOU FOOL! GET AWAY! GET AWAY NOW!
WHUP!
SPLOOSH
BY THE SEVEN SEAS... NO SIGN OF HIM. COULD IT BE THAT THE SURFACE DWELLER CANNOT SWIM?
ALL RIGHT, NAMOR, WHAT DO YOU DO...? TAME THE BEAST, OR SAVE THE STUPID, STUPID HUMAN?
=SIGH=
THE HUMAN WINS...AS USUAL.

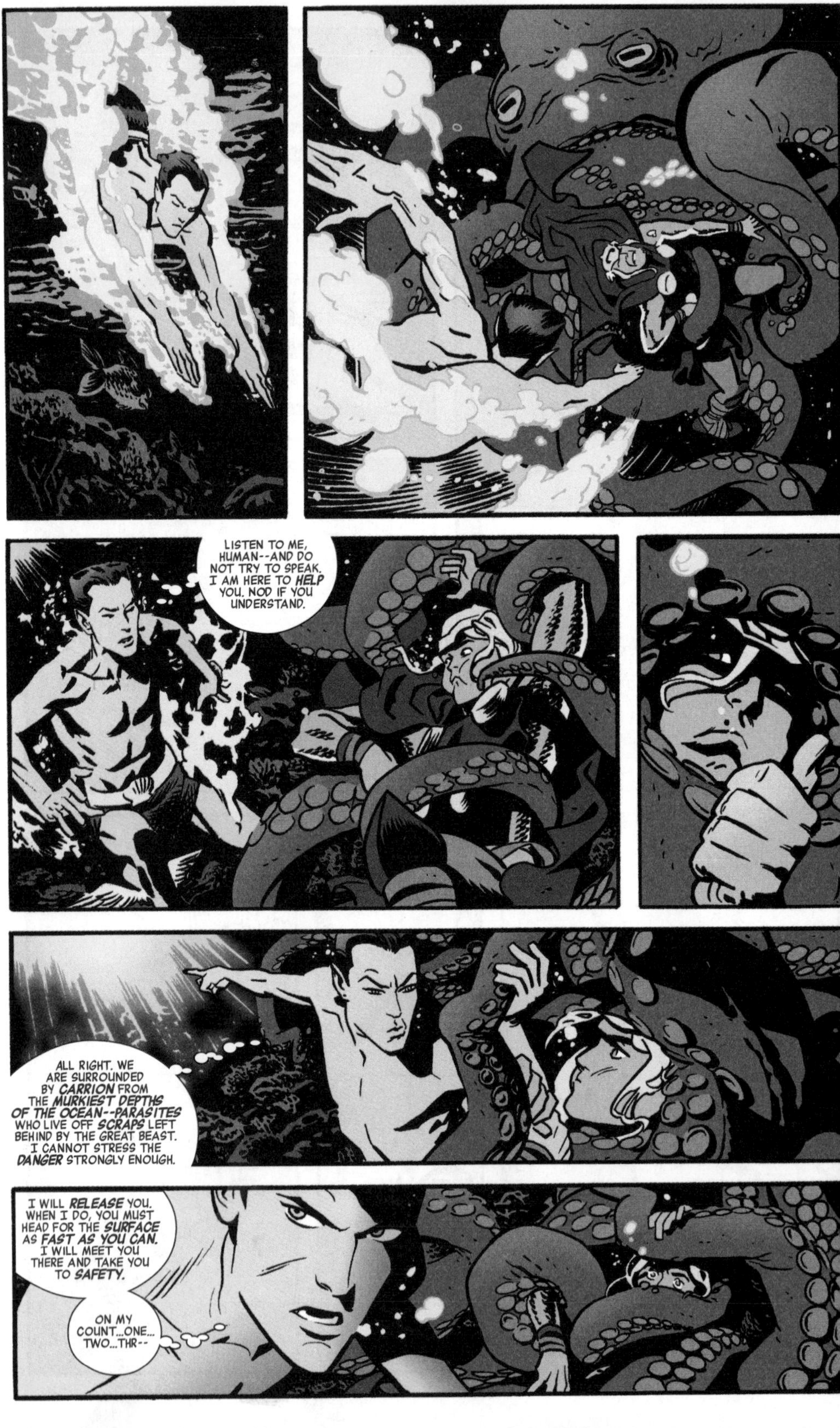
LISTEN TO ME, HUMAN--AND DO NOT TRY TO SPEAK. I AM HERE TO HELP YOU. NOD IF YOU UNDERSTAND.
ALL RIGHT. WE ARE SURROUNDED BY CARRION FROM THE MURKIEST DEPTHS OF THE OCEAN--PARASITES WHO LIVE OFF SCRAPS LEFT BEHIND BY THE GREAT BEAST. I CANNOT STRESS THE DANGER STRONGLY ENOUGH.
I WILL RELEASE YOU. WHEN I DO, YOU MUST HEAD FOR THE SURFACE AS FAST AS YOU CAN. I WILL MEET YOU THERE AND TAKE YOU TO SAFETY.
ON MY COUNT...ONE... TWO...THR--

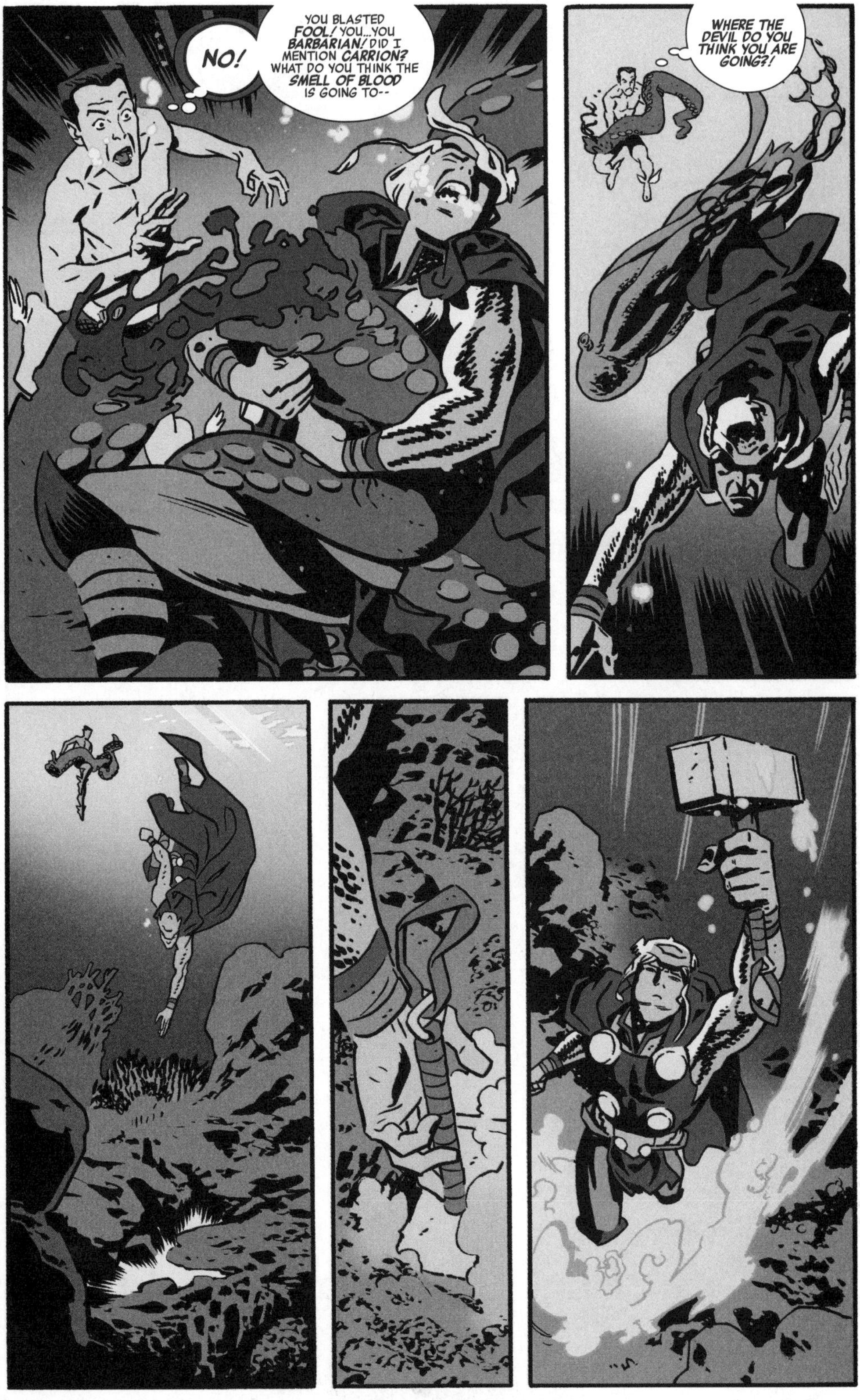
NO!
YOU BLASTED FOOL! YOU...YOU BARBARIAN! DID I MENTION CARRION? WHAT DO YOU THINK THE SMELL OF BLOOD IS GOING TO--
WHERE THE DEVIL DO YOU THINK YOU ARE GOING?!

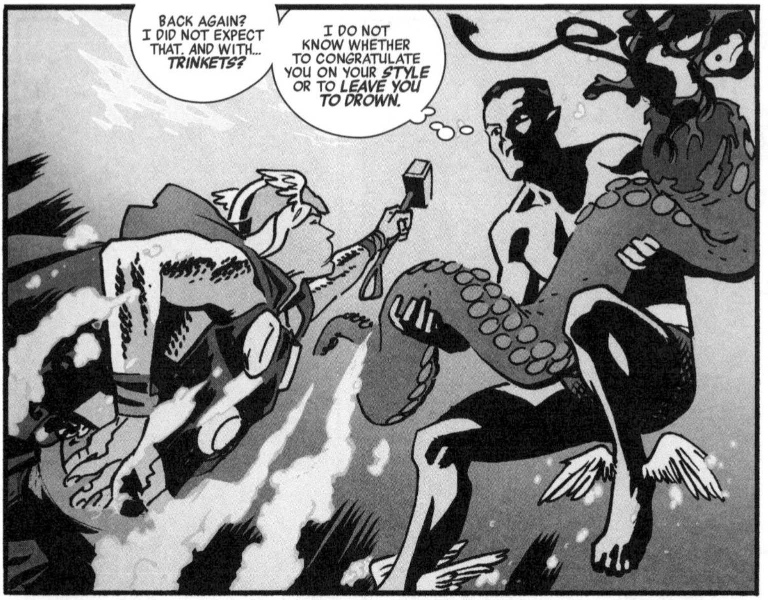
BACK AGAIN? I DID NOT EXPECT THAT. AND WITH... TRINKETS?
I DO NOT KNOW WHETHER TO CONGRATULATE YOU ON YOUR STYLE OR TO LEAVE YOU TO DROWN.

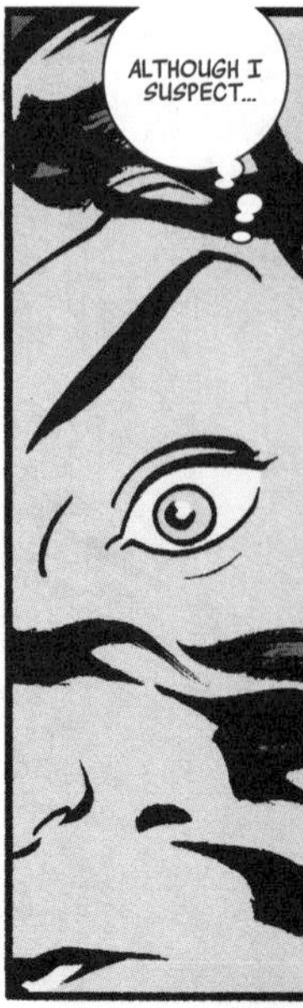
ALTHOUGH I SUSPECT...

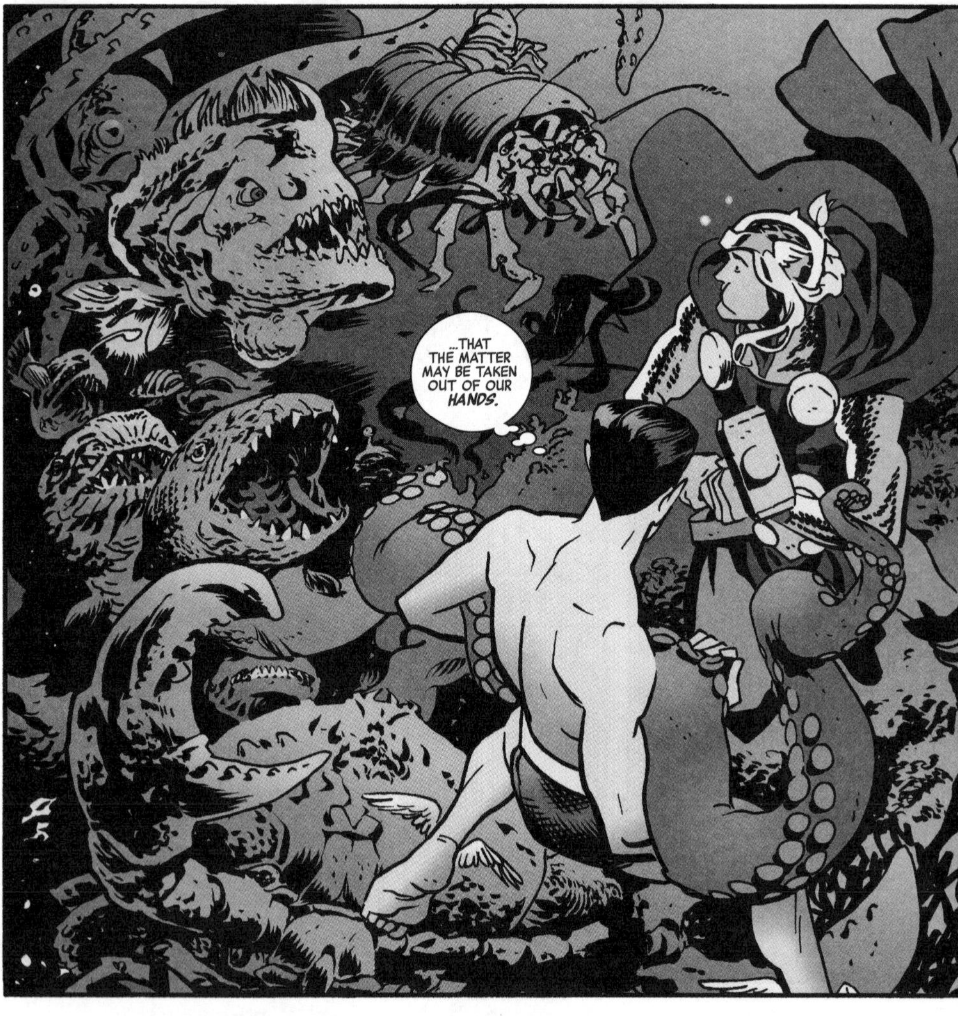
...THAT THE MATTER MAY BE TAKEN OUT OF OUR HANDS.

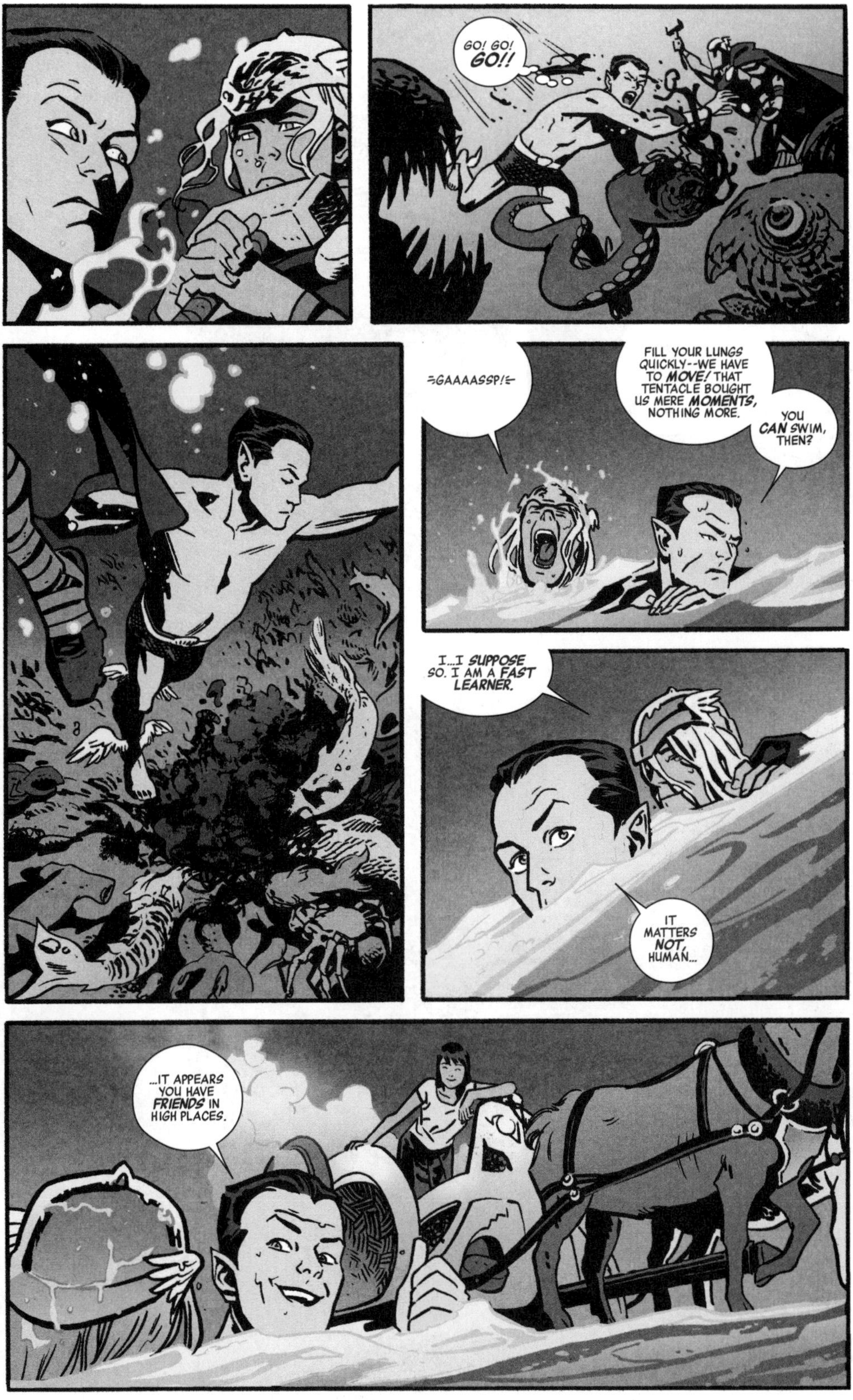
GO! GO! GO!!
=GAAAASSP!=
FILL YOUR LUNGS QUICKLY--WE HAVE TO MOVE! THAT TENTACLE BOUGHT US MERE MOMENTS, NOTHING MORE.
YOU CAN SWIM, THEN?
I...I SUPPOSE SO. I AM A FAST LEARNER.
IT MATTERS NOT, HUMAN...
...IT APPEARS YOU HAVE FRIENDS IN HIGH PLACES.

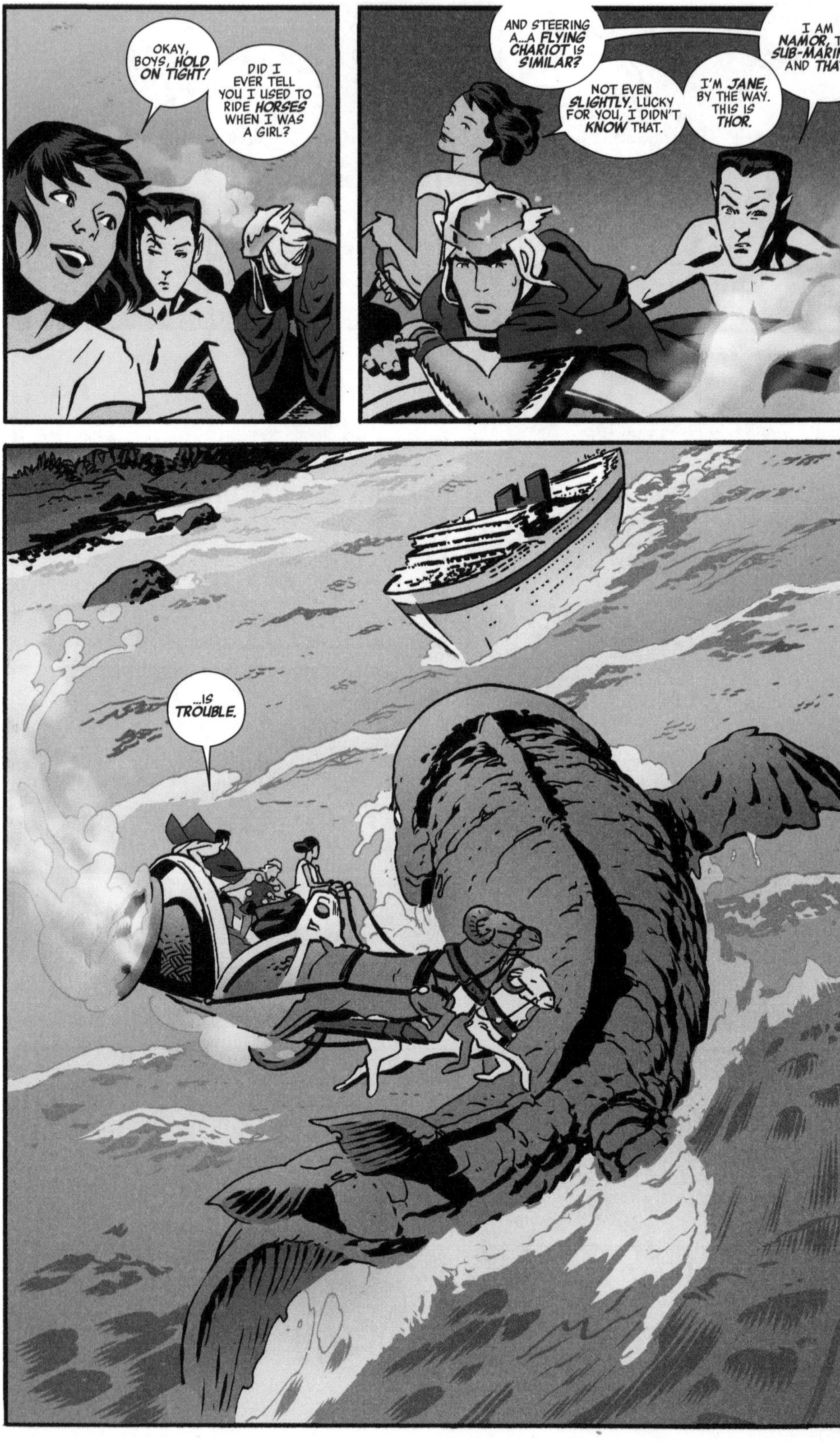
OKAY, BOYS, HOLD ON TIGHT!
DID I EVER TELL YOU I USED TO RIDE HORSES WHEN I WAS A GIRL?
AND STEERING A...A FLYING CHARIOT IS SIMILAR?
NOT EVEN SLIGHTLY. LUCKY FOR YOU, I DIDN'T KNOW THAT.
I'M JANE, BY THE WAY. THIS IS THOR.
I AM NAMOR, THE SUB-MARINER... AND THAT...
...IS TROUBLE.

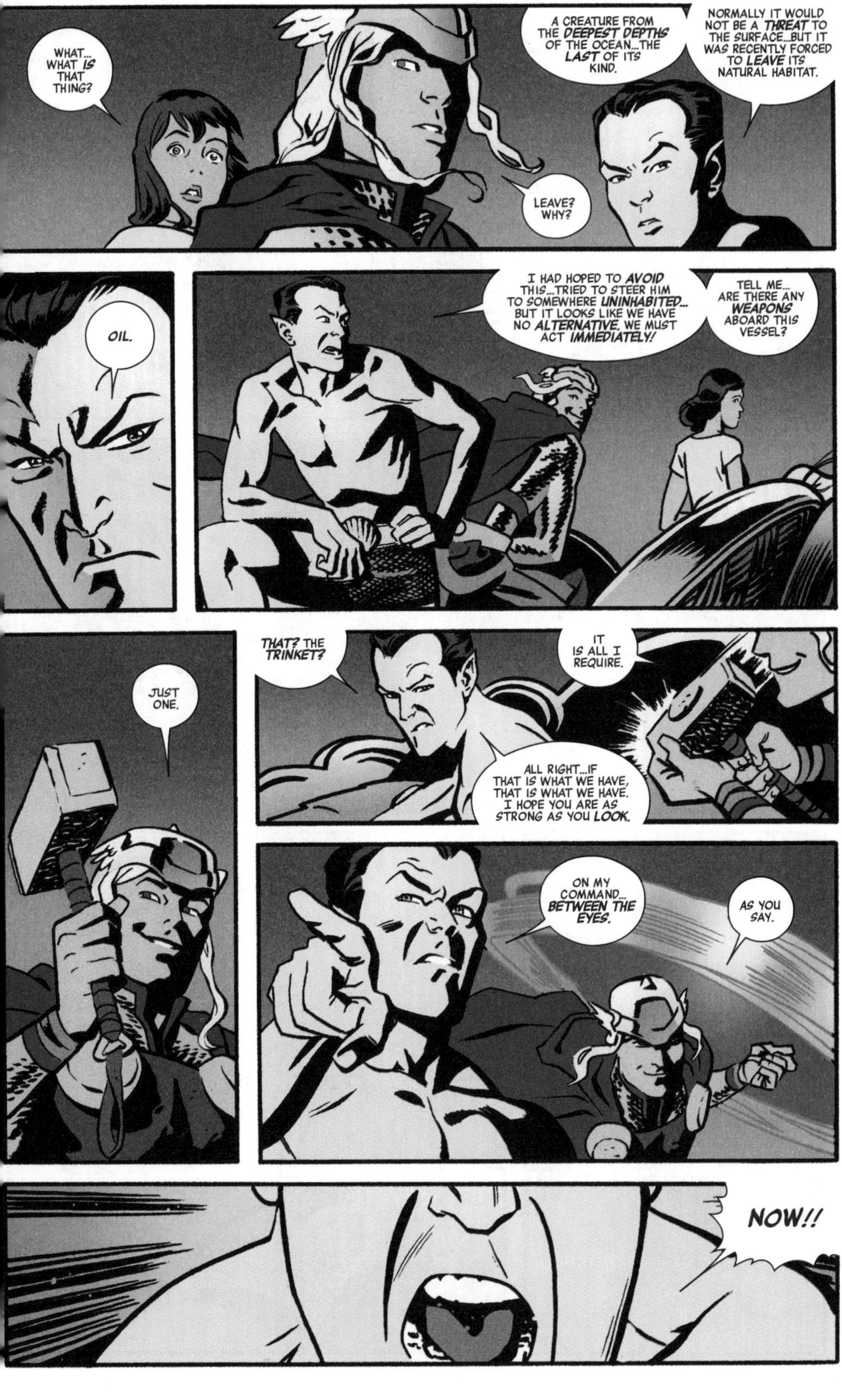
WHAT... WHAT IS THAT THING?
A CREATURE FROM THE DEEPEST DEPTHS OF THE OCEAN...THE LAST OF ITS KIND.
NORMALLY IT WOULD NOT BE A THREAT TO THE SURFACE...BUT IT WAS RECENTLY FORCED TO LEAVE ITS NATURAL HABITAT.
LEAVE? WHY?
OIL.
I HAD HOPED TO AVOID THIS...TRIED TO STEER HIM TO SOMEWHERE UNINHABITED... BUT IT LOOKS LIKE WE HAVE NO ALTERNATIVE. WE MUST ACT IMMEDIATELY!
TELL ME... ARE THERE ANY WEAPONS ABOARD THIS VESSEL?
JUST ONE.
THAT? THE TRINKET?
IT IS ALL I REQUIRE.
ALL RIGHT...IF THAT IS WHAT WE HAVE, THAT IS WHAT WE HAVE. I HOPE YOU ARE AS STRONG AS YOU LOOK.
ON MY COMMAND... BETWEEN THE EYES.
AS YOU SAY.
NOW!!

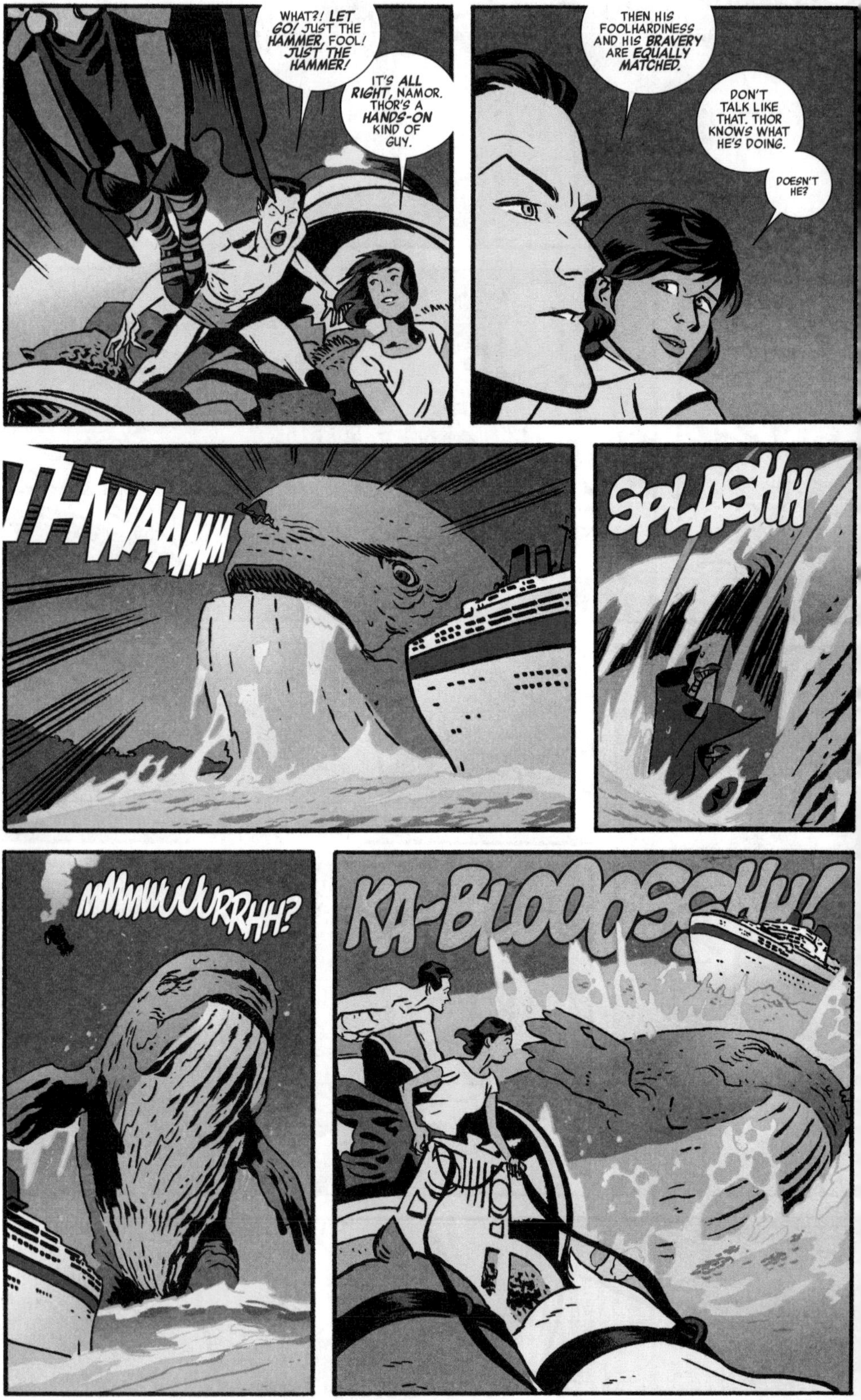

WHAT?! LET GO! JUST THE HAMMER, FOOL! JUST THE HAMMER!
IT'S ALL RIGHT, NAMOR. THOR'S A HANDS-ON KIND OF GUY.
THEN HIS FOOLHARDINESS AND HIS BRAVERY ARE EQUALLY MATCHED.
DON'T TALK LIKE THAT. THOR KNOWS WHAT HE'S DOING.
DOESN'T HE?
THWAAMM
SPLASHH
MMMWUURRHH?
KA-BLOOOSCHH!

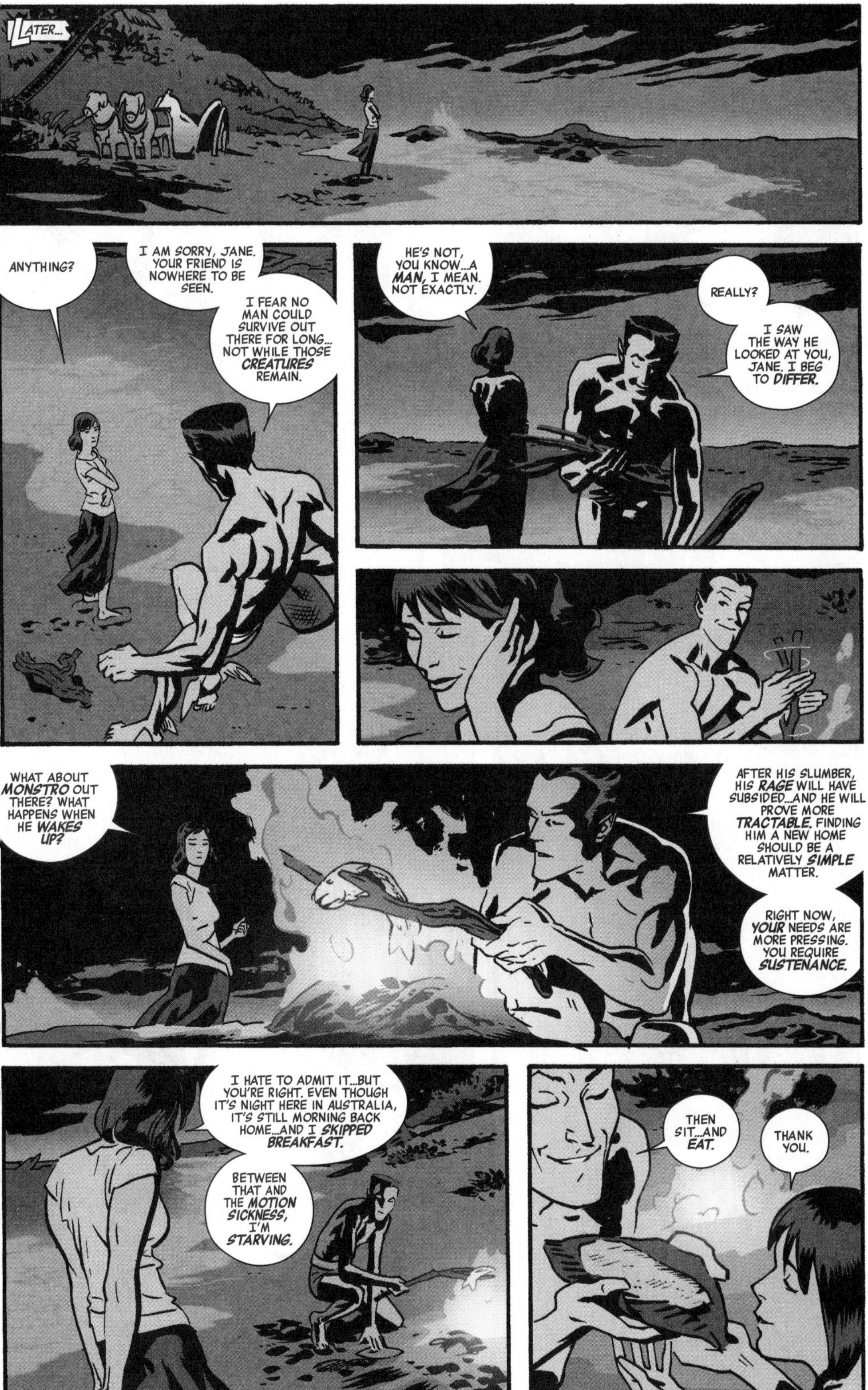
LATER...
ANYTHING?
I AM SORRY, JANE. YOUR FRIEND IS NOWHERE TO BE SEEN.
I FEAR NO MAN COULD SURVIVE OUT THERE FOR LONG... NOT WHILE THOSE CREATURES REMAIN.
HE'S NOT, YOU KNOW...A MAN, I MEAN. NOT EXACTLY.
REALLY?
I SAW THE WAY HE LOOKED AT YOU, JANE. I BEG TO DIFFER.
WHAT ABOUT MONSTRO OUT THERE? WHAT HAPPENS WHEN HE WAKES UP?
AFTER HIS SLUMBER, HIS RAGE WILL HAVE SUBSIDED...AND HE WILL PROVE MORE TRACTABLE. FINDING HIM A NEW HOME SHOULD BE A RELATIVELY SIMPLE MATTER.
RIGHT NOW, YOUR NEEDS ARE MORE PRESSING. YOU REQUIRE SUSTENANCE.
I HATE TO ADMIT IT...BUT YOU'RE RIGHT. EVEN THOUGH IT'S NIGHT HERE IN AUSTRALIA, IT'S STILL MORNING BACK HOME...AND I SKIPPED BREAKFAST.
BETWEEN THAT AND THE MOTION SICKNESS, I'M STARVING.
THEN SIT...AND EAT.
THANK YOU.

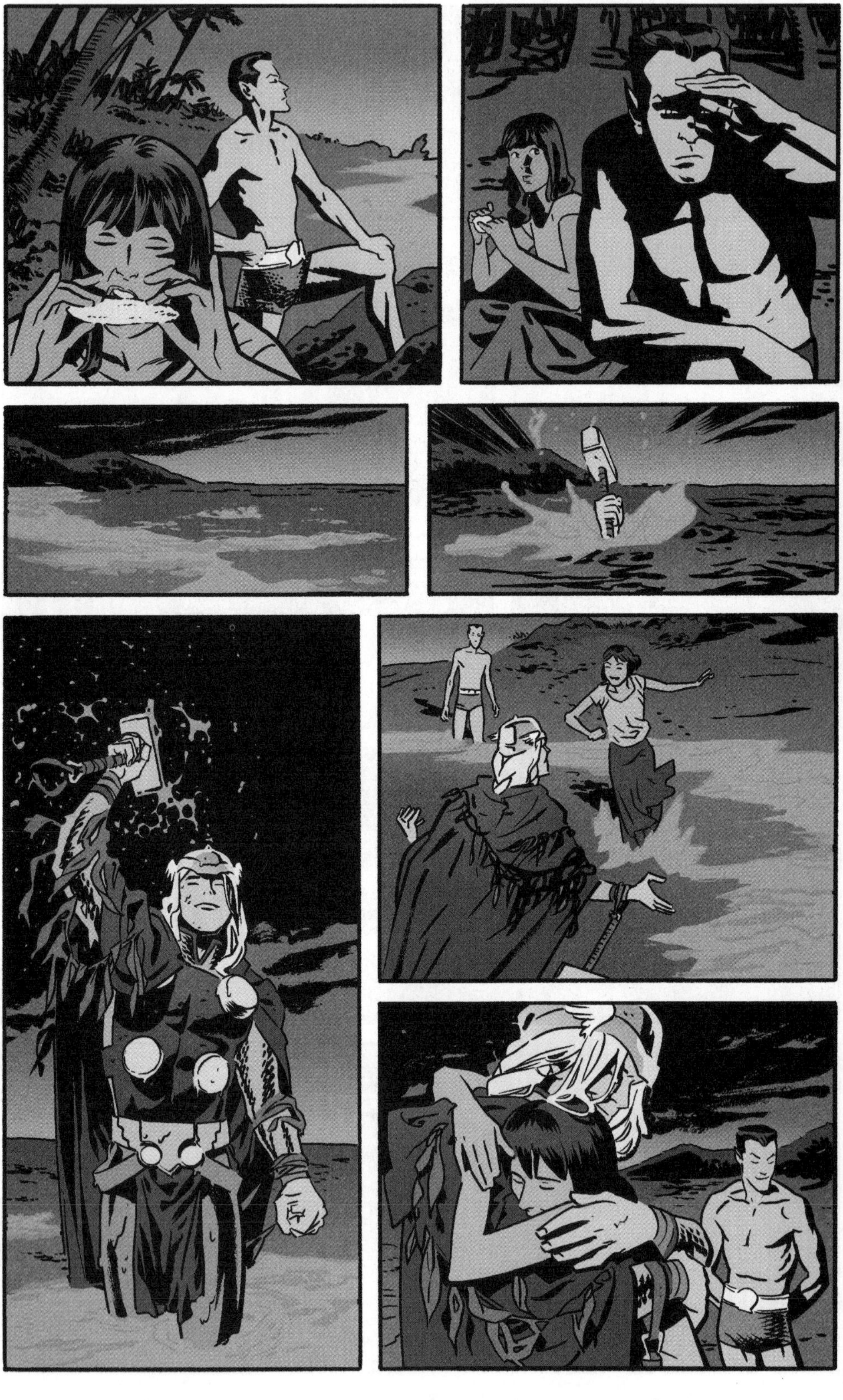

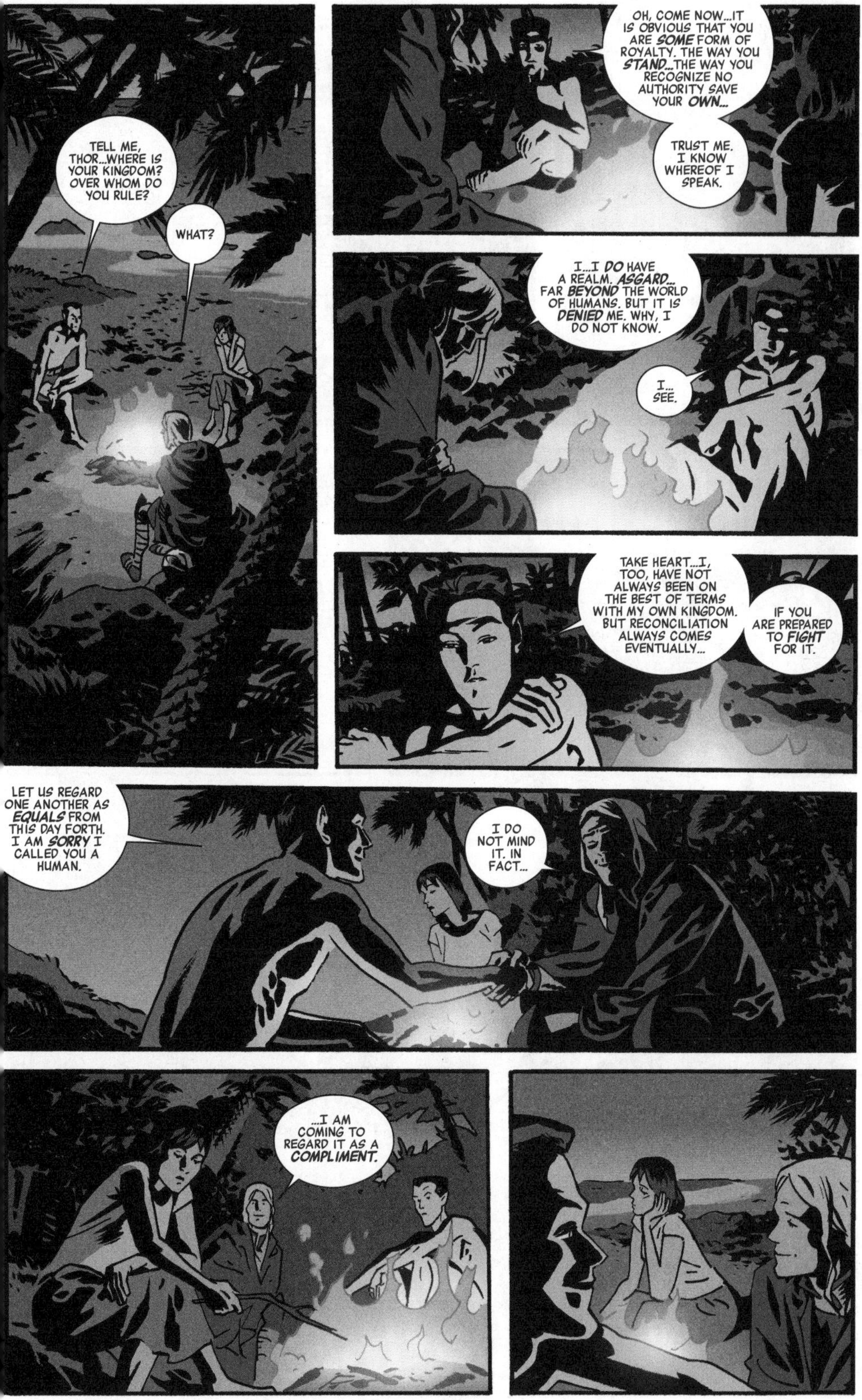
TELL ME, THOR...WHERE IS YOUR KINGDOM? OVER WHOM DO YOU RULE?
WHAT?
OH, COME NOW...IT IS OBVIOUS THAT YOU ARE SOME FORM OF ROYALTY. THE WAY YOU STAND...THE WAY YOU RECOGNIZE NO AUTHORITY SAVE YOUR OWN...
TRUST ME. I KNOW WHEREOF I SPEAK.
I...I DO HAVE A REALM. ASGARD... FAR BEYOND THE WORLD OF HUMANS. BUT IT IS DENIED ME. WHY, I DO NOT KNOW.
I... SEE.
TAKE HEART...I, TOO, HAVE NOT ALWAYS BEEN ON THE BEST OF TERMS WITH MY OWN KINGDOM. BUT RECONCILIATION ALWAYS COMES EVENTUALLY...
IF YOU ARE PREPARED TO FIGHT FOR IT.
LET US REGARD ONE ANOTHER AS EQUALS FROM THIS DAY FORTH. I AM SORRY I CALLED YOU A HUMAN.
I DO NOT MIND IT. IN FACT...
...I AM COMING TO REGARD IT AS A COMPLIMENT.

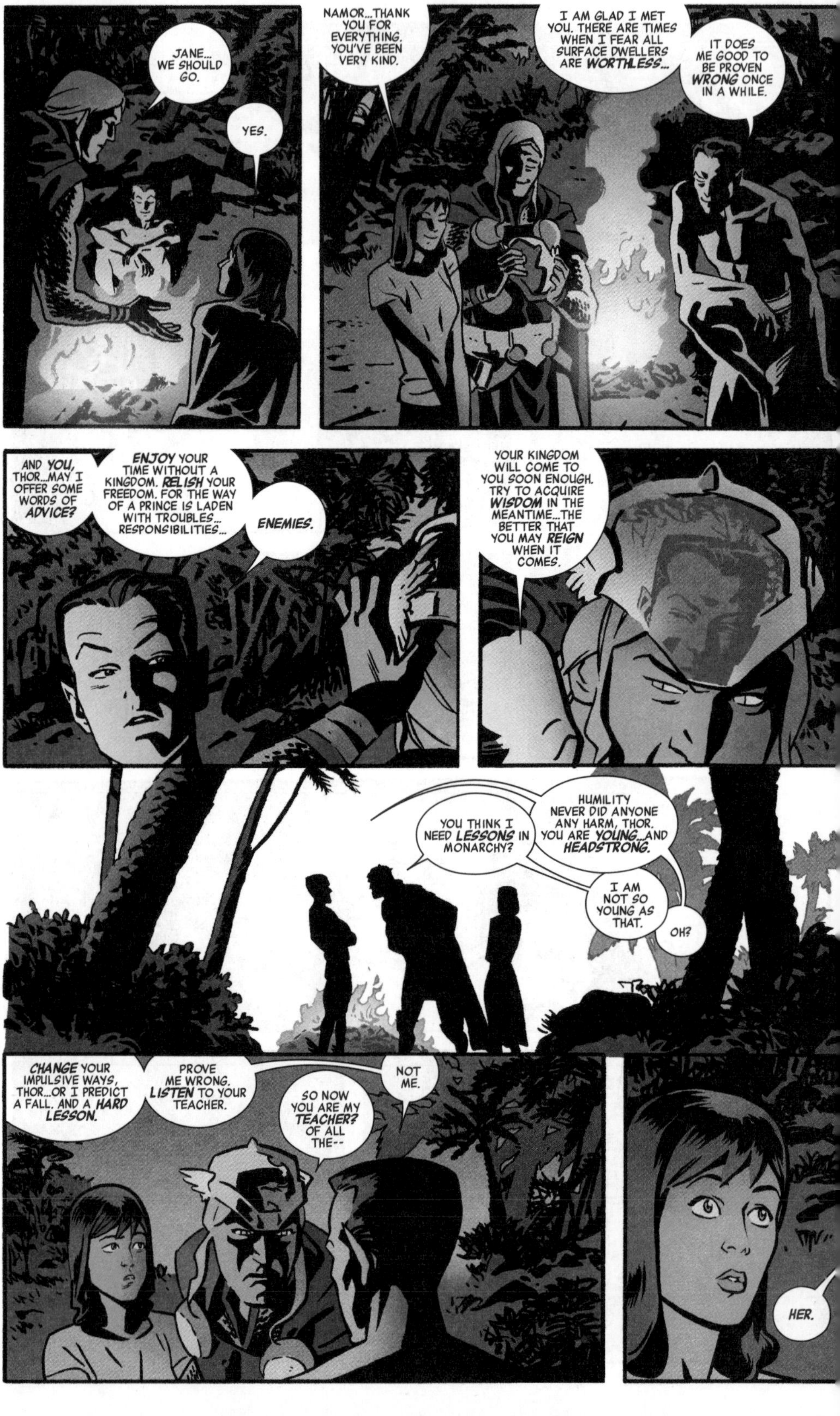

JANE... WE SHOULD GO.
YES.
NAMOR...THANK YOU FOR EVERYTHING. YOU'VE BEEN VERY KIND.
I AM GLAD I MET YOU. THERE ARE TIMES WHEN I FEAR ALL SURFACE DWELLERS ARE WORTHLESS...
IT DOES ME GOOD TO BE PROVEN WRONG ONCE IN A WHILE.
AND YOU, THOR...MAY I OFFER SOME WORDS OF ADVICE?
ENJOY YOUR TIME WITHOUT A KINGDOM. RELISH YOUR FREEDOM. FOR THE WAY OF A PRINCE IS LADEN WITH TROUBLES... RESPONSIBILITIES...
ENEMIES.
YOUR KINGDOM WILL COME TO YOU SOON ENOUGH. TRY TO ACQUIRE WISDOM IN THE MEANTIME...THE BETTER THAT YOU MAY REIGN WHEN IT COMES.
YOU THINK I NEED LESSONS IN MONARCHY?
HUMILITY NEVER DID ANYONE ANY HARM, THOR. YOU ARE YOUNG...AND HEADSTRONG.
I AM NOT SO YOUNG AS THAT.
OH?
CHANGE YOUR IMPULSIVE WAYS, THOR...OR I PREDICT A FALL. AND A HARD LESSON.
PROVE ME WRONG. LISTEN TO YOUR TEACHER.
SO NOW YOU ARE MY TEACHER? OF ALL THE--
NOT ME.
HER.

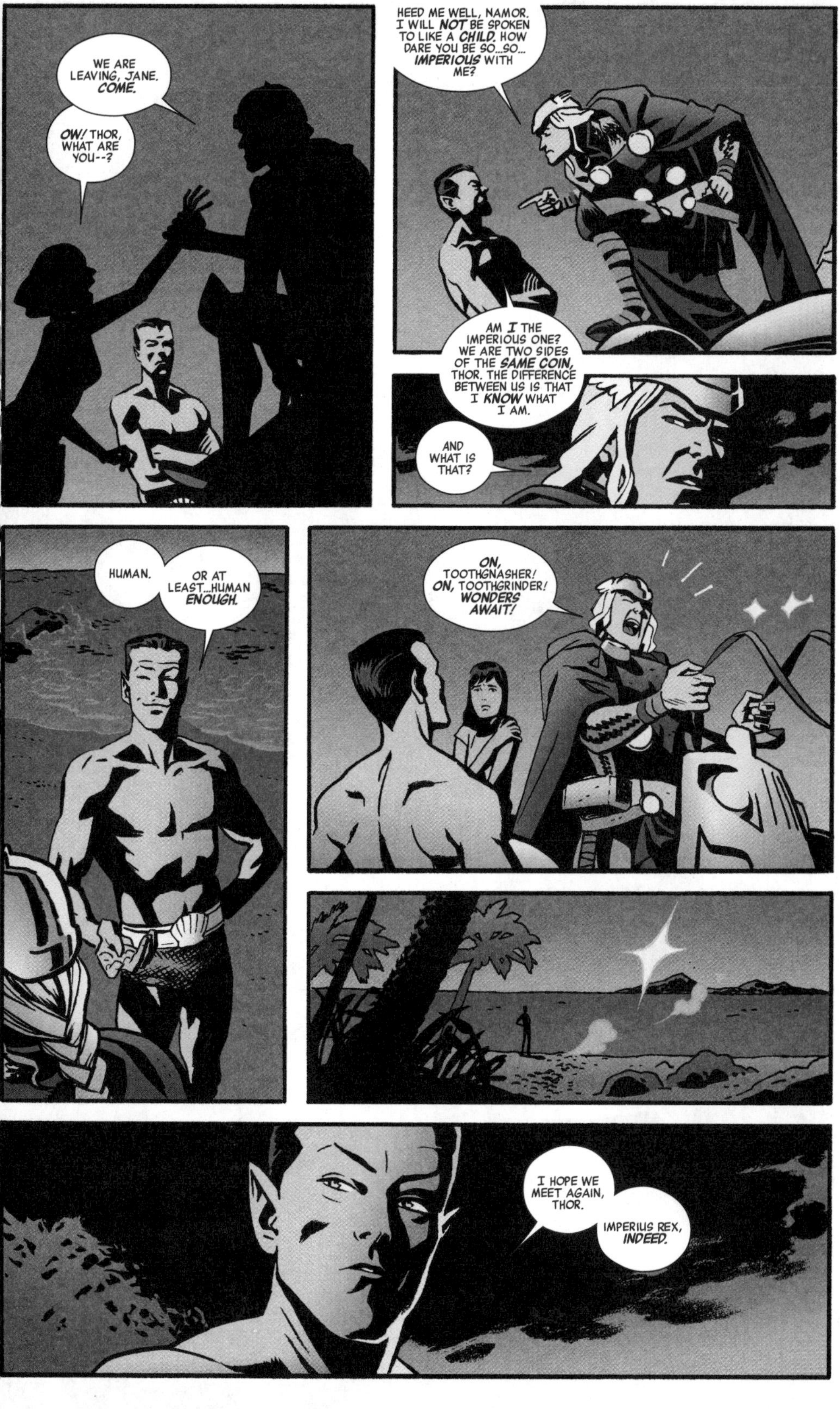
WE ARE LEAVING, JANE. COME.
OW! THOR, WHAT ARE YOU--?
HEED ME WELL, NAMOR. I WILL NOT BE SPOKEN TO LIKE A CHILD. HOW DARE YOU BE SO...SO... IMPERIOUS WITH ME?
AM I THE IMPERIOUS ONE? WE ARE TWO SIDES OF THE SAME COIN, THOR. THE DIFFERENCE BETWEEN US IS THAT I KNOW WHAT I AM.
AND WHAT IS THAT?
HUMAN.
OR AT LEAST...HUMAN ENOUGH.
ON, TOOTHGNASHER! ON, TOOTHGRINDER! WONDERS AWAIT!
I HOPE WE MEET AGAIN, THOR.
IMPERIUS REX, INDEED.

THOR THE MIGHTY AVENGER #6

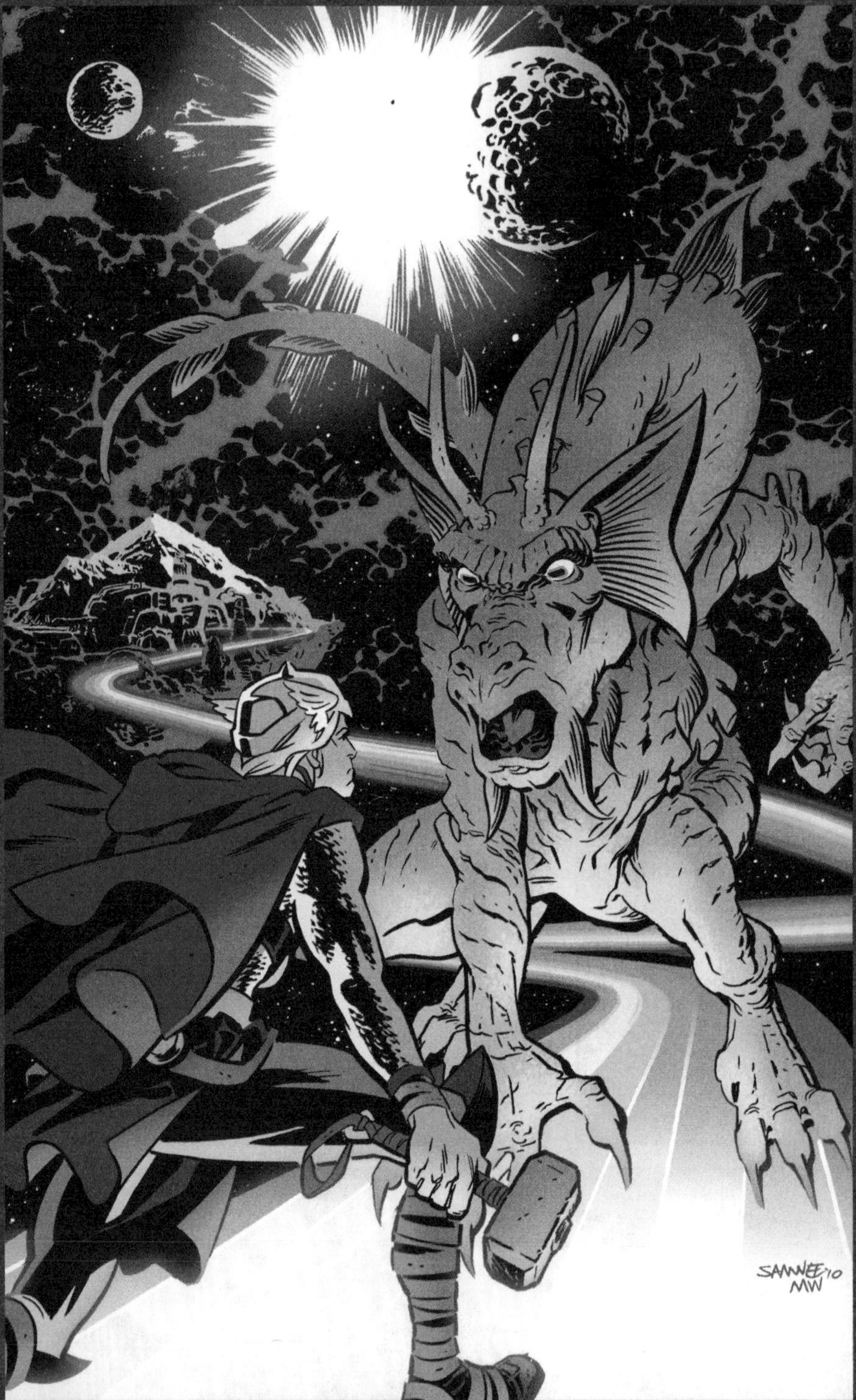
SAMNEE '10
MW

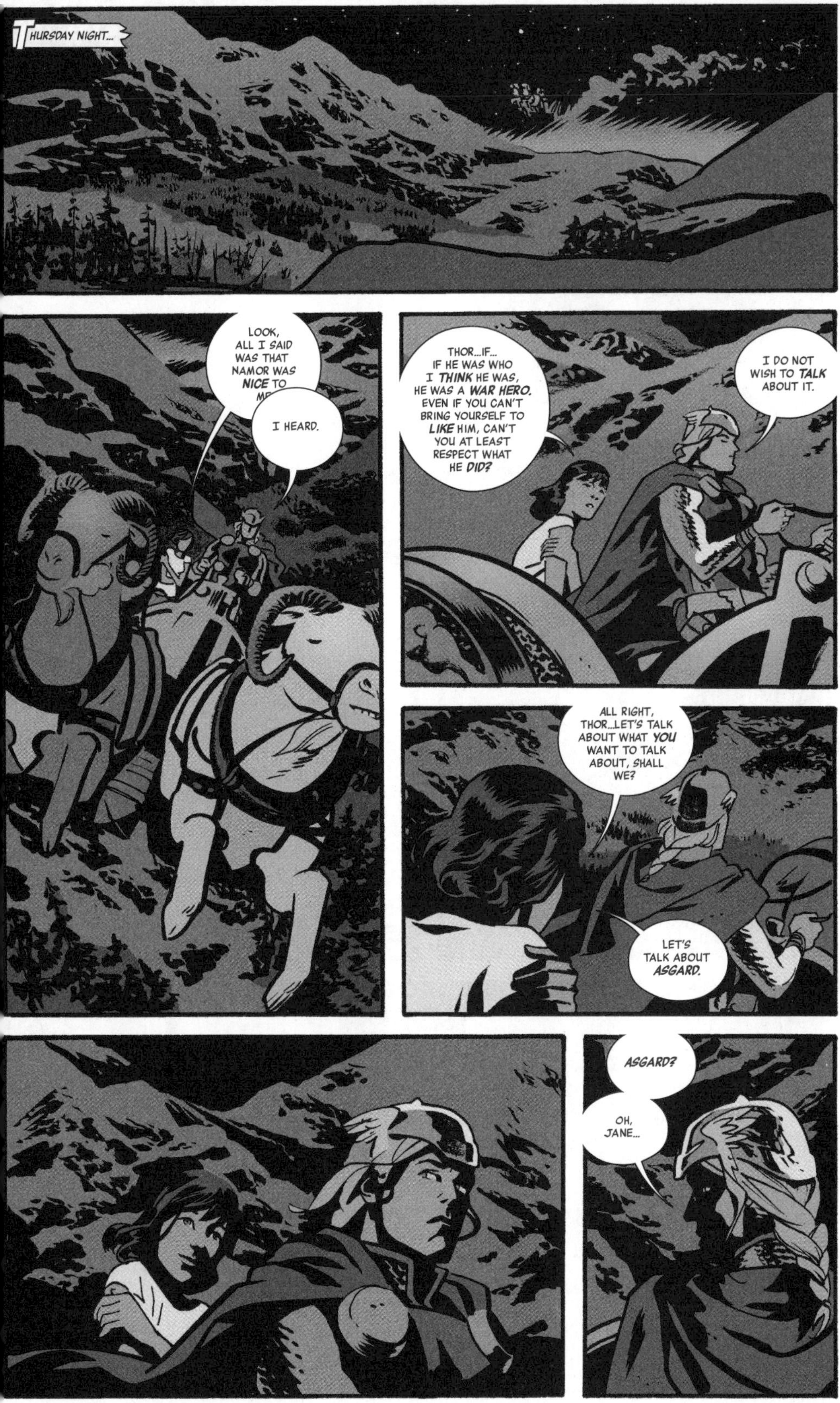
THURSDAY NIGHT...
LOOK, ALL I SAID WAS THAT NAMOR WAS NICE TO ME
I HEARD.
THOR...IF... IF HE WAS WHO I THINK HE WAS, HE WAS A WAR HERO. EVEN IF YOU CAN'T BRING YOURSELF TO LIKE HIM, CAN'T YOU AT LEAST RESPECT WHAT HE DID?
I DO NOT WISH TO TALK ABOUT IT.
ALL RIGHT, THOR...LET'S TALK ABOUT WHAT YOU WANT TO TALK ABOUT, SHALL WE?
LET'S TALK ABOUT ASGARD.
ASGARD?
OH, JANE...

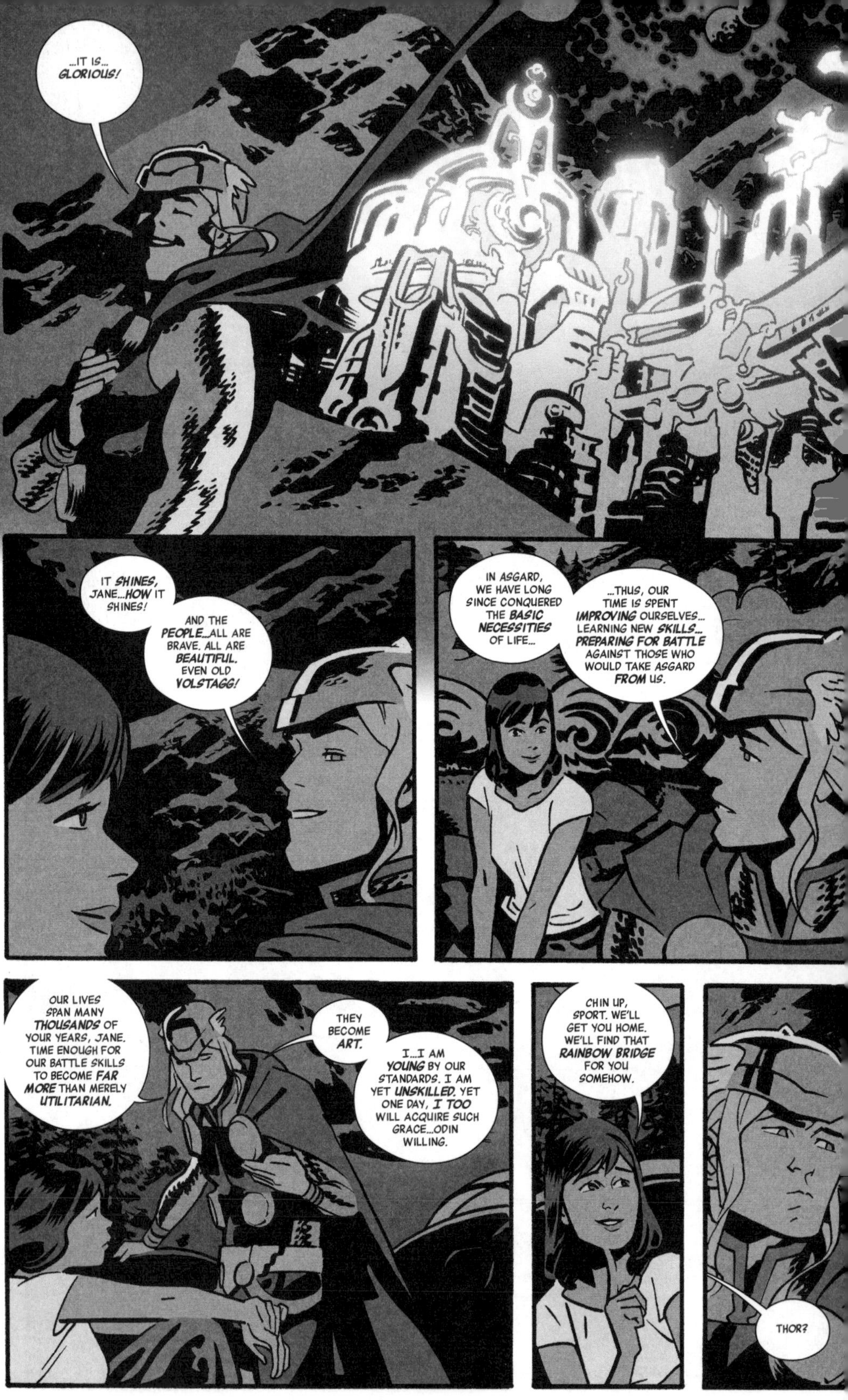
...IT IS... GLORIOUS!
IT SHINES, JANE...HOW IT SHINES!
AND THE PEOPLE...ALL ARE BRAVE. ALL ARE BEAUTIFUL. EVEN OLD VOLSTAGG!
IN ASGARD, WE HAVE LONG SINCE CONQUERED THE BASIC NECESSITIES OF LIFE...
...THUS, OUR TIME IS SPENT IMPROVING OURSELVES... LEARNING NEW SKILLS... PREPARING FOR BATTLE AGAINST THOSE WHO WOULD TAKE ASGARD FROM US.
OUR LIVES SPAN MANY THOUSANDS OF YOUR YEARS, JANE. TIME ENOUGH FOR OUR BATTLE SKILLS TO BECOME FAR MORE THAN MERELY UTILITARIAN.
THEY BECOME ART.
I...I AM YOUNG BY OUR STANDARDS. I AM YET UNSKILLED. YET ONE DAY, I TOO WILL ACQUIRE SUCH GRACE...ODIN WILLING.
CHIN UP, SPORT. WE'LL GET YOU HOME. WE'LL FIND THAT RAINBOW BRIDGE FOR YOU SOMEHOW.
THOR?

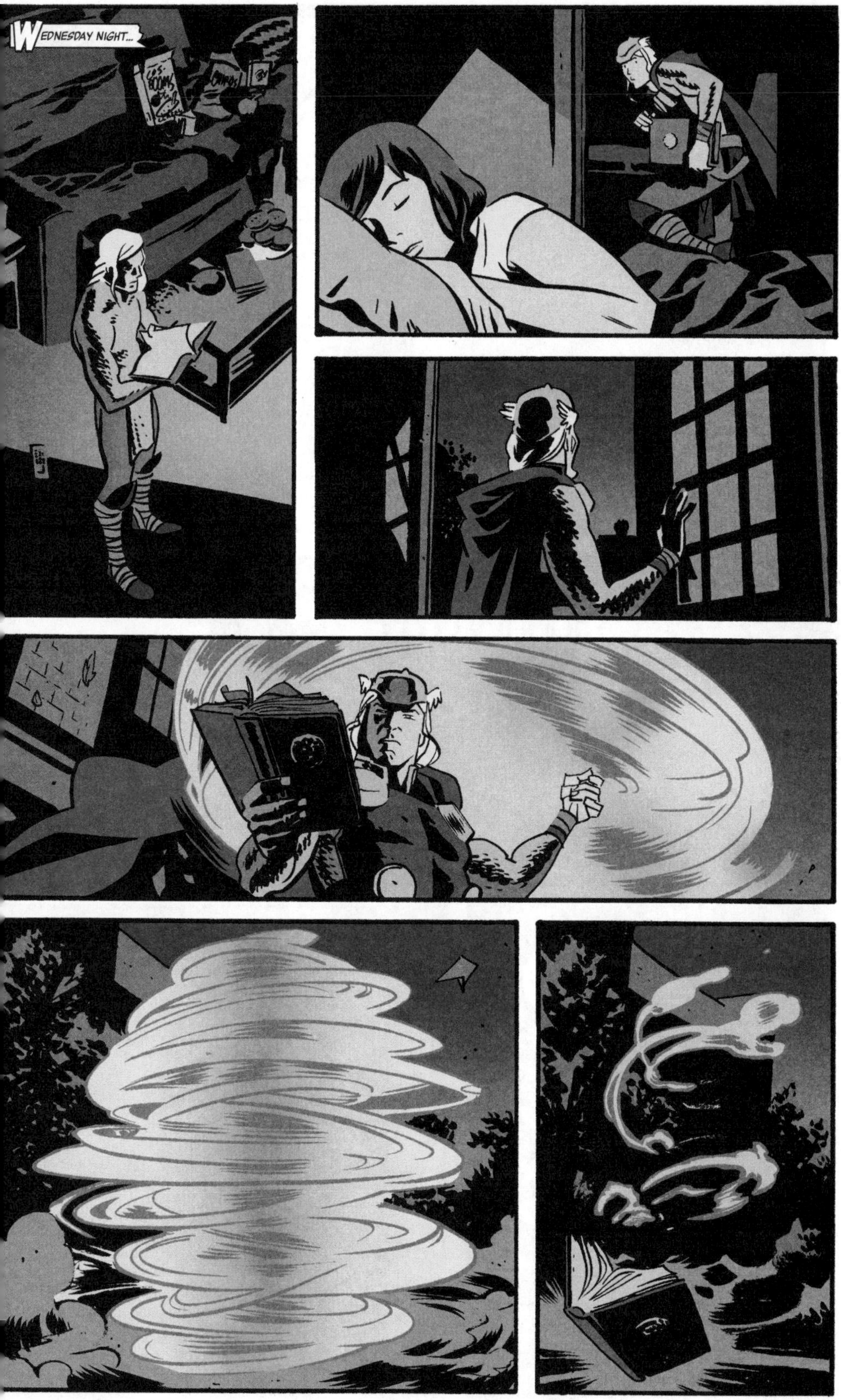
WEDNESDAY NIGHT...

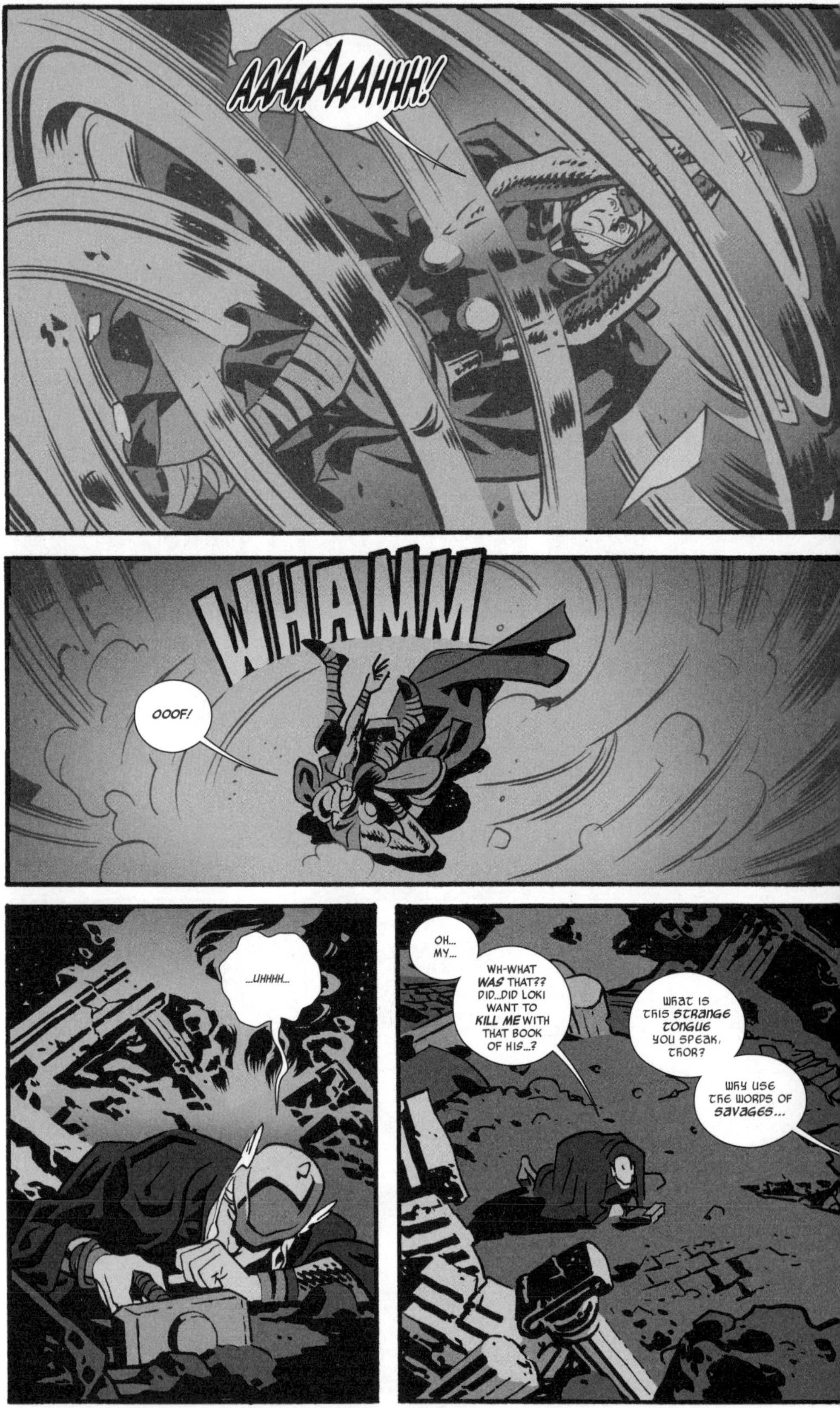
AAAAAAAHHH!
WHAMM
OOOF!
...UHHHH...
OH... MY...
WH-WHAT WAS THAT?? DID...DID LOKI WANT TO KILL ME WITH THAT BOOK OF HIS...?
WHAT IS THIS STRANGE TONGUE YOU SPEAK, THOR?
WHY USE THE WORDS OF SAVAGES...

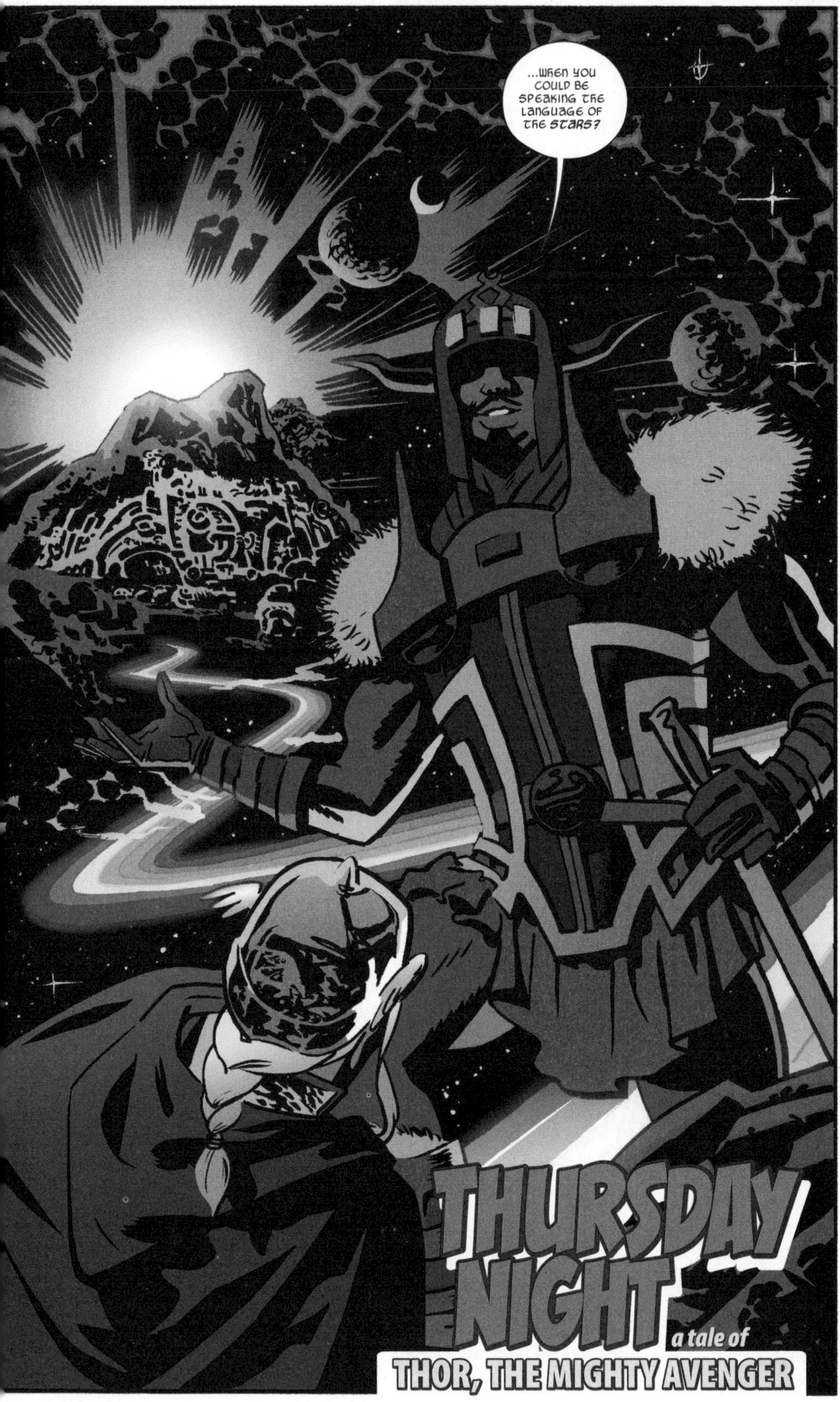
...WHEN YOU COULD BE SPEAKING THE LANGUAGE OF THE STARS?
THURSDAY NIGHT
a tale of
THOR, THE MIGHTY AVENGER

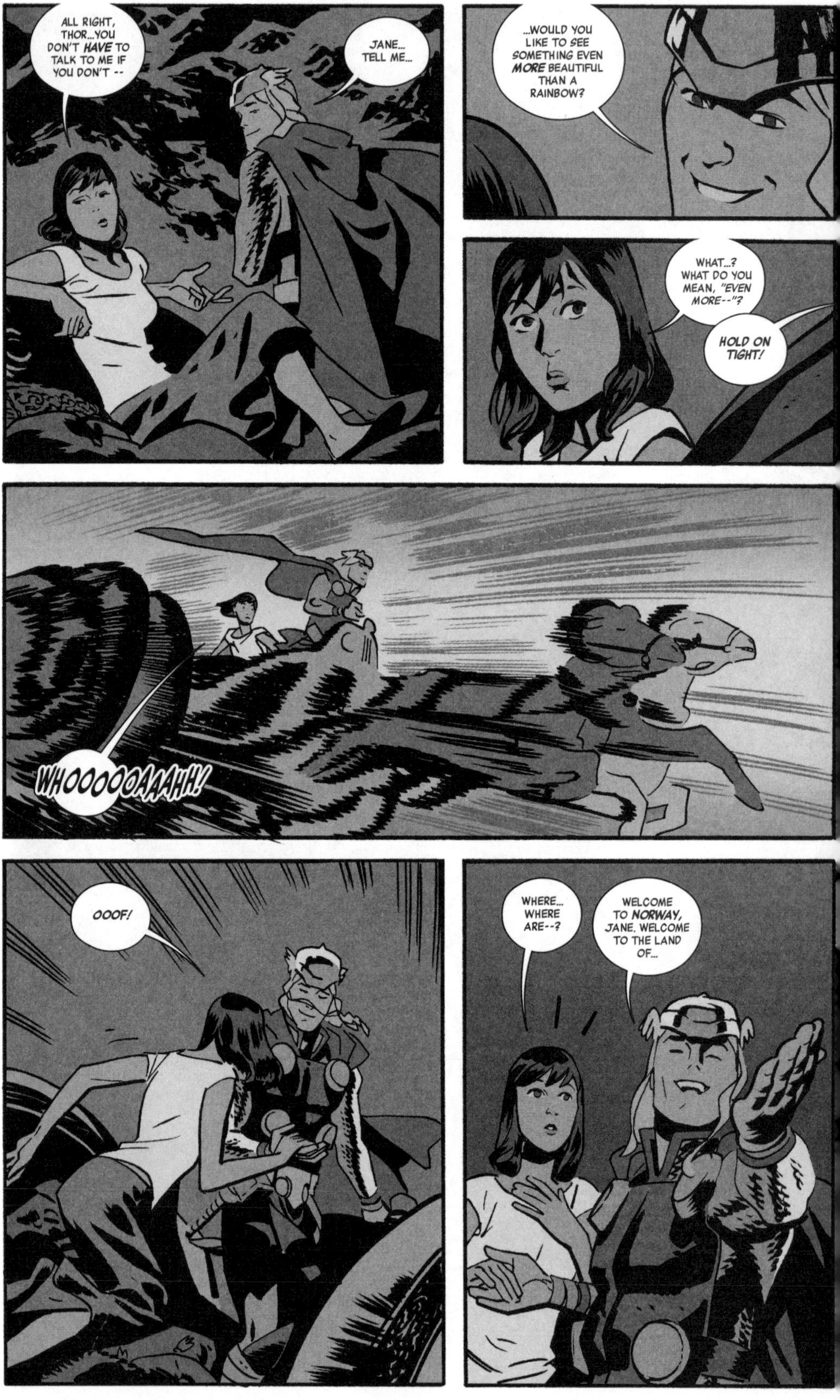
ALL RIGHT, THOR...YOU DON'T HAVE TO TALK TO ME IF YOU DON'T --
JANE... TELL ME...
...WOULD YOU LIKE TO SEE SOMETHING EVEN MORE BEAUTIFUL THAN A RAINBOW?
WHAT...? WHAT DO YOU MEAN, "EVEN MORE--"?
HOLD ON TIGHT!
WHOOOOOAAAHH!
OOOF!
WHERE... WHERE ARE--?
WELCOME TO NORWAY, JANE. WELCOME TO THE LAND OF...

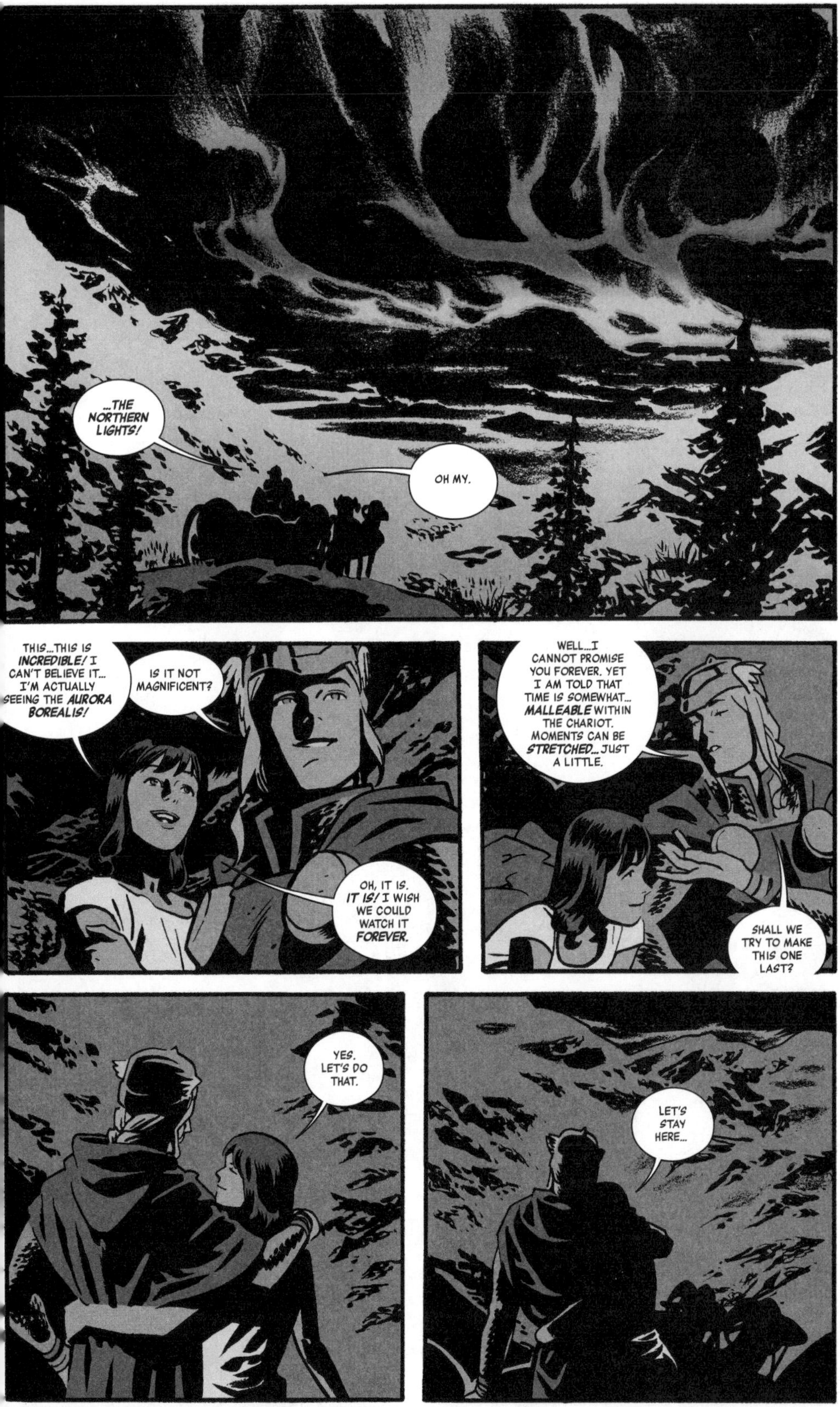

...THE NORTHERN LIGHTS!
OH MY.
THIS...THIS IS INCREDIBLE! I CAN'T BELIEVE IT... I'M ACTUALLY SEEING THE AURORA BOREALIS!
IS IT NOT MAGNIFICENT?
OH, IT IS. IT IS! I WISH WE COULD WATCH IT FOREVER.
WELL...I CANNOT PROMISE YOU FOREVER. YET I AM TOLD THAT TIME IS SOMEWHAT... MALLEABLE WITHIN THE CHARIOT. MOMENTS CAN BE STRETCHED... JUST A LITTLE.
SHALL WE TRY TO MAKE THIS ONE LAST?
YES. LET'S DO THAT.
LET'S STAY HERE...

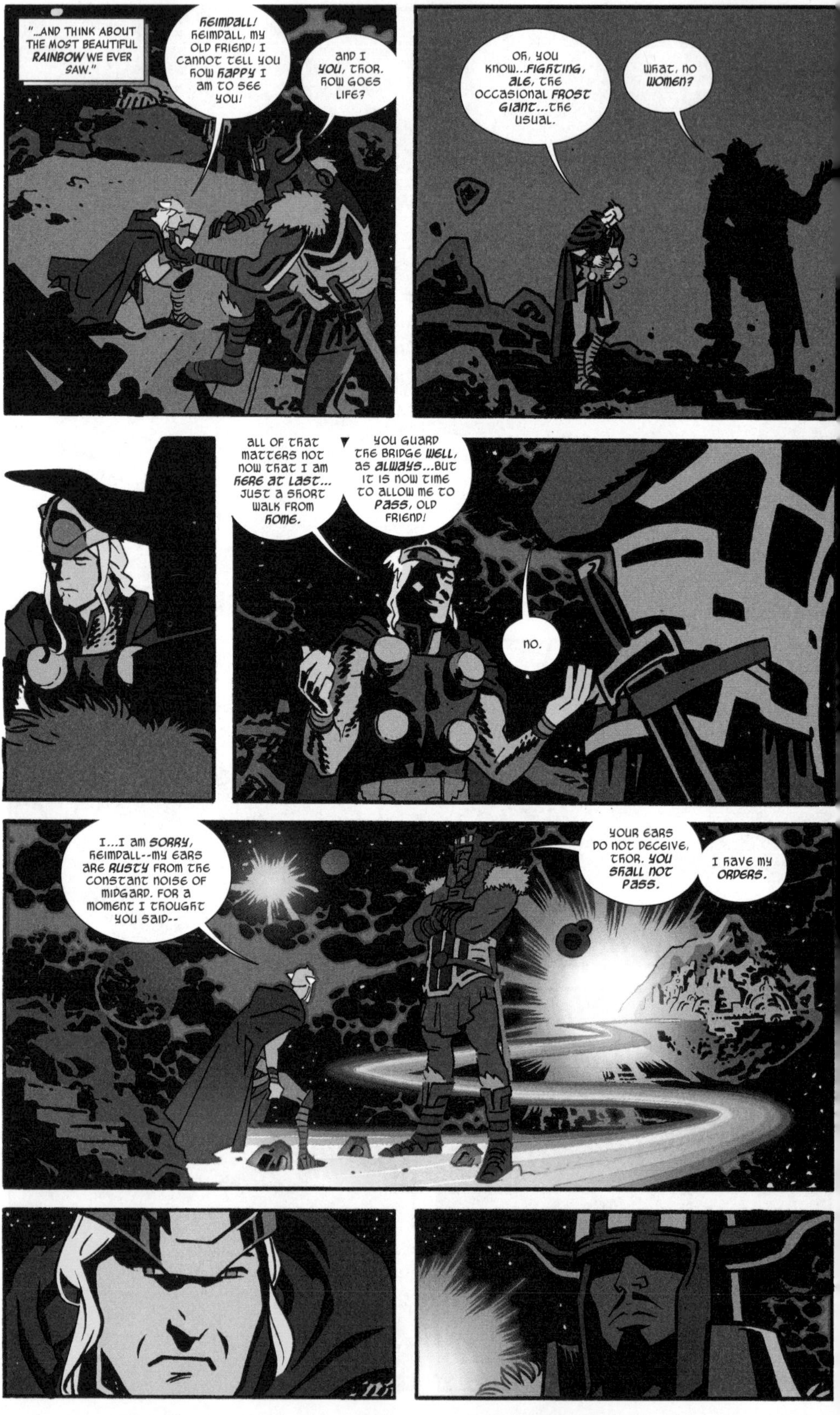
"...AND THINK ABOUT THE MOST BEAUTIFUL RAINBOW WE EVER SAW."
HEIMDALL! HEIMDALL, MY OLD FRIEND! I CANNOT TELL YOU HOW HAPPY I AM TO SEE YOU!
AND I YOU, THOR. HOW GOES LIFE?
OH, YOU KNOW...FIGHTING, ALE, THE OCCASIONAL FROST GIANT...THE USUAL.
WHAT, NO WOMEN?
ALL OF THAT MATTERS NOT NOW THAT I AM HERE AT LAST... JUST A SHORT WALK FROM HOME.
YOU GUARD THE BRIDGE WELL, AS ALWAYS...BUT IT IS NOW TIME TO ALLOW ME TO PASS, OLD FRIEND!
NO.
I...I AM SORRY, HEIMDALL--MY EARS ARE RUSTY FROM THE CONSTANT NOISE OF MIDGARD. FOR A MOMENT I THOUGHT YOU SAID--
YOUR EARS DO NOT DECEIVE, THOR. YOU SHALL NOT PASS.
I HAVE MY ORDERS.

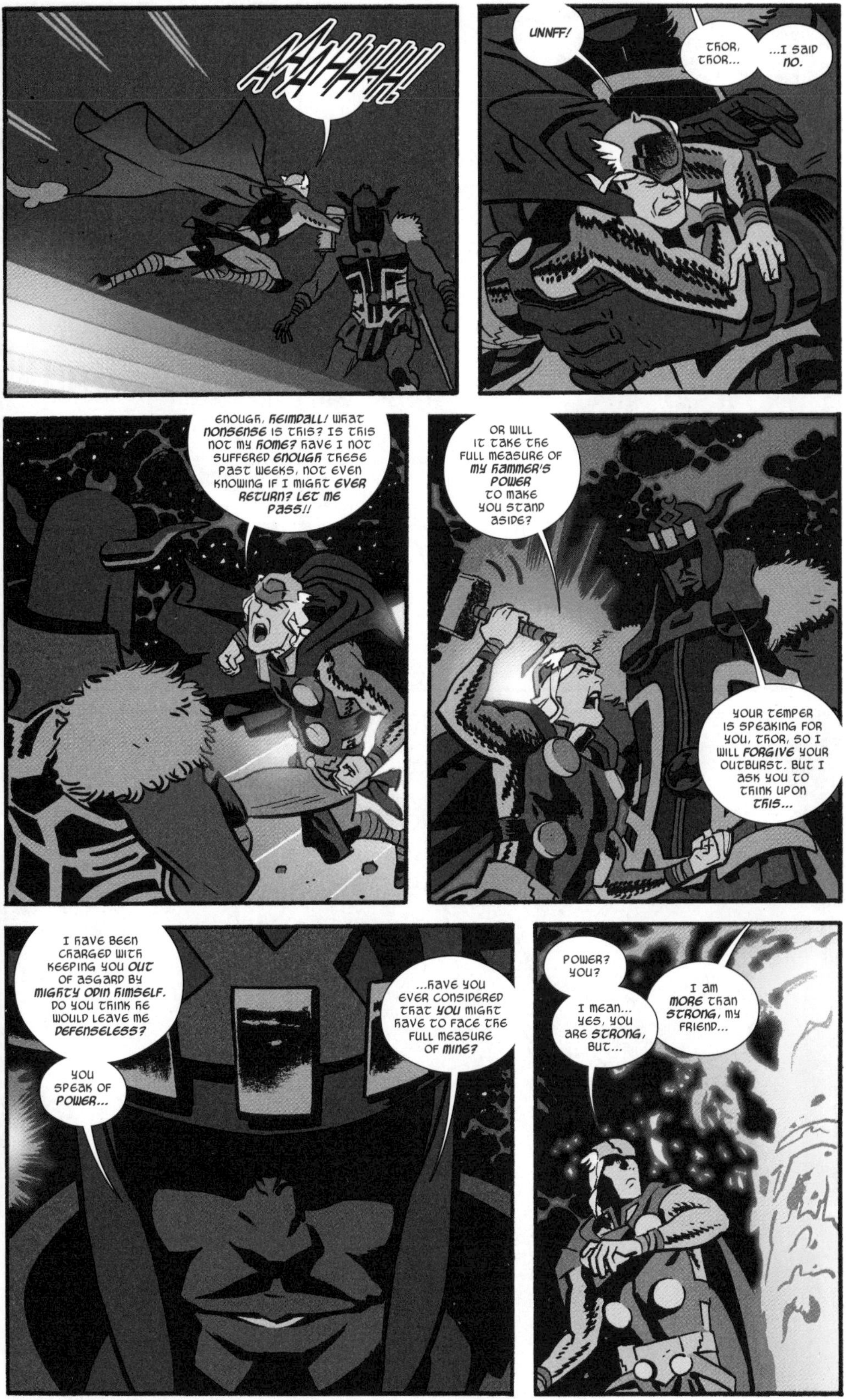
AAHHHH!
UNNFF!
THOR, THOR...
...I SAID NO.
ENOUGH, HEIMDALL! WHAT NONSENSE IS THIS? IS THIS NOT MY HOME? HAVE I NOT SUFFERED ENOUGH THESE PAST WEEKS, NOT EVEN KNOWING IF I MIGHT EVER RETURN? LET ME PASS!!
OR WILL IT TAKE THE FULL MEASURE OF MY HAMMER'S POWER TO MAKE YOU STAND ASIDE?
YOUR TEMPER IS SPEAKING FOR YOU, THOR, SO I WILL FORGIVE YOUR OUTBURST. BUT I ASK YOU TO THINK UPON THIS...
I HAVE BEEN CHARGED WITH KEEPING YOU OUT OF ASGARD BY MIGHTY ODIN HIMSELF. DO YOU THINK HE WOULD LEAVE ME DEFENSELESS?
YOU SPEAK OF POWER...
...HAVE YOU EVER CONSIDERED THAT YOU MIGHT HAVE TO FACE THE FULL MEASURE OF MINE?
POWER? YOU?
I MEAN... YES, YOU ARE STRONG, BUT...
I AM MORE THAN STRONG, MY FRIEND...

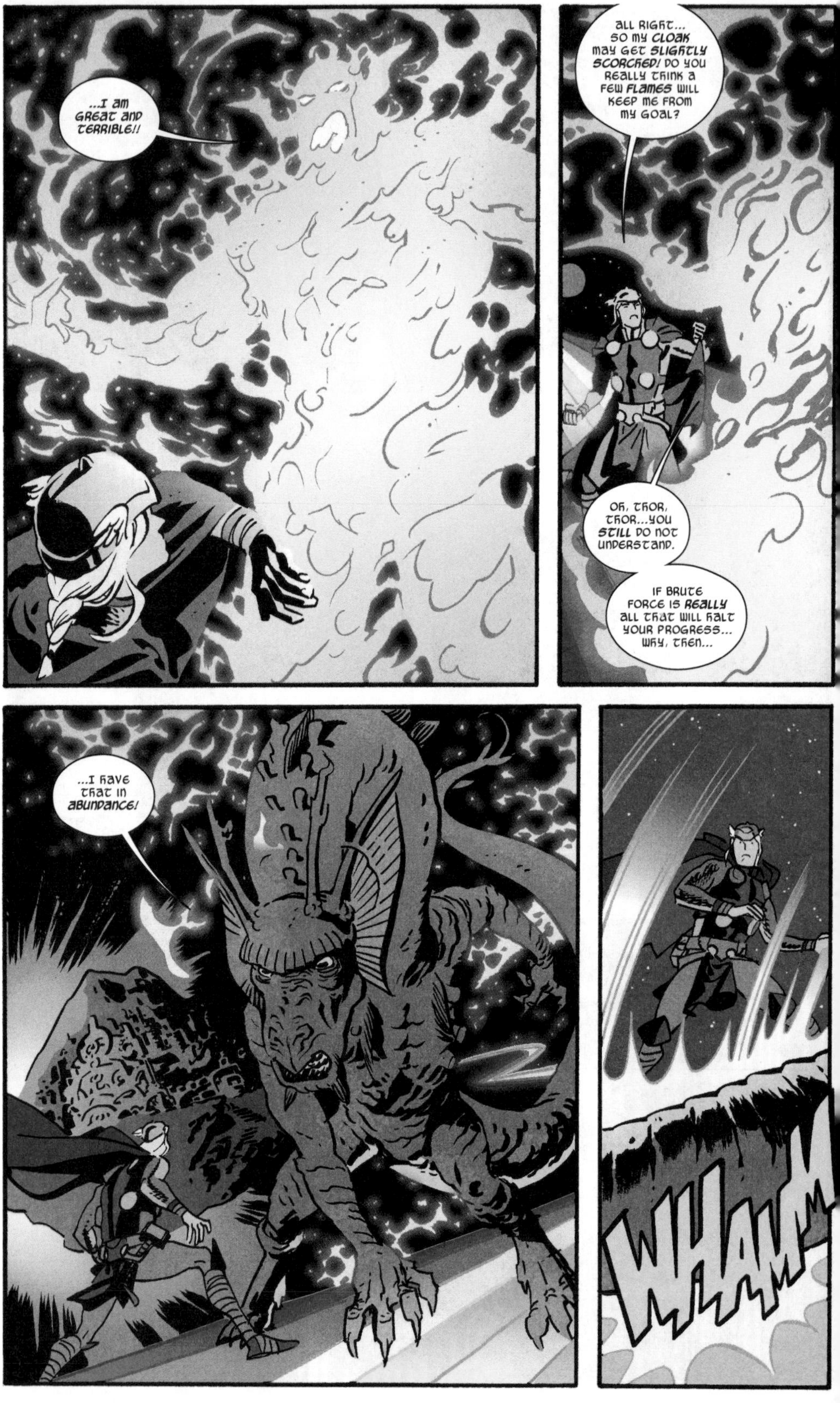

...I AM GREAT AND TERRIBLE!!
ALL RIGHT... SO MY CLOAK MAY GET SLIGHTLY SCORCHED! DO YOU REALLY THINK A FEW FLAMES WILL KEEP ME FROM MY GOAL?
OH, THOR, THOR...YOU STILL DO NOT UNDERSTAND.
IF BRUTE FORCE IS REALLY ALL THAT WILL HALT YOUR PROGRESS... WHY, THEN...
...I HAVE THAT IN ABUNDANCE!
WHAM

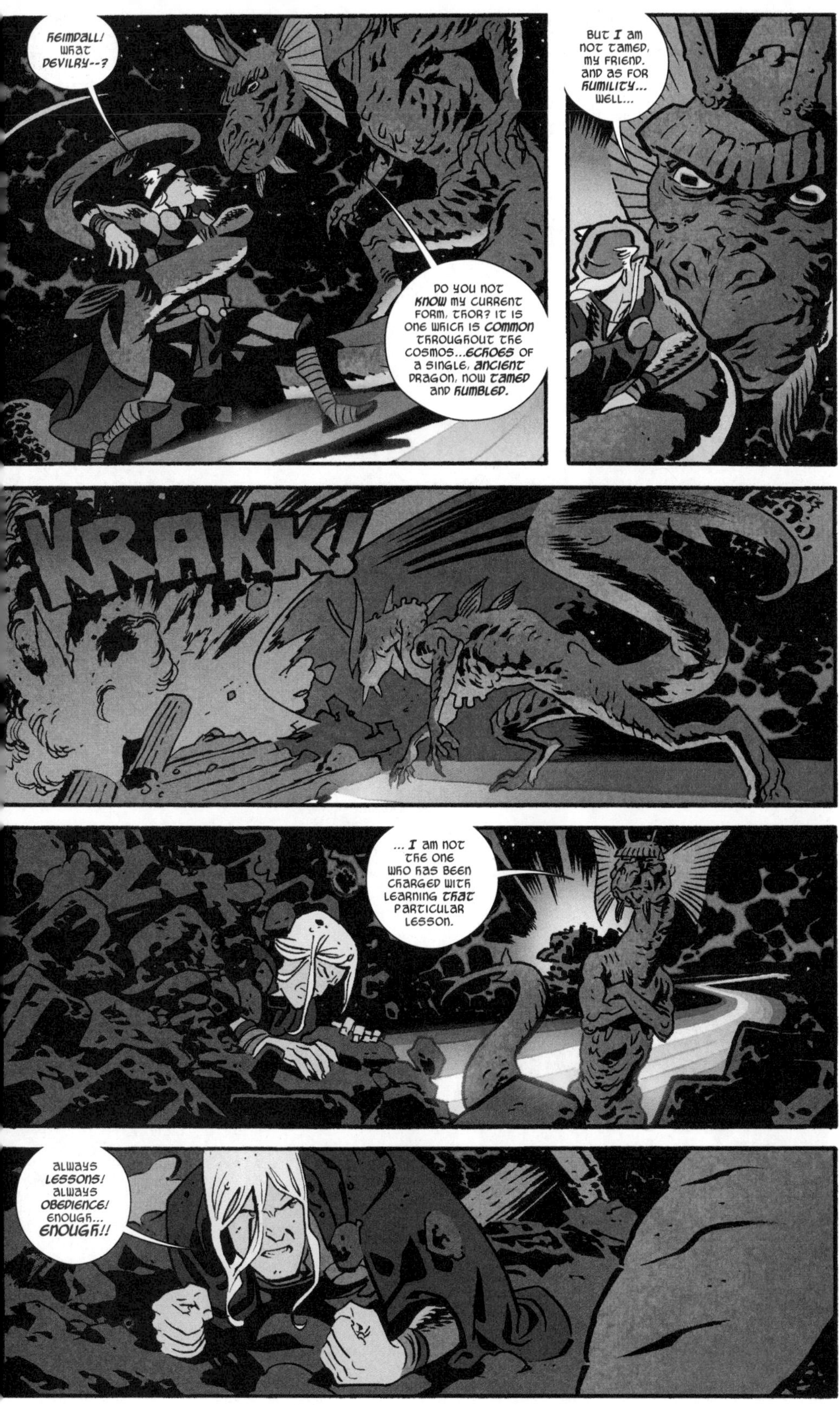
HEIMDALL! WHAT DEVILRY--?
DO YOU NOT KNOW MY CURRENT FORM, THOR? IT IS ONE WHICH IS COMMON THROUGHOUT THE COSMOS...ECHOES OF A SINGLE, ANCIENT DRAGON, NOW TAMED AND HUMBLED.
BUT I AM NOT TAMED, MY FRIEND. AND AS FOR HUMILITY... WELL...
KRAKK!
...I AM NOT THE ONE WHO HAS BEEN CHARGED WITH LEARNING THAT PARTICULAR LESSON.
ALWAYS LESSONS! ALWAYS OBEDIENCE! ENOUGH... ENOUGH!!

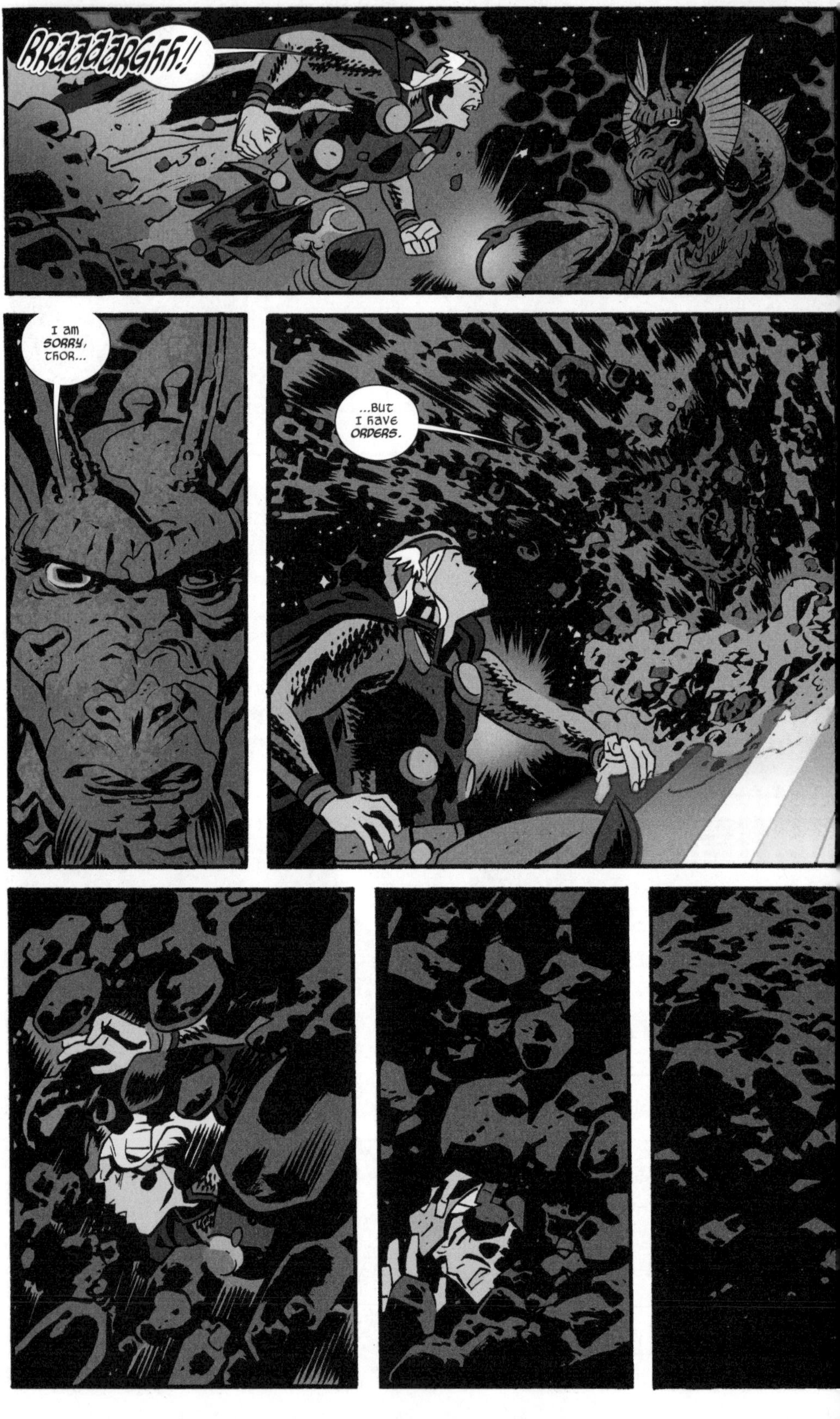
RRAAAAARGHH!!
I am SORRY, THOR...
...BUT I HAVE ORDERS.

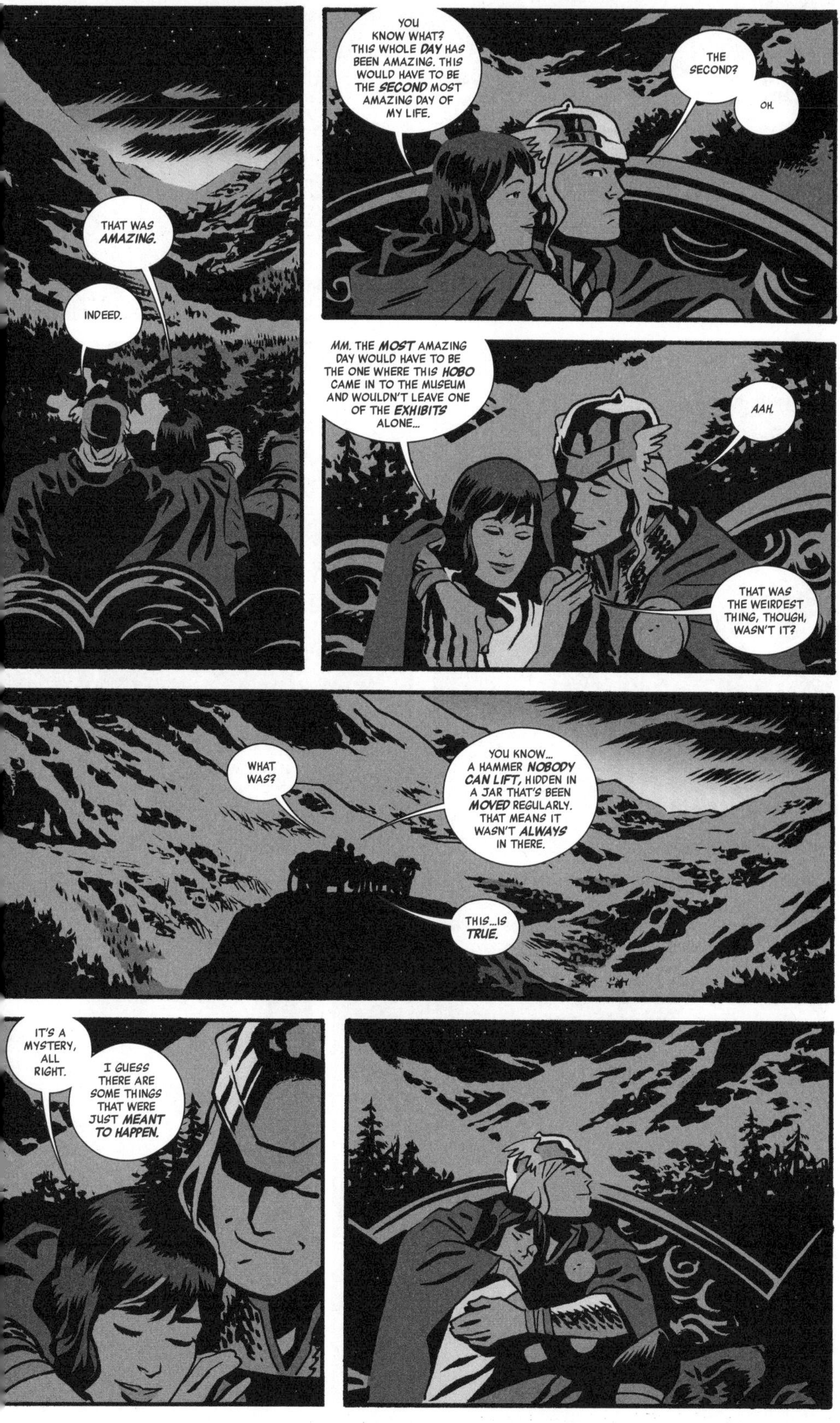
THAT WAS AMAZING.
INDEED.
YOU KNOW WHAT? THIS WHOLE DAY HAS BEEN AMAZING. THIS WOULD HAVE TO BE THE SECOND MOST AMAZING DAY OF MY LIFE.
THE SECOND?
OH.
MM. THE MOST AMAZING DAY WOULD HAVE TO BE THE ONE WHERE THIS HOBO CAME IN TO THE MUSEUM AND WOULDN'T LEAVE ONE OF THE EXHIBITS ALONE...
AAH.
THAT WAS THE WEIRDEST THING, THOUGH, WASN'T IT?
WHAT WAS?
YOU KNOW... A HAMMER NOBODY CAN LIFT, HIDDEN IN A JAR THAT'S BEEN MOVED REGULARLY. THAT MEANS IT WASN'T ALWAYS IN THERE.
THIS...IS TRUE.
IT'S A MYSTERY, ALL RIGHT.
I GUESS THERE ARE SOME THINGS THAT WERE JUST MEANT TO HAPPEN.

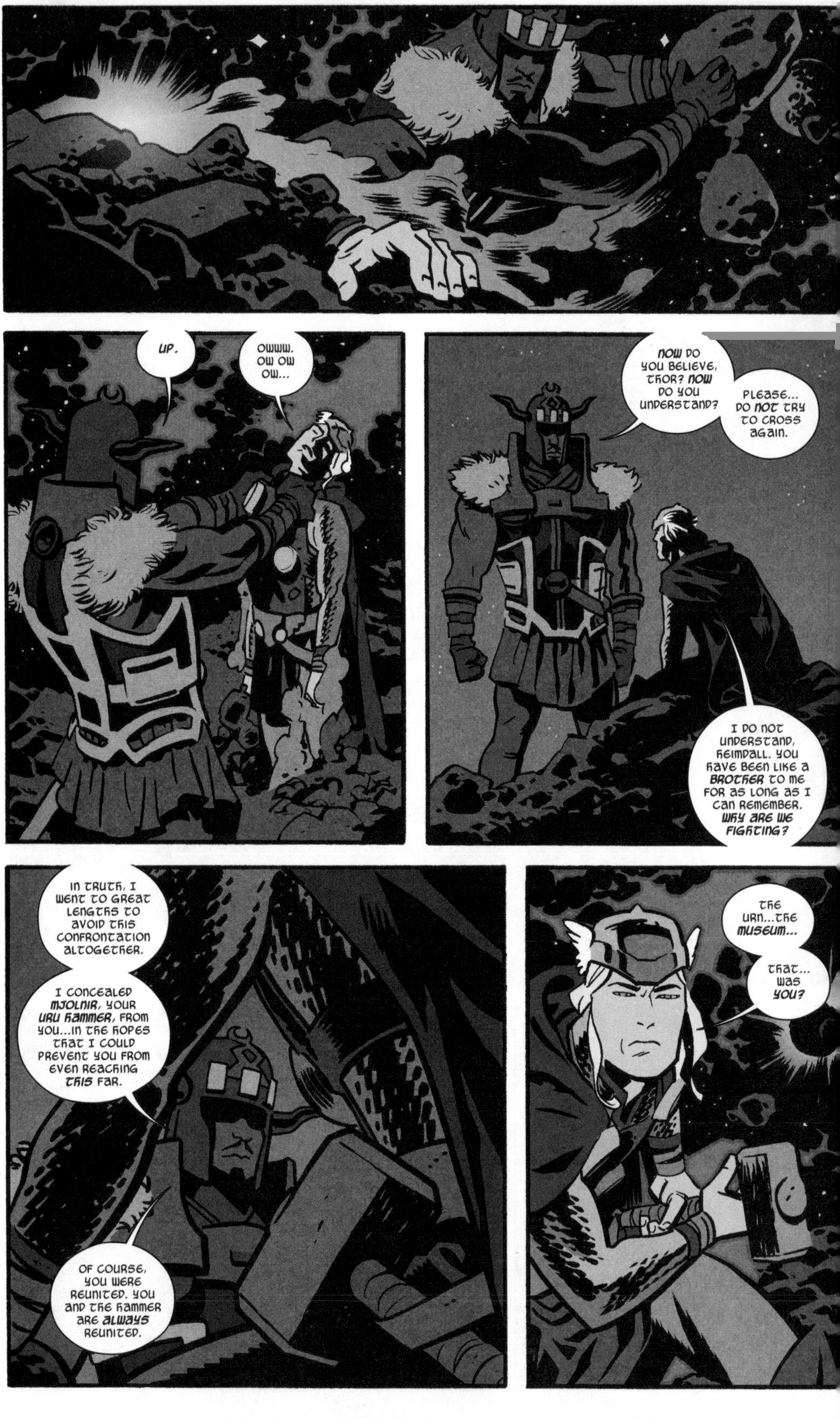
UP.
OWWW. OW OW OW...
NOW DO YOU BELIEVE, THOR? NOW DO YOU UNDERSTAND?
PLEASE... DO NOT TRY TO CROSS AGAIN.
I DO NOT UNDERSTAND, HEIMDALL. YOU HAVE BEEN LIKE A BROTHER TO ME FOR AS LONG AS I CAN REMEMBER. WHY ARE WE FIGHTING?
IN TRUTH, I WENT TO GREAT LENGTHS TO AVOID THIS CONFRONTATION ALTOGETHER.
I CONCEALED MJOLNIR, YOUR URU HAMMER, FROM YOU...IN THE HOPES THAT I COULD PREVENT YOU FROM EVEN REACHING THIS FAR.
OF COURSE, YOU WERE REUNITED. YOU AND THE HAMMER ARE ALWAYS REUNITED.
THE URN...THE MUSEUM...
THAT... WAS YOU?

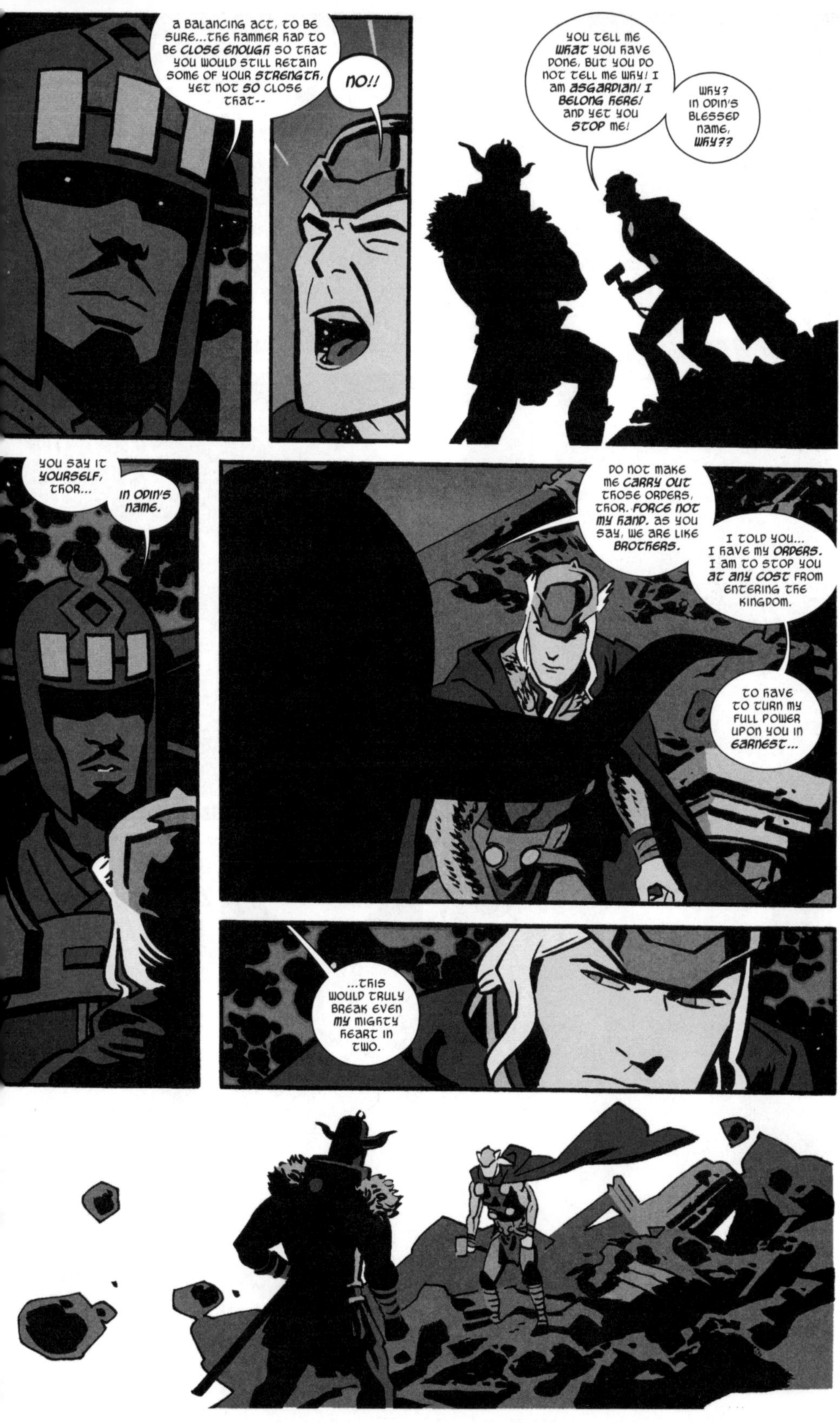
A BALANCING ACT, TO BE SURE...THE HAMMER HAD TO BE CLOSE ENOUGH SO THAT YOU WOULD STILL RETAIN SOME OF YOUR STRENGTH, YET NOT SO CLOSE THAT--
NO!!
YOU TELL ME WHAT YOU HAVE DONE, BUT YOU DO NOT TELL ME WHY! I AM ASGARDIAN! I BELONG HERE! AND YET YOU STOP ME!
WHY? IN ODIN'S BLESSED NAME, WHY??
YOU SAY IT YOURSELF, THOR...
IN ODIN'S NAME.
DO NOT MAKE ME CARRY OUT THOSE ORDERS, THOR. FORCE NOT MY HAND. AS YOU SAY, WE ARE LIKE BROTHERS.
I TOLD YOU... I HAVE MY ORDERS. I AM TO STOP YOU AT ANY COST FROM ENTERING THE KINGDOM.
TO HAVE TO TURN MY FULL POWER UPON YOU IN EARNEST...
...THIS WOULD TRULY BREAK EVEN MY MIGHTY HEART IN TWO.

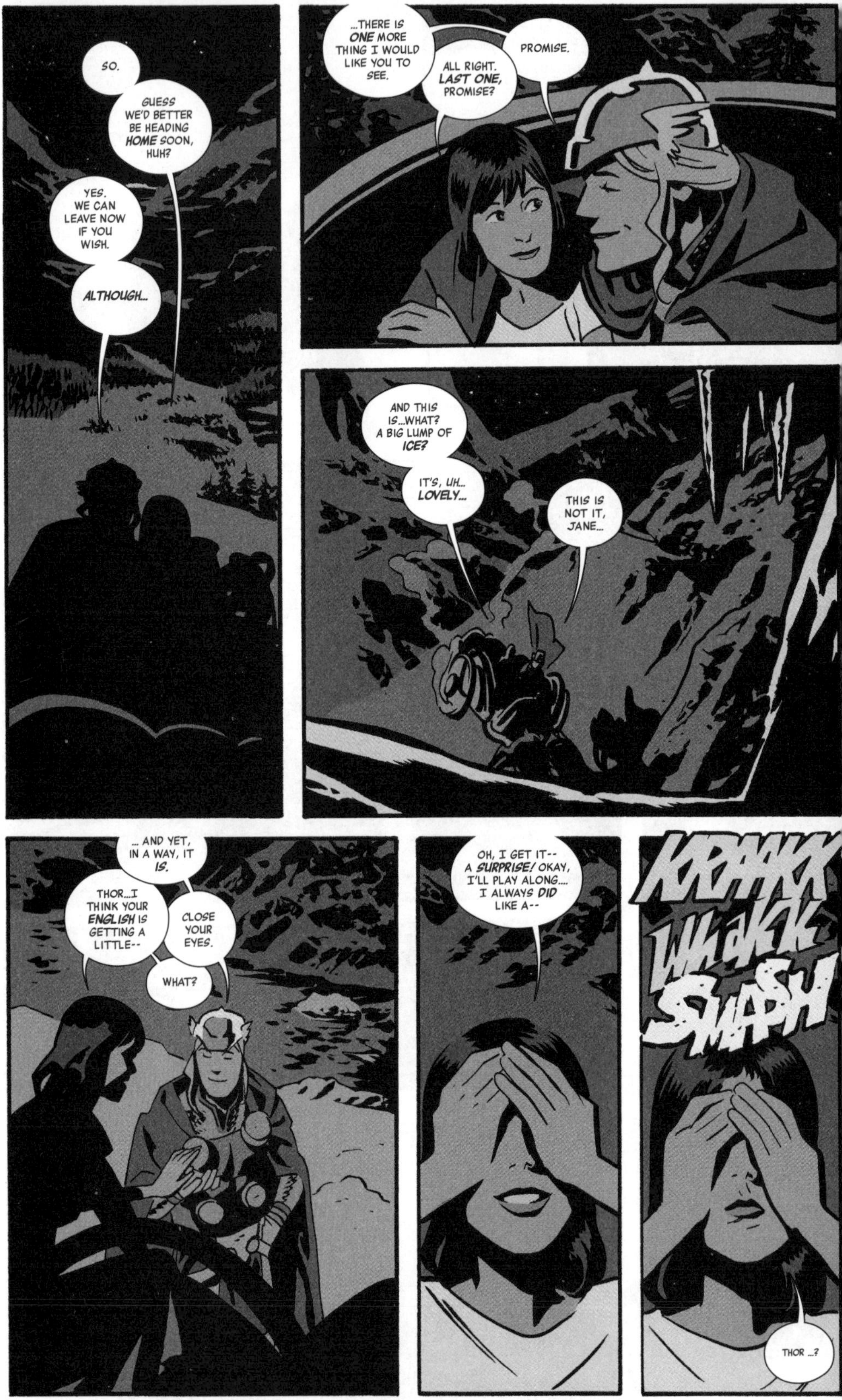
SO.
GUESS WE'D BETTER BE HEADING HOME SOON, HUH?
YES. WE CAN LEAVE NOW IF YOU WISH.
ALTHOUGH...
...THERE IS ONE MORE THING I WOULD LIKE YOU TO SEE.
ALL RIGHT. LAST ONE, PROMISE?
PROMISE.
AND THIS IS...WHAT? A BIG LUMP OF ICE?
IT'S, UH... LOVELY...
THIS IS NOT IT, JANE...
... AND YET, IN A WAY, IT IS.
THOR...I THINK YOUR ENGLISH IS GETTING A LITTLE--
CLOSE YOUR EYES.
WHAT?
OH, I GET IT-- A SURPRISE! OKAY, I'LL PLAY ALONG.... I ALWAYS DID LIKE A--
KRAAKK
WHAKK
SMASH
THOR ...?

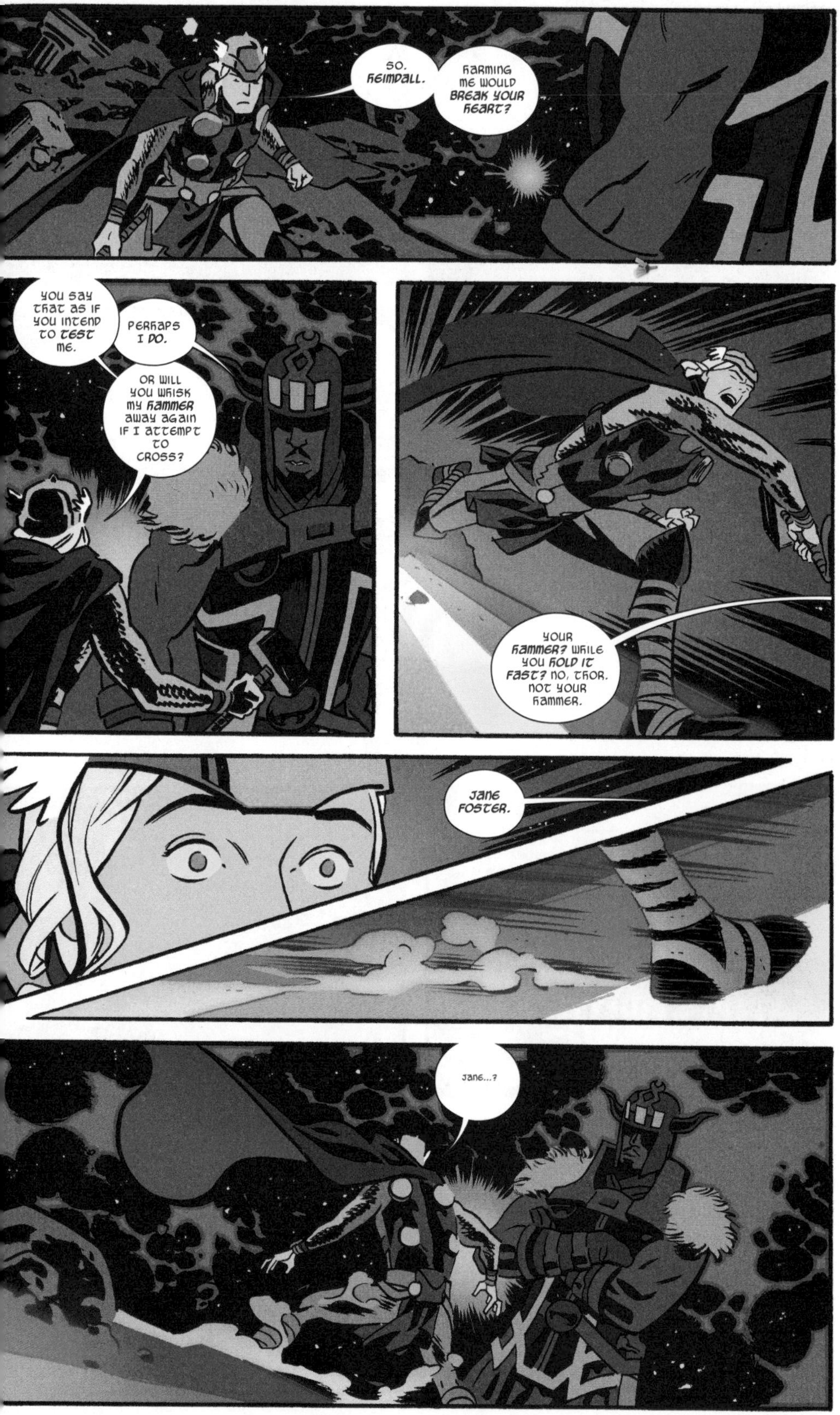

SO. HEIMDALL.
HARMING ME WOULD BREAK YOUR HEART?
YOU SAY THAT AS IF YOU INTEND TO TEST ME.
PERHAPS I DO.
OR WILL YOU WHISK MY HAMMER AWAY AGAIN IF I ATTEMPT TO CROSS?
YOUR HAMMER? WHILE YOU HOLD IT FAST? NO, THOR. NOT YOUR HAMMER.
JANE FOSTER.
JANE...?

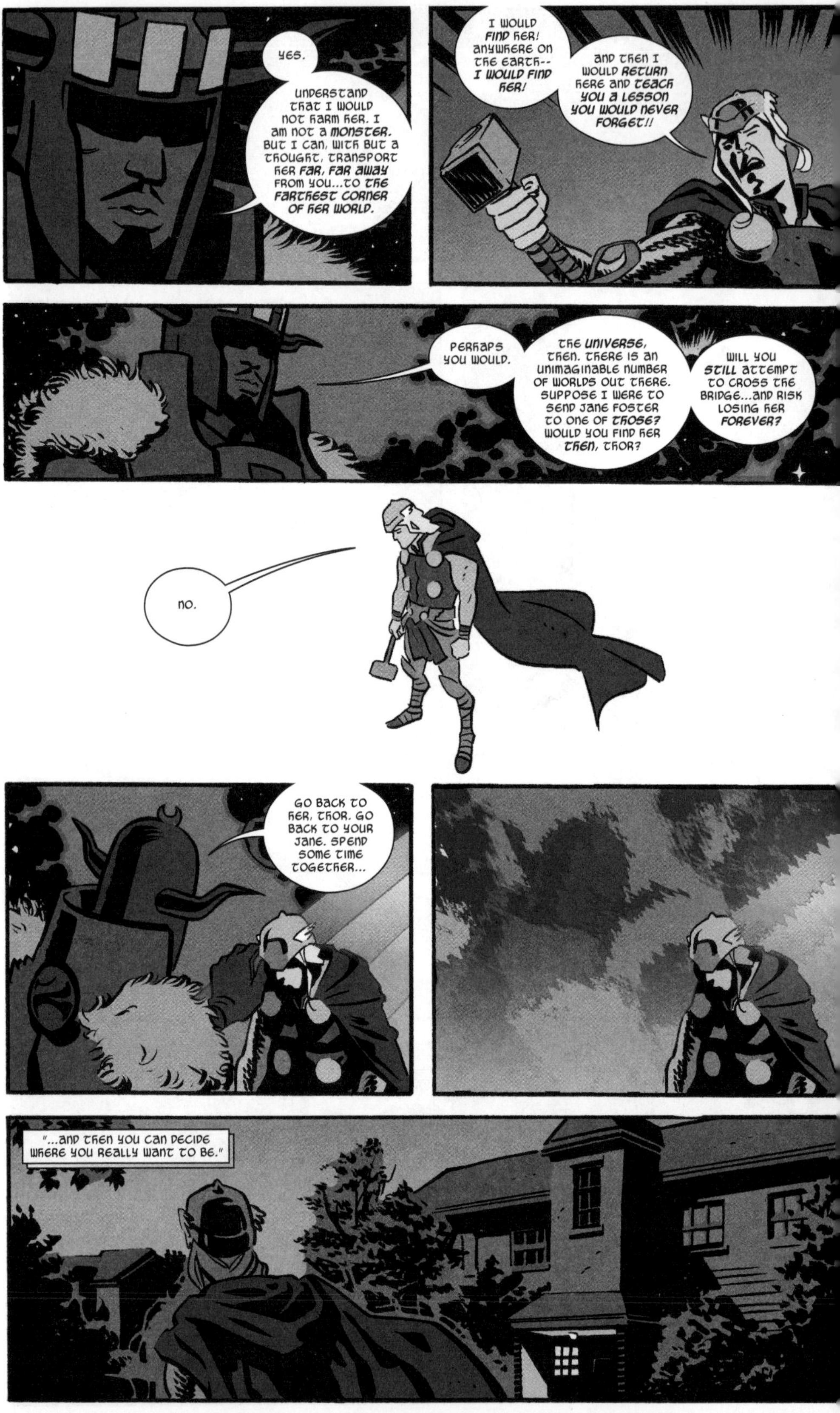
YES.
UNDERSTAND THAT I WOULD NOT HARM HER. I AM NOT A MONSTER. BUT I CAN, WITH BUT A THOUGHT, TRANSPORT HER FAR, FAR AWAY FROM YOU...TO THE FARTHEST CORNER OF HER WORLD.
I WOULD FIND HER! ANYWHERE ON THE EARTH-- I WOULD FIND HER!
AND THEN I WOULD RETURN HERE AND TEACH YOU A LESSON YOU WOULD NEVER FORGET!!
PERHAPS YOU WOULD.
THE UNIVERSE, THEN. THERE IS AN UNIMAGINABLE NUMBER OF WORLDS OUT THERE. SUPPOSE I WERE TO SEND JANE FOSTER TO ONE OF THOSE? WOULD YOU FIND HER THEN, THOR?
WILL YOU STILL ATTEMPT TO CROSS THE BRIDGE...AND RISK LOSING HER FOREVER?
NO.
GO BACK TO HER, THOR. GO BACK TO YOUR JANE. SPEND SOME TIME TOGETHER...
"...AND THEN YOU CAN DECIDE WHERE YOU REALLY WANT TO BE."

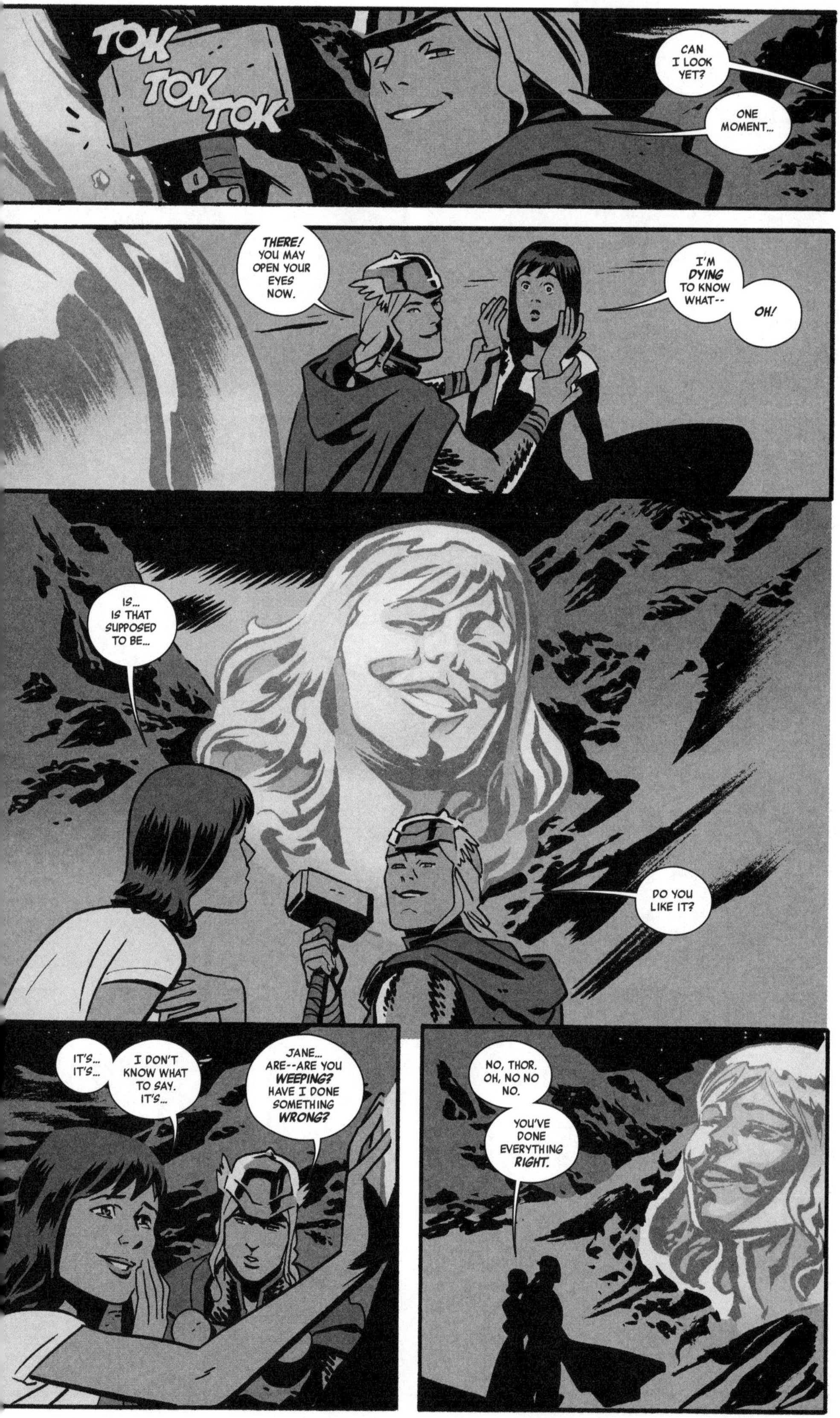
TOK
TOK TOK
CAN I LOOK YET?
ONE MOMENT...
THERE! YOU MAY OPEN YOUR EYES NOW.
I'M DYING TO KNOW WHAT--
OH!
IS... IS THAT SUPPOSED TO BE...
DO YOU LIKE IT?
IT'S... IT'S...
I DON'T KNOW WHAT TO SAY. IT'S...
JANE... ARE--ARE YOU WEEPING? HAVE I DONE SOMETHING WRONG?
NO, THOR. OH, NO NO NO.
YOU'VE DONE EVERYTHING RIGHT.

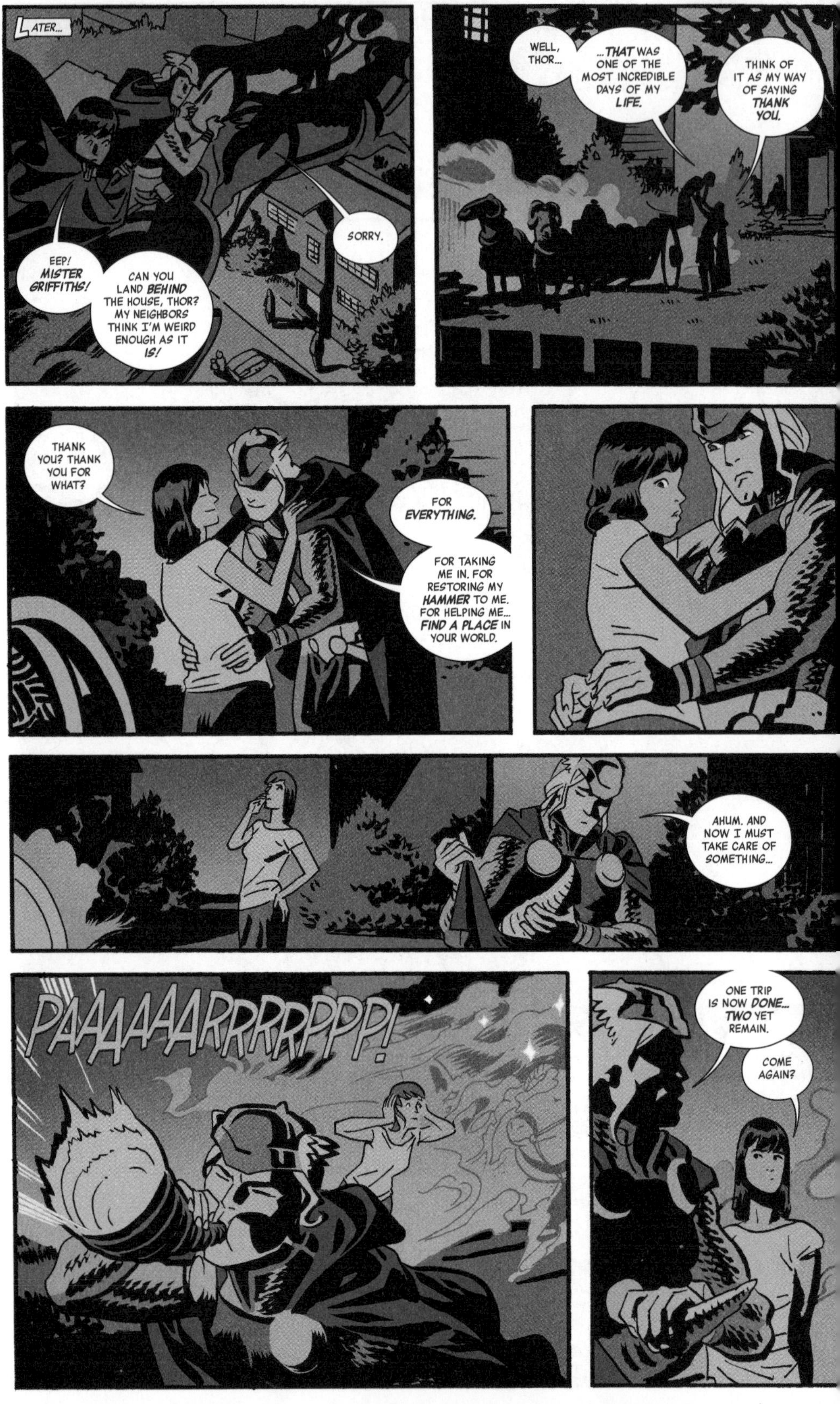
LATER...
EEP! MISTER GRIFFITHS!
CAN YOU LAND BEHIND THE HOUSE, THOR? MY NEIGHBORS THINK I'M WEIRD ENOUGH AS IT IS!
SORRY.
WELL, THOR...
...THAT WAS ONE OF THE MOST INCREDIBLE DAYS OF MY LIFE.
THINK OF IT AS MY WAY OF SAYING THANK YOU.
THANK YOU? THANK YOU FOR WHAT?
FOR EVERYTHING.
FOR TAKING ME IN. FOR RESTORING MY HAMMER TO ME. FOR HELPING ME... FIND A PLACE IN YOUR WORLD.
AHUM. AND NOW I MUST TAKE CARE OF SOMETHING...
PAAAAAARRRRRPPPP!
ONE TRIP IS NOW DONE... TWO YET REMAIN.
COME AGAIN?

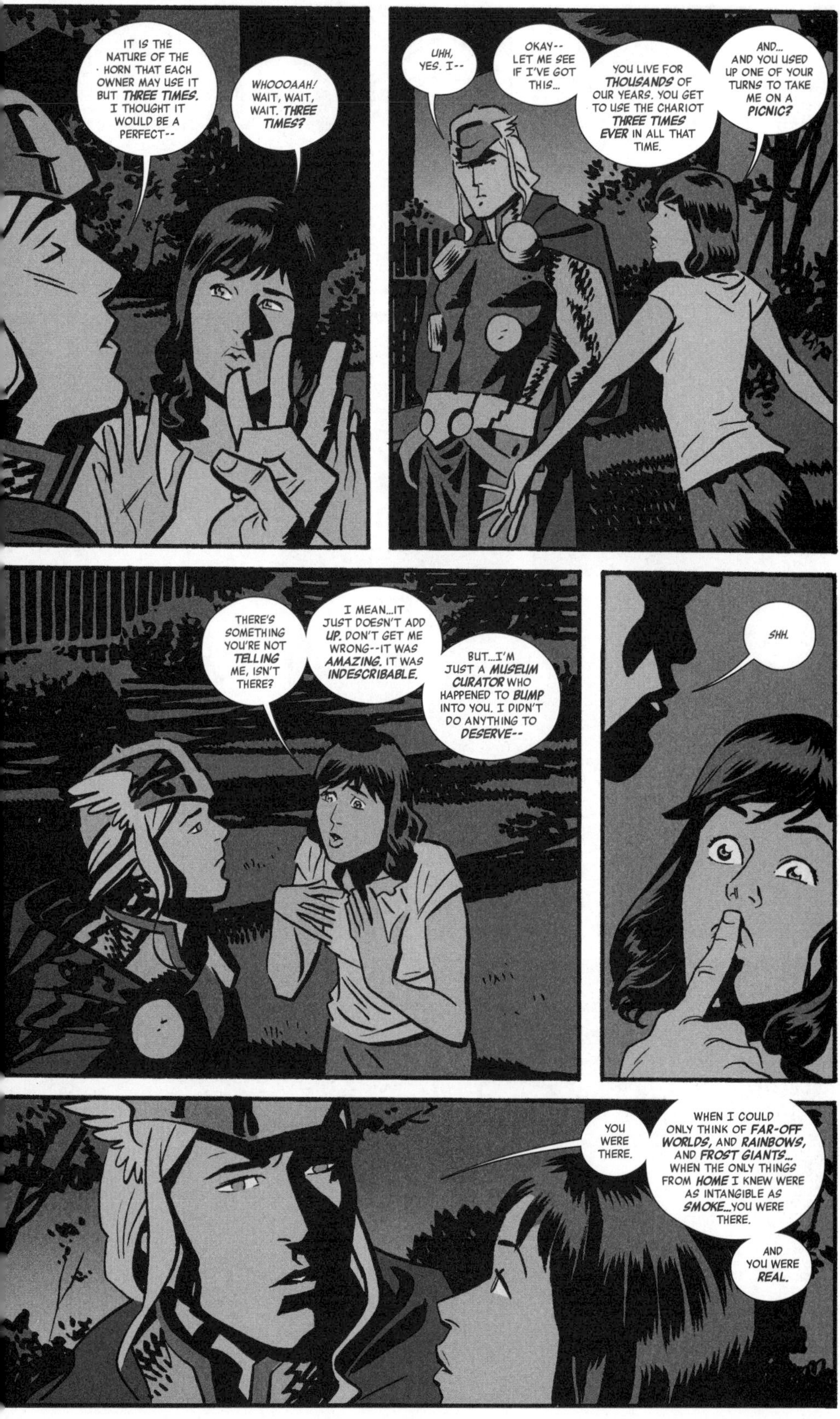
IT IS THE NATURE OF THE HORN THAT EACH OWNER MAY USE IT BUT THREE TIMES. I THOUGHT IT WOULD BE A PERFECT--
WHOOOAAH! WAIT, WAIT, WAIT. THREE TIMES?
UHH, YES. I--
OKAY-- LET ME SEE IF I'VE GOT THIS...
YOU LIVE FOR THOUSANDS OF OUR YEARS. YOU GET TO USE THE CHARIOT THREE TIMES EVER IN ALL THAT TIME.
AND... AND YOU USED UP ONE OF YOUR TURNS TO TAKE ME ON A PICNIC?
I MEAN...IT JUST DOESN'T ADD UP. DON'T GET ME WRONG--IT WAS AMAZING. IT WAS INDESCRIBABLE.
BUT...I'M JUST A MUSEUM CURATOR WHO HAPPENED TO BUMP INTO YOU. I DIDN'T DO ANYTHING TO DESERVE--
THERE'S SOMETHING YOU'RE NOT TELLING ME, ISN'T THERE?
SHH.
YOU WERE THERE.
WHEN I COULD ONLY THINK OF FAR-OFF WORLDS, AND RAINBOWS, AND FROST GIANTS... WHEN THE ONLY THINGS FROM HOME I KNEW WERE AS INTANGIBLE AS SMOKE...YOU WERE THERE.
AND YOU WERE REAL.

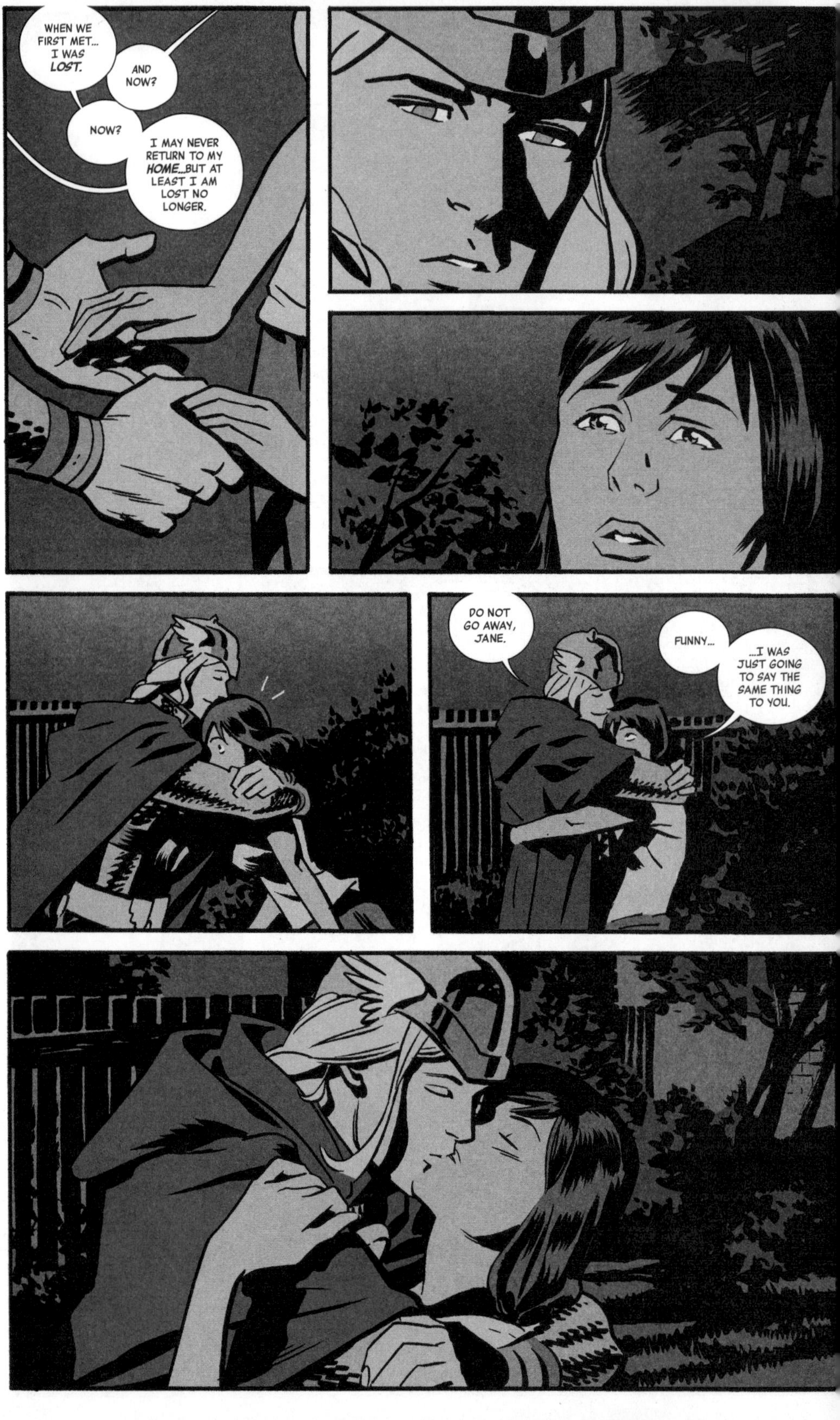
WHEN WE FIRST MET... I WAS LOST.
AND NOW?
NOW?
I MAY NEVER RETURN TO MY HOME...BUT AT LEAST I AM LOST NO LONGER.
DO NOT GO AWAY, JANE.
FUNNY...
...I WAS JUST GOING TO SAY THE SAME THING TO YOU.

THOR THE MIGHTY AVENGER #7

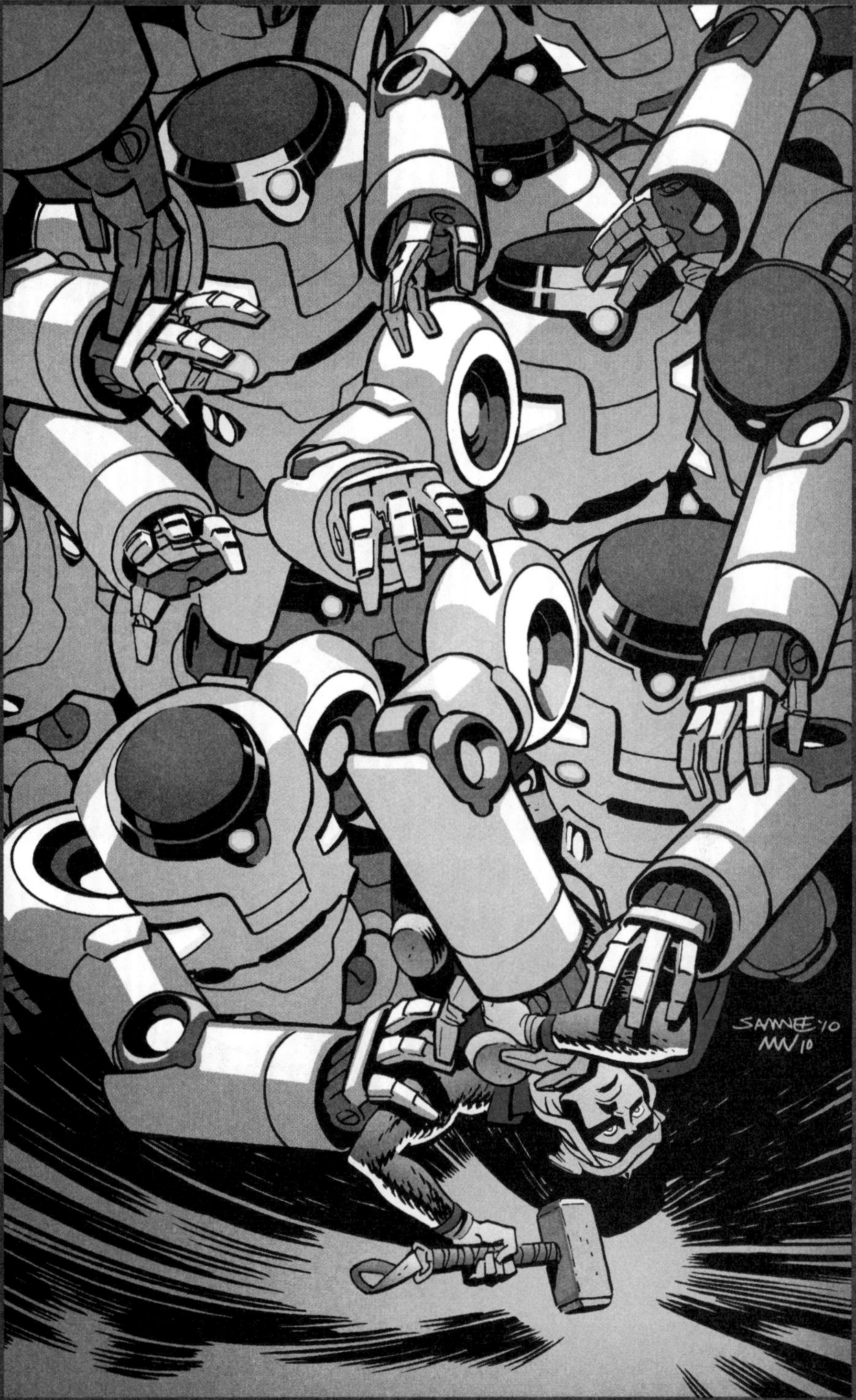
SAMNEE '10
MW 10

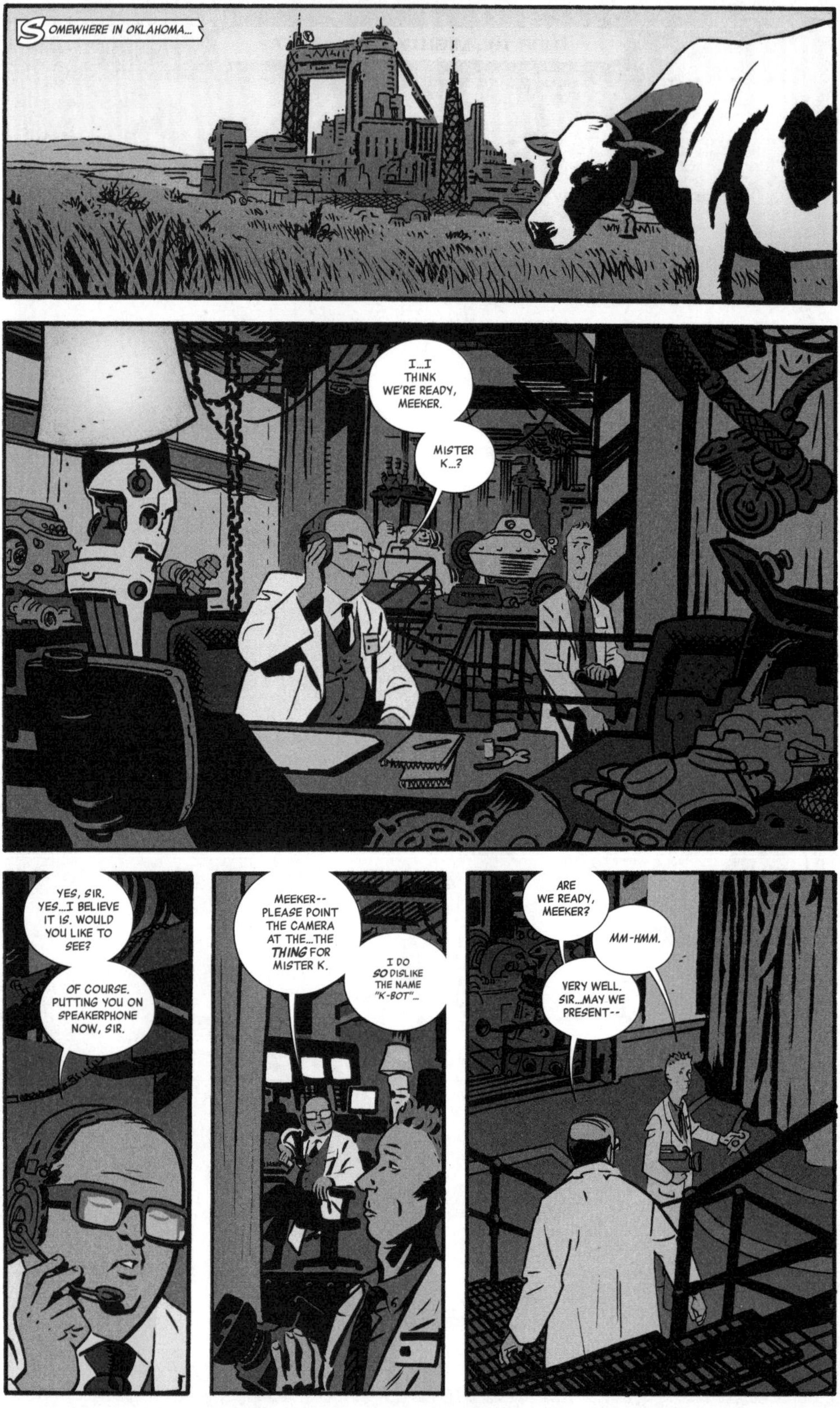
SOMEWHERE IN OKLAHOMA...
I...I THINK WE'RE READY, MEEKER.
MISTER K...?
YES, SIR. YES...I BELIEVE IT IS. WOULD YOU LIKE TO SEE?
OF COURSE. PUTTING YOU ON SPEAKERPHONE NOW, SIR.
MEEKER-- PLEASE POINT THE CAMERA AT THE...THE THING FOR MISTER K.
I DO SO DISLIKE THE NAME "K-BOT"...
ARE WE READY, MEEKER?
MM-HMM.
VERY WELL. SIR...MAY WE PRESENT--

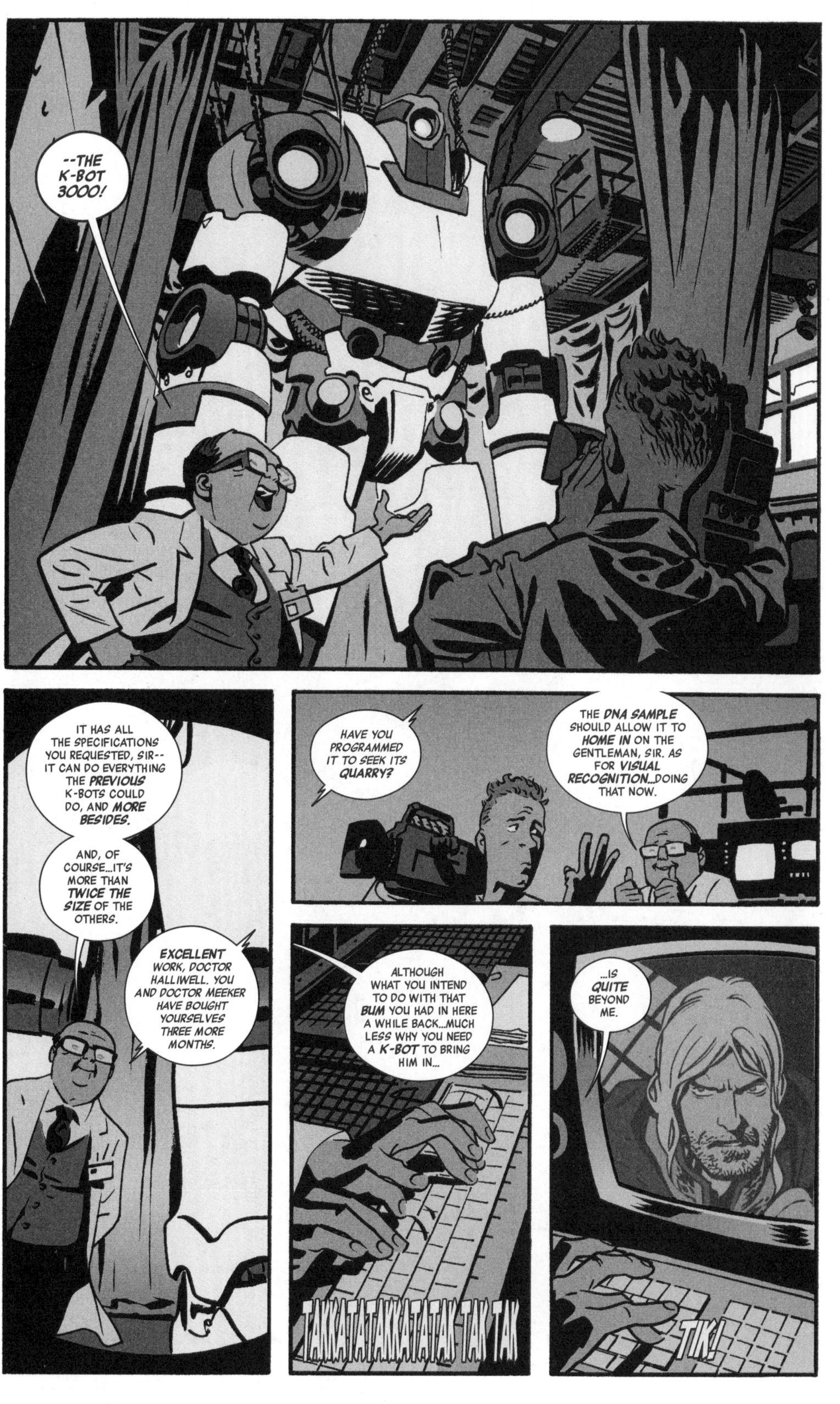
--THE K-BOT 3000!
IT HAS ALL THE SPECIFICATIONS YOU REQUESTED, SIR-- IT CAN DO EVERYTHING THE PREVIOUS K-BOTS COULD DO, AND MORE BESIDES.
AND, OF COURSE...IT'S MORE THAN TWICE THE SIZE OF THE OTHERS.
EXCELLENT WORK, DOCTOR HALLIWELL. YOU AND DOCTOR MEEKER HAVE BOUGHT YOURSELVES THREE MORE MONTHS.
HAVE YOU PROGRAMMED IT TO SEEK ITS QUARRY?
THE DNA SAMPLE SHOULD ALLOW IT TO HOME IN ON THE GENTLEMAN, SIR. AS FOR VISUAL RECOGNITION...DOING THAT NOW.
ALTHOUGH WHAT YOU INTEND TO DO WITH THAT BUM YOU HAD IN HERE A WHILE BACK...MUCH LESS WHY YOU NEED A K-BOT TO BRING HIM IN...
TAKKATATAKKATATAK TAK TAK
...IS QUITE BEYOND ME.
TIK!

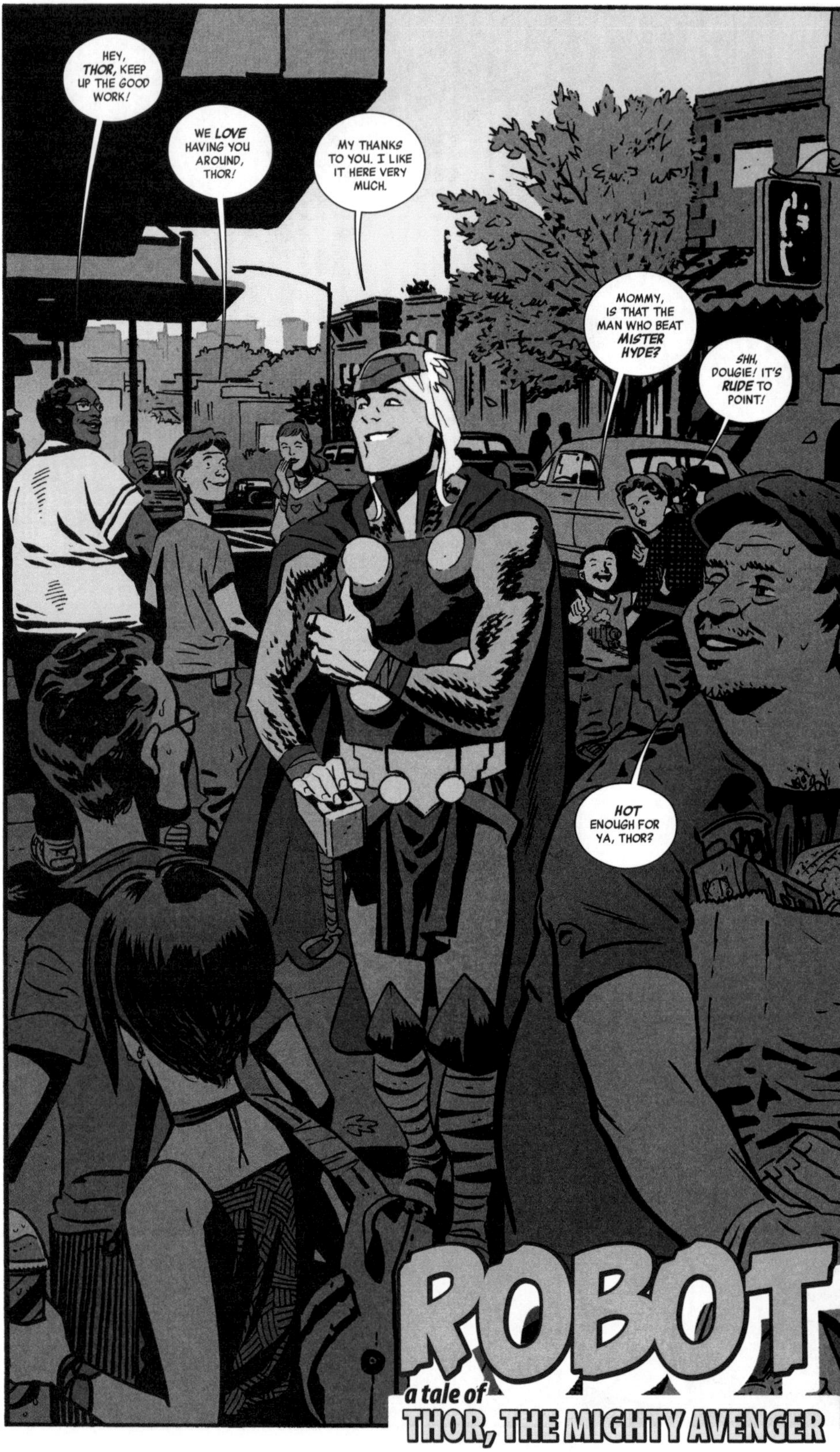
HEY, THOR, KEEP UP THE GOOD WORK!
WE LOVE HAVING YOU AROUND, THOR!
MY THANKS TO YOU. I LIKE IT HERE VERY MUCH.
MOMMY, IS THAT THE MAN WHO BEAT MISTER HYDE?
SHH, DOUGIE! IT'S RUDE TO POINT!
HOT ENOUGH FOR YA, THOR?
ROBOT
a tale of
THOR, THE MIGHTY AVENGER

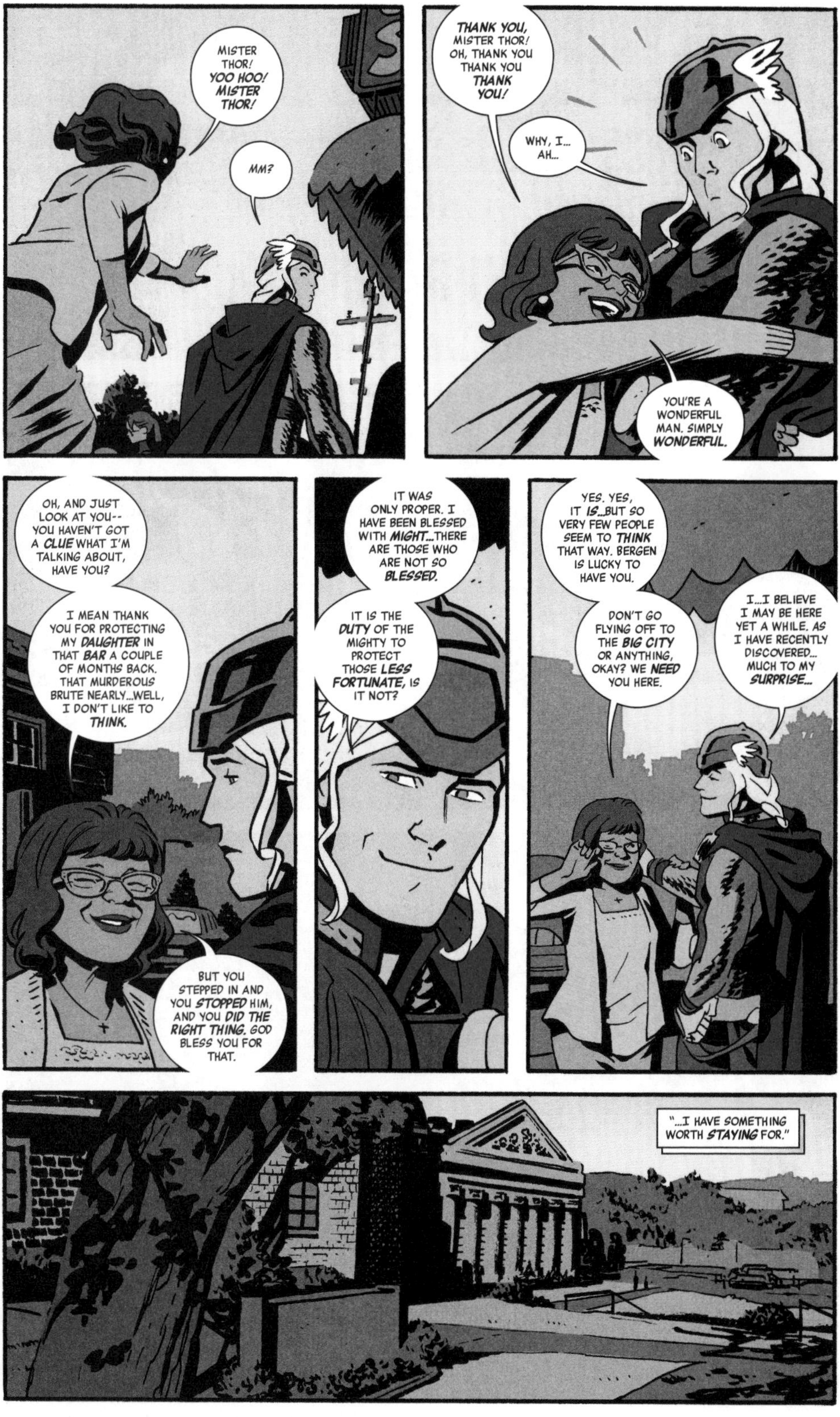

MISTER THOR! YOO HOO! MISTER THOR!
MM?
THANK YOU, MISTER THOR! OH, THANK YOU THANK YOU THANK YOU!
WHY, I... AH...
YOU'RE A WONDERFUL MAN. SIMPLY WONDERFUL.
OH, AND JUST LOOK AT YOU-- YOU HAVEN'T GOT A CLUE WHAT I'M TALKING ABOUT, HAVE YOU?
I MEAN THANK YOU FOR PROTECTING MY DAUGHTER IN THAT BAR A COUPLE OF MONTHS BACK. THAT MURDEROUS BRUTE NEARLY...WELL, I DON'T LIKE TO THINK.
BUT YOU STEPPED IN AND YOU STOPPED HIM, AND YOU DID THE RIGHT THING. GOD BLESS YOU FOR THAT.
IT WAS ONLY PROPER. I HAVE BEEN BLESSED WITH MIGHT...THERE ARE THOSE WHO ARE NOT SO BLESSED.
IT IS THE DUTY OF THE MIGHTY TO PROTECT THOSE LESS FORTUNATE, IS IT NOT?
YES. YES, IT IS...BUT SO VERY FEW PEOPLE SEEM TO THINK THAT WAY. BERGEN IS LUCKY TO HAVE YOU.
DON'T GO FLYING OFF TO THE BIG CITY OR ANYTHING, OKAY? WE NEED YOU HERE.
I...I BELIEVE I MAY BE HERE YET A WHILE. AS I HAVE RECENTLY DISCOVERED... MUCH TO MY SURPRISE...
"...I HAVE SOMETHING WORTH STAYING FOR."

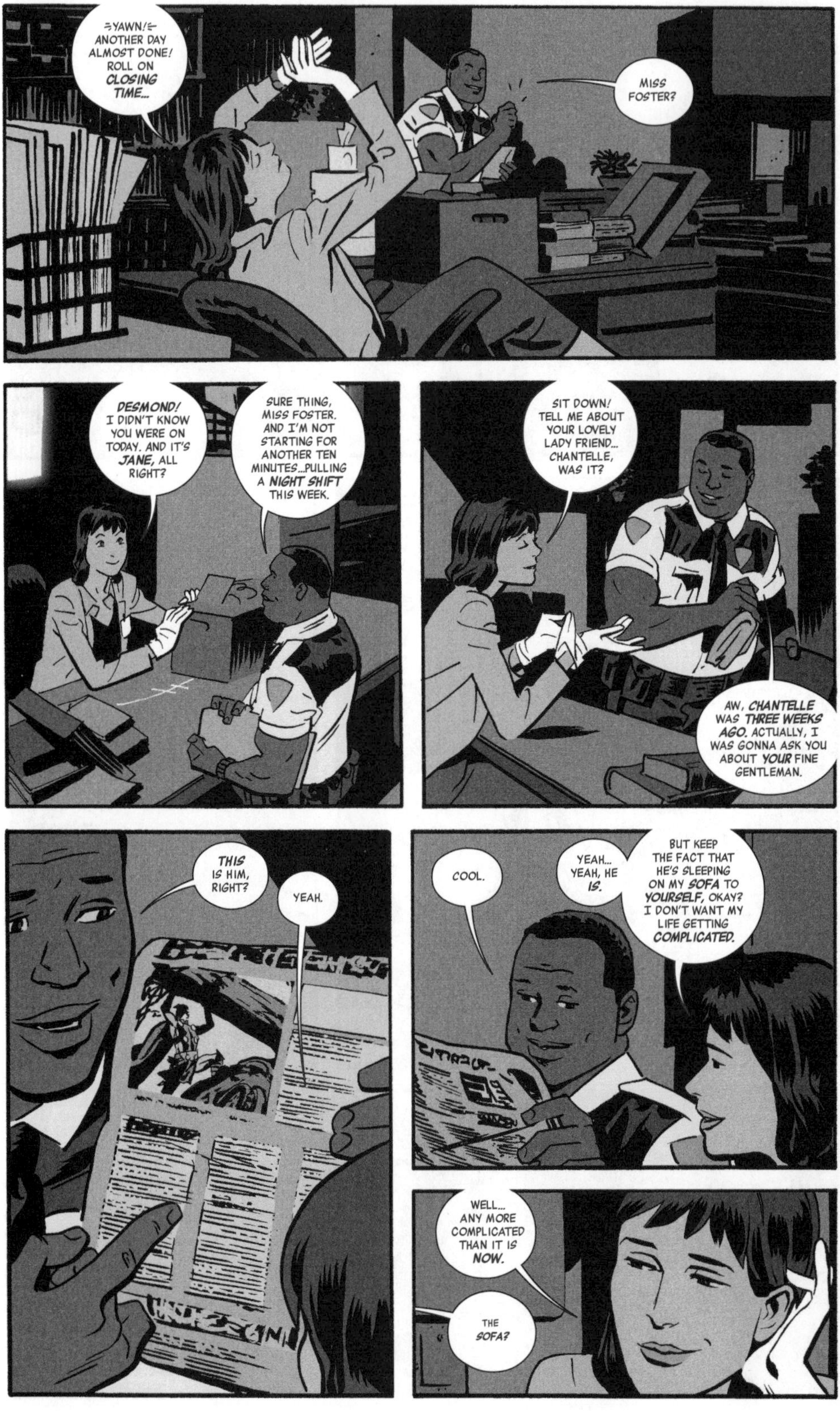

=YAWN!= ANOTHER DAY ALMOST DONE! ROLL ON CLOSING TIME...
MISS FOSTER?
DESMOND! I DIDN'T KNOW YOU WERE ON TODAY. AND IT'S JANE, ALL RIGHT?
SURE THING, MISS FOSTER. AND I'M NOT STARTING FOR ANOTHER TEN MINUTES...PULLING A NIGHT SHIFT THIS WEEK.
SIT DOWN! TELL ME ABOUT YOUR LOVELY LADY FRIEND... CHANTELLE, WAS IT?
AW, CHANTELLE WAS THREE WEEKS AGO. ACTUALLY, I WAS GONNA ASK YOU ABOUT YOUR FINE GENTLEMAN.
THIS IS HIM, RIGHT?
YEAH.
COOL.
YEAH... YEAH, HE IS.
BUT KEEP THE FACT THAT HE'S SLEEPING ON MY SOFA TO YOURSELF, OKAY? I DON'T WANT MY LIFE GETTING COMPLICATED.
WELL... ANY MORE COMPLICATED THAN IT IS NOW.
THE SOFA?

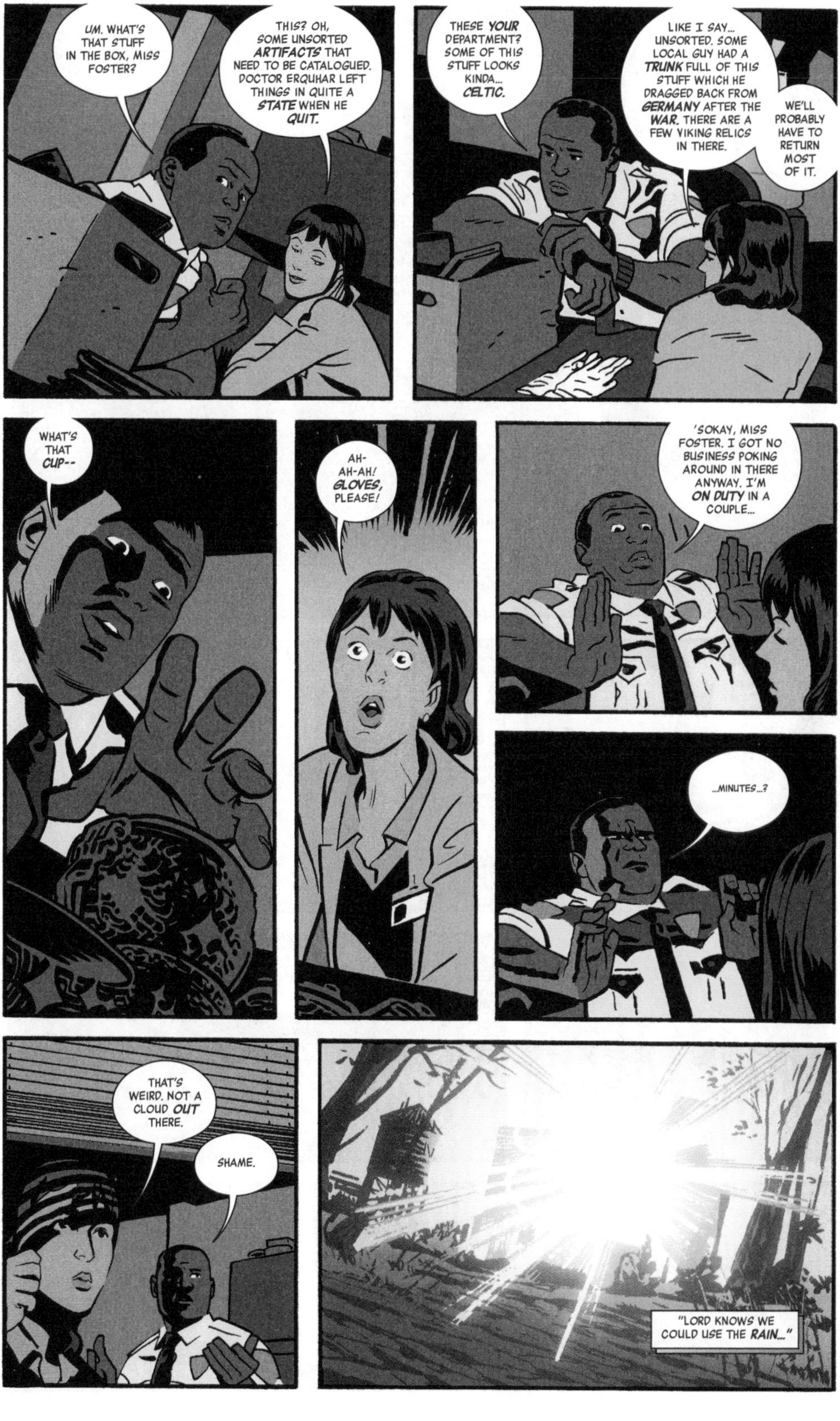
UM. WHAT'S THAT STUFF IN THE BOX, MISS FOSTER?
THIS? OH, SOME UNSORTED ARTIFACTS THAT NEED TO BE CATALOGUED. DOCTOR ERQUHAR LEFT THINGS IN QUITE A STATE WHEN HE QUIT.
THESE YOUR DEPARTMENT? SOME OF THIS STUFF LOOKS KINDA... CELTIC.
LIKE I SAY... UNSORTED. SOME LOCAL GUY HAD A TRUNK FULL OF THIS STUFF WHICH HE DRAGGED BACK FROM GERMANY AFTER THE WAR. THERE ARE A FEW VIKING RELICS IN THERE.
WE'LL PROBABLY HAVE TO RETURN MOST OF IT.
WHAT'S THAT CUP--
AH-AH-AH! GLOVES, PLEASE!
'SOKAY, MISS FOSTER. I GOT NO BUSINESS POKING AROUND IN THERE ANYWAY. I'M ON DUTY IN A COUPLE...
...MINUTES...?
THAT'S WEIRD. NOT A CLOUD OUT THERE.
SHAME.
"LORD KNOWS WE COULD USE THE RAIN..."

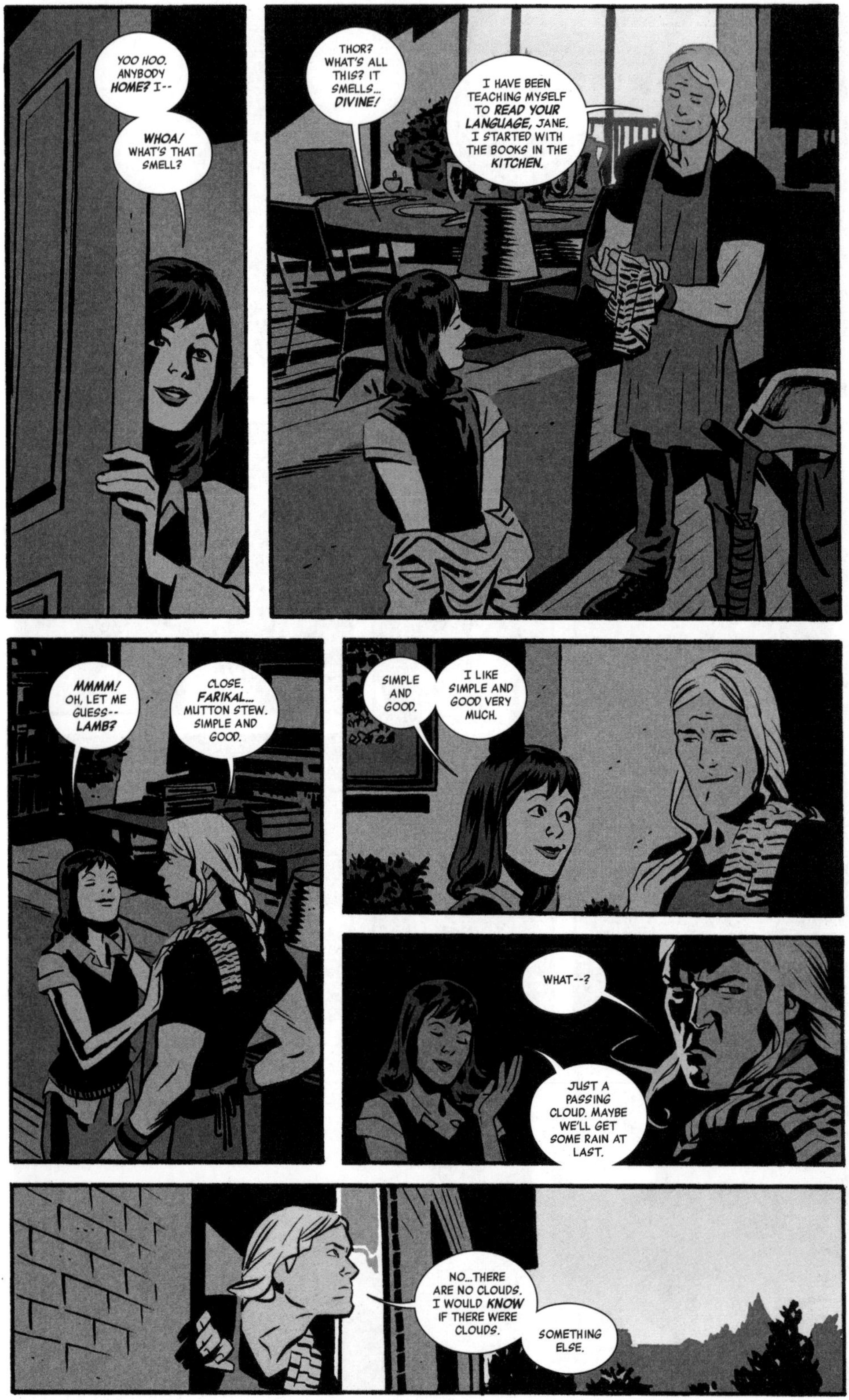
YOO HOO. ANYBODY HOME? I--
WHOA! WHAT'S THAT SMELL?
THOR? WHAT'S ALL THIS? IT SMELLS... DIVINE!
I HAVE BEEN TEACHING MYSELF TO READ YOUR LANGUAGE, JANE. I STARTED WITH THE BOOKS IN THE KITCHEN.
MMMM! OH, LET ME GUESS-- LAMB?
CLOSE. FARIKAL... MUTTON STEW. SIMPLE AND GOOD.
SIMPLE AND GOOD.
I LIKE SIMPLE AND GOOD VERY MUCH.
WHAT--?
JUST A PASSING CLOUD. MAYBE WE'LL GET SOME RAIN AT LAST.
NO...THERE ARE NO CLOUDS. I WOULD KNOW IF THERE WERE CLOUDS.
SOMETHING ELSE.

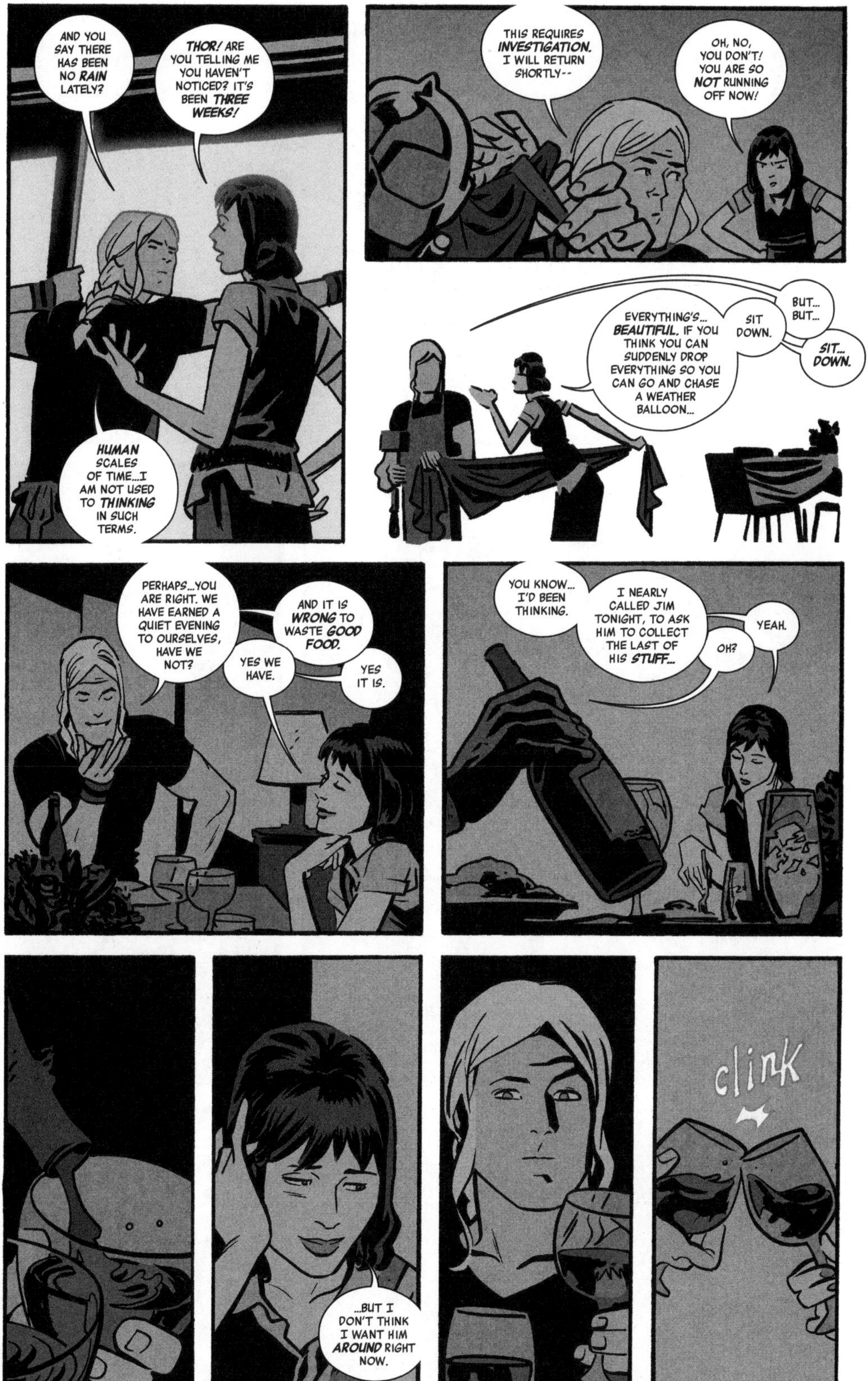
AND YOU SAY THERE HAS BEEN NO RAIN LATELY?
THOR! ARE YOU TELLING ME YOU HAVEN'T NOTICED? IT'S BEEN THREE WEEKS!
HUMAN SCALES OF TIME...I AM NOT USED TO THINKING IN SUCH TERMS.
THIS REQUIRES INVESTIGATION. I WILL RETURN SHORTLY--
OH, NO, YOU DON'T! YOU ARE SO NOT RUNNING OFF NOW!
EVERYTHING'S... BEAUTIFUL. IF YOU THINK YOU CAN SUDDENLY DROP EVERYTHING SO YOU CAN GO AND CHASE A WEATHER BALLOON...
SIT DOWN.
BUT... BUT...
SIT... DOWN.
PERHAPS...YOU ARE RIGHT. WE HAVE EARNED A QUIET EVENING TO OURSELVES, HAVE WE NOT?
YES WE HAVE.
AND IT IS WRONG TO WASTE GOOD FOOD.
YES IT IS.
YOU KNOW... I'D BEEN THINKING.
I NEARLY CALLED JIM TONIGHT, TO ASK HIM TO COLLECT THE LAST OF HIS STUFF...
OH?
YEAH.
...BUT I DON'T THINK I WANT HIM AROUND RIGHT NOW.
clink

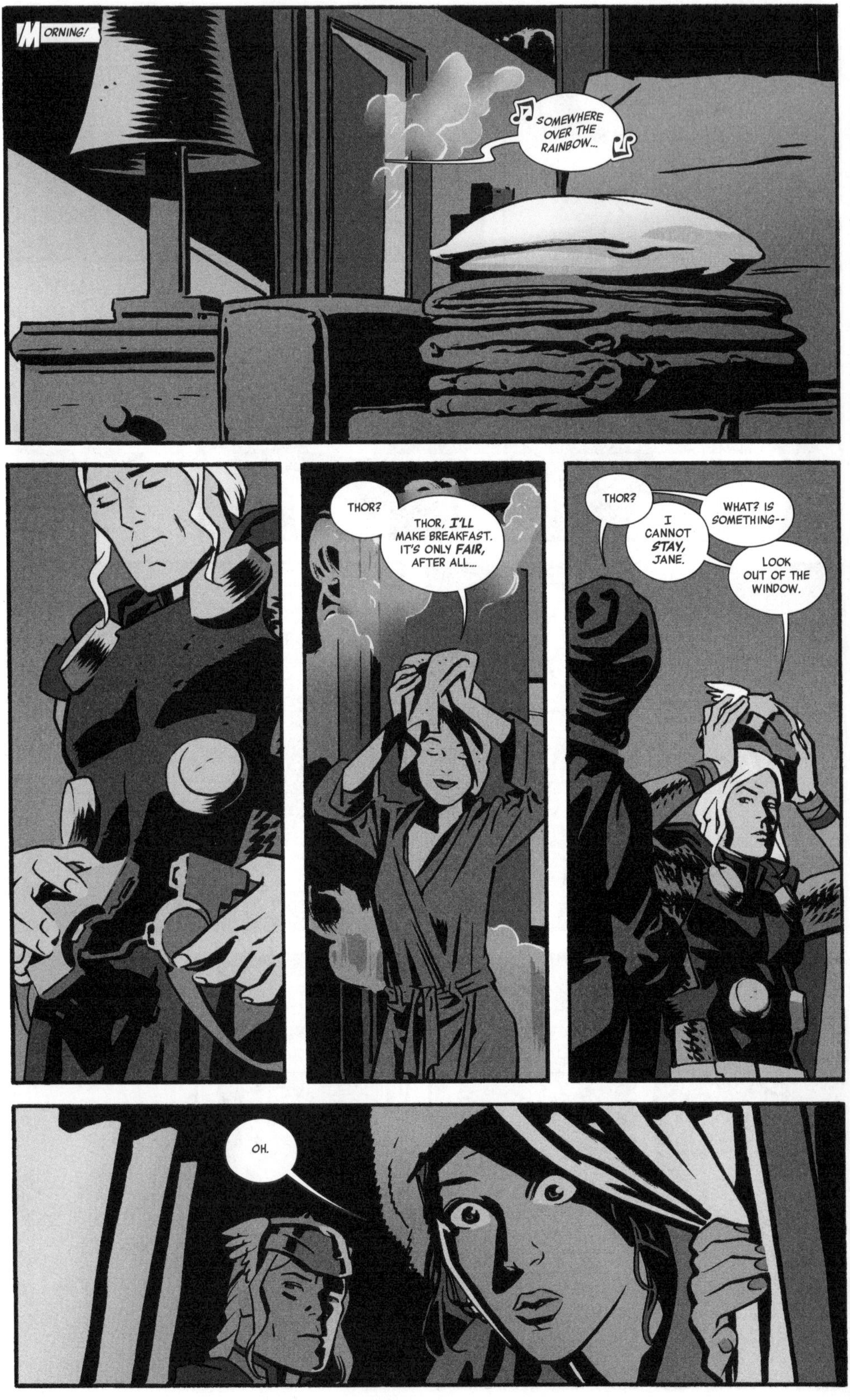
MORNING!
SOMEWHERE OVER THE RAINBOW...
THOR?
THOR, I'LL MAKE BREAKFAST. IT'S ONLY FAIR, AFTER ALL...
THOR?
WHAT? IS SOMETHING--
I CANNOT STAY, JANE.
LOOK OUT OF THE WINDOW.
OH.

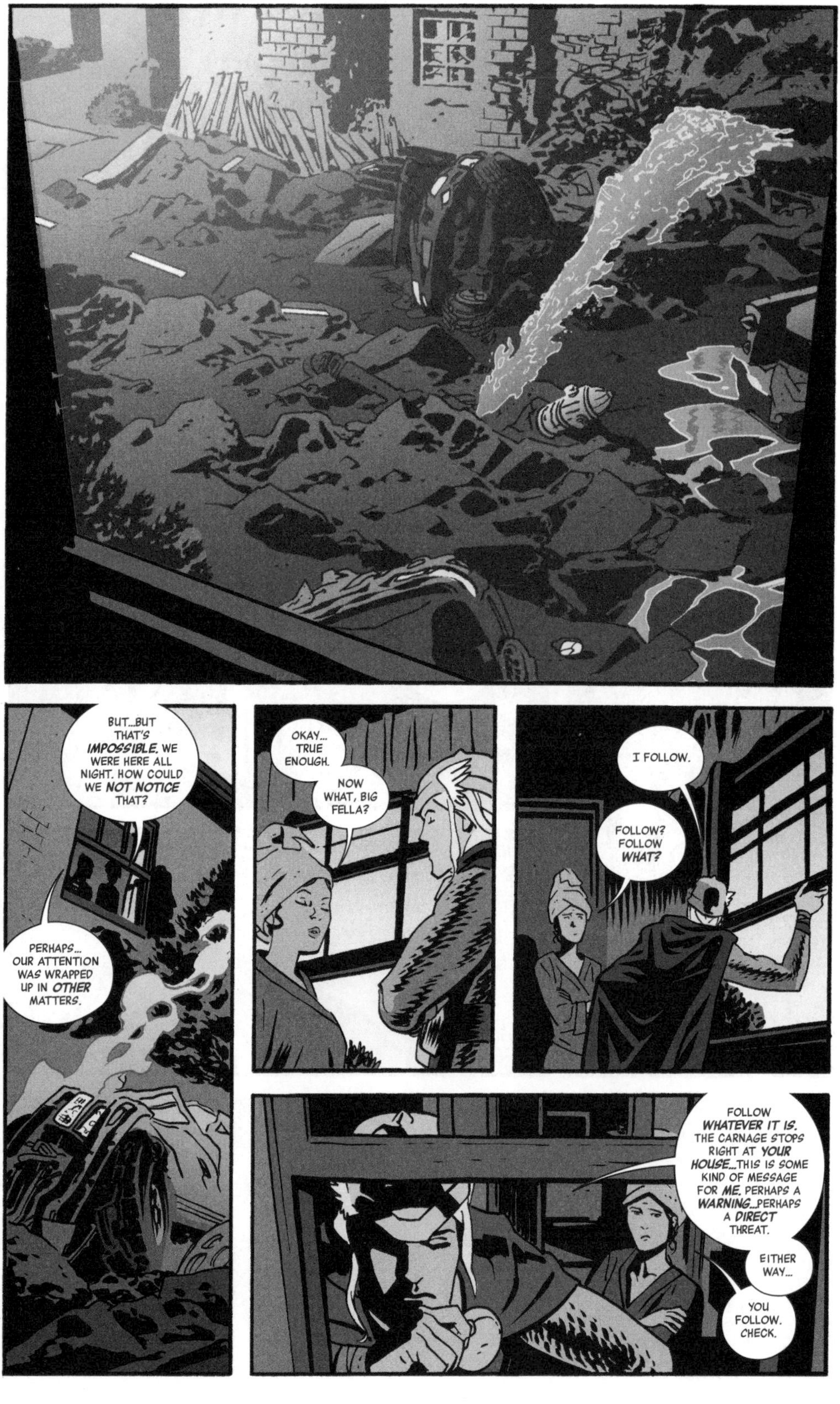
BUT...BUT THAT'S IMPOSSIBLE. WE WERE HERE ALL NIGHT. HOW COULD WE NOT NOTICE THAT?
PERHAPS... OUR ATTENTION WAS WRAPPED UP IN OTHER MATTERS.
OKAY... TRUE ENOUGH.
NOW WHAT, BIG FELLA?
I FOLLOW.
FOLLOW? FOLLOW WHAT?
FOLLOW WHATEVER IT IS. THE CARNAGE STOPS RIGHT AT YOUR HOUSE...THIS IS SOME KIND OF MESSAGE FOR ME. PERHAPS A WARNING...PERHAPS A DIRECT THREAT.
EITHER WAY...
YOU FOLLOW. CHECK.

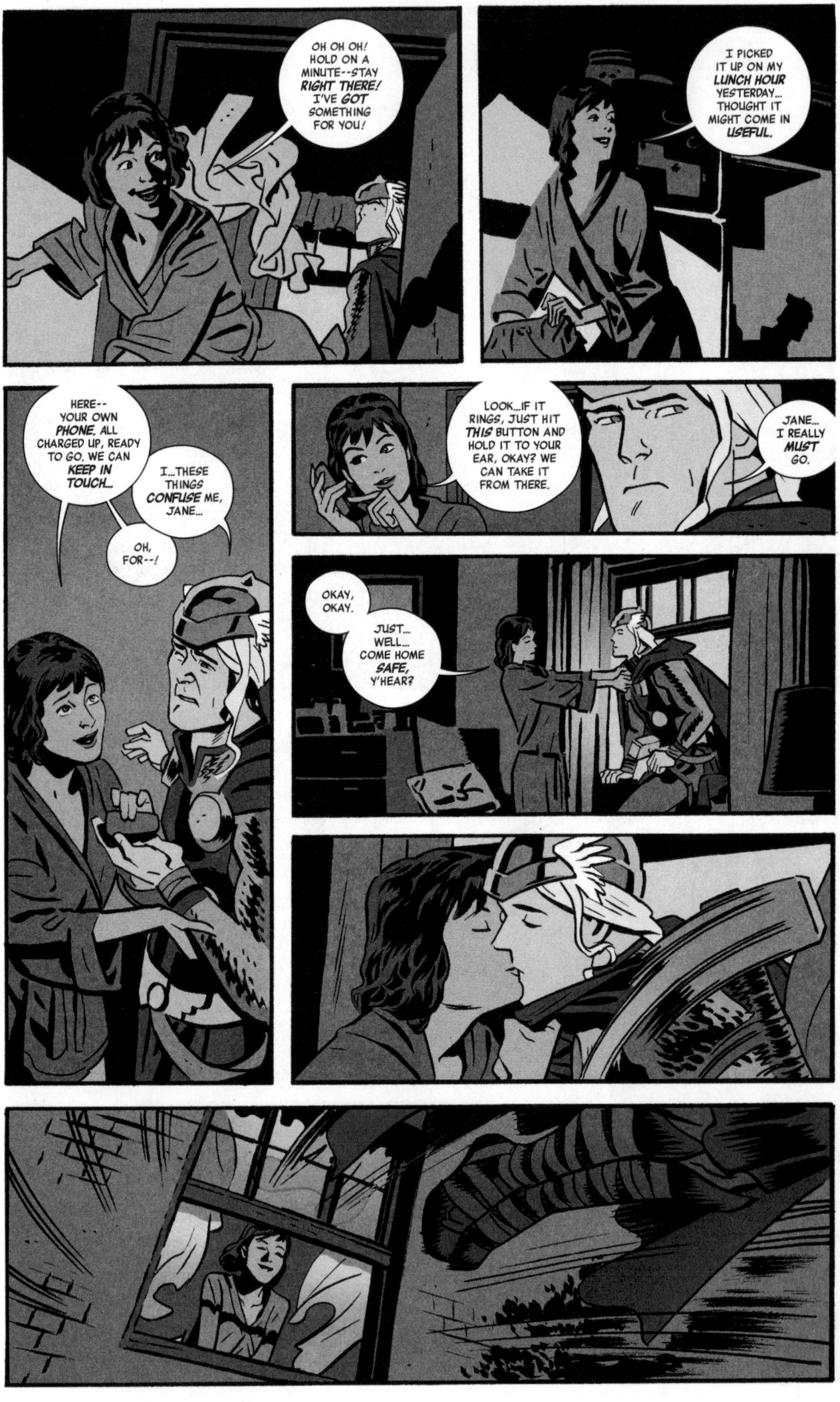
OH OH OH! HOLD ON A MINUTE--STAY RIGHT THERE! I'VE GOT SOMETHING FOR YOU!
I PICKED IT UP ON MY LUNCH HOUR YESTERDAY... THOUGHT IT MIGHT COME IN USEFUL.
HERE-- YOUR OWN PHONE. ALL CHARGED UP, READY TO GO. WE CAN KEEP IN TOUCH...
I...THESE THINGS CONFUSE ME, JANE...
OH, FOR--!
LOOK...IF IT RINGS, JUST HIT THIS BUTTON AND HOLD IT TO YOUR EAR, OKAY? WE CAN TAKE IT FROM THERE.
JANE... I REALLY MUST GO.
OKAY, OKAY.
JUST... WELL... COME HOME SAFE, Y'HEAR?

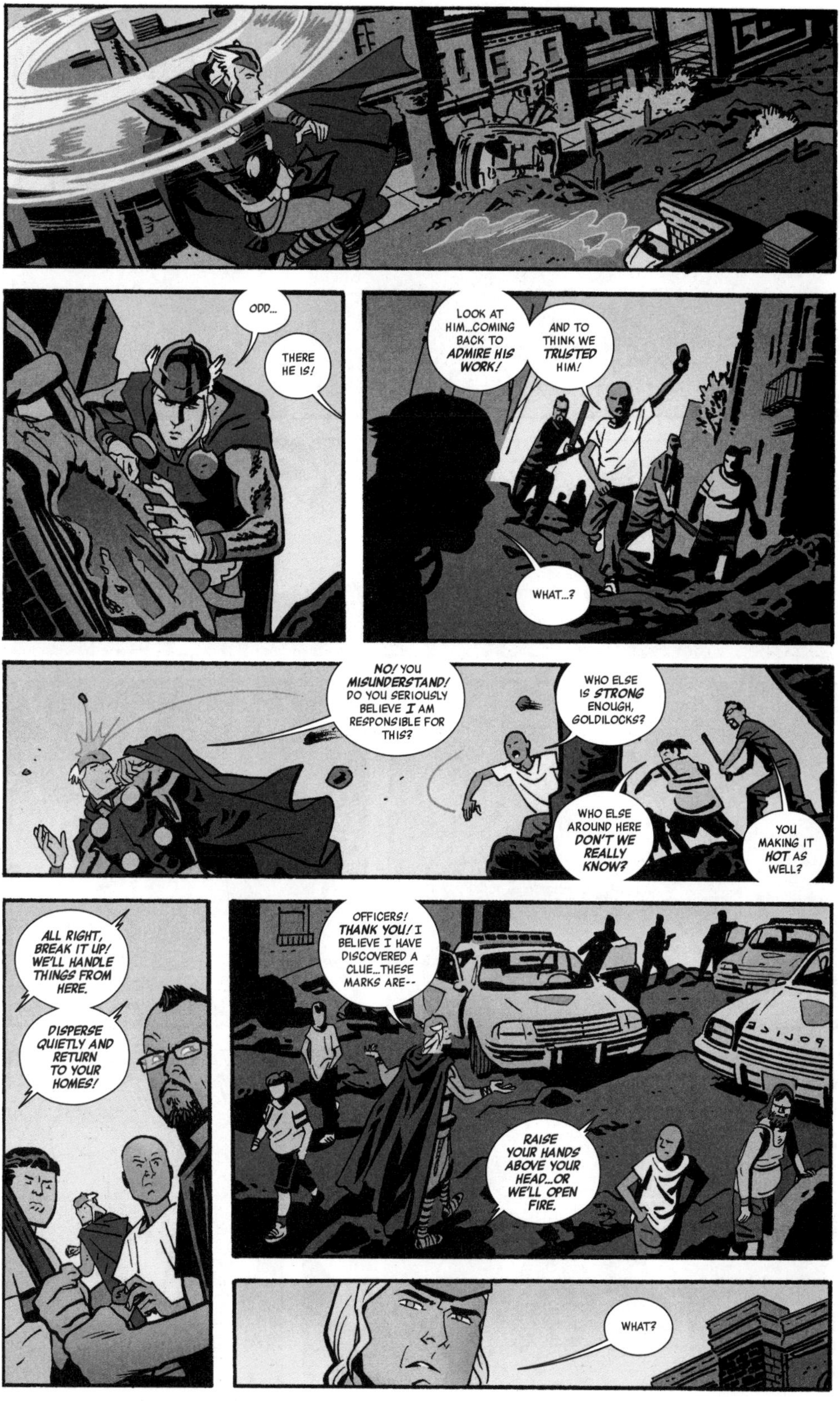
ODD...
THERE HE IS!
LOOK AT HIM...COMING BACK TO ADMIRE HIS WORK!
AND TO THINK WE TRUSTED HIM!
WHAT...?
NO! YOU MISUNDERSTAND! DO YOU SERIOUSLY BELIEVE I AM RESPONSIBLE FOR THIS?
WHO ELSE IS STRONG ENOUGH, GOLDILOCKS?
WHO ELSE AROUND HERE DON'T WE REALLY KNOW?
YOU MAKING IT HOT AS WELL?
ALL RIGHT, BREAK IT UP! WE'LL HANDLE THINGS FROM HERE.
DISPERSE QUIETLY AND RETURN TO YOUR HOMES!
OFFICERS! THANK YOU! I BELIEVE I HAVE DISCOVERED A CLUE...THESE MARKS ARE--
RAISE YOUR HANDS ABOVE YOUR HEAD...OR WE'LL OPEN FIRE.
WHAT?

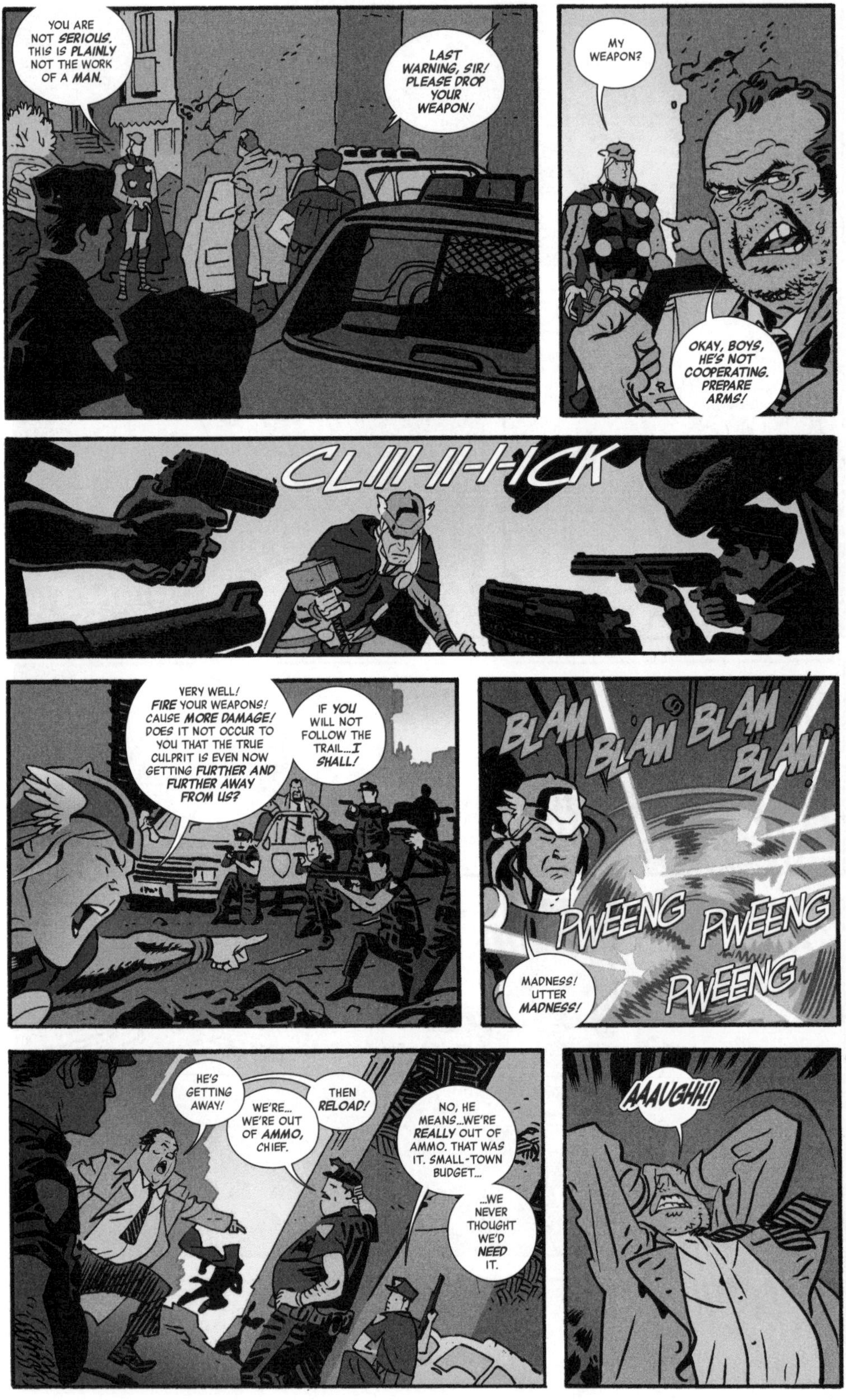
YOU ARE NOT SERIOUS. THIS IS PLAINLY NOT THE WORK OF A MAN.
LAST WARNING, SIR! PLEASE DROP YOUR WEAPON!
MY WEAPON?
OKAY, BOYS, HE'S NOT COOPERATING. PREPARE ARMS!
CLIII-II-I-ICK
VERY WELL! FIRE YOUR WEAPONS! CAUSE MORE DAMAGE! DOES IT NOT OCCUR TO YOU THAT THE TRUE CULPRIT IS EVEN NOW GETTING FURTHER AND FURTHER AWAY FROM US?
IF YOU WILL NOT FOLLOW THE TRAIL...I SHALL!
BLAM BLAM BLAM BLAM
PWEENG PWEENG PWEENG
MADNESS! UTTER MADNESS!
HE'S GETTING AWAY!
THEN RELOAD!
WE'RE... WE'RE OUT OF AMMO, CHIEF.
NO, HE MEANS...WE'RE REALLY OUT OF AMMO. THAT WAS IT. SMALL-TOWN BUDGET...
...WE NEVER THOUGHT WE'D NEED IT.
AAAUGHH!

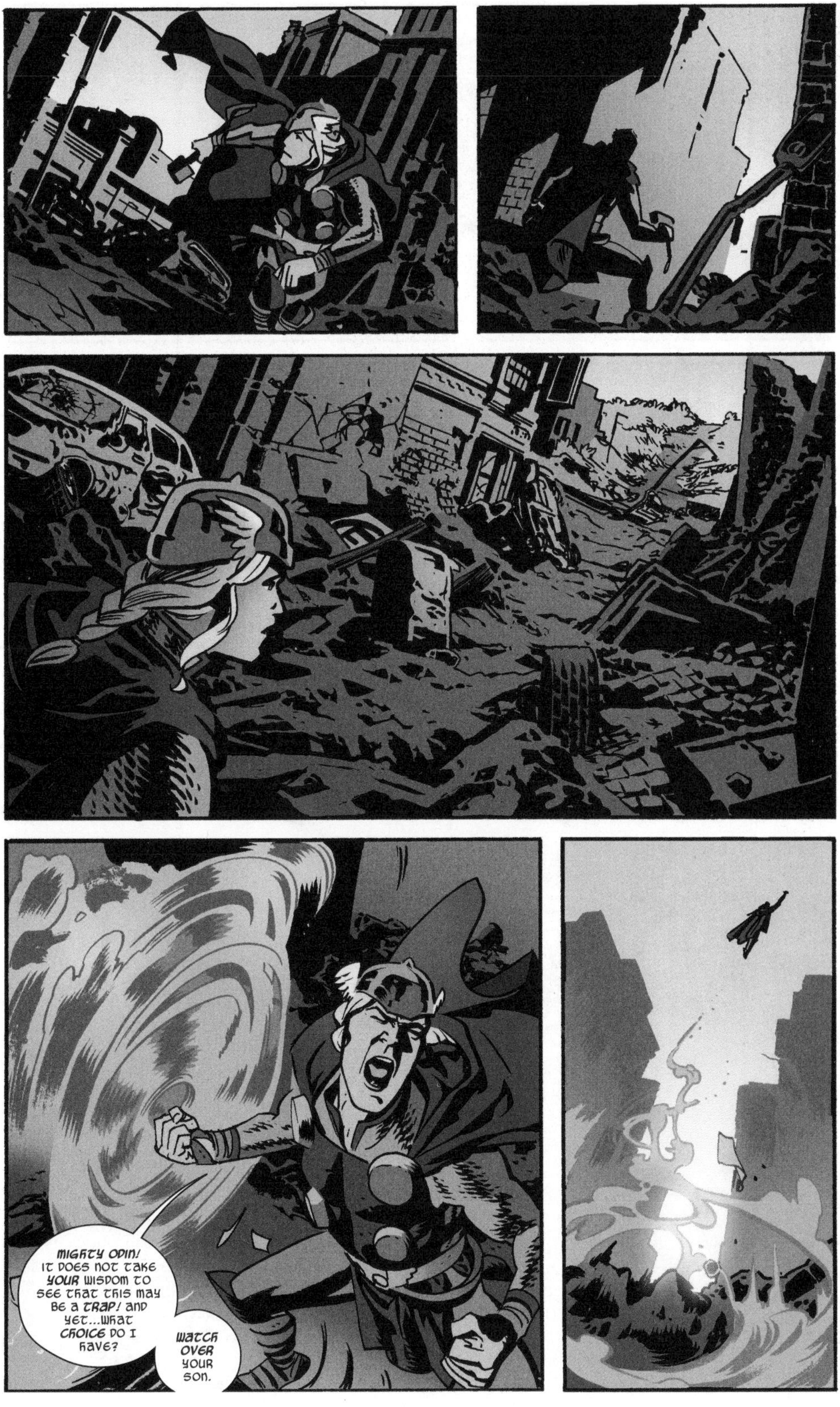
MIGHTY ODIN! IT DOES NOT TAKE YOUR WISDOM TO SEE THAT THIS MAY BE A TRAP! AND YET...WHAT CHOICE DO I HAVE?
WATCH OVER YOUR SON.

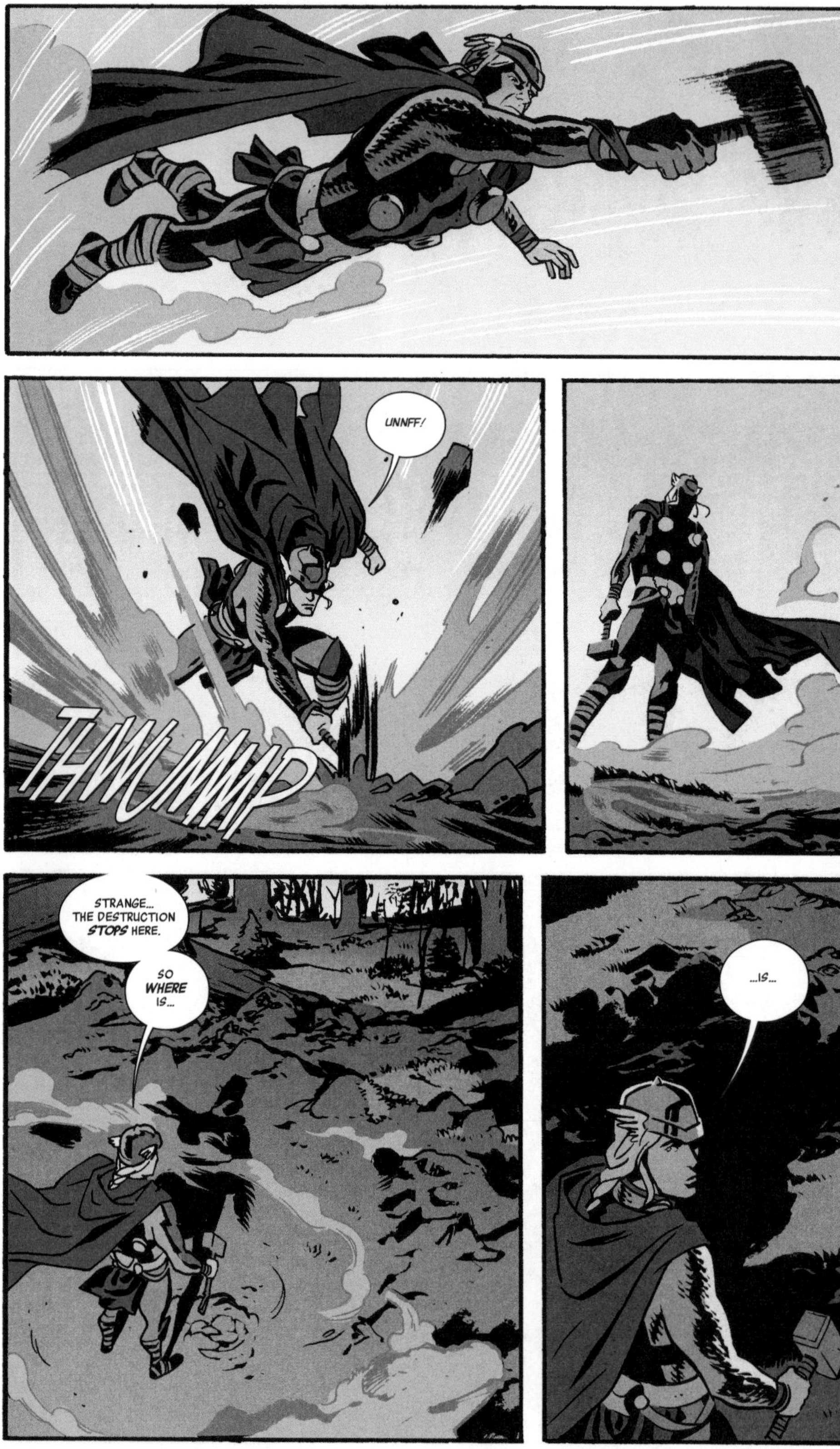
UNNFF!
THWUMMP
STRANGE... THE DESTRUCTION STOPS HERE.
SO WHERE IS...
...IS...

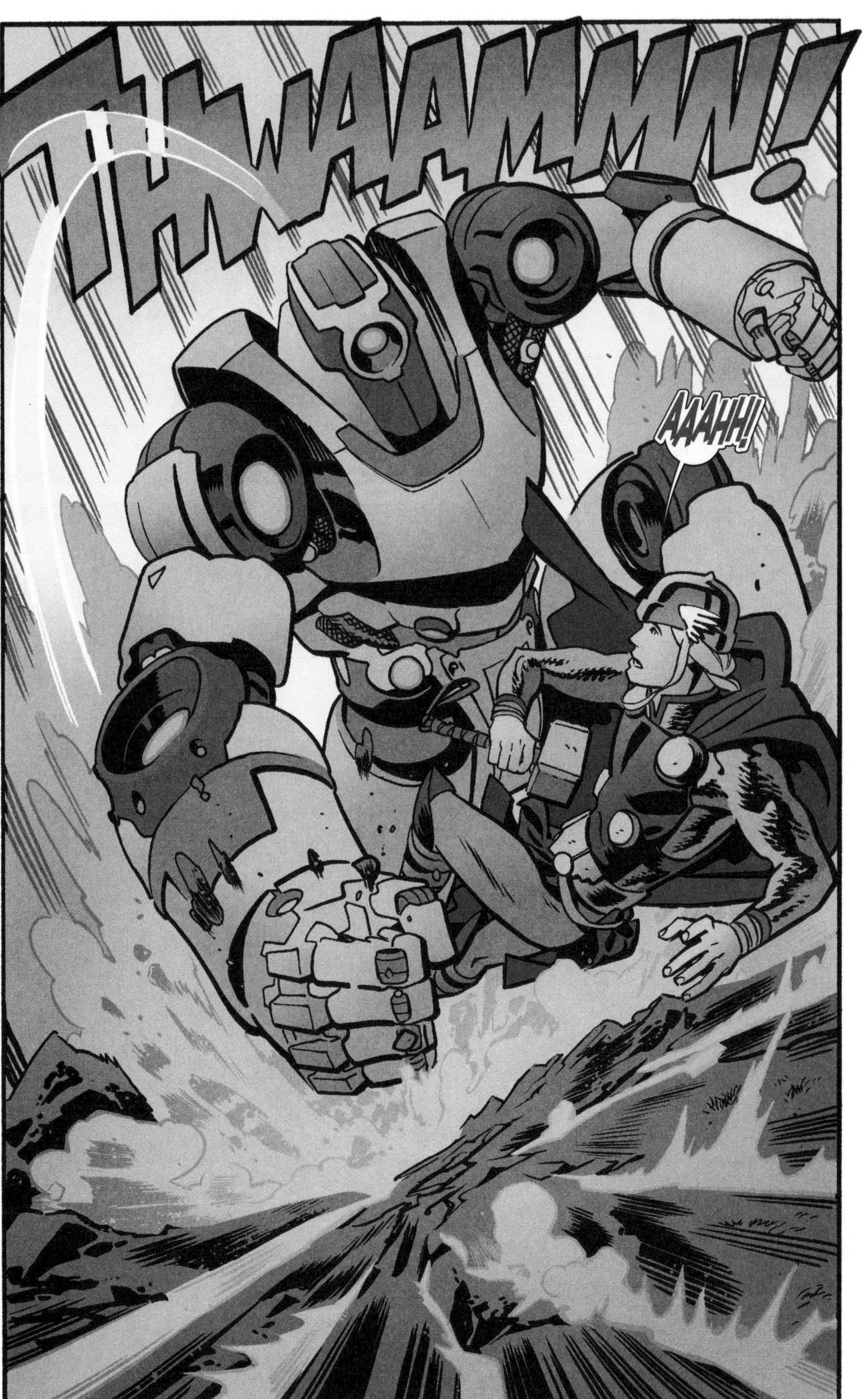
THWAAMM!
AAAHH!

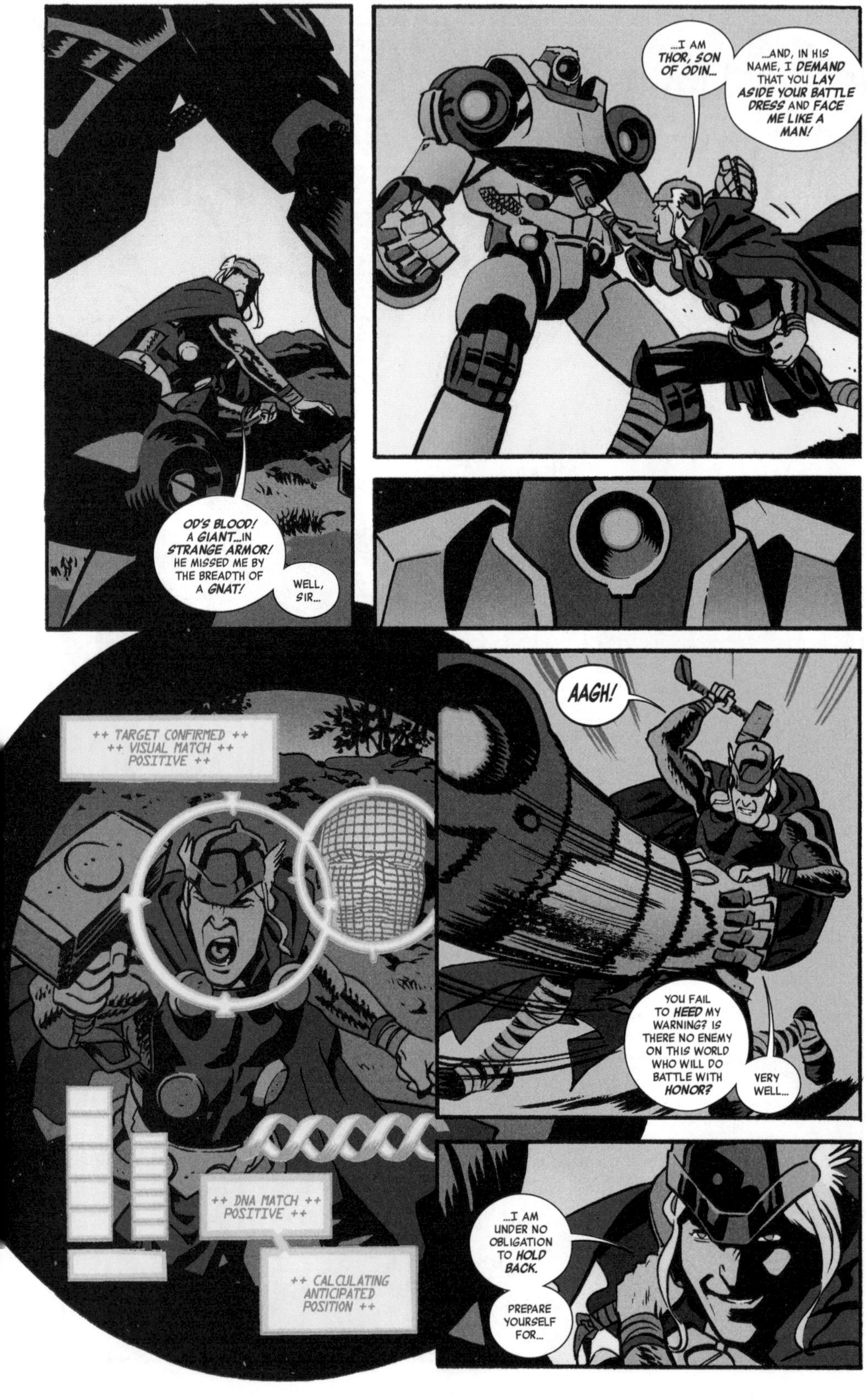
OD'S BLOOD! A GIANT...IN STRANGE ARMOR! HE MISSED ME BY THE BREADTH OF A GNAT!
WELL, SIR...
...I AM THOR, SON OF ODIN...
...AND, IN HIS NAME, I DEMAND THAT YOU LAY ASIDE YOUR BATTLE DRESS AND FACE ME LIKE A MAN!
++ TARGET CONFIRMED ++ ++ VISUAL MATCH ++ POSITIVE ++
++ DNA MATCH ++ POSITIVE ++
++ CALCULATING ANTICIPATED POSITION ++
AAGH!
YOU FAIL TO HEED MY WARNING? IS THERE NO ENEMY ON THIS WORLD WHO WILL DO BATTLE WITH HONOR?
VERY WELL...
...I AM UNDER NO OBLIGATION TO HOLD BACK.
PREPARE YOURSELF FOR...

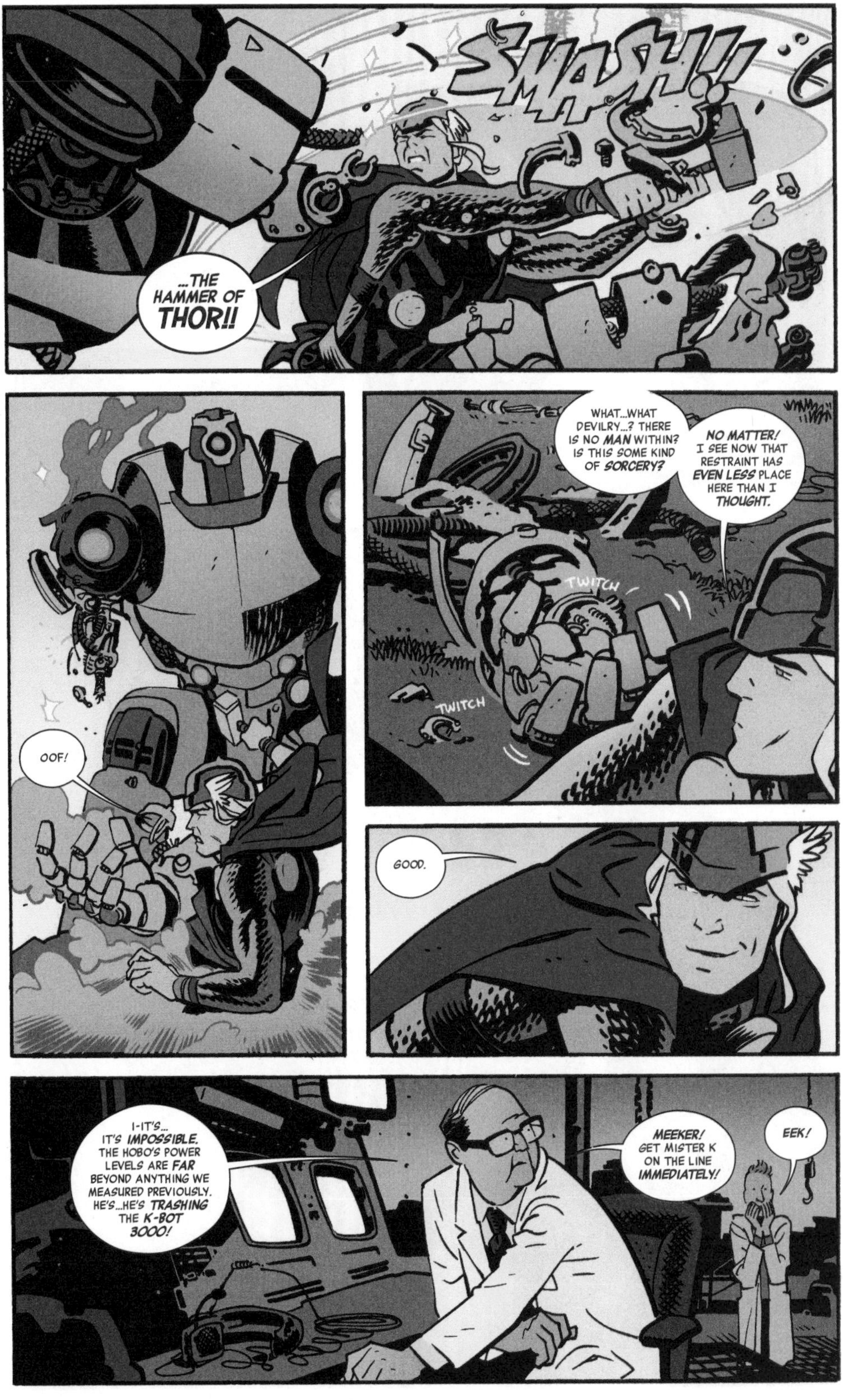
SMASH!!
...THE HAMMER OF THOR!!
OOF!
WHAT...WHAT DEVILRY...? THERE IS NO MAN WITHIN? IS THIS SOME KIND OF SORCERY?
NO MATTER! I SEE NOW THAT RESTRAINT HAS EVEN LESS PLACE HERE THAN I THOUGHT.
TWITCH
TWITCH
GOOD.
I-IT'S... IT'S IMPOSSIBLE. THE HOBO'S POWER LEVELS ARE FAR BEYOND ANYTHING WE MEASURED PREVIOUSLY. HE'S...HE'S TRASHING THE K-BOT 3000!
MEEKER! GET MISTER K ON THE LINE IMMEDIATELY!
EEK!

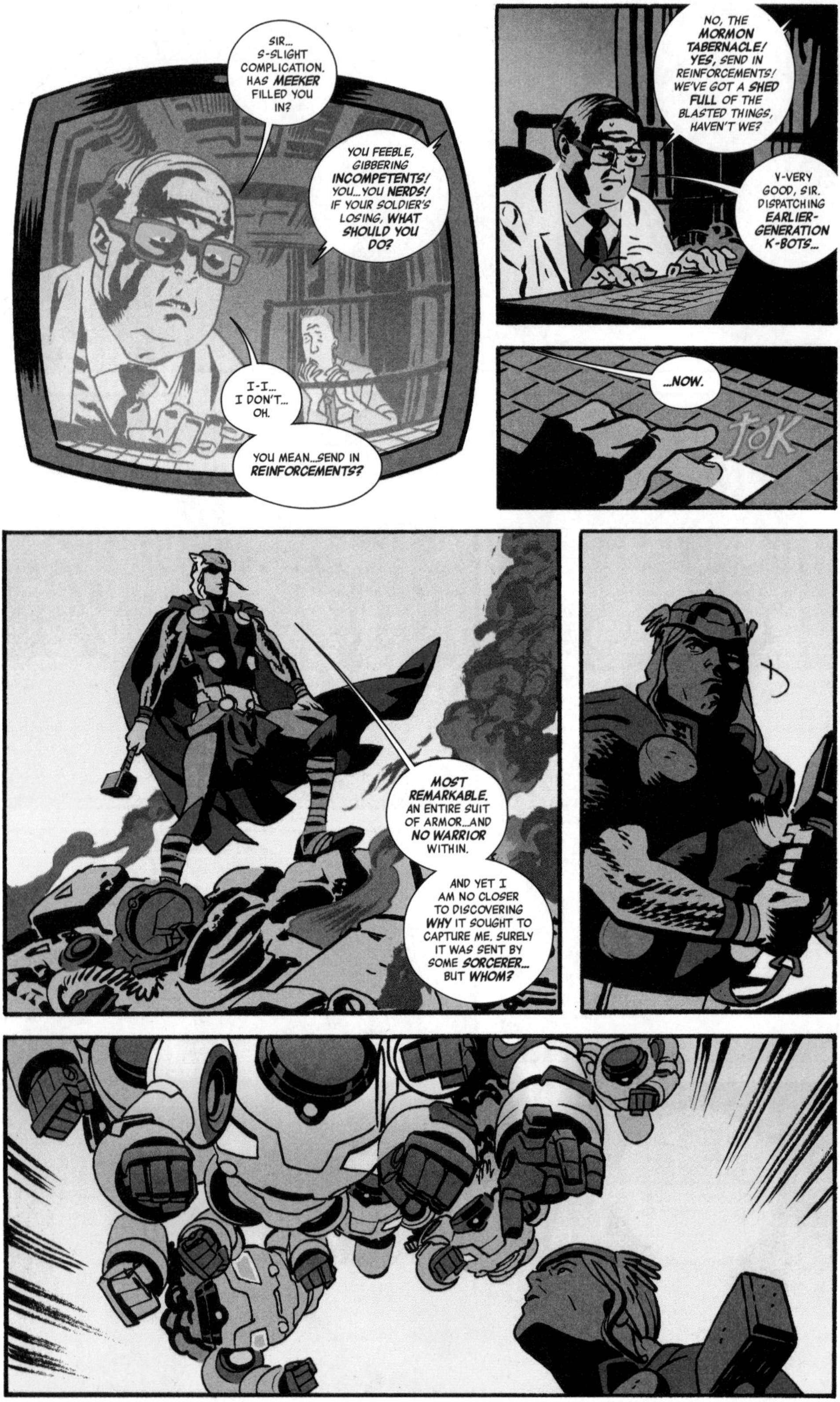
SIR... S-SLIGHT COMPLICATION. HAS MEEKER FILLED YOU IN?
YOU FEEBLE, GIBBERING INCOMPETENTS! YOU...YOU NERDS! IF YOUR SOLDIER'S LOSING, WHAT SHOULD YOU DO?
I-I... I DON'T... OH.
YOU MEAN...SEND IN REINFORCEMENTS?
NO, THE MORMON TABERNACLE! YES, SEND IN REINFORCEMENTS! WE'VE GOT A SHED FULL OF THE BLASTED THINGS, HAVEN'T WE?
V-VERY GOOD, SIR. DISPATCHING EARLIER-GENERATION K-BOTS...
...NOW.
TOK
MOST REMARKABLE. AN ENTIRE SUIT OF ARMOR...AND NO WARRIOR WITHIN.
AND YET I AM NO CLOSER TO DISCOVERING WHY IT SOUGHT TO CAPTURE ME. SURELY IT WAS SENT BY SOME SORCERER... BUT WHOM?

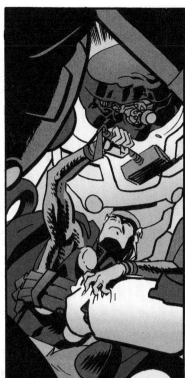

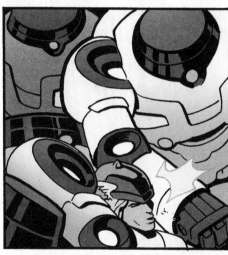

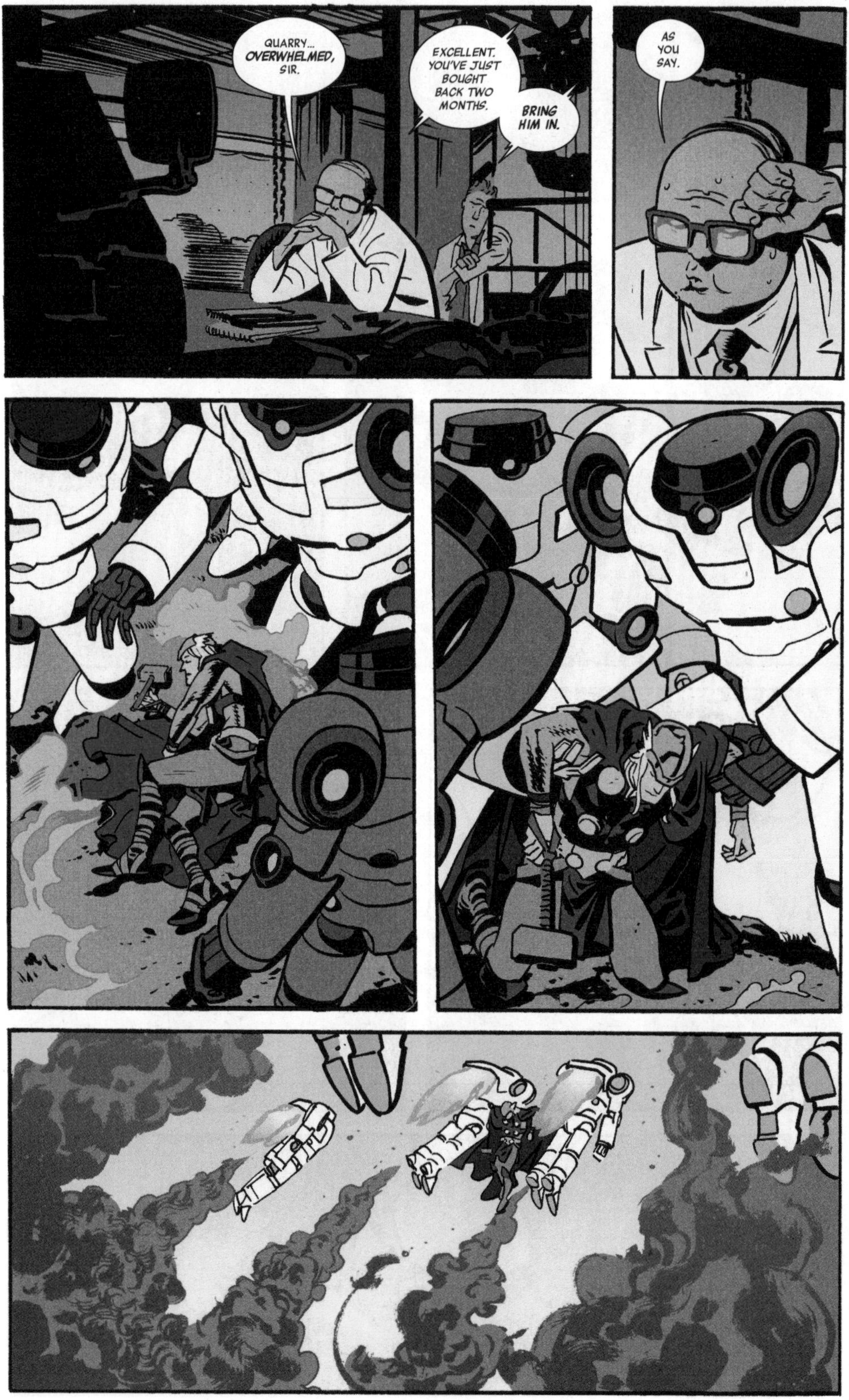
QUARRY... OVERWHELMED, SIR.
EXCELLENT. YOU'VE JUST BOUGHT BACK TWO MONTHS.
BRING HIM IN.
AS YOU SAY.

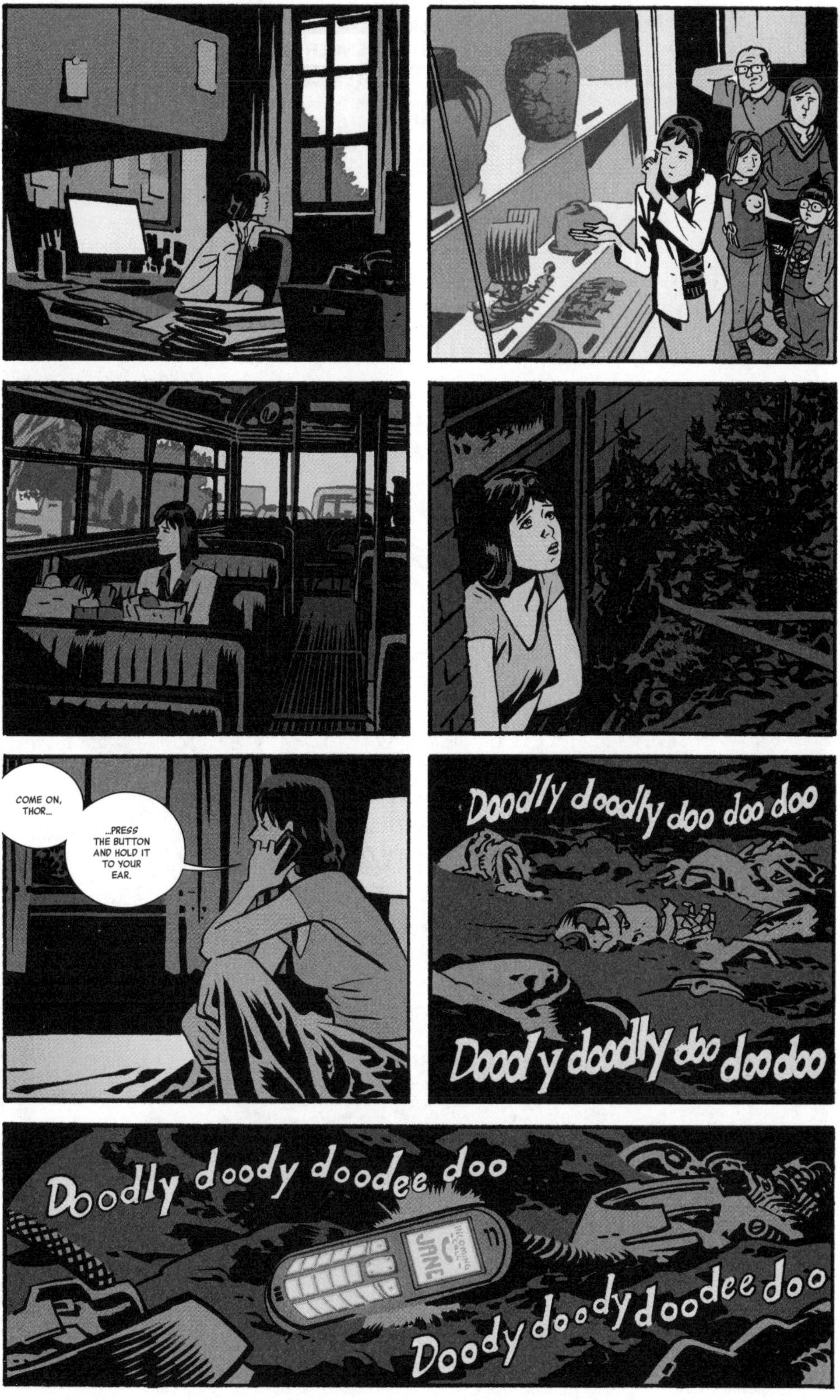

COME ON, THOR...
...PRESS THE BUTTON AND HOLD IT TO YOUR EAR.
Doodly doodly doo doo doo
Doodly doodly doo doo doo
Doodly doody doodee doo
INCOMING CALL
JANE
Doody doody doodee doo

THOR THE MIGHTY AVENGER #8

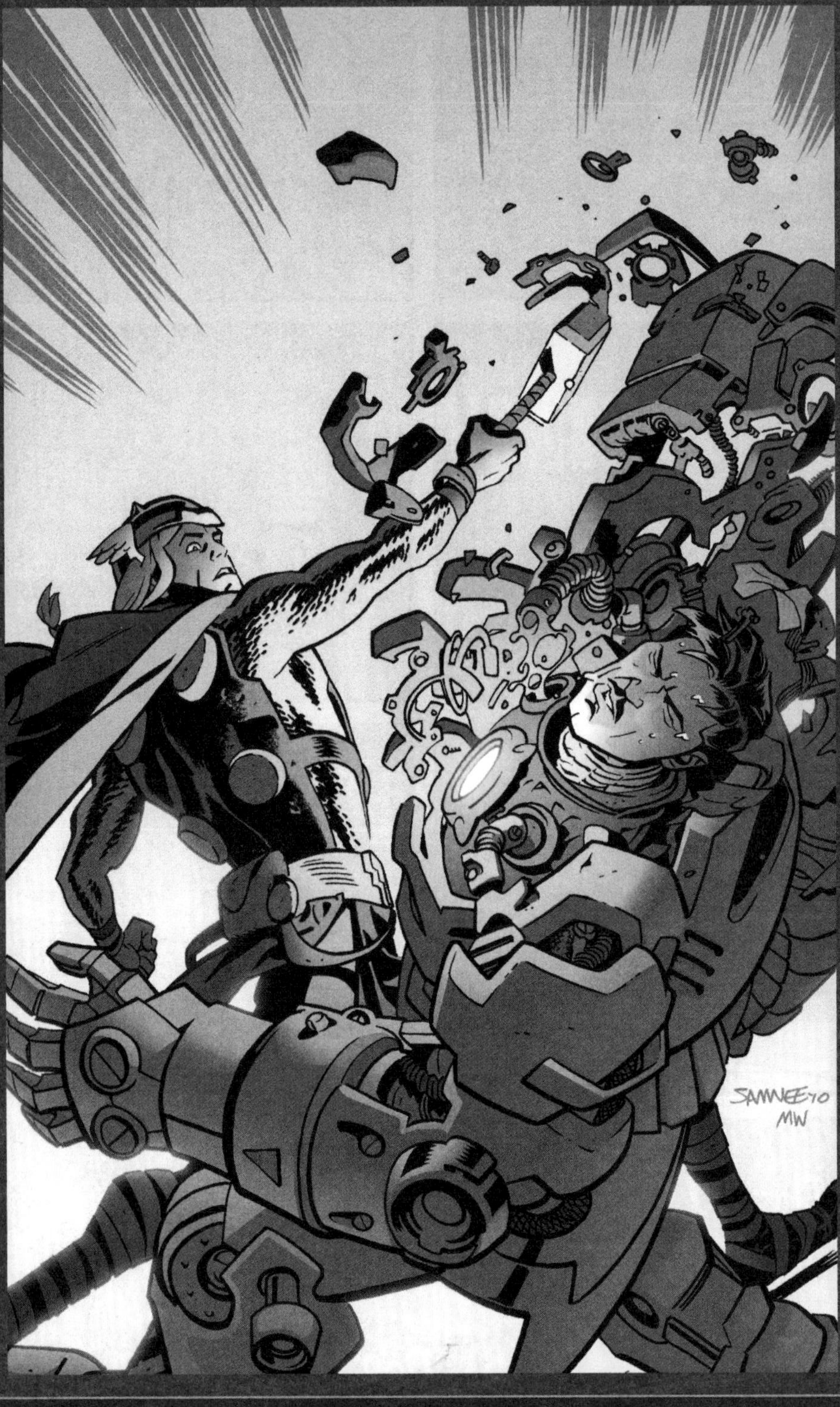
SAMNEE '10
MW

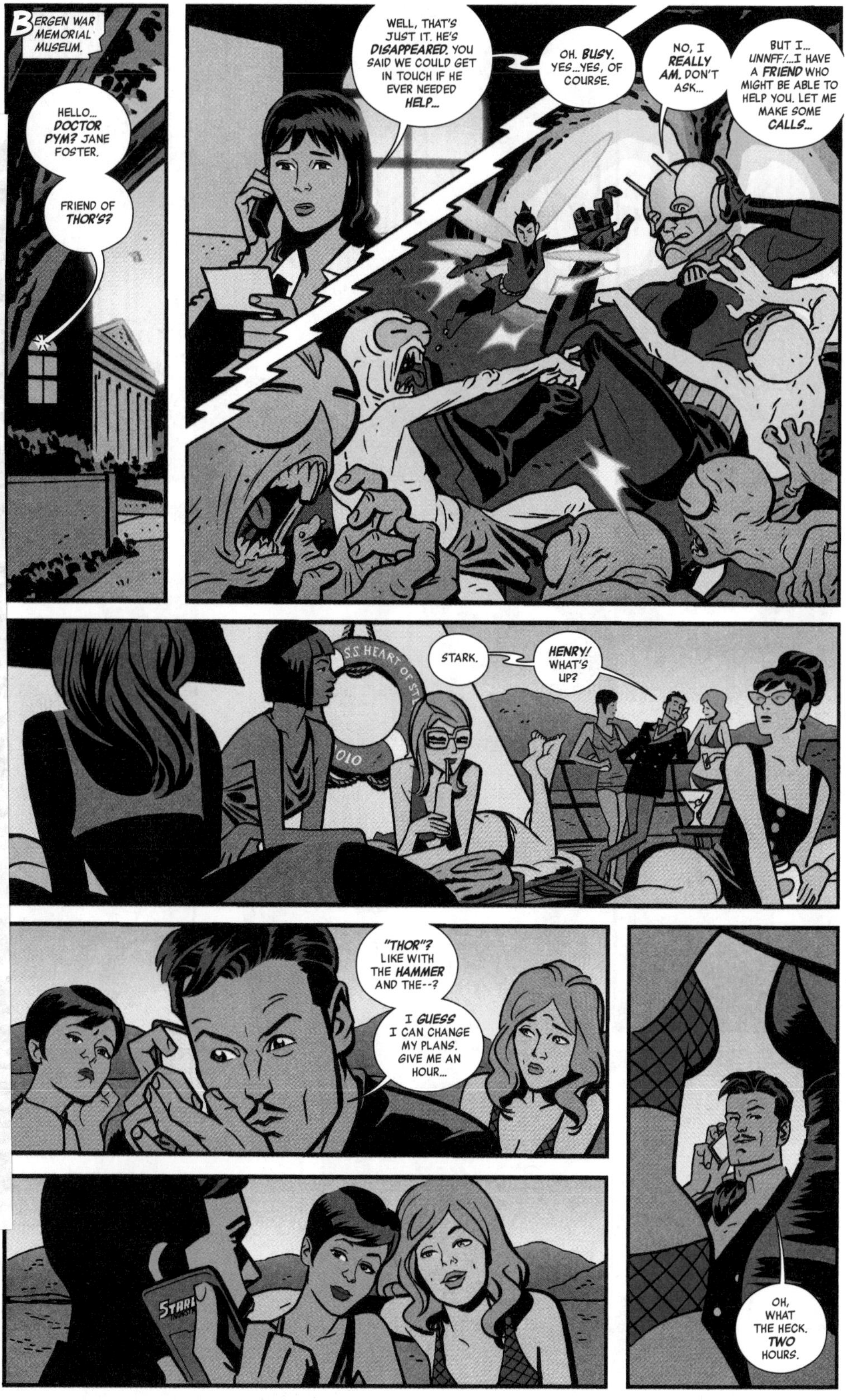
BERGEN WAR MEMORIAL MUSEUM.
HELLO... DOCTOR PYM? JANE FOSTER.
FRIEND OF THOR'S?
WELL, THAT'S JUST IT. HE'S DISAPPEARED. YOU SAID WE COULD GET IN TOUCH IF HE EVER NEEDED HELP...
OH. BUSY. YES...YES, OF COURSE.
NO, I REALLY AM. DON'T ASK...
BUT I... UNNFF!...I HAVE A FRIEND WHO MIGHT BE ABLE TO HELP YOU. LET ME MAKE SOME CALLS...
STARK.
HENRY! WHAT'S UP?
"THOR"? LIKE WITH THE HAMMER AND THE--?
I GUESS I CAN CHANGE MY PLANS. GIVE ME AN HOUR...
OH, WHAT THE HECK. TWO HOURS.

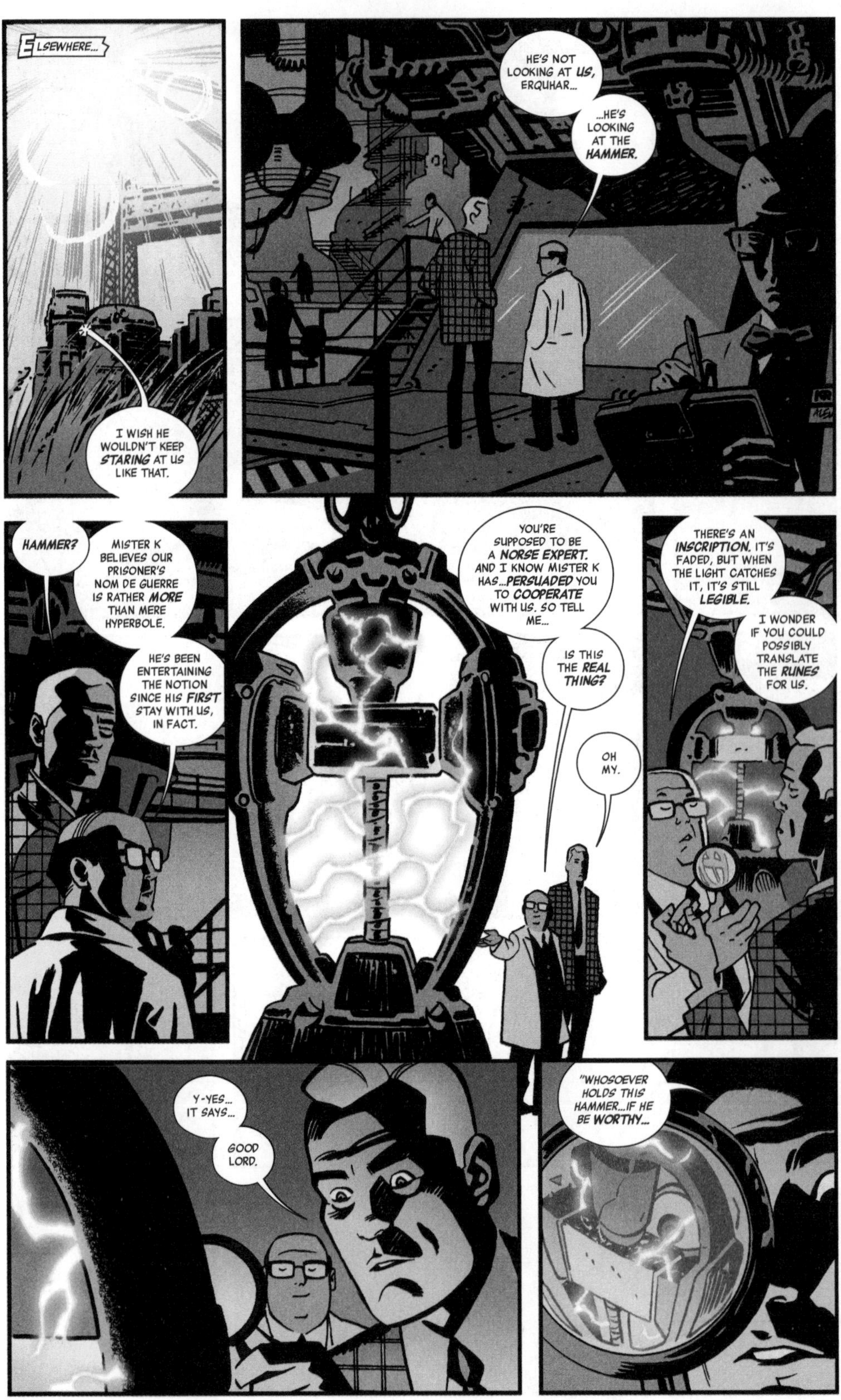
ELSEWHERE...
I WISH HE WOULDN'T KEEP STARING AT US LIKE THAT.
HE'S NOT LOOKING AT US, ERQUHAR...
...HE'S LOOKING AT THE HAMMER.
HAMMER?
MISTER K BELIEVES OUR PRISONER'S NOM DE GUERRE IS RATHER MORE THAN MERE HYPERBOLE.
HE'S BEEN ENTERTAINING THE NOTION SINCE HIS FIRST STAY WITH US, IN FACT.
YOU'RE SUPPOSED TO BE A NORSE EXPERT. AND I KNOW MISTER K HAS...PERSUADED YOU TO COOPERATE WITH US. SO TELL ME...
IS THIS THE REAL THING?
OH MY.
THERE'S AN INSCRIPTION. IT'S FADED, BUT WHEN THE LIGHT CATCHES IT, IT'S STILL LEGIBLE.
I WONDER IF YOU COULD POSSIBLY TRANSLATE THE RUNES FOR US.
Y-YES... IT SAYS...
GOOD LORD.
"WHOSOEVER HOLDS THIS HAMMER...IF HE BE WORTHY...

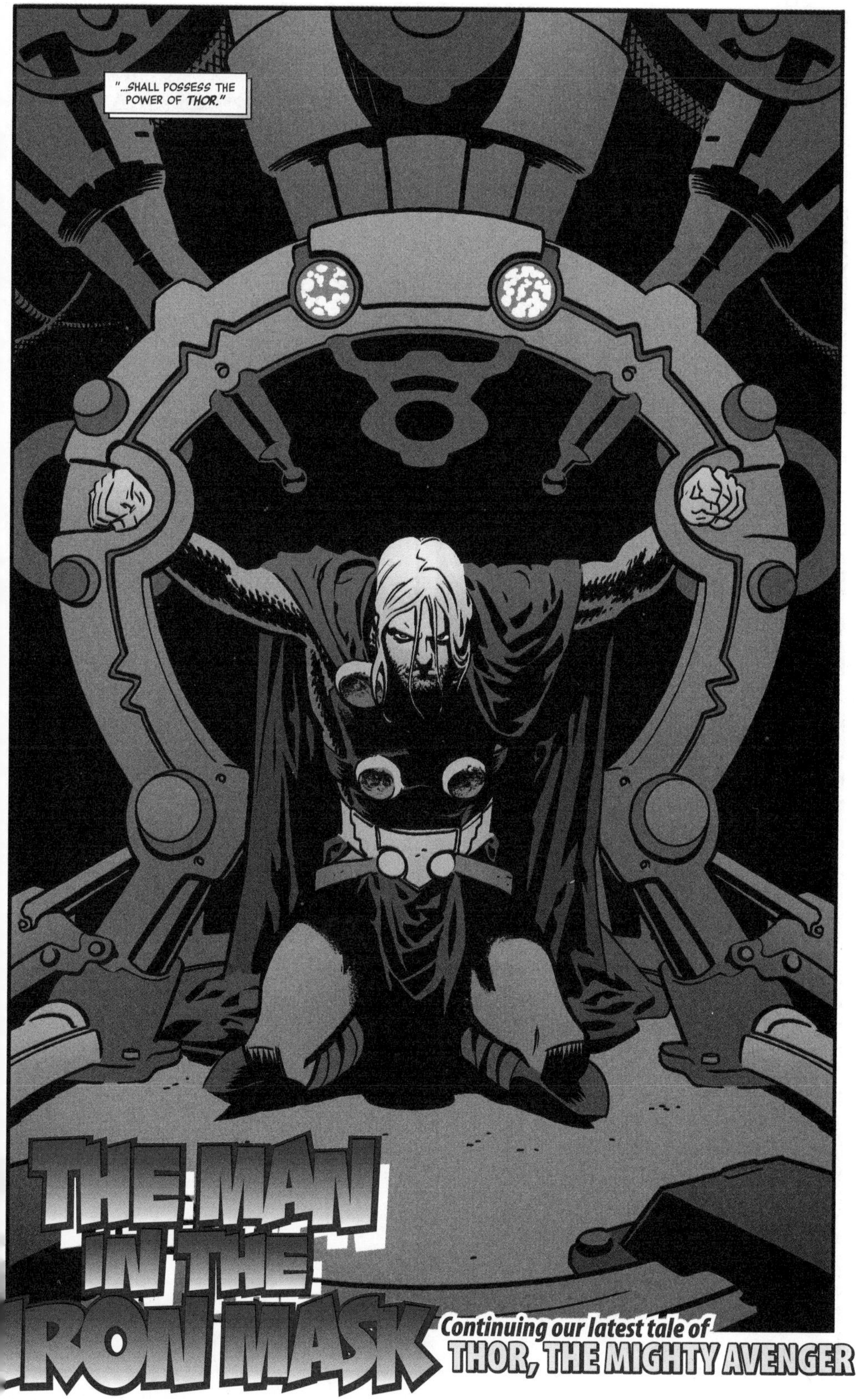
"...SHALL POSSESS THE POWER OF THOR."
THE MAN IN THE IRON MASK
Continuing our latest tale of
THOR, THE MIGHTY AVENGER

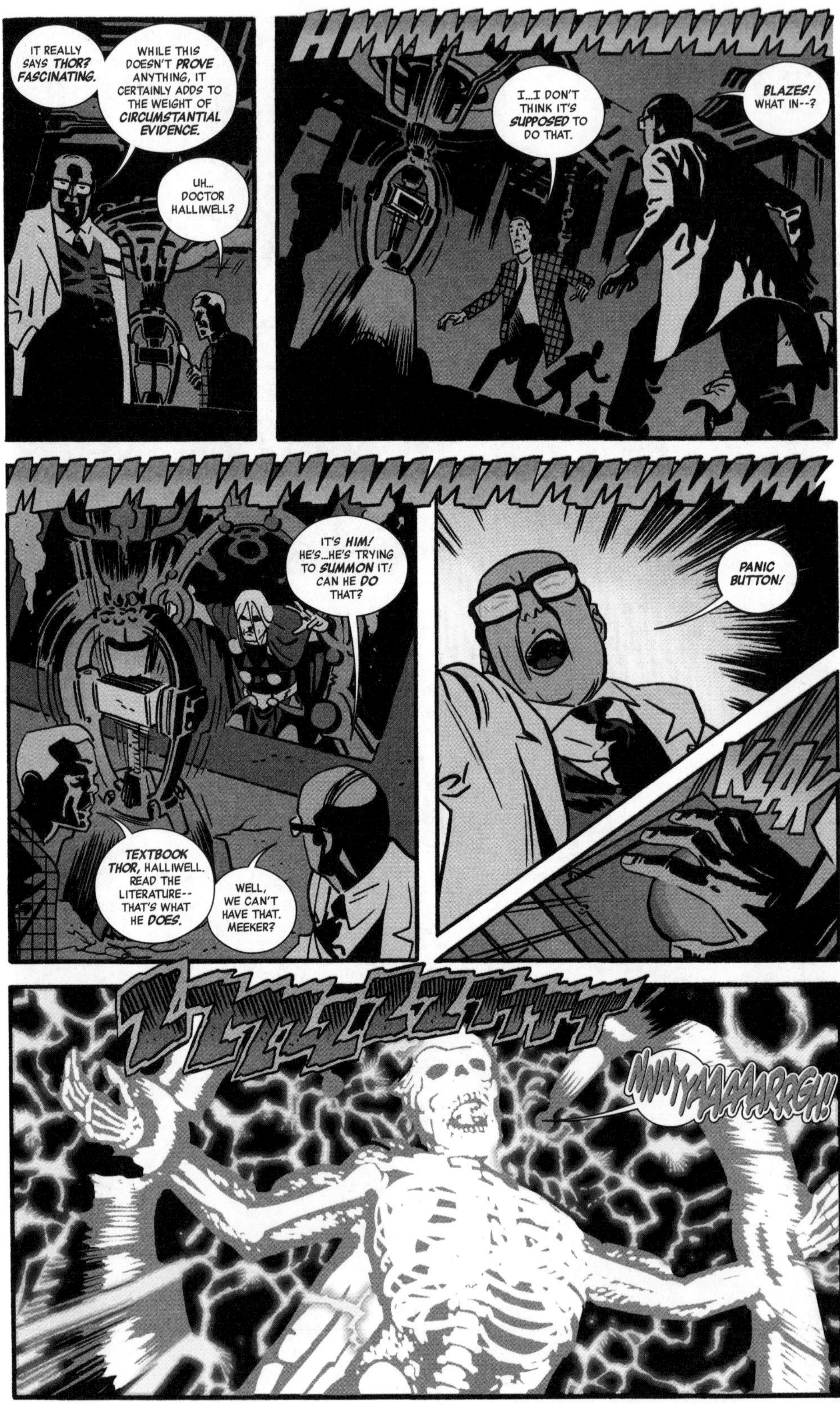
IT REALLY SAYS THOR? FASCINATING.
WHILE THIS DOESN'T PROVE ANYTHING, IT CERTAINLY ADDS TO THE WEIGHT OF CIRCUMSTANTIAL EVIDENCE.
UH... DOCTOR HALLIWELL?
HMMMMMMMMMMMMMMMMM
I...I DON'T THINK IT'S SUPPOSED TO DO THAT.
BLAZES! WHAT IN--?
MMMMMMMMMMMMMMMMMMMMMMMMMMMM
IT'S HIM! HE'S...HE'S TRYING TO SUMMON IT! CAN HE DO THAT?
TEXTBOOK THOR, HALLIWELL. READ THE LITERATURE-- THAT'S WHAT HE DOES.
WELL, WE CAN'T HAVE THAT. MEEKER?
PANIC BUTTON!
KLAK
ZZZZZZZZTTTTT
NNNYAAAAAARRGH!

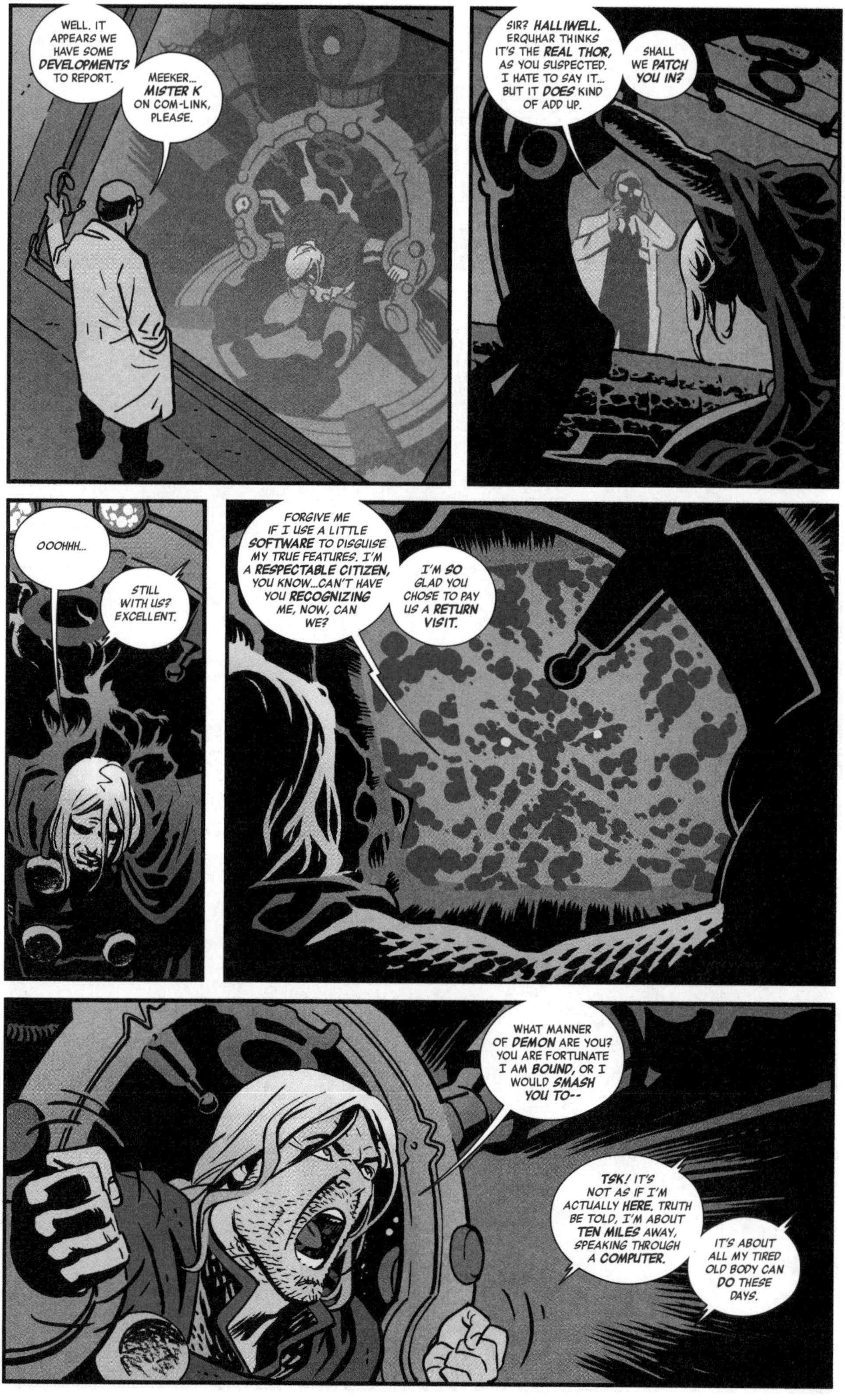

WELL. IT APPEARS WE HAVE SOME DEVELOPMENTS TO REPORT.
MEEKER... MISTER K ON COM-LINK, PLEASE.
SIR? HALLIWELL. ERQUHAR THINKS IT'S THE REAL THOR, AS YOU SUSPECTED. I HATE TO SAY IT... BUT IT DOES KIND OF ADD UP.
SHALL WE PATCH YOU IN?
OOOHHH...
STILL WITH US? EXCELLENT.
FORGIVE ME IF I USE A LITTLE SOFTWARE TO DISGUISE MY TRUE FEATURES. I'M A RESPECTABLE CITIZEN, YOU KNOW...CAN'T HAVE YOU RECOGNIZING ME, NOW, CAN WE?
I'M SO GLAD YOU CHOSE TO PAY US A RETURN VISIT.
WHAT MANNER OF DEMON ARE YOU? YOU ARE FORTUNATE I AM BOUND, OR I WOULD SMASH YOU TO--
TSK! IT'S NOT AS IF I'M ACTUALLY HERE. TRUTH BE TOLD, I'M ABOUT TEN MILES AWAY, SPEAKING THROUGH A COMPUTER.
IT'S ABOUT ALL MY TIRED OLD BODY CAN DO THESE DAYS.

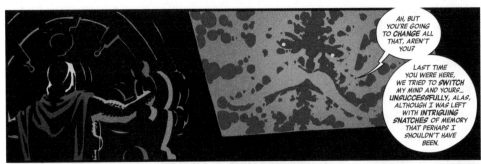

AH, BUT YOU'RE GOING TO *CHANGE* ALL THAT, AREN'T YOU?

LAST TIME YOU WERE HERE, WE TRIED TO *SWITCH* MY MIND AND YOURS... *UNSUCCESSFULLY*, ALAS, ALTHOUGH I WAS LEFT WITH *INTRIGUING SNATCHES* OF MEMORY THAT PERHAPS I SHOULDN'T HAVE BEEN.

YOU... YOU *STOLE* MY MEMORIES?

ALL THESE WEEKS I HAVE THOUGHT MY FATHER WAS *TOYING* WITH ME... OR THAT I WAS *LOSING MY MIND*...AND IT WAS *YOU* ALL ALONG?

"*STOLE*"? SUCH AN UGLY WORD...AND QUITE *INCORRECT*, I'M SURE. YOU NO DOUBT GOT *SOMETHING* BACK FROM THE EXCHANGE... THOUGH *WHAT*, I CAN'T IMAGINE.

IRREGULAR VERBS, PERHAPS?

OH, AND I'D *STOP STRAINING* IF I WERE YOU. YOU MIGHT DAMAGE THE *BODY*. THOSE BONDS HAVE BEEN THOROUGHLY TESTED... *ARNOLD SCHWARZENEGGER* AT HIS PEAK COULDN'T BREAK OUT OF--

SNAP?

SNAP

AH.

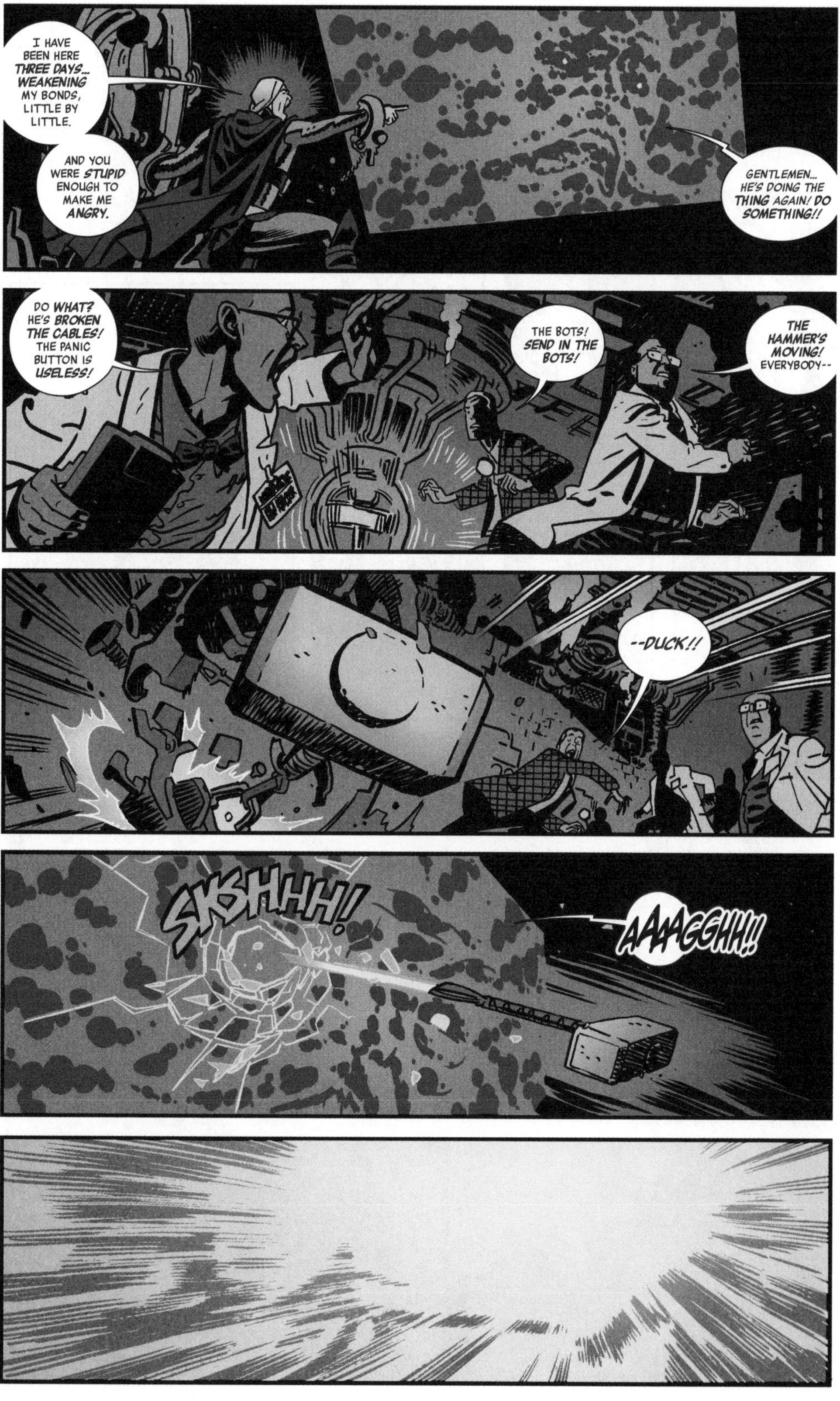
I HAVE BEEN HERE THREE DAYS... WEAKENING MY BONDS, LITTLE BY LITTLE.
AND YOU WERE STUPID ENOUGH TO MAKE ME ANGRY.
GENTLEMEN... HE'S DOING THE THING AGAIN! DO SOMETHING!!
DO WHAT? HE'S BROKEN THE CABLES! THE PANIC BUTTON IS USELESS!
THE BOTS! SEND IN THE BOTS!
THE HAMMER'S MOVING! EVERYBODY--
--DUCK!!
SKSHHH!
AAAAGGHH!!

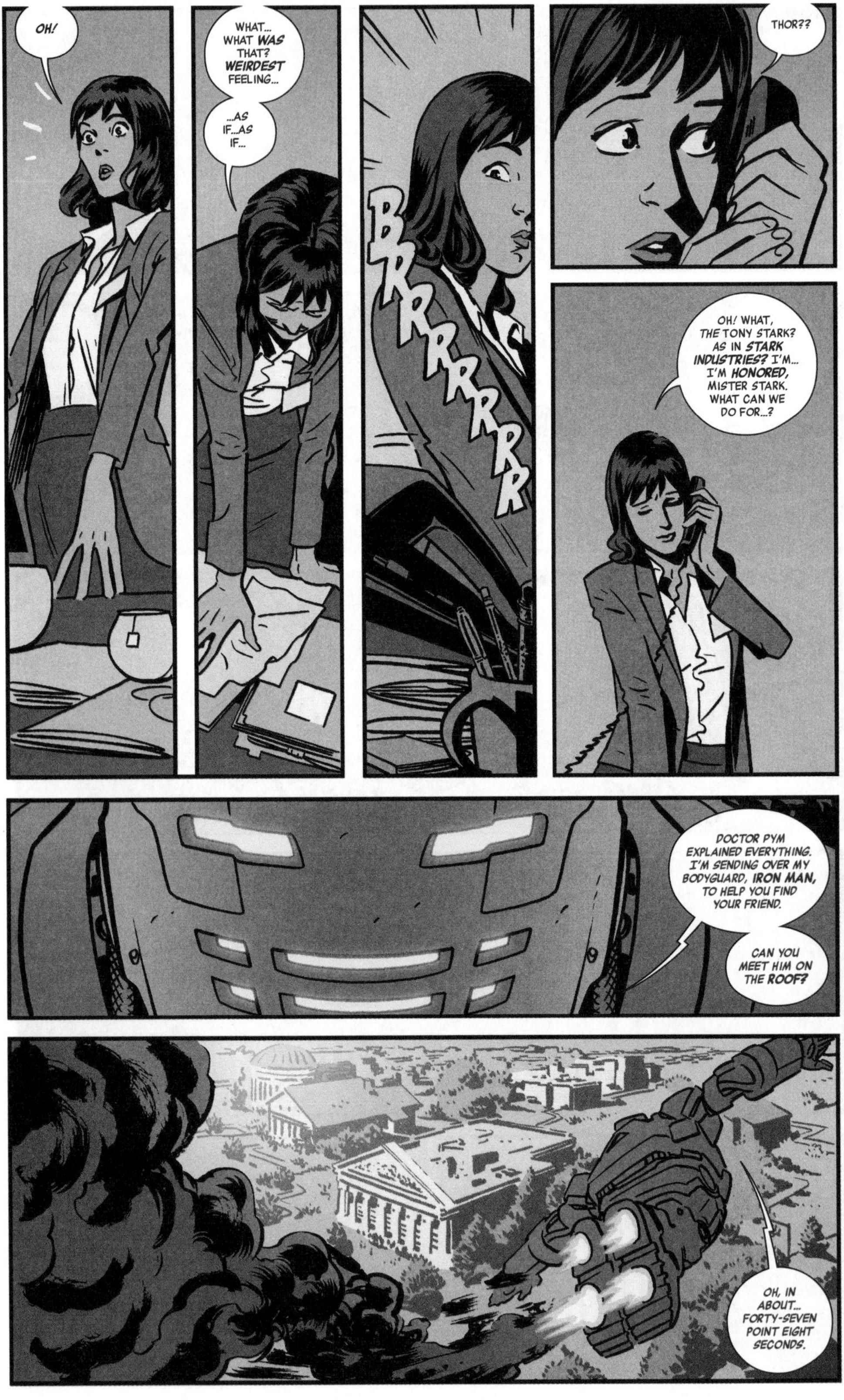
OH!
WHAT... WHAT WAS THAT? WEIRDEST FEELING...
...AS IF...AS IF...
BRRRRRRRR
THOR??
OH! WHAT, THE TONY STARK? AS IN STARK INDUSTRIES? I'M... I'M HONORED, MISTER STARK. WHAT CAN WE DO FOR...?
DOCTOR PYM EXPLAINED EVERYTHING. I'M SENDING OVER MY BODYGUARD, IRON MAN, TO HELP YOU FIND YOUR FRIEND.
CAN YOU MEET HIM ON THE ROOF?
OH, IN ABOUT... FORTY-SEVEN POINT EIGHT SECONDS.

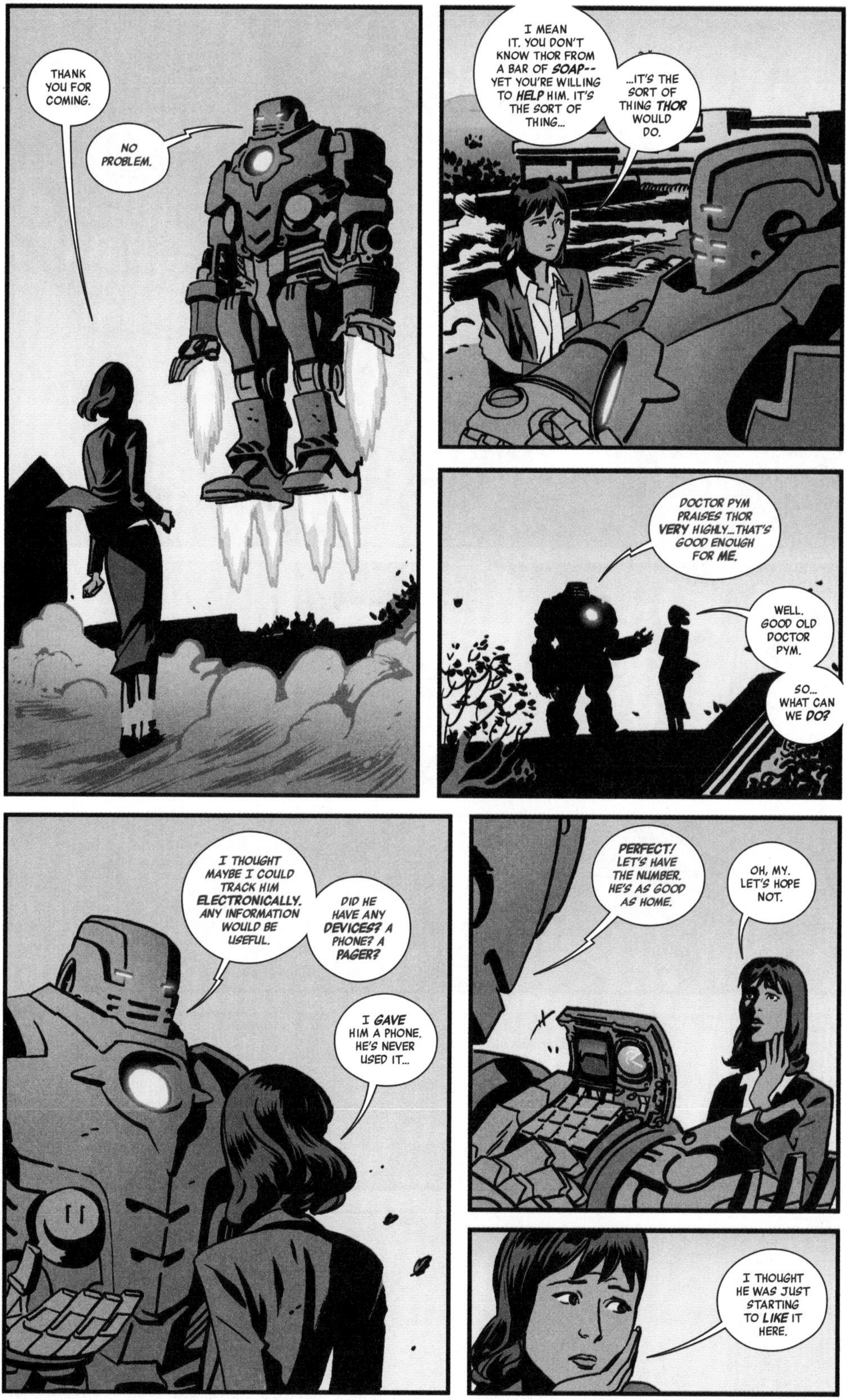

THANK YOU FOR COMING.
NO PROBLEM.
I MEAN IT. YOU DON'T KNOW THOR FROM A BAR OF SOAP-- YET YOU'RE WILLING TO HELP HIM. IT'S THE SORT OF THING...
...IT'S THE SORT OF THING THOR WOULD DO.
DOCTOR PYM PRAISES THOR VERY HIGHLY...THAT'S GOOD ENOUGH FOR ME.
WELL. GOOD OLD DOCTOR PYM.
SO... WHAT CAN WE DO?
I THOUGHT MAYBE I COULD TRACK HIM ELECTRONICALLY. ANY INFORMATION WOULD BE USEFUL.
DID HE HAVE ANY DEVICES? A PHONE? A PAGER?
I GAVE HIM A PHONE. HE'S NEVER USED IT...
PERFECT! LET'S HAVE THE NUMBER. HE'S AS GOOD AS HOME.
OH, MY. LET'S HOPE NOT.
I THOUGHT HE WAS JUST STARTING TO LIKE IT HERE.

FIGHT, THOR-- FIGHT, FOR ALL THE GOOD IT WILL DO YOU! MY K-BOTS WILL DEFEAT YOU EVENTUALLY-- AND THEN MY SCIENTISTS WILL--

UH... SIR...?

WHAT?

WE'RE, UH, WE'RE ACTUALLY EVACUATING, SIR. WE'RE ALL HEADING DOWN INTO BUNKER FOUR.

WE DON'T WANT TO DIE, SIR.

COWARDS! AFTER ALL I'VE DONE FOR YOU! GIVEN YOU THE FINEST SCIENTIFIC FACILITIES MONEY CAN BUY...!

YOU...YOU BLACKMAILED US, SIR. YOU BLACKMAILED US AND THREATENED TO KILL US. FRANKLY, SIR, GIVEN OUR OPTIONS...

...WE'VE GOT NOTHING TO LOSE.

CLUNK

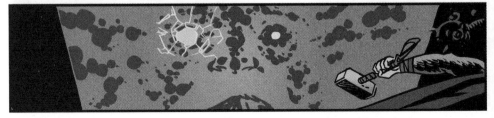

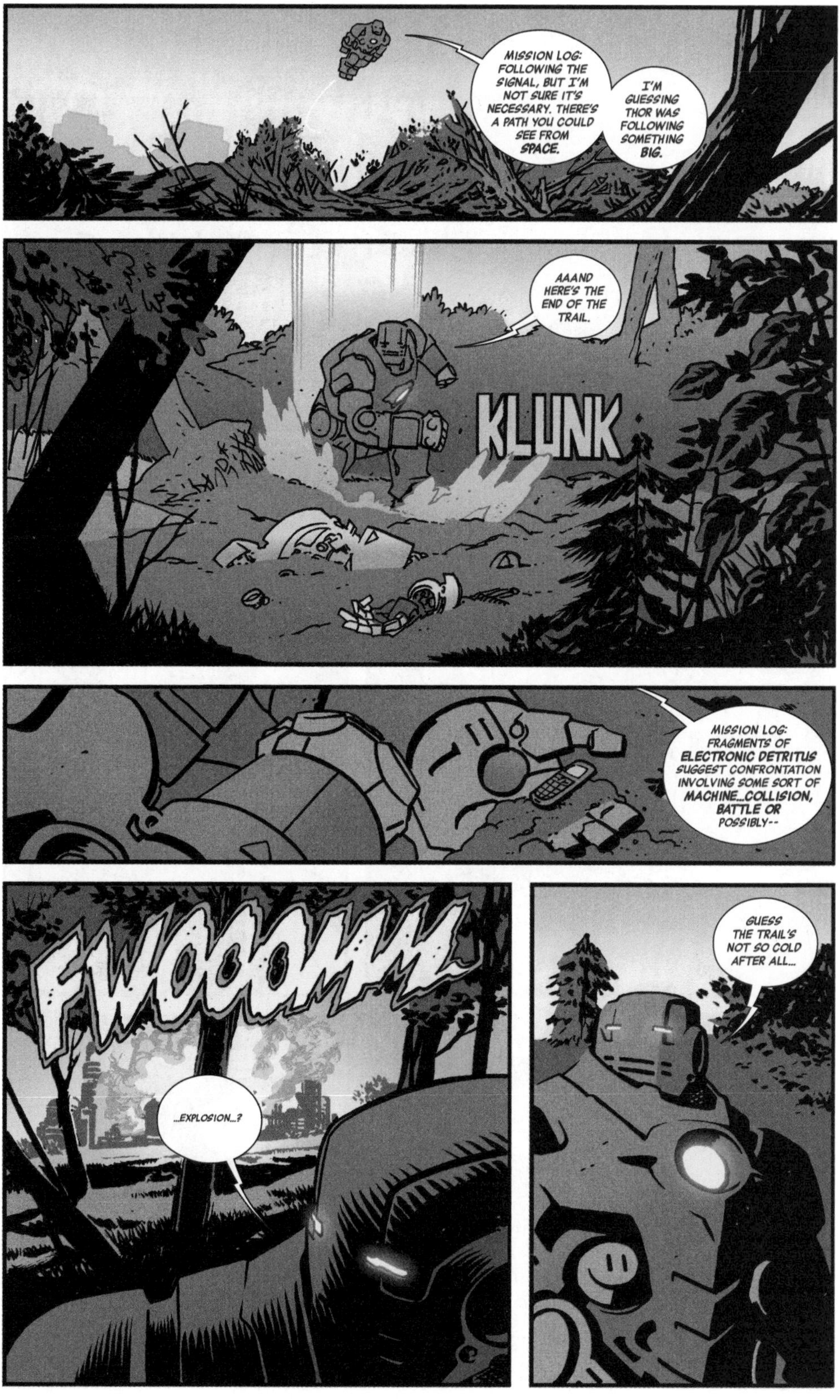
MISSION LOG: FOLLOWING THE SIGNAL, BUT I'M NOT SURE IT'S NECESSARY. THERE'S A PATH YOU COULD SEE FROM SPACE.
I'M GUESSING THOR WAS FOLLOWING SOMETHING BIG.
AAAND HERE'S THE END OF THE TRAIL.
KLUNK
MISSION LOG: FRAGMENTS OF ELECTRONIC DETRITUS SUGGEST CONFRONTATION INVOLVING SOME SORT OF MACHINE...COLLISION, BATTLE OR POSSIBLY--
FWOOOMM
...EXPLOSION...?
GUESS THE TRAIL'S NOT SO COLD AFTER ALL...

=KOFF! KOFF!= WHAT IN ODIN'S NAME--?

SURPRISED?

AFTER YOUR THOROUGH **TRASHING** OF MY K-BOT 3000, I HAD SOME **ADJUSTMENTS** MADE TO THE REST OF THE FLEET.

IF THEIR **CHEST CASINGS** ARE BREACHED, THEY'RE NOW PRIMED TO **BLOW UP.**

I HAVE NO DOUBT YOU CAN SURVIVE **ONE** SUCH EXPLOSION... POSSIBLY EVEN **TWO** OR **THREE...**

...BUT A **DOZEN?**

GIVE UP QUIETLY AND I'LL MAKE...WHATEVER FOLLOWS...AS **PAINLESS** AS POSSIBLE.

EEEEEEEEEEEEEEEEEEEEEEEE

+++ 111000111100 +++

WHAT... ?

+++ 000111010111100 +++

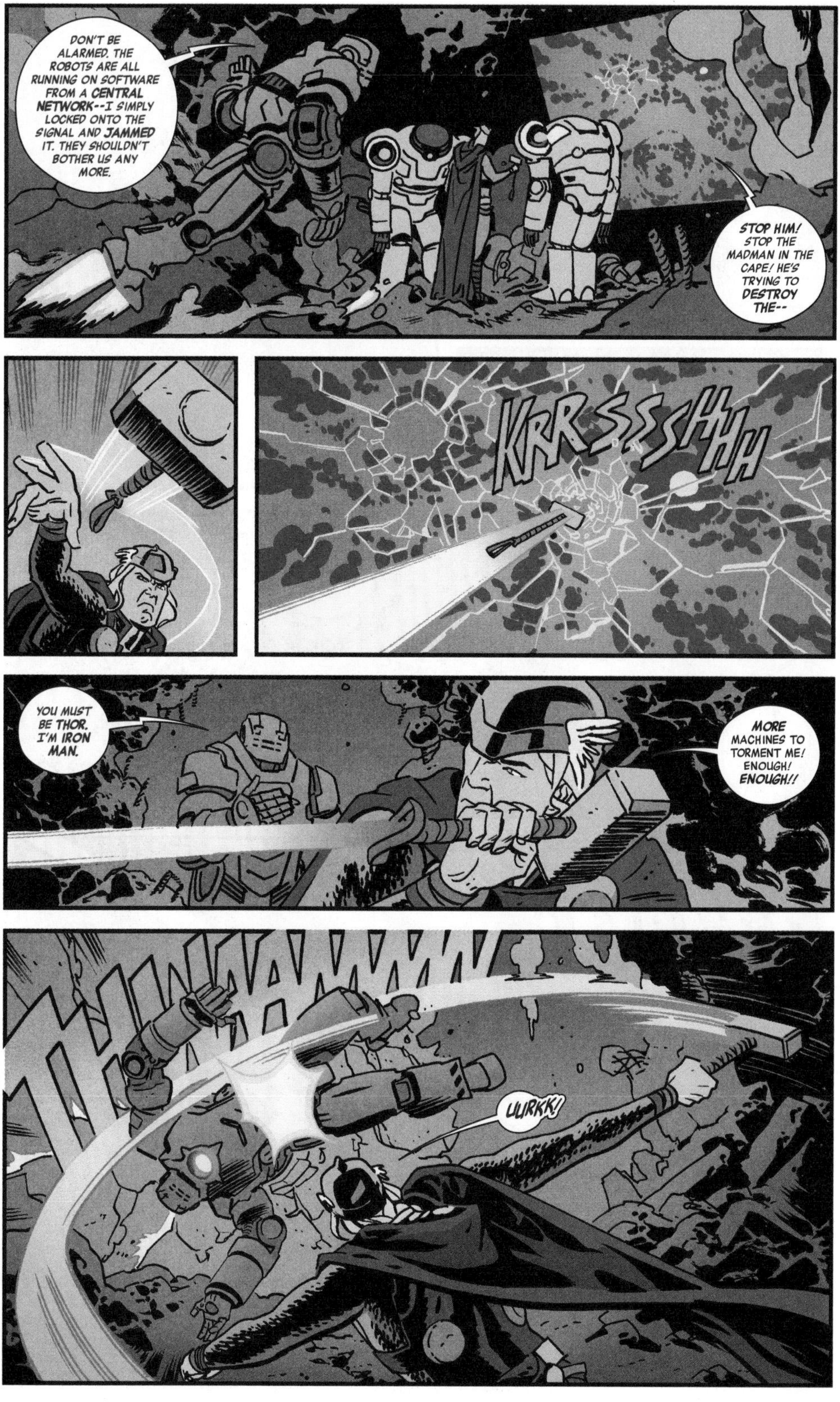
DON'T BE ALARMED. THE ROBOTS ARE ALL RUNNING ON SOFTWARE FROM A CENTRAL NETWORK--I SIMPLY LOCKED ONTO THE SIGNAL AND JAMMED IT. THEY SHOULDN'T BOTHER US ANY MORE.
STOP HIM! STOP THE MADMAN IN THE CAPE! HE'S TRYING TO DESTROY THE--
KRRSSSHHH
YOU MUST BE THOR. I'M IRON MAN.
MORE MACHINES TO TORMENT ME! ENOUGH! ENOUGH!!
UURKK!

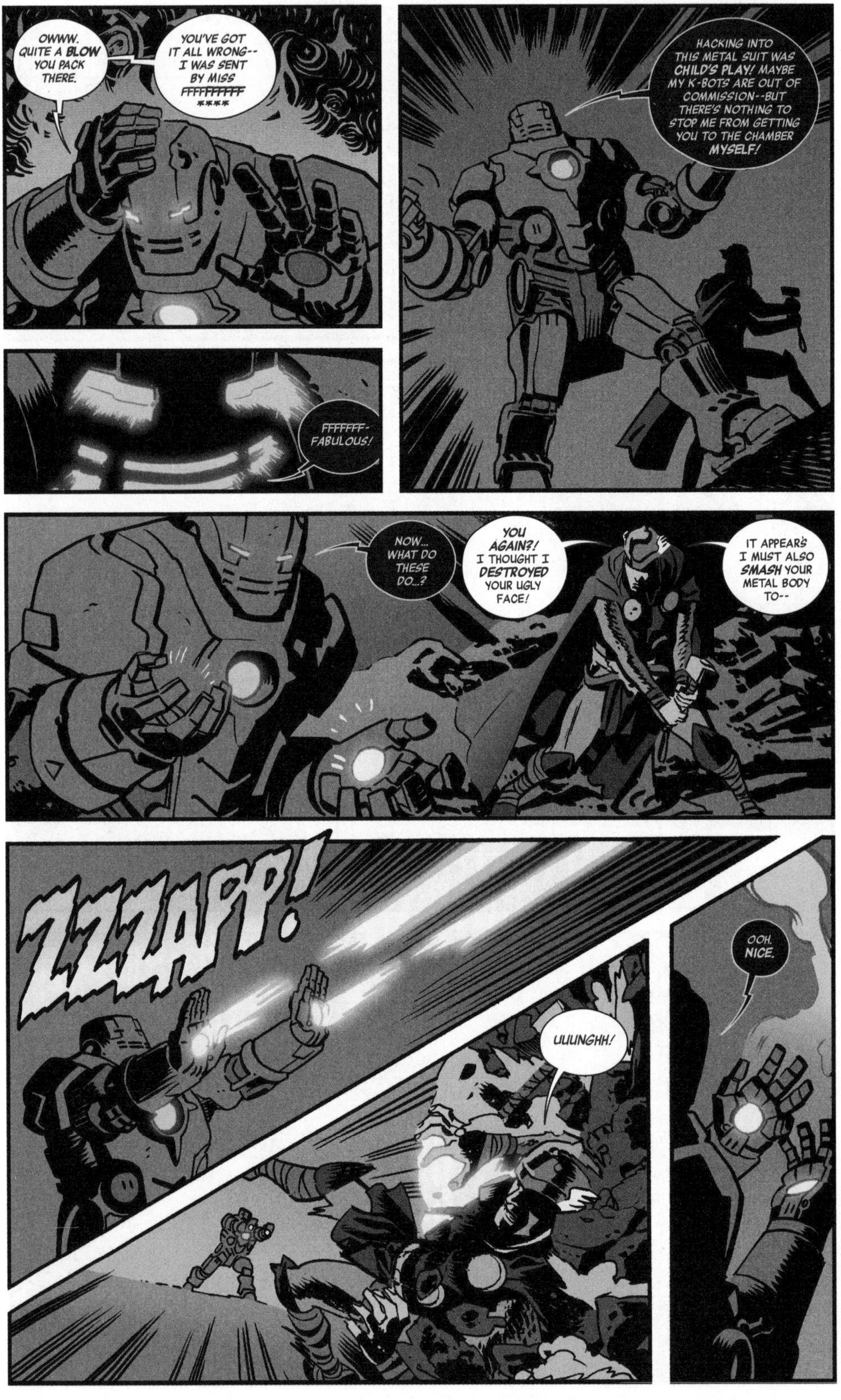
OWWW. QUITE A BLOW YOU PACK THERE.
YOU'VE GOT IT ALL WRONG-- I WAS SENT BY MISS FFFFFFFFFF ****
FFFFFFF- FABULOUS!
HACKING INTO THIS METAL SUIT WAS CHILD'S PLAY! MAYBE MY K-BOTS ARE OUT OF COMMISSION--BUT THERE'S NOTHING TO STOP ME FROM GETTING YOU TO THE CHAMBER MYSELF!
NOW... WHAT DO THESE DO...?
YOU AGAIN?! I THOUGHT I DESTROYED YOUR UGLY FACE!
IT APPEARS I MUST ALSO SMASH YOUR METAL BODY TO--
ZZZAPP!
UUUNGHH!
OOH. NICE.

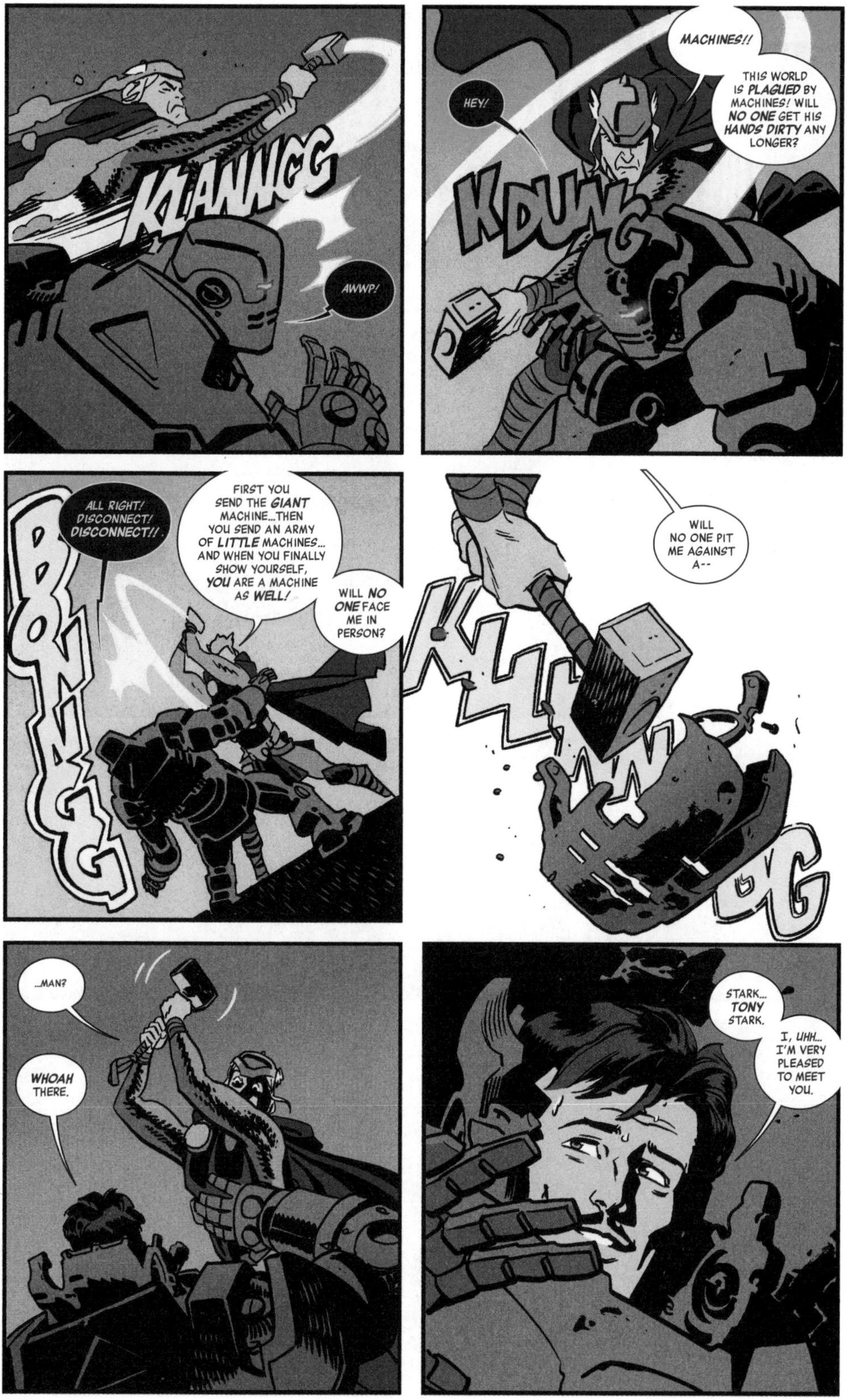
KLANNGG
AWWP!
HEY!
MACHINES!!
THIS WORLD IS PLAGUED BY MACHINES! WILL NO ONE GET HIS HANDS DIRTY ANY LONGER?
KDUNG
BONNG
ALL RIGHT! DISCONNECT! DISCONNECT!!
FIRST YOU SEND THE GIANT MACHINE...THEN YOU SEND AN ARMY OF LITTLE MACHINES... AND WHEN YOU FINALLY SHOW YOURSELF, YOU ARE A MACHINE AS WELL!
WILL NO ONE FACE ME IN PERSON?
WILL NO ONE PIT ME AGAINST A--
...MAN?
WHOAH THERE.
STARK... TONY STARK.
I, UHH... I'M VERY PLEASED TO MEET YOU.

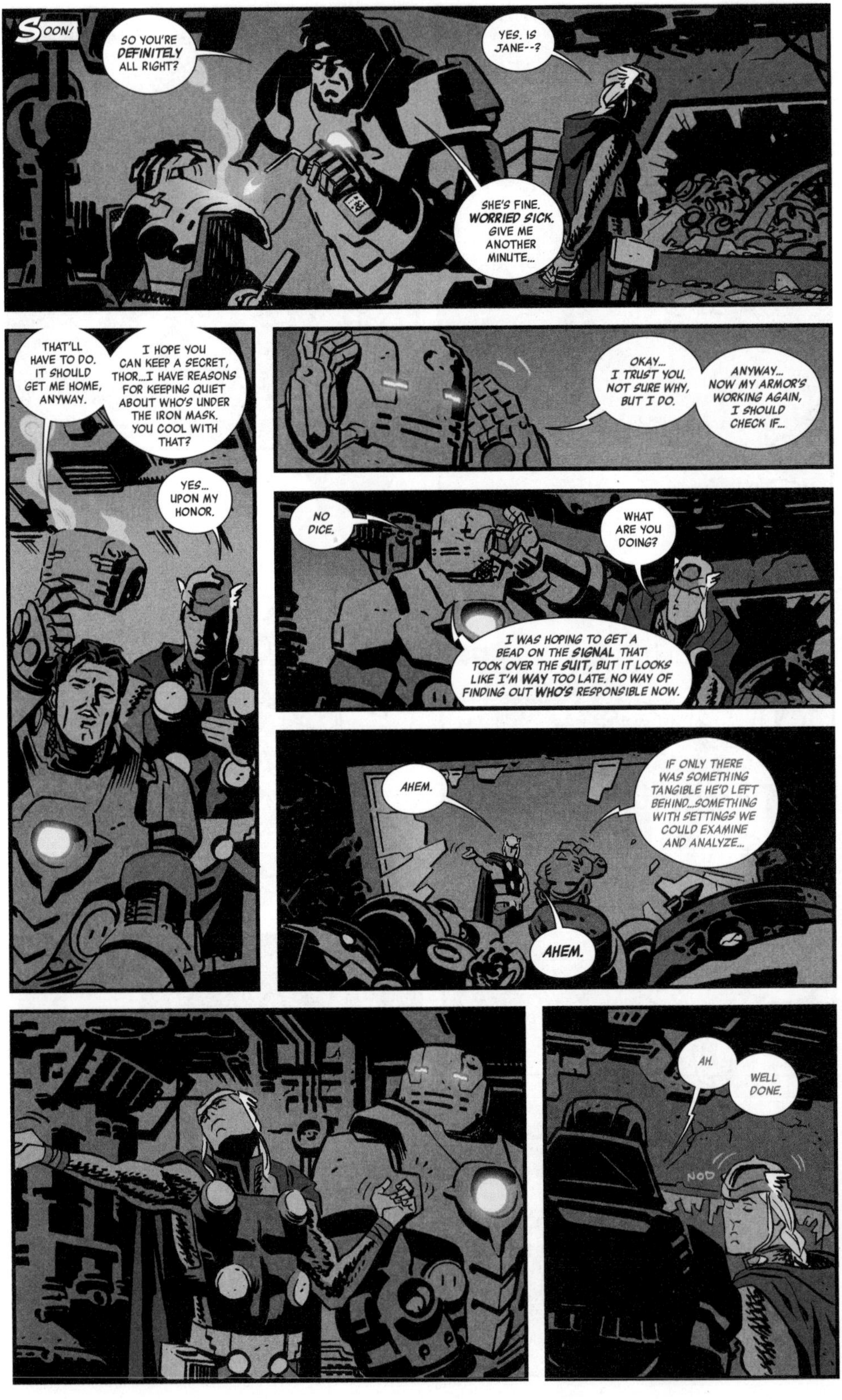
SOON!
SO YOU'RE DEFINITELY ALL RIGHT?
YES. IS JANE--?
SHE'S FINE. WORRIED SICK. GIVE ME ANOTHER MINUTE...
THAT'LL HAVE TO DO. IT SHOULD GET ME HOME, ANYWAY.
I HOPE YOU CAN KEEP A SECRET, THOR...I HAVE REASONS FOR KEEPING QUIET ABOUT WHO'S UNDER THE IRON MASK. YOU COOL WITH THAT?
YES... UPON MY HONOR.
OKAY... I TRUST YOU. NOT SURE WHY, BUT I DO.
ANYWAY... NOW MY ARMOR'S WORKING AGAIN, I SHOULD CHECK IF...
NO DICE.
WHAT ARE YOU DOING?
I WAS HOPING TO GET A BEAD ON THE SIGNAL THAT TOOK OVER THE SUIT, BUT IT LOOKS LIKE I'M WAY TOO LATE. NO WAY OF FINDING OUT WHO'S RESPONSIBLE NOW.
AHEM.
IF ONLY THERE WAS SOMETHING TANGIBLE HE'D LEFT BEHIND...SOMETHING WITH SETTINGS WE COULD EXAMINE AND ANALYZE...
AHEM.
AH.
WELL DONE.
NOD

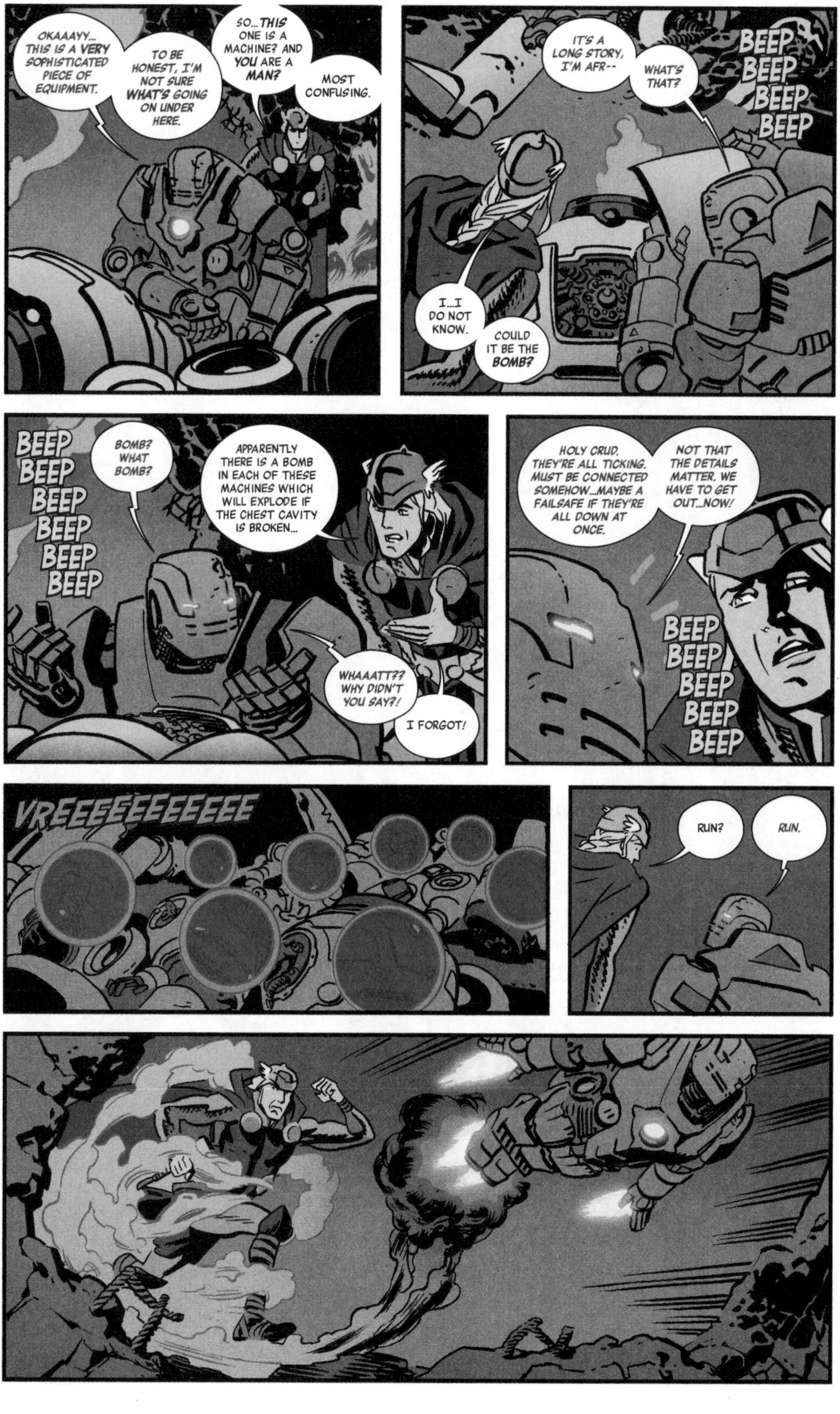
OKAAAYY... THIS IS A VERY SOPHISTICATED PIECE OF EQUIPMENT.
TO BE HONEST, I'M NOT SURE WHAT'S GOING ON UNDER HERE.
SO... THIS ONE IS A MACHINE? AND YOU ARE A MAN?
MOST CONFUSING.
IT'S A LONG STORY, I'M AFR--
WHAT'S THAT?
BEEP BEEP BEEP BEEP
I...I DO NOT KNOW.
COULD IT BE THE BOMB?
BEEP BEEP BEEP BEEP BEEP BEEP
BOMB? WHAT BOMB?
APPARENTLY THERE IS A BOMB IN EACH OF THESE MACHINES WHICH WILL EXPLODE IF THE CHEST CAVITY IS BROKEN...
WHAAATT?? WHY DIDN'T YOU SAY?!
I FORGOT!
HOLY CRUD. THEY'RE ALL TICKING. MUST BE CONNECTED SOMEHOW...MAYBE A FAILSAFE IF THEY'RE ALL DOWN AT ONCE.
NOT THAT THE DETAILS MATTER. WE HAVE TO GET OUT...NOW!
BEEP BEEP BEEP BEEP BEEP
VREEEEEEEEEEE
RUN?
RUN.

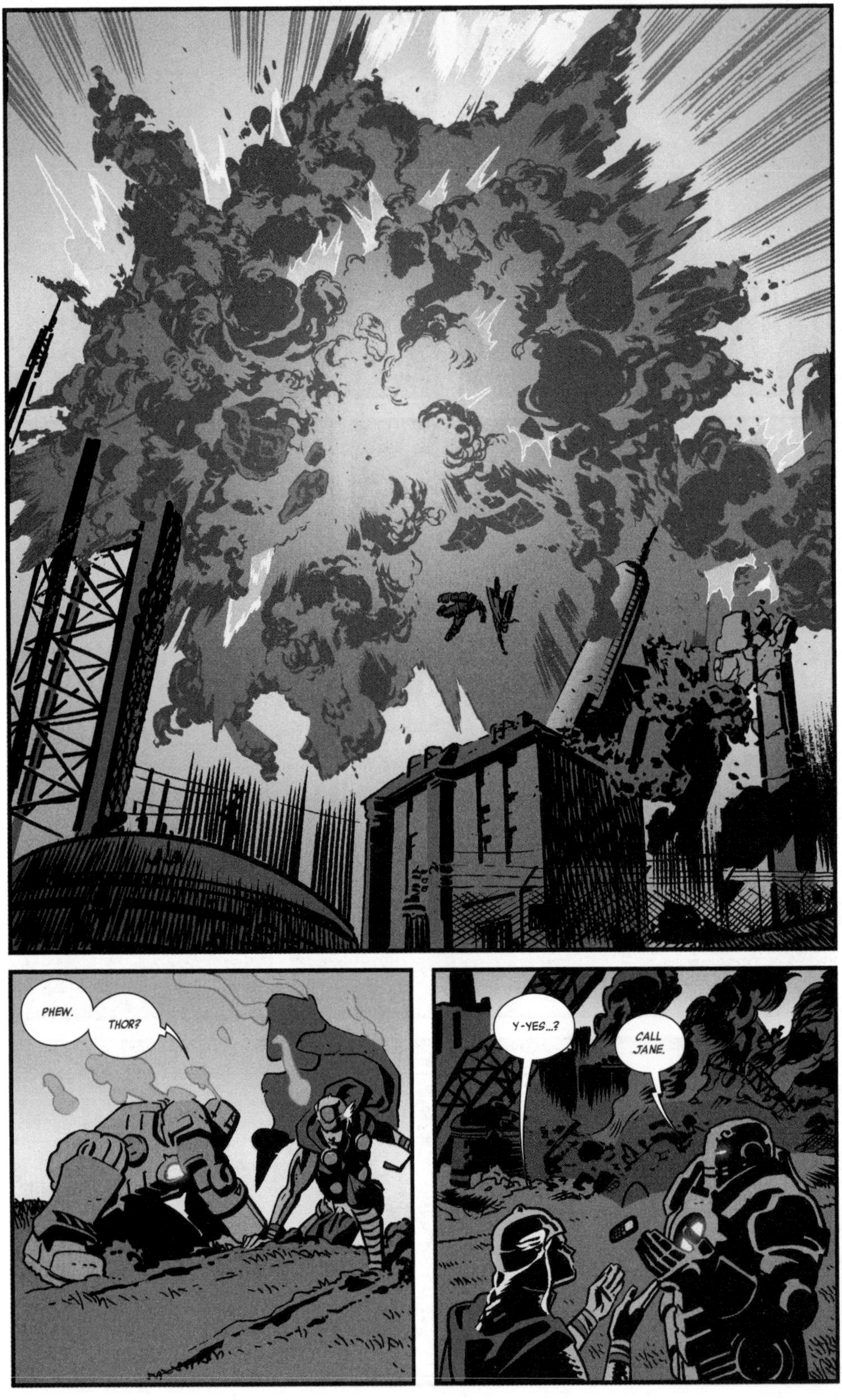
PHEW.
THOR?
Y-YES...?
CALL JANE.

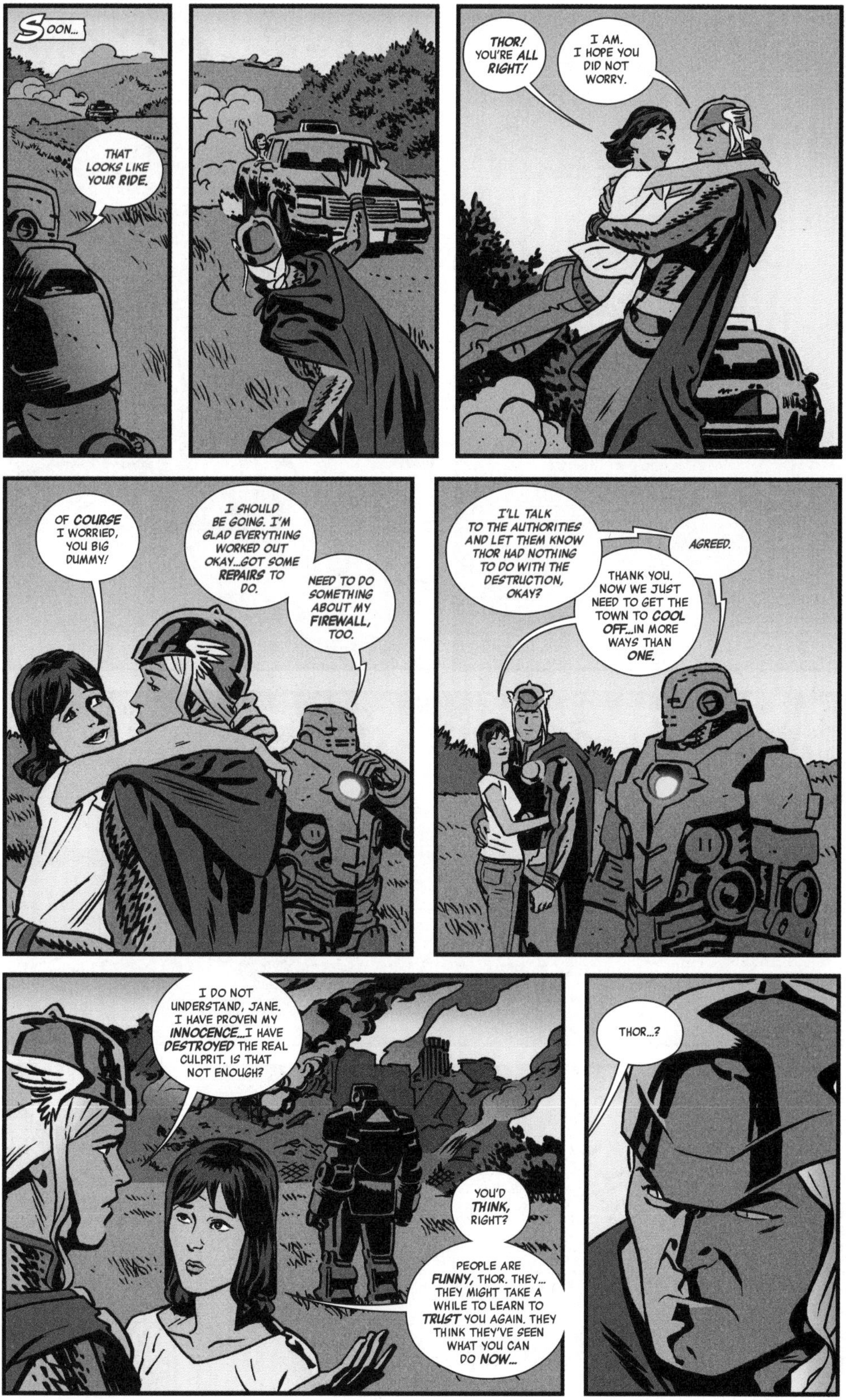
SOON...
THAT LOOKS LIKE YOUR RIDE.
THOR! YOU'RE ALL RIGHT!
I AM. I HOPE YOU DID NOT WORRY.
OF COURSE I WORRIED, YOU BIG DUMMY!
I SHOULD BE GOING. I'M GLAD EVERYTHING WORKED OUT OKAY...GOT SOME REPAIRS TO DO.
NEED TO DO SOMETHING ABOUT MY FIREWALL, TOO.
I'LL TALK TO THE AUTHORITIES AND LET THEM KNOW THOR HAD NOTHING TO DO WITH THE DESTRUCTION, OKAY?
AGREED.
THANK YOU. NOW WE JUST NEED TO GET THE TOWN TO COOL OFF...IN MORE WAYS THAN ONE.
I DO NOT UNDERSTAND, JANE. I HAVE PROVEN MY INNOCENCE...I HAVE DESTROYED THE REAL CULPRIT. IS THAT NOT ENOUGH?
YOU'D THINK, RIGHT?
PEOPLE ARE FUNNY, THOR. THEY... THEY MIGHT TAKE A WHILE TO LEARN TO TRUST YOU AGAIN. THEY THINK THEY'VE SEEN WHAT YOU CAN DO NOW...
THOR...?

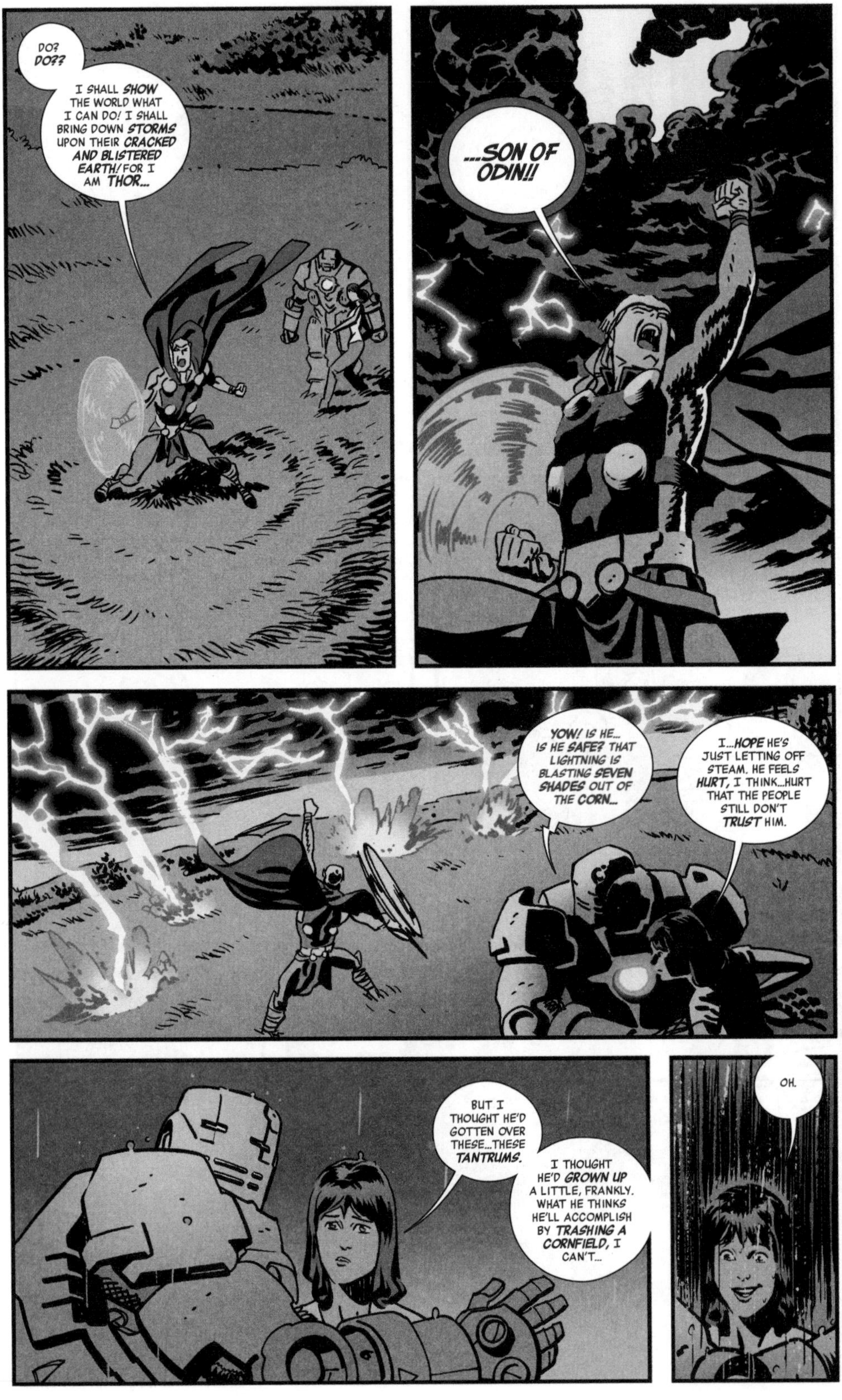
DO? DO??
I SHALL SHOW THE WORLD WHAT I CAN DO! I SHALL BRING DOWN STORMS UPON THEIR CRACKED AND BLISTERED EARTH! FOR I AM THOR...
...SON OF ODIN!!
YOW! IS HE... IS HE SAFE? THAT LIGHTNING IS BLASTING SEVEN SHADES OUT OF THE CORN...
I...HOPE HE'S JUST LETTING OFF STEAM. HE FEELS HURT, I THINK...HURT THAT THE PEOPLE STILL DON'T TRUST HIM.
BUT I THOUGHT HE'D GOTTEN OVER THESE...THESE TANTRUMS.
I THOUGHT HE'D GROWN UP A LITTLE, FRANKLY. WHAT HE THINKS HE'LL ACCOMPLISH BY TRASHING A CORNFIELD, I CAN'T...
OH.

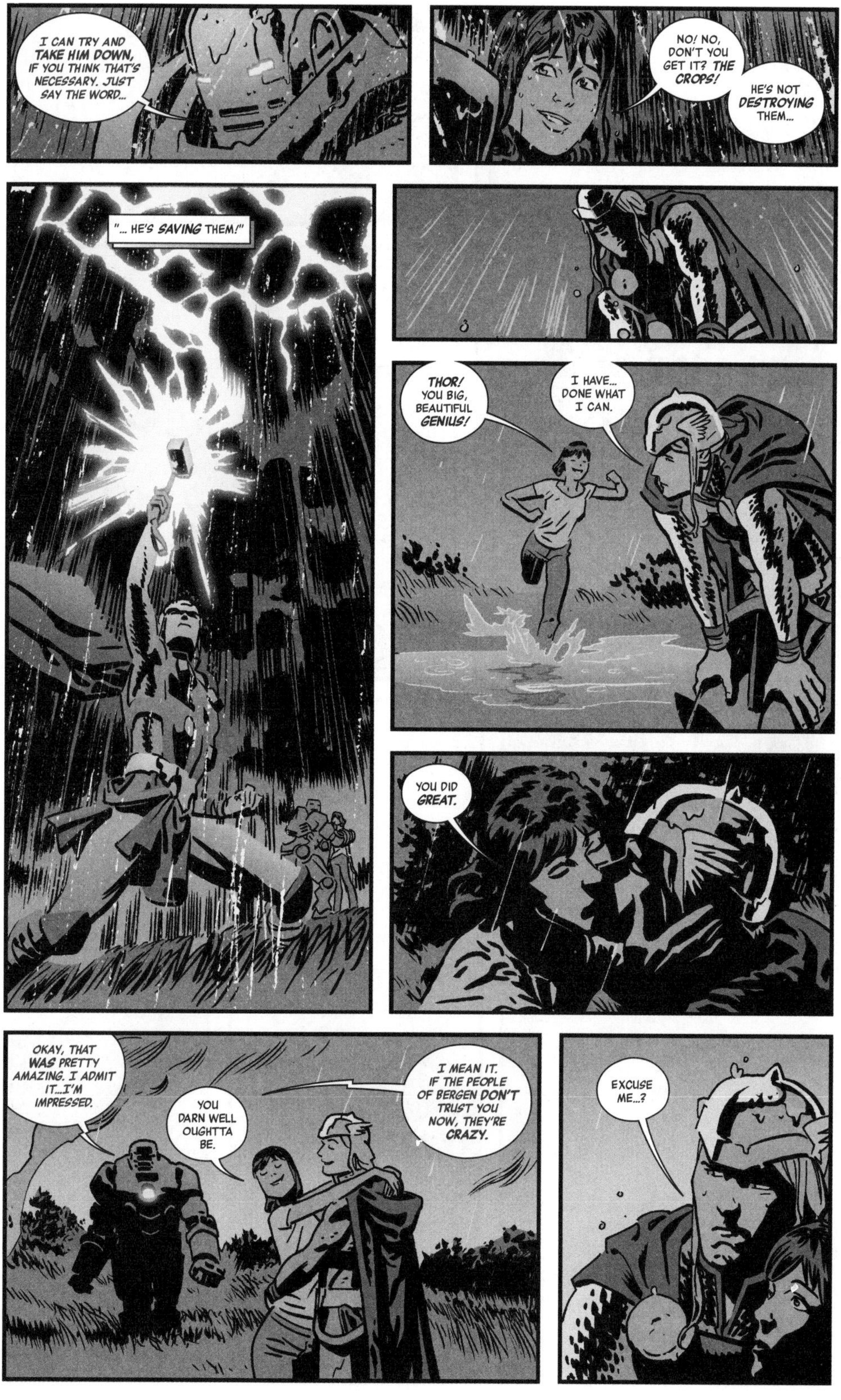
I CAN TRY AND TAKE HIM DOWN, IF YOU THINK THAT'S NECESSARY. JUST SAY THE WORD...
NO! NO, DON'T YOU GET IT? THE CROPS!
HE'S NOT DESTROYING THEM...
"... HE'S SAVING THEM!"
THOR! YOU BIG, BEAUTIFUL GENIUS!
I HAVE... DONE WHAT I CAN.
YOU DID GREAT.
OKAY, THAT WAS PRETTY AMAZING. I ADMIT IT...I'M IMPRESSED.
YOU DARN WELL OUGHTTA BE.
I MEAN IT. IF THE PEOPLE OF BERGEN DON'T TRUST YOU NOW, THEY'RE CRAZY.
EXCUSE ME...?

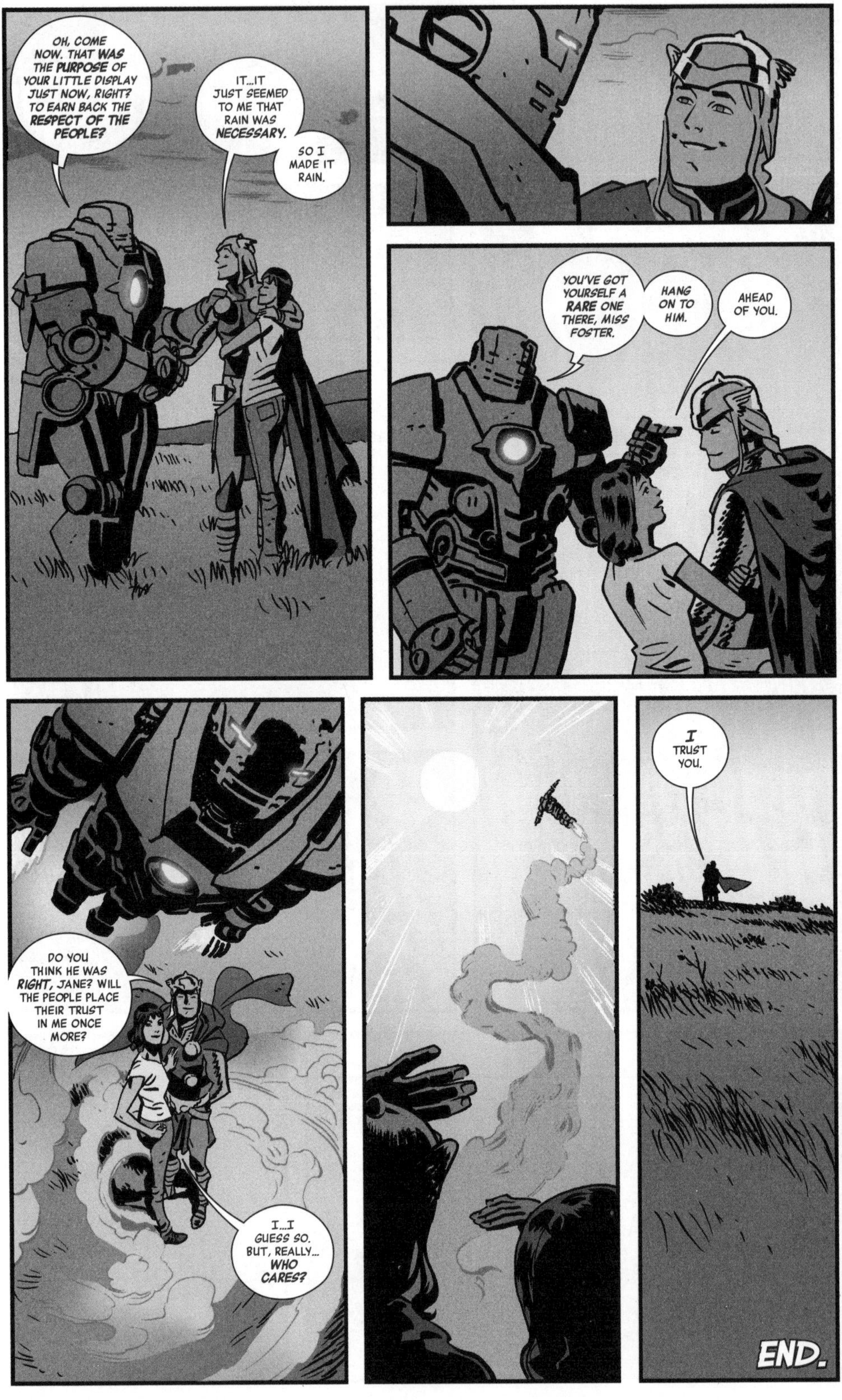
OH, COME NOW. THAT WAS THE PURPOSE OF YOUR LITTLE DISPLAY JUST NOW, RIGHT? TO EARN BACK THE RESPECT OF THE PEOPLE?
IT...IT JUST SEEMED TO ME THAT RAIN WAS NECESSARY.
SO I MADE IT RAIN.
YOU'VE GOT YOURSELF A RARE ONE THERE, MISS FOSTER.
HANG ON TO HIM.
AHEAD OF YOU.
DO YOU THINK HE WAS RIGHT, JANE? WILL THE PEOPLE PLACE THEIR TRUST IN ME ONCE MORE?
I...I GUESS SO. BUT, REALLY... WHO CARES?
I TRUST YOU.
END.

AND IT CAME TO PASS THAT
THOR: THE MIGHTY AVENGER
DID END. AND THE READERS CAME AND THEY
WERE ALL A-TWITTER. AND THEY DID OPEN THE
FINAL ISSUE AND TURN TO THE LAST PAGE, AND
LO! THERE THEY DID READ THESE
SIMPLE INSCRIPTIONS:

Whosoever holds this comic book, if they should have romance in their hearts, shall possess the everlasting gratitude of THOR, THE MIGHTY AVENGER.
- Roger Langridge

I can't believe this journey is coming to an end. Working on THOR: THE MIGHTY AVENGER with this wonderful team has been the most fun I've ever had making comics. What an amazing experience it has been to have a book that I love so much be so well received by fans. My sincere gratitude to all of you who supported the series.
- Chris Samnee

THOR THE MIGHTY AVENGER will always be a career highlight for me, and that's all thanks to the top notch creative team and the most amazing fans in comics.
Thanks so much to all of you!
- Matt Wilson

THOR THE MIGHTY AVENGER has been a blast, and I'm sad to see it end. I'm proud to have been a part of this amazing creative team. Thanks to everyone who supported this book!
- Rus Wooton

Y'know how you think back to when you were a kid, and you fondly remember stories you read that made you laugh, blew your mind, took you on fantastic journeys and made you feel like all the characters were your friends? When the children of today think back in ten years, I think that's how they're gonna remember what Roger, Chris, Matt & Rus did on THOR THE MIGHTY AVENGER. I'm too lucky and so proud that I got to be a part of such a special tale.
- Nate Cosby

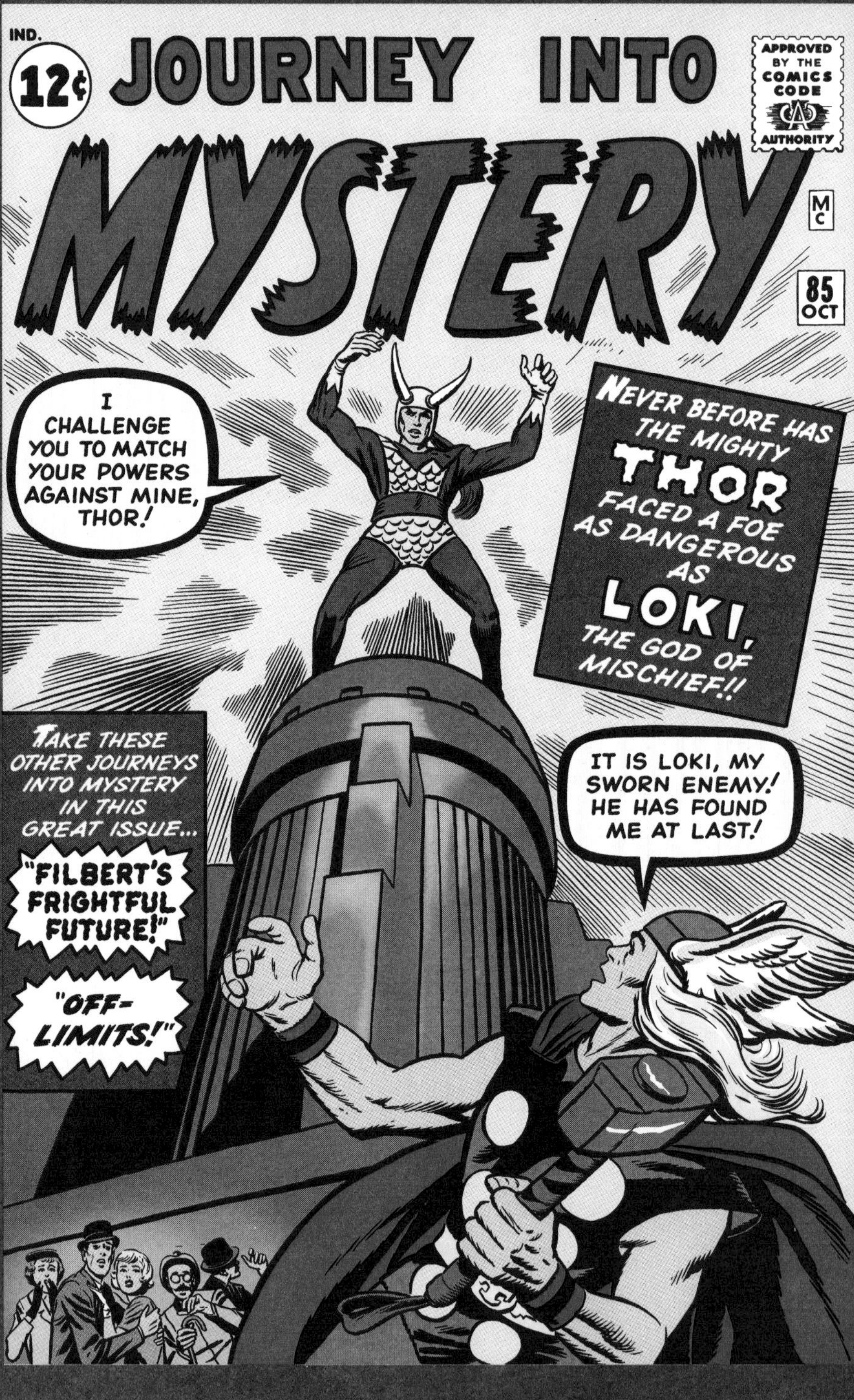
IND.
12¢
JOURNEY INTO
MYSTERY
APPROVED BY THE COMICS CODE AUTHORITY
MC
85 OCT
I CHALLENGE YOU TO MATCH YOUR POWERS AGAINST MINE, THOR!
NEVER BEFORE HAS THE MIGHTY THOR FACED A FOE AS DANGEROUS AS LOKI, THE GOD OF MISCHIEF!!
TAKE THESE OTHER JOURNEYS INTO MYSTERY IN THIS GREAT ISSUE...
"FILBERT'S FRIGHTFUL FUTURE!"
"OFF-LIMITS!"
IT IS LOKI, MY SWORN ENEMY! HE HAS FOUND ME AT LAST!

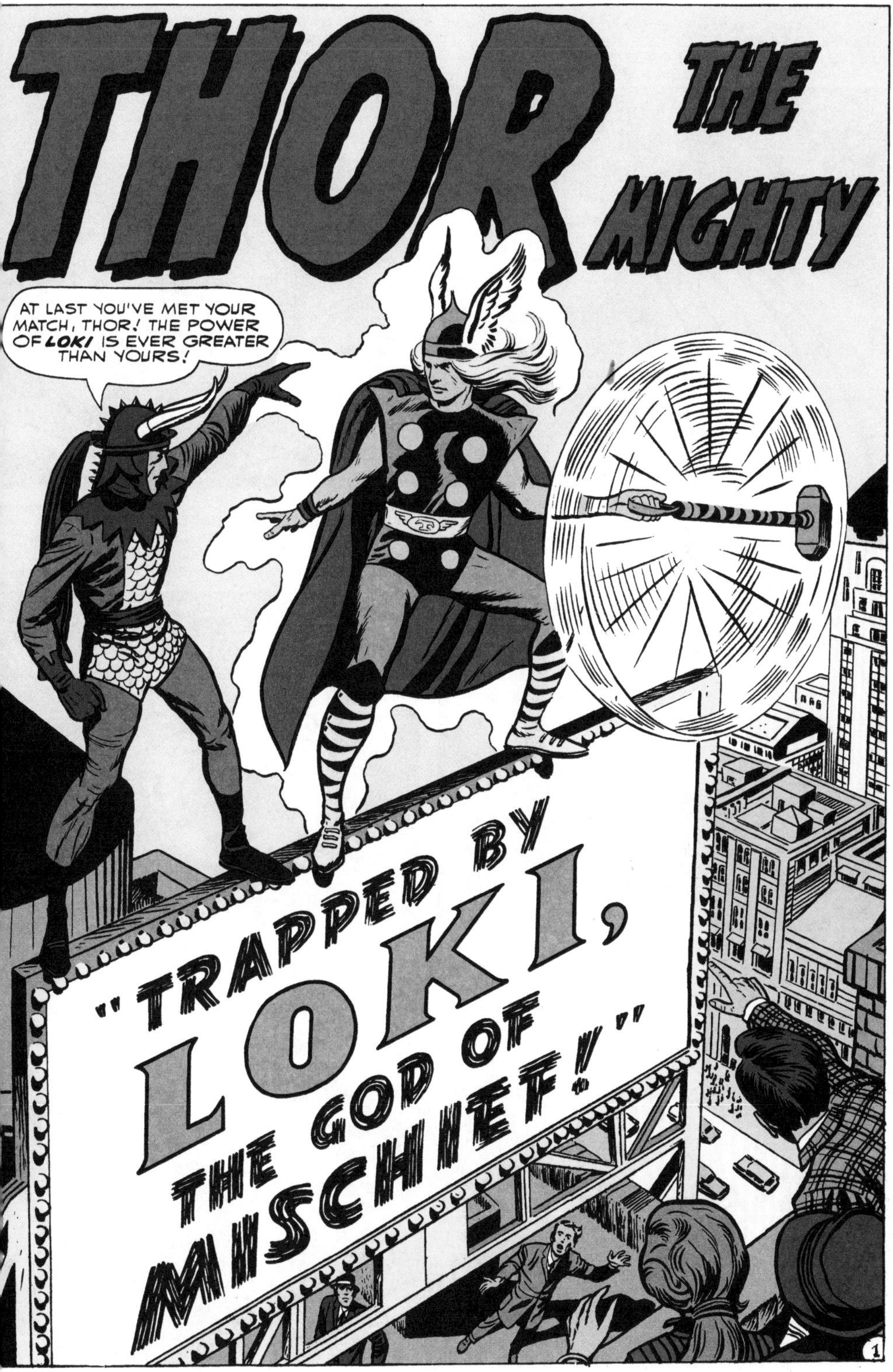
THOR THE MIGHTY
AT LAST YOU'VE MET YOUR MATCH, THOR! THE POWER OF LOKI IS EVER GREATER THAN YOURS!
"TRAPPED BY LOKI, THE GOD OF MISCHIEF!"
1

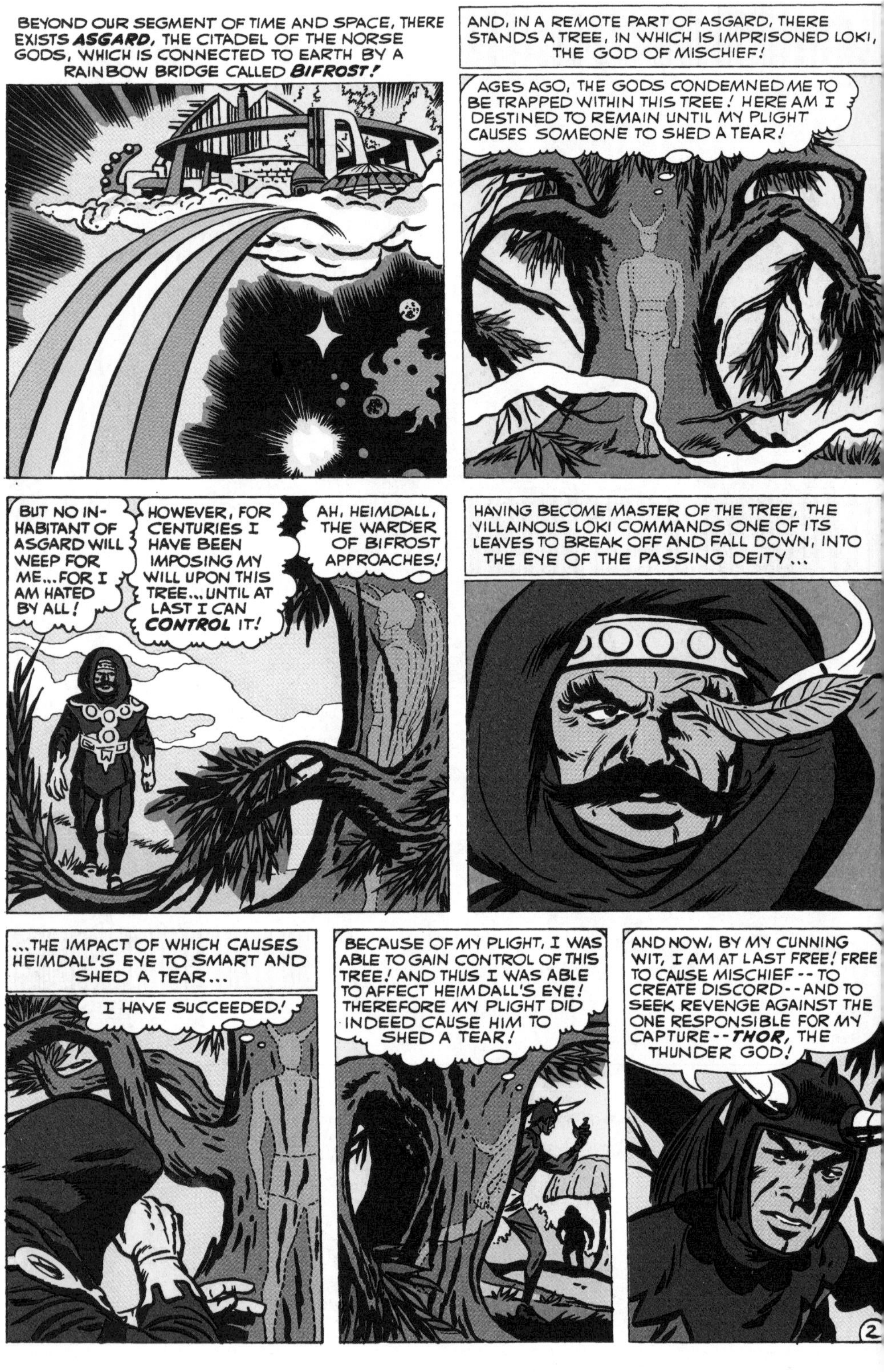
BEYOND OUR SEGMENT OF TIME AND SPACE, THERE EXISTS ASGARD, THE CITADEL OF THE NORSE GODS, WHICH IS CONNECTED TO EARTH BY A RAINBOW BRIDGE CALLED BIFROST!
AND, IN A REMOTE PART OF ASGARD, THERE STANDS A TREE, IN WHICH IS IMPRISONED LOKI, THE GOD OF MISCHIEF!
AGES AGO, THE GODS CONDEMNED ME TO BE TRAPPED WITHIN THIS TREE! HERE AM I DESTINED TO REMAIN UNTIL MY PLIGHT CAUSES SOMEONE TO SHED A TEAR!
BUT NO INHABITANT OF ASGARD WILL WEEP FOR ME...FOR I AM HATED BY ALL!
HOWEVER, FOR CENTURIES I HAVE BEEN IMPOSING MY WILL UPON THIS TREE...UNTIL AT LAST I CAN CONTROL IT!
AH, HEIMDALL, THE WARDER OF BIFROST APPROACHES!
HAVING BECOME MASTER OF THE TREE, THE VILLAINOUS LOKI COMMANDS ONE OF ITS LEAVES TO BREAK OFF AND FALL DOWN, INTO THE EYE OF THE PASSING DEITY...
...THE IMPACT OF WHICH CAUSES HEIMDALL'S EYE TO SMART AND SHED A TEAR...
I HAVE SUCCEEDED!
BECAUSE OF MY PLIGHT, I WAS ABLE TO GAIN CONTROL OF THIS TREE! AND THUS I WAS ABLE TO AFFECT HEIMDALL'S EYE! THEREFORE MY PLIGHT DID INDEED CAUSE HIM TO SHED A TEAR!
AND NOW, BY MY CUNNING WIT, I AM AT LAST FREE! FREE TO CAUSE MISCHIEF -- TO CREATE DISCORD -- AND TO SEEK REVENGE AGAINST THE ONE RESPONSIBLE FOR MY CAPTURE -- THOR, THE THUNDER GOD!
2

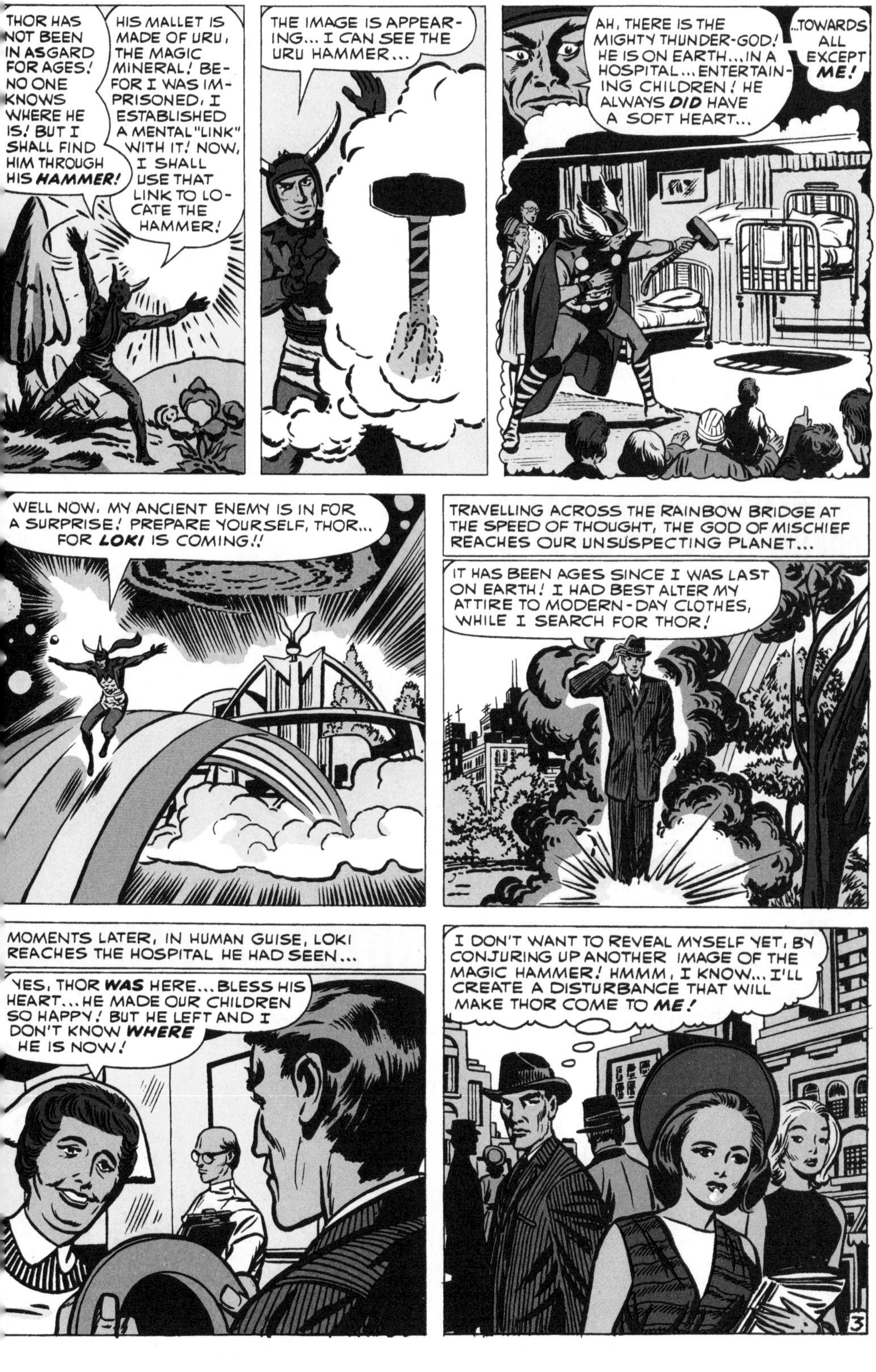
THOR HAS NOT BEEN IN ASGARD FOR AGES! NO ONE KNOWS WHERE HE IS! BUT I SHALL FIND HIM THROUGH HIS **HAMMER!**
HIS MALLET IS MADE OF URU, THE MAGIC MINERAL! BEFOR I WAS IMPRISONED, I ESTABLISHED A MENTAL "LINK" WITH IT! NOW, I SHALL USE THAT LINK TO LOCATE THE HAMMER!
THE IMAGE IS APPEARING... I CAN SEE THE URU HAMMER...
AH, THERE IS THE MIGHTY THUNDER-GOD! HE IS ON EARTH...IN A HOSPITAL...ENTERTAINING CHILDREN! HE ALWAYS **DID** HAVE A SOFT HEART...
...TOWARDS ALL EXCEPT **ME!**
WELL NOW, MY ANCIENT ENEMY IS IN FOR A SURPRISE! PREPARE YOURSELF, THOR... FOR **LOKI** IS COMING!!
TRAVELLING ACROSS THE RAINBOW BRIDGE AT THE SPEED OF THOUGHT, THE GOD OF MISCHIEF REACHES OUR UNSUSPECTING PLANET...
IT HAS BEEN AGES SINCE I WAS LAST ON EARTH! I HAD BEST ALTER MY ATTIRE TO MODERN-DAY CLOTHES, WHILE I SEARCH FOR THOR!
MOMENTS LATER, IN HUMAN GUISE, LOKI REACHES THE HOSPITAL HE HAD SEEN...
YES, THOR **WAS** HERE... BLESS HIS HEART... HE MADE OUR CHILDREN SO HAPPY! BUT HE LEFT AND I DON'T KNOW **WHERE** HE IS NOW!
I DON'T WANT TO REVEAL MYSELF YET, BY CONJURING UP ANOTHER IMAGE OF THE MAGIC HAMMER! HMMM, I KNOW... I'LL CREATE A DISTURBANCE THAT WILL MAKE THOR COME TO **ME!**
3

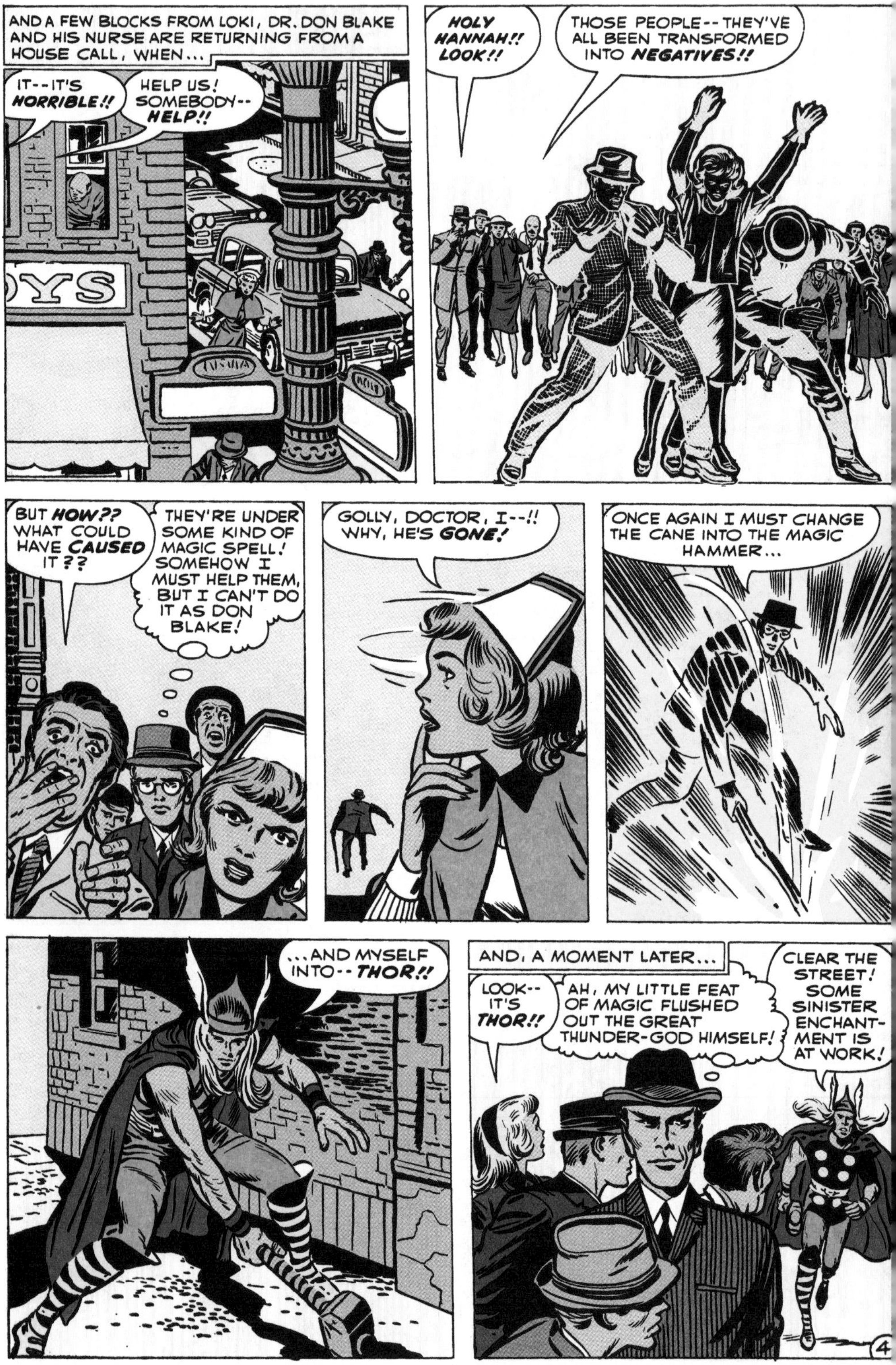
AND A FEW BLOCKS FROM LOKI, DR. DON BLAKE AND HIS NURSE ARE RETURNING FROM A HOUSE CALL, WHEN...
IT--IT'S **HORRIBLE!!**
HELP US! SOMEBODY-- **HELP!!**
OYS
HOLY HANNAH!! LOOK!!
THOSE PEOPLE--THEY'VE ALL BEEN TRANSFORMED INTO **NEGATIVES!!**
BUT **HOW??** WHAT COULD HAVE **CAUSED** IT??
THEY'RE UNDER SOME KIND OF MAGIC SPELL! SOMEHOW I MUST HELP THEM, BUT I CAN'T DO IT AS DON BLAKE!
GOLLY, DOCTOR, I--!! WHY, HE'S **GONE!**
ONCE AGAIN I MUST CHANGE THE CANE INTO THE MAGIC HAMMER...
...AND MYSELF INTO--**THOR!!**
AND, A MOMENT LATER...
LOOK-- IT'S **THOR!!**
AH, MY LITTLE FEAT OF MAGIC FLUSHED OUT THE GREAT THUNDER-GOD HIMSELF!
CLEAR THE STREET! SOME SINISTER ENCHANTMENT IS AT WORK!
4

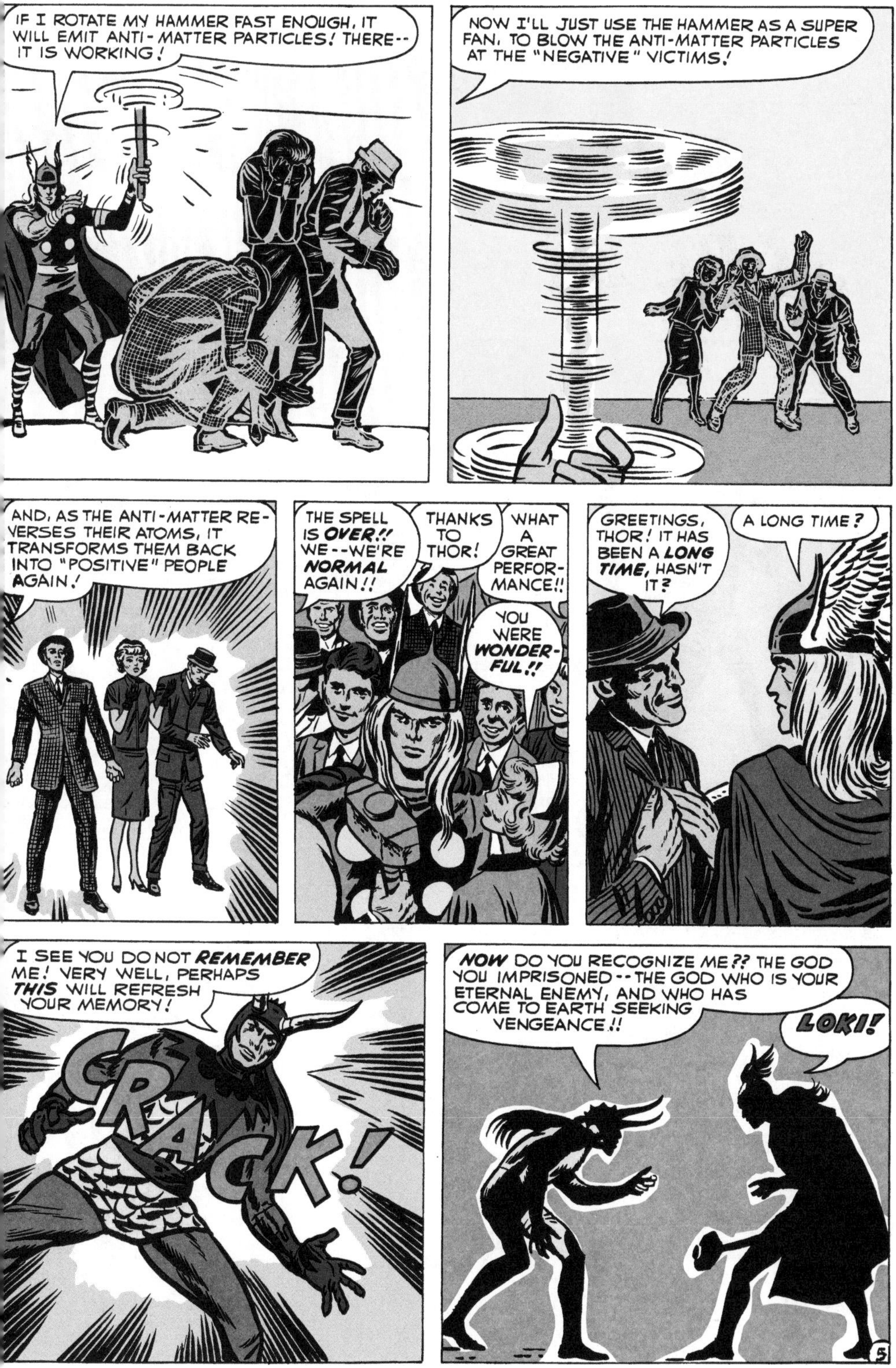
IF I ROTATE MY HAMMER FAST ENOUGH, IT WILL EMIT ANTI-MATTER PARTICLES! THERE-- IT IS WORKING!
NOW I'LL JUST USE THE HAMMER AS A SUPER FAN, TO BLOW THE ANTI-MATTER PARTICLES AT THE "NEGATIVE" VICTIMS!
AND, AS THE ANTI-MATTER REVERSES THEIR ATOMS, IT TRANSFORMS THEM BACK INTO "POSITIVE" PEOPLE AGAIN!
THE SPELL IS OVER!! WE--WE'RE NORMAL AGAIN!!
THANKS TO THOR!
WHAT A GREAT PERFORMANCE!!
YOU WERE WONDERFUL!!
GREETINGS, THOR! IT HAS BEEN A LONG TIME, HASN'T IT?
A LONG TIME?
I SEE YOU DO NOT REMEMBER ME! VERY WELL, PERHAPS THIS WILL REFRESH YOUR MEMORY!
CRACK!
NOW DO YOU RECOGNIZE ME?? THE GOD YOU IMPRISONED--THE GOD WHO IS YOUR ETERNAL ENEMY, AND WHO HAS COME TO EARTH SEEKING VENGEANCE!!
LOKI!
5

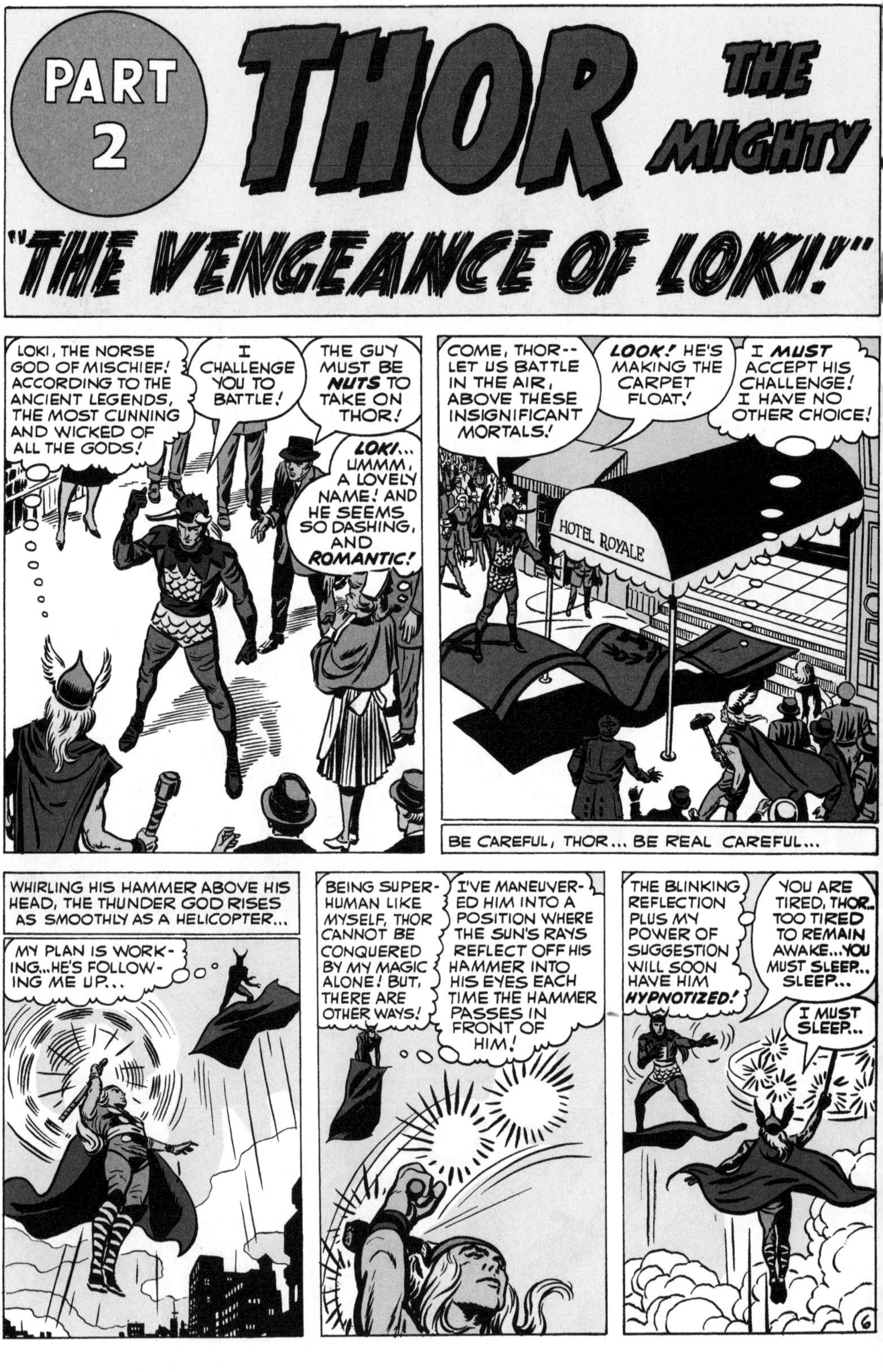
PART 2
THOR THE MIGHTY
"THE VENGEANCE OF LOKI!"
LOKI, THE NORSE GOD OF MISCHIEF! ACCORDING TO THE ANCIENT LEGENDS, THE MOST CUNNING AND WICKED OF ALL THE GODS!
I CHALLENGE YOU TO BATTLE!
THE GUY MUST BE NUTS TO TAKE ON THOR!
LOKI... UMMM, A LOVELY NAME! AND HE SEEMS SO DASHING, AND ROMANTIC!
COME, THOR-- LET US BATTLE IN THE AIR, ABOVE THESE INSIGNIFICANT MORTALS!
LOOK! HE'S MAKING THE CARPET FLOAT!
I MUST ACCEPT HIS CHALLENGE! I HAVE NO OTHER CHOICE!
HOTEL ROYALE
BE CAREFUL, THOR... BE REAL CAREFUL...
WHIRLING HIS HAMMER ABOVE HIS HEAD, THE THUNDER GOD RISES AS SMOOTHLY AS A HELICOPTER...
MY PLAN IS WORKING...HE'S FOLLOWING ME UP...
BEING SUPER-HUMAN LIKE MYSELF, THOR CANNOT BE CONQUERED BY MY MAGIC ALONE! BUT, THERE ARE OTHER WAYS!
I'VE MANEUVERED HIM INTO A POSITION WHERE THE SUN'S RAYS REFLECT OFF HIS HAMMER INTO HIS EYES EACH TIME THE HAMMER PASSES IN FRONT OF HIM!
THE BLINKING REFLECTION PLUS MY POWER OF SUGGESTION WILL SOON HAVE HIM HYPNOTIZED!
YOU ARE TIRED, THOR... TOO TIRED TO REMAIN AWAKE...YOU MUST SLEEP... SLEEP...
I MUST SLEEP...
6

"YOU ARE IN MY POWER....I AM YOUR MASTER...YOU MUST OBEY ME..."

"I MUST... OBEY YOU..."

"I HAVE *TRIUMPHED!* NOW TO HAVE MY REVENGE! I SHALL USE *THOR* AS MY INSTRUMENT FOR CREATING MISCHIEF!"

"DESCEND TO EARTH, THOR!"

"YES, LOKI!"

BUT, WHEN THE TWO LIVING LEGENDS TOUCH THE GROUND, ONE SUDDEN FEAR SWEEPS THROUGH LOKI...

"SOME ACCIDENTAL SHOCK MIGHT SUDDENLY SNAP HIM OUT OF HIS TRANCE! IF THAT HAPPENED AND HE HAD HIS HAMMER WITH HIM, IT WOULD BE TOO DANGEROUS FOR ME!"

"I MUST GET THOR'S HAMMER *AWAY* FROM HIM!"

"I COMMAND YOU TO GIVE ME THE ENCHANTED HAMMER!"

"I...I CANNOT OBEY YOU, LOKI! BY THE WILL OF ODIN* THE MAGIC WEAPON MUST NEVER BE WRESTED FROM THOR!"

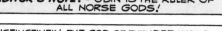
EDITOR'S NOTE! ODIN IS THE RULER OF ALL NORSE GODS!*

"HIS ATTACHMENT TO THE HAMMER IS TOO STRONG FOR EVEN *HYPNOSIS* TO OVERCOME!"

"I WILL HAVE TO RESORT TO TRICKERY!"

"*LOOK*, THOR--THERE IS A *SEA BEAST* BENEATH THE SURFACE! IT IS ATTACKING THAT SMALL BOAT!"

INSTINCTIVELY, THE GOD OF THUNDER HURLS HIS MIGHTY HAMMER IN THE DIRECTION INDICATED BY LOKI...

"*HAH!* IT WORKED! HE BELIEVED THERE REALLY *WAS* A MENACE AND HE TRIED TO DESTROY IT!"

BUT, AN INSTANT LATER...

"OHH--I *FORGOT*--THE HAMMER'S GREATEST POWER---WHENEVER THOR THROWS IT, IT *RETURNS* TO HIM!"

7

I *MUST* GET THE HAMMER AWAY FROM HIM! WAIT-- I HAVE A PLAN! I SHALL CONJURE UP *ANOTHER* THOR!

IN HIS HYPNOTIC TRANCE, HE MIGHT JUST BE DECEIVED BY THE IMAGE I'VE CREATED!

BEHOLD *THOR*, THE MIGHTY-- THE THUNDER GOD! THE HAMMER IS *HIS!* GIVE IT TO HIM!

YES, LOKI. THE HAMMER BELONGS TO THOR!

IT *WORKED!*

NOW GO TO YONDER HOUSE OF ANIMALS AND SET FREE THE BEASTS!

SET FREE THE BEASTS...

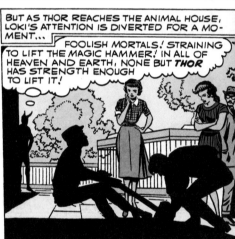

BUT AS THOR REACHES THE ANIMAL HOUSE, LOKI'S ATTENTION IS DIVERTED FOR A MOMENT...

FOOLISH MORTALS! STRAINING TO LIFT THE MAGIC HAMMER! IN ALL OF HEAVEN AND EARTH, NONE BUT *THOR* HAS STRENGTH ENOUGH TO LIFT IT!

AND, IN THAT FATEFUL MOMENT, THE TRANSFORMATION TAKES PLACE! FOR WHEN THE GOD OF THUNDER AND HIS HAMMER ARE SEPARATED FOR MORE THAN SIXTY SECONDS, HE REVERTS BACK TO HIS NORMAL FORM...

...AND THE HYPNOTIC SPELL WHICH THOR WAS UNDER HAS NO EFFECT UPON THE PERSON OF DR. DON BLAKE...

WHAT CAN BE TAKING THOR SO LONG? WHY HAS HE NOT RELEASED THE BEASTS?

I MUST MANAGE TO TOUCH THE HAMMER AGAIN!

ANIMAL HOUSE

I DON'T *GET* IT! I CAN'T LIFT THIS THING CLEAR OFF THE GROUND!

WHEW! I STRAINED EVERY MUSCLE IN MY ARM AND *STILL* COULDN'T BUDGE IT!

LET *ME* TRY!

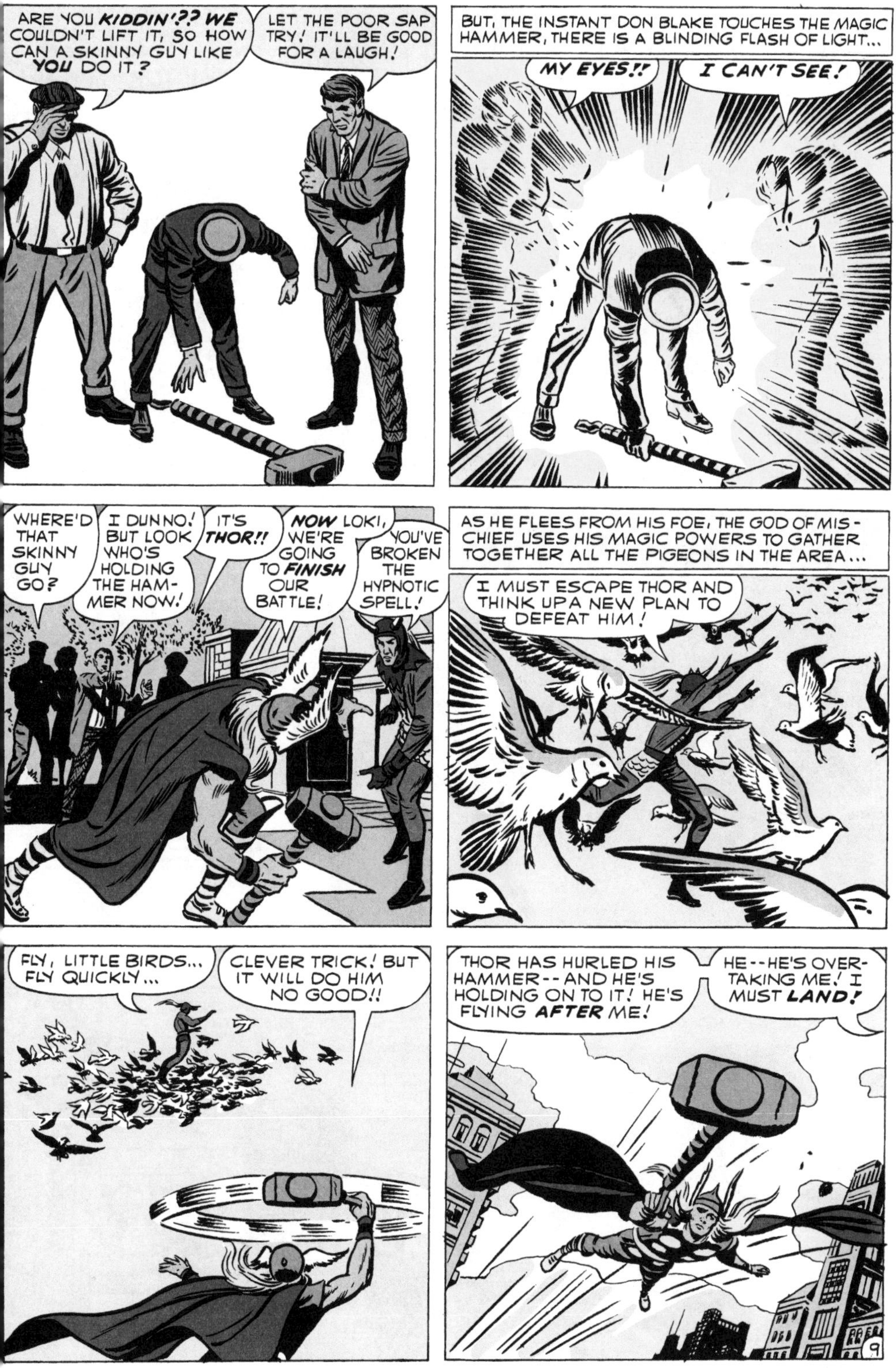
ARE YOU KIDDIN'?? WE COULDN'T LIFT IT, SO HOW CAN A SKINNY GUY LIKE YOU DO IT?
LET THE POOR SAP TRY! IT'LL BE GOOD FOR A LAUGH!
BUT, THE INSTANT DON BLAKE TOUCHES THE MAGIC HAMMER, THERE IS A BLINDING FLASH OF LIGHT...
MY EYES!!
I CAN'T SEE!
WHERE'D THAT SKINNY GUY GO?
I DUNNO! BUT LOOK WHO'S HOLDING THE HAMMER NOW!
IT'S THOR!!
NOW LOKI, WE'RE GOING TO FINISH OUR BATTLE!
YOU'VE BROKEN THE HYPNOTIC SPELL!
AS HE FLEES FROM HIS FOE, THE GOD OF MISCHIEF USES HIS MAGIC POWERS TO GATHER TOGETHER ALL THE PIGEONS IN THE AREA...
I MUST ESCAPE THOR AND THINK UP A NEW PLAN TO DEFEAT HIM!
FLY, LITTLE BIRDS... FLY QUICKLY...
CLEVER TRICK! BUT IT WILL DO HIM NO GOOD!!
THOR HAS HURLED HIS HAMMER -- AND HE'S HOLDING ON TO IT! HE'S FLYING AFTER ME!
HE -- HE'S OVERTAKING ME! I MUST LAND!
9

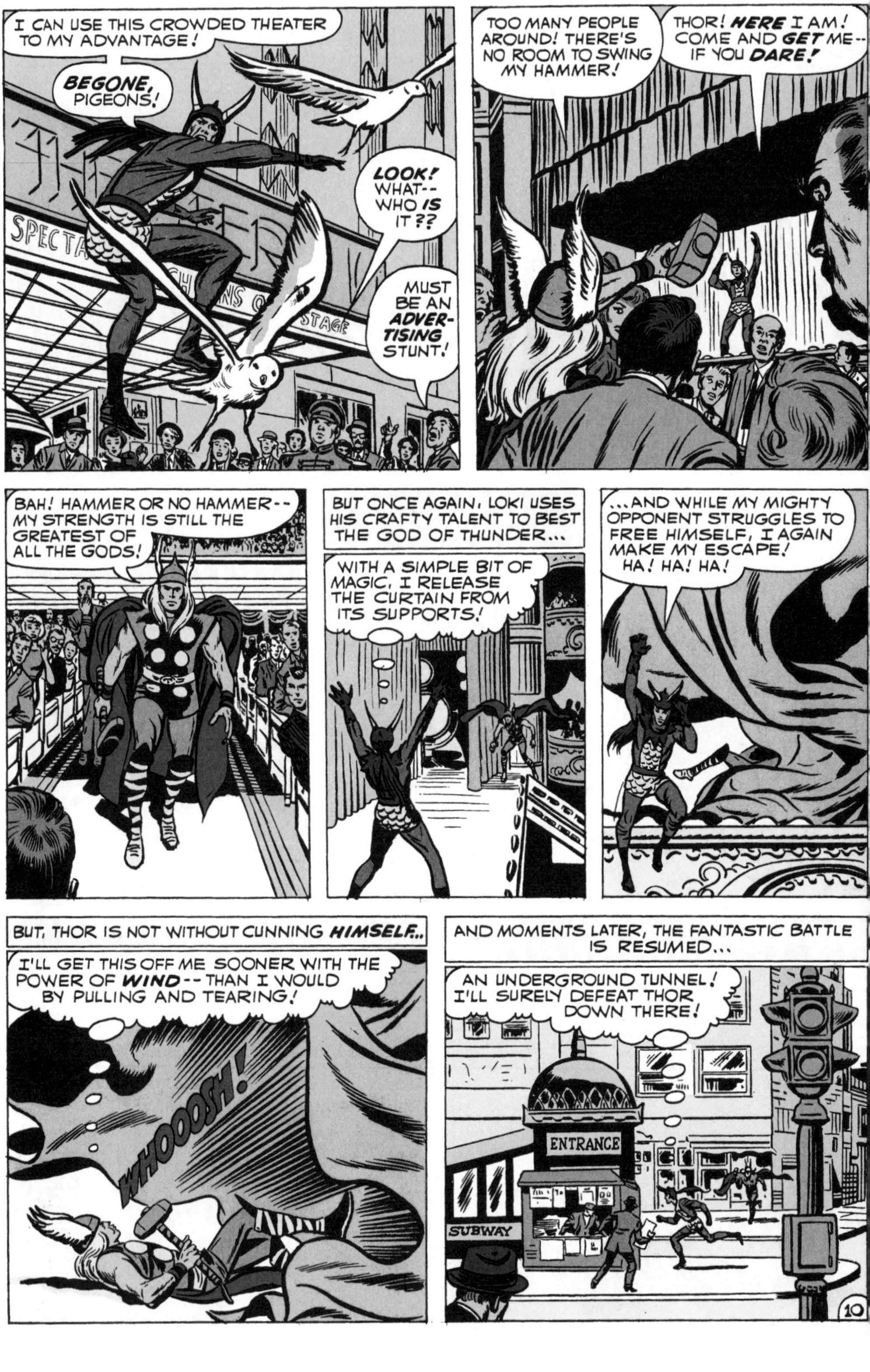
I CAN USE THIS CROWDED THEATER TO MY ADVANTAGE!
BEGONE, PIGEONS!
SPECTA
STAGE
LOOK! WHAT-- WHO IS IT??
MUST BE AN ADVERTISING STUNT!
TOO MANY PEOPLE AROUND! THERE'S NO ROOM TO SWING MY HAMMER!
THOR! HERE I AM! COME AND GET ME-- IF YOU DARE!
BAH! HAMMER OR NO HAMMER-- MY STRENGTH IS STILL THE GREATEST OF ALL THE GODS!
BUT ONCE AGAIN, LOKI USES HIS CRAFTY TALENT TO BEST THE GOD OF THUNDER...
WITH A SIMPLE BIT OF MAGIC, I RELEASE THE CURTAIN FROM ITS SUPPORTS!
...AND WHILE MY MIGHTY OPPONENT STRUGGLES TO FREE HIMSELF, I AGAIN MAKE MY ESCAPE! HA! HA! HA!
BUT, THOR IS NOT WITHOUT CUNNING HIMSELF...
I'LL GET THIS OFF ME SOONER WITH THE POWER OF WIND-- THAN I WOULD BY PULLING AND TEARING!
WHOOOSH!
AND MOMENTS LATER, THE FANTASTIC BATTLE IS RESUMED...
AN UNDERGROUND TUNNEL! I'LL SURELY DEFEAT THOR DOWN THERE!
ENTRANCE
SUBWAY
10

HE'S PUSHING THOSE PEOPLE OFF THE PLATFORM -- AND A *TRAIN'S COMING!*

AWAY, PUNY MORTALS!

HAH! I *KNEW* THE SOFT-HEARTED THOR WOULD STOP TO HELP THE USELESS HUMANS!

NO TIME TO LOSE! THE TRAIN WILL PASS WITHIN SECONDS!

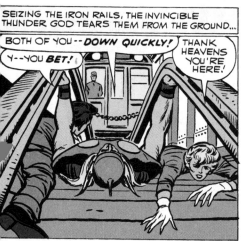

SEIZING THE IRON RAILS, THE INVINCIBLE THUNDER GOD TEARS THEM FROM THE GROUND...

BOTH OF YOU -- *DOWN QUICKLY!*

Y--YOU *BET!*

THANK HEAVENS YOU'RE HERE!

IF I DIDN'T SEE IT WITH MY OWN EYES --

I *DO* SEE IT AND I *STILL* DON'T BELIEVE IT!

NOBODY CAN DO THAT!

NOBODY EXCEPT-- *THOR!!*

WE'RE *SAVED!!*

NOW TO FIND LOKI, BEFORE HE DOES ANY *MORE* HARM!

UP *THERE!* HE'S BROUGHT THE WINGED HORSE OF A GASOLINE SIGN TO LIFE! NOW HE CAN *FLY* AGAIN!

AND IN THIS TIMES SQUARE CROWD, I CAN'T SWING MY HAMMER! I CAN'T FLY AFTER HIM!

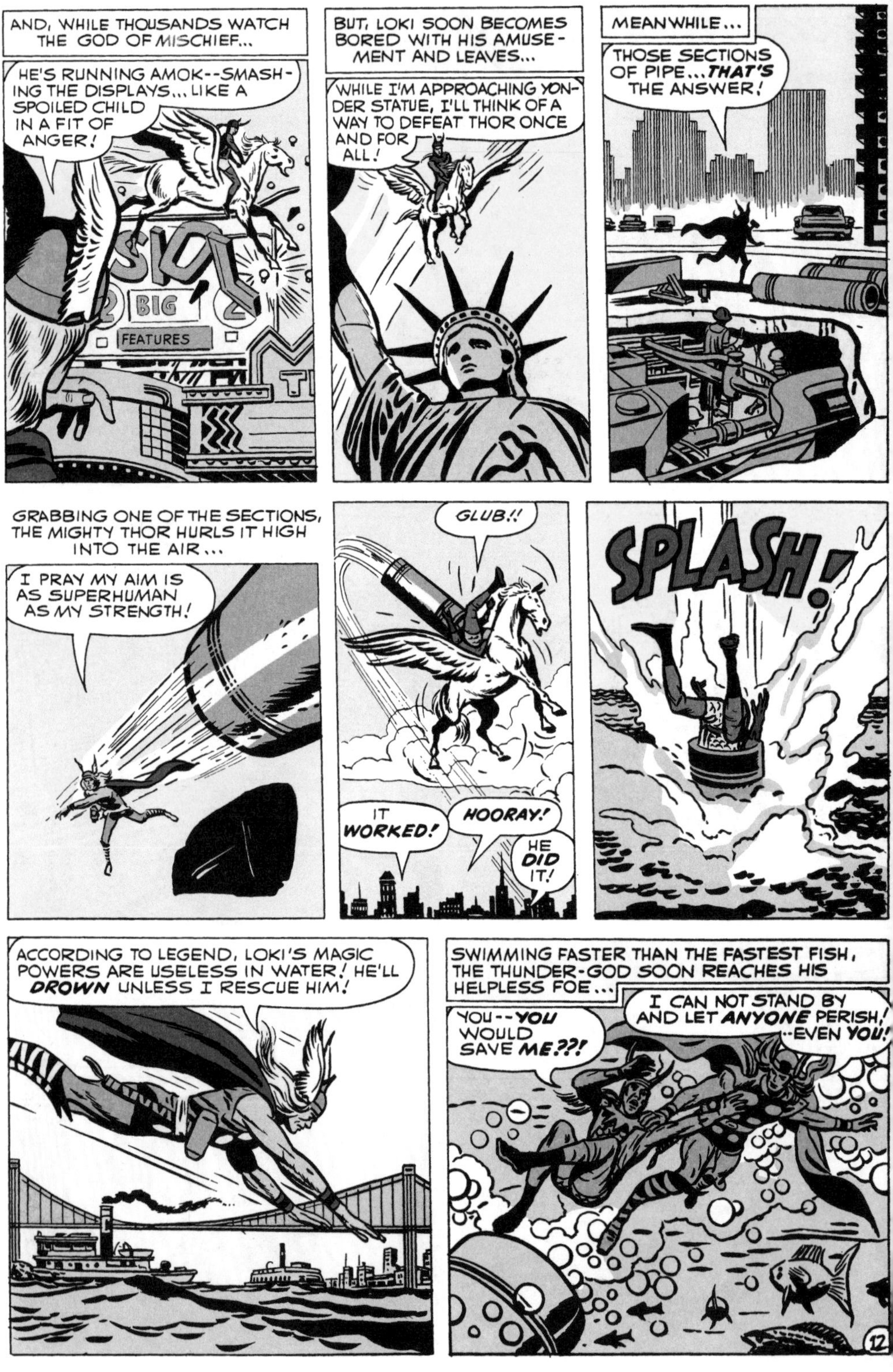
AND, WHILE THOUSANDS WATCH THE GOD OF MISCHIEF...
HE'S RUNNING AMOK--SMASHING THE DISPLAYS... LIKE A SPOILED CHILD IN A FIT OF ANGER!
2 BIG 2
FEATURES
BUT, LOKI SOON BECOMES BORED WITH HIS AMUSEMENT AND LEAVES...
WHILE I'M APPROACHING YONDER STATUE, I'LL THINK OF A WAY TO DEFEAT THOR ONCE AND FOR ALL!
MEANWHILE...
THOSE SECTIONS OF PIPE...THAT'S THE ANSWER!
GRABBING ONE OF THE SECTIONS, THE MIGHTY THOR HURLS IT HIGH INTO THE AIR...
I PRAY MY AIM IS AS SUPERHUMAN AS MY STRENGTH!
GLUB!!
IT WORKED!
HOORAY!
HE DID IT!
SPLASH!
ACCORDING TO LEGEND, LOKI'S MAGIC POWERS ARE USELESS IN WATER! HE'LL DROWN UNLESS I RESCUE HIM!
SWIMMING FASTER THAN THE FASTEST FISH, THE THUNDER-GOD SOON REACHES HIS HELPLESS FOE...
YOU--YOU WOULD SAVE ME??!
I CAN NOT STAND BY AND LET ANYONE PERISH! ..EVEN YOU!
12

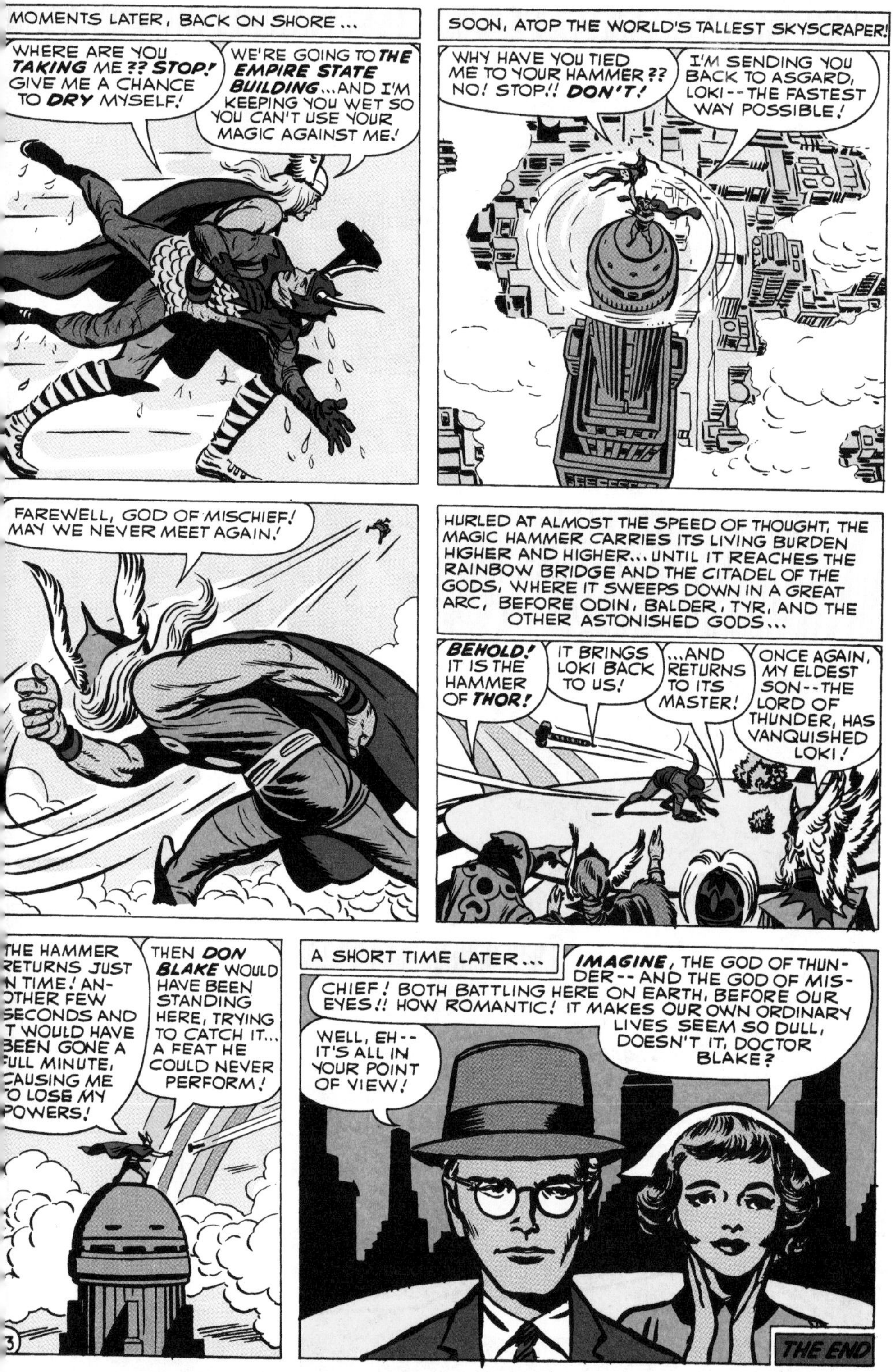
MOMENTS LATER, BACK ON SHORE...
WHERE ARE YOU TAKING ME?? STOP! GIVE ME A CHANCE TO DRY MYSELF!
WE'RE GOING TO THE EMPIRE STATE BUILDING...AND I'M KEEPING YOU WET SO YOU CAN'T USE YOUR MAGIC AGAINST ME!
SOON, ATOP THE WORLD'S TALLEST SKYSCRAPER!
WHY HAVE YOU TIED ME TO YOUR HAMMER?? NO! STOP!! DON'T!
I'M SENDING YOU BACK TO ASGARD, LOKI--THE FASTEST WAY POSSIBLE!
FAREWELL, GOD OF MISCHIEF! MAY WE NEVER MEET AGAIN!
HURLED AT ALMOST THE SPEED OF THOUGHT, THE MAGIC HAMMER CARRIES ITS LIVING BURDEN HIGHER AND HIGHER... UNTIL IT REACHES THE RAINBOW BRIDGE AND THE CITADEL OF THE GODS, WHERE IT SWEEPS DOWN IN A GREAT ARC, BEFORE ODIN, BALDER, TYR, AND THE OTHER ASTONISHED GODS...
BEHOLD! IT IS THE HAMMER OF THOR!
IT BRINGS LOKI BACK TO US!
...AND RETURNS TO ITS MASTER!
ONCE AGAIN, MY ELDEST SON--THE LORD OF THUNDER, HAS VANQUISHED LOKI!
THE HAMMER RETURNS JUST IN TIME! ANOTHER FEW SECONDS AND IT WOULD HAVE BEEN GONE A FULL MINUTE, CAUSING ME TO LOSE MY POWERS!
THEN DON BLAKE WOULD HAVE BEEN STANDING HERE, TRYING TO CATCH IT... A FEAT HE COULD NEVER PERFORM!
A SHORT TIME LATER...
IMAGINE, THE GOD OF THUNDER--AND THE GOD OF MISCHIEF! BOTH BATTLING HERE ON EARTH, BEFORE OUR EYES!! HOW ROMANTIC! IT MAKES OUR OWN ORDINARY LIVES SEEM SO DULL, DOESN'T IT, DOCTOR BLAKE?
WELL, EH--IT'S ALL IN YOUR POINT OF VIEW!
THE END

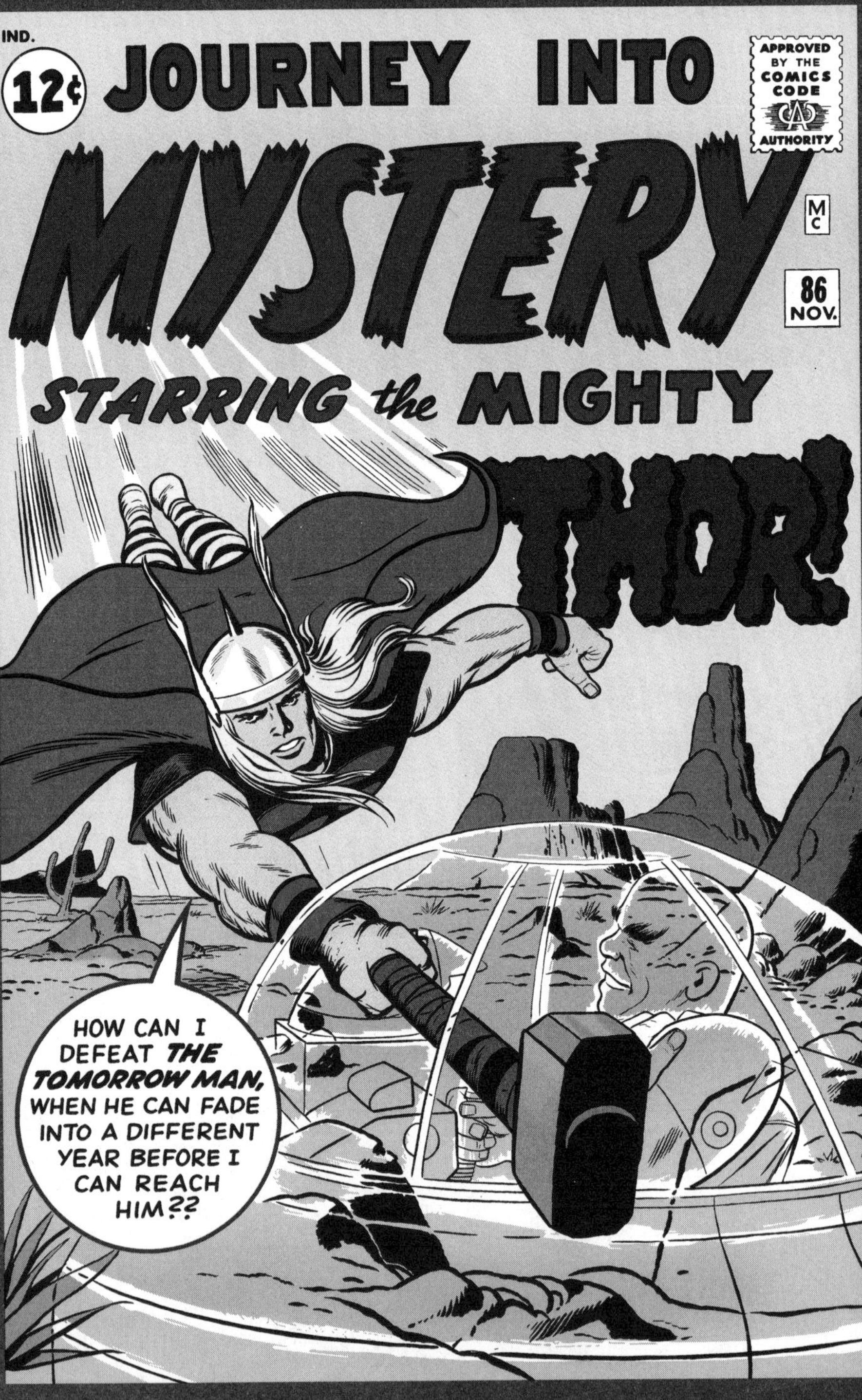
IND.
12¢
JOURNEY INTO
MYSTERY
APPROVED BY THE COMICS CODE AUTHORITY
MC
86
NOV.
STARRING the MIGHTY
THOR!
HOW CAN I DEFEAT THE TOMORROW MAN, WHEN HE CAN FADE INTO A DIFFERENT YEAR BEFORE I CAN REACH HIM??

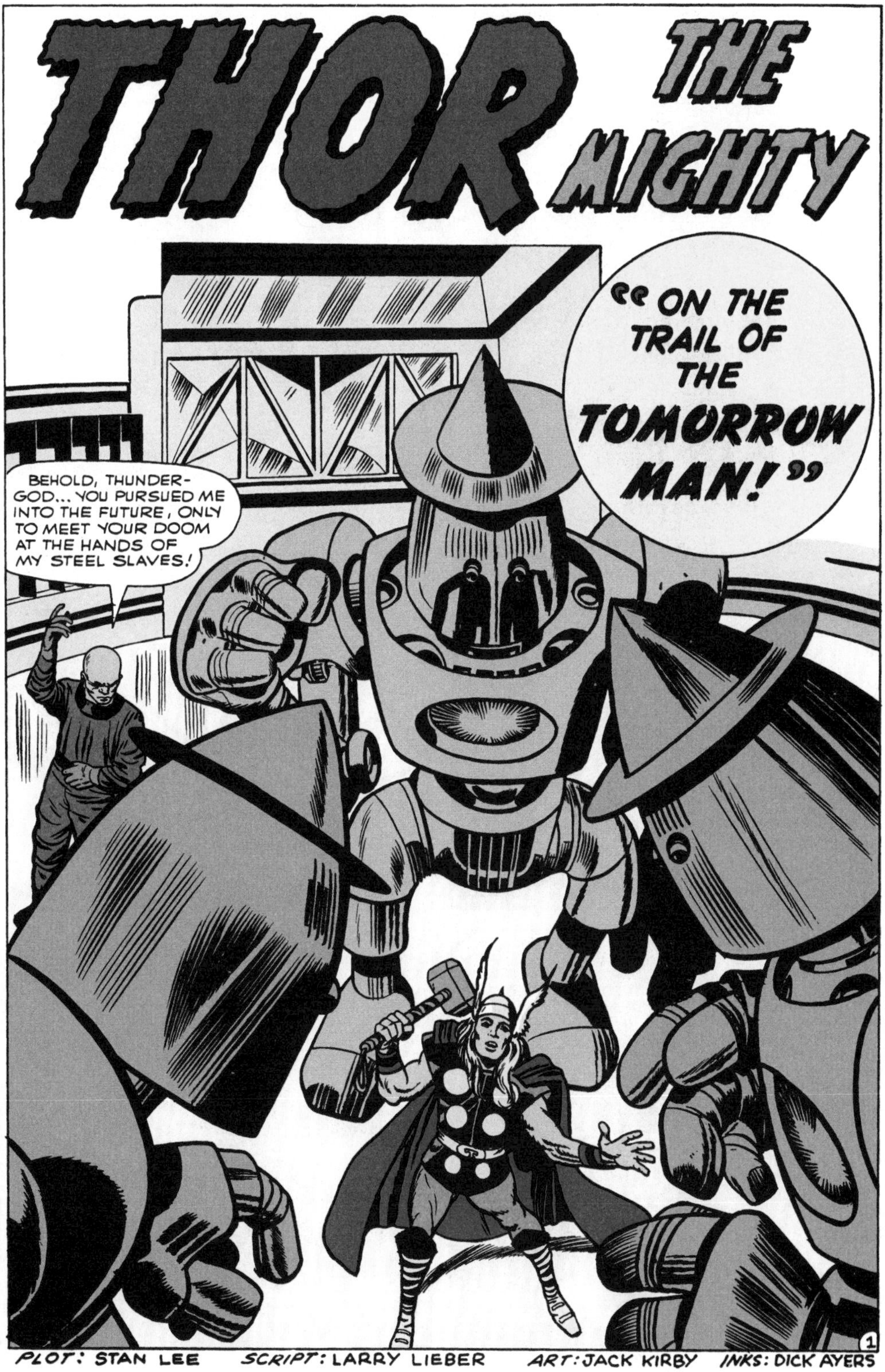
THOR THE MIGHTY
"ON THE TRAIL OF THE TOMORROW MAN!"
BEHOLD, THUNDER-GOD... YOU PURSUED ME INTO THE FUTURE, ONLY TO MEET YOUR DOOM AT THE HANDS OF MY STEEL SLAVES!
1
PLOT: STAN LEE SCRIPT: LARRY LIEBER ART: JACK KIRBY INKS: DICK AYERS

NO, WHAT YOU ARE LOOKING AT IS **NOT** ANOTHER WORLD! IT IS OUR VERY OWN EARTH, **THREE CENTURIES** FROM NOW! MANKIND HAS ABOLISHED WAR AND SCRAPPED ITS WEAPONS! PEACE AND CONTENTMENT PREVAIL THROUGHOUT THE GLOBE...

BUT THERE IS ONE WHO IS **NOT** PEACE-LOVING! HE IS A SCIENTIST NAMED ZARRKO... AND WITHIN HIS HEART LURKS AN EVIL AMBITION...

MY FELLOW MEN ARE WEAK, TENDER-HEARTED FOOLS! IT WILL BE EASY TO CONQUER THEM!

OTHER SCIENTISTS DEVOTE THEMSELVES TO HELPING CIVILIZATION... BUT **I** HAVE INVENTED A WAY OF **LEAVING** OUR CIVILIZATION! I HAVE CONSTRUCTED EARTH'S ONLY **TIME MACHINE!**

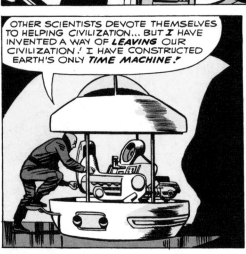

FIRST, I MUST VIEW THE PAST, THROUGH MY **TIME-SCOPE!** I MUST DISCOVER AN AGE WHEN MANKIND POSSESSED **MIGHTY WEAPONS!**

AHHH--AN ANCIENT EXPLOSION OF A NUCLEAR BOMB! THE PERFECT DEVICE WITH WHICH TO CONQUER THE TWENTY-THIRD CENTURY!

THOSE BOMBS EXISTED ON EARTH DURING THE TWENTIETH CENTURY! I SHALL GO BACK THERE AT ONCE!

MEANWHILE, TRAVELLING AT THE STILL FASTER SPEED OF OUR IMAGINATION, LET US RETURN TO 1962! THE SCENE IS A REMOTE DESERT AREA...

WE APPRECIATE YOUR HELPING US TEST OUR NEWEST EXPERIMENTAL WEAPONS, THOR!

I'M HAPPY TO PLAY A PART IN KEEPING THE FREE WORLD STRONG AND SECURE AGAINST THE FORCES OF TYRANNY!

2

SUDDENLY, WITH A TREMENDOUS ROAR...

THE MISSILE'S BEEN FIRED.!

GET READY, THOR...

THERE GOES THE ANTI-MISSILE MISSILE!

AND THERE GOES *THOR!!*

WITH FANTASTIC SPEED, MAN AND MISSILE SOAR HIGHER AND HIGHER IN PURSUIT OF THE ROCKET...

BUT IT IS THE THUNDER-GOD WHO REACHES THE TARGET FIRST...

THE MISSILES ARE GETTING FASTER! I ALMOST LOST THIS ROCKET!

THOR WAS FASTER THAN THE ANTI-MISSILE MISSILE!

YES, BUT THIS TIME HE BEAT IT ONLY BY AN INSTANT!

USING HIM AS A MEASURING DEVICE, WE'RE ABLE TO CONSTANTLY IMPROVE OUR WEAPONS.'

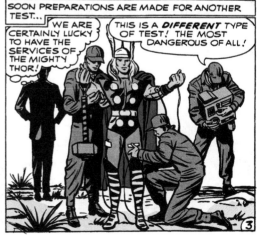

SOON PREPARATIONS ARE MADE FOR ANOTHER TEST...

WE ARE CERTAINLY LUCKY TO HAVE THE SERVICES OF THE MIGHTY THOR!

THIS IS A *DIFFERENT* TYPE OF TEST! THE MOST DANGEROUS OF ALL!

3

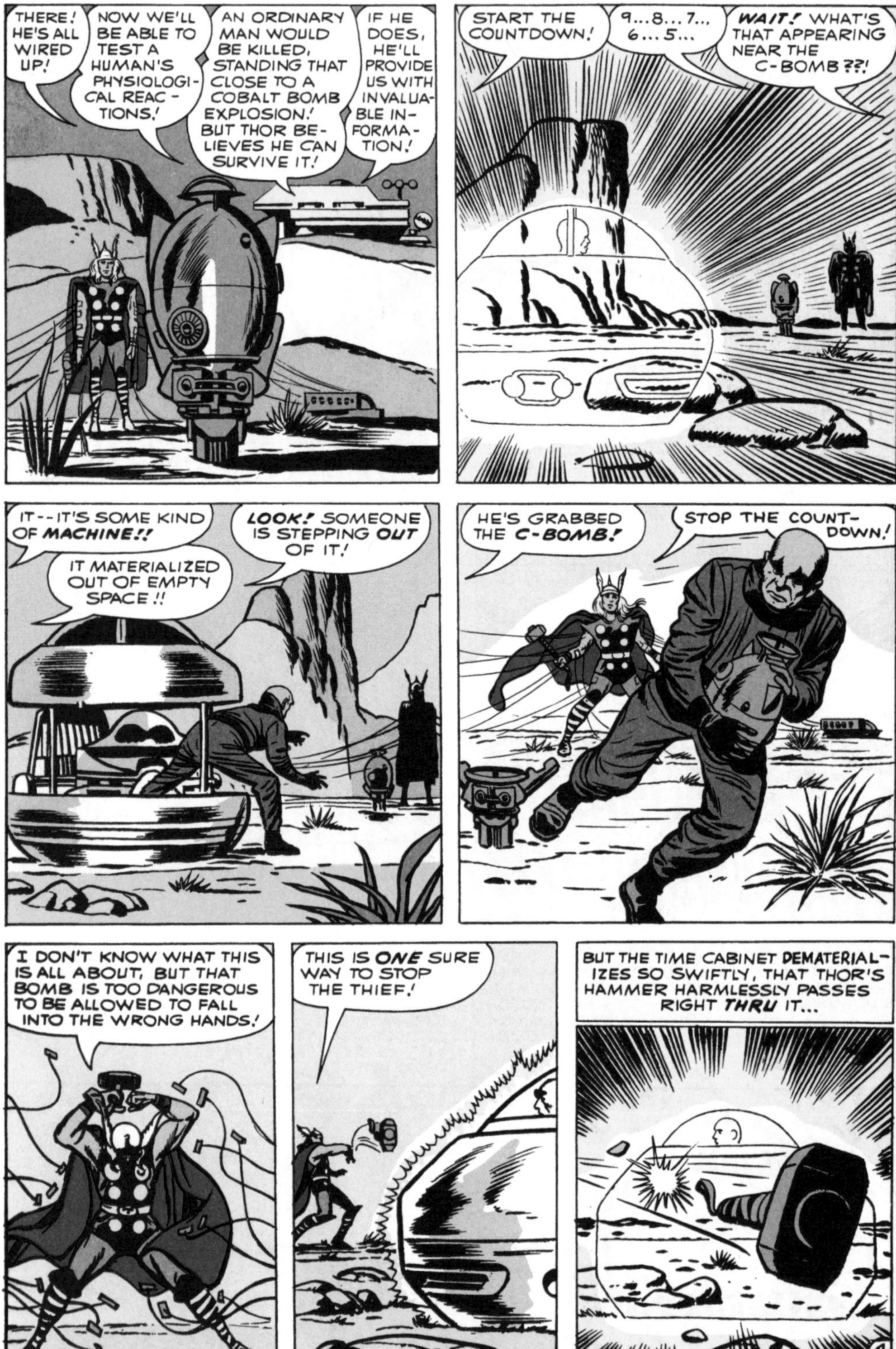

THERE! HE'S ALL WIRED UP!
NOW WE'LL BE ABLE TO TEST A HUMAN'S PHYSIOLOGICAL REACTIONS!
AN ORDINARY MAN WOULD BE KILLED, STANDING THAT CLOSE TO A COBALT BOMB EXPLOSION! BUT THOR BELIEVES HE CAN SURVIVE IT!
IF HE DOES, HE'LL PROVIDE US WITH INVALUABLE INFORMATION!
START THE COUNTDOWN!
9...8...7... 6...5...
WAIT! WHAT'S THAT APPEARING NEAR THE C-BOMB??!
IT--IT'S SOME KIND OF MACHINE!!
IT MATERIALIZED OUT OF EMPTY SPACE!!
LOOK! SOMEONE IS STEPPING OUT OF IT!
HE'S GRABBED THE C-BOMB!
STOP THE COUNT-DOWN!
I DON'T KNOW WHAT THIS IS ALL ABOUT, BUT THAT BOMB IS TOO DANGEROUS TO BE ALLOWED TO FALL INTO THE WRONG HANDS!
THIS IS ONE SURE WAY TO STOP THE THIEF!
BUT THE TIME CABINET DEMATERIALIZES SO SWIFTLY, THAT THOR'S HAMMER HARMLESSLY PASSES RIGHT THRU IT...
4

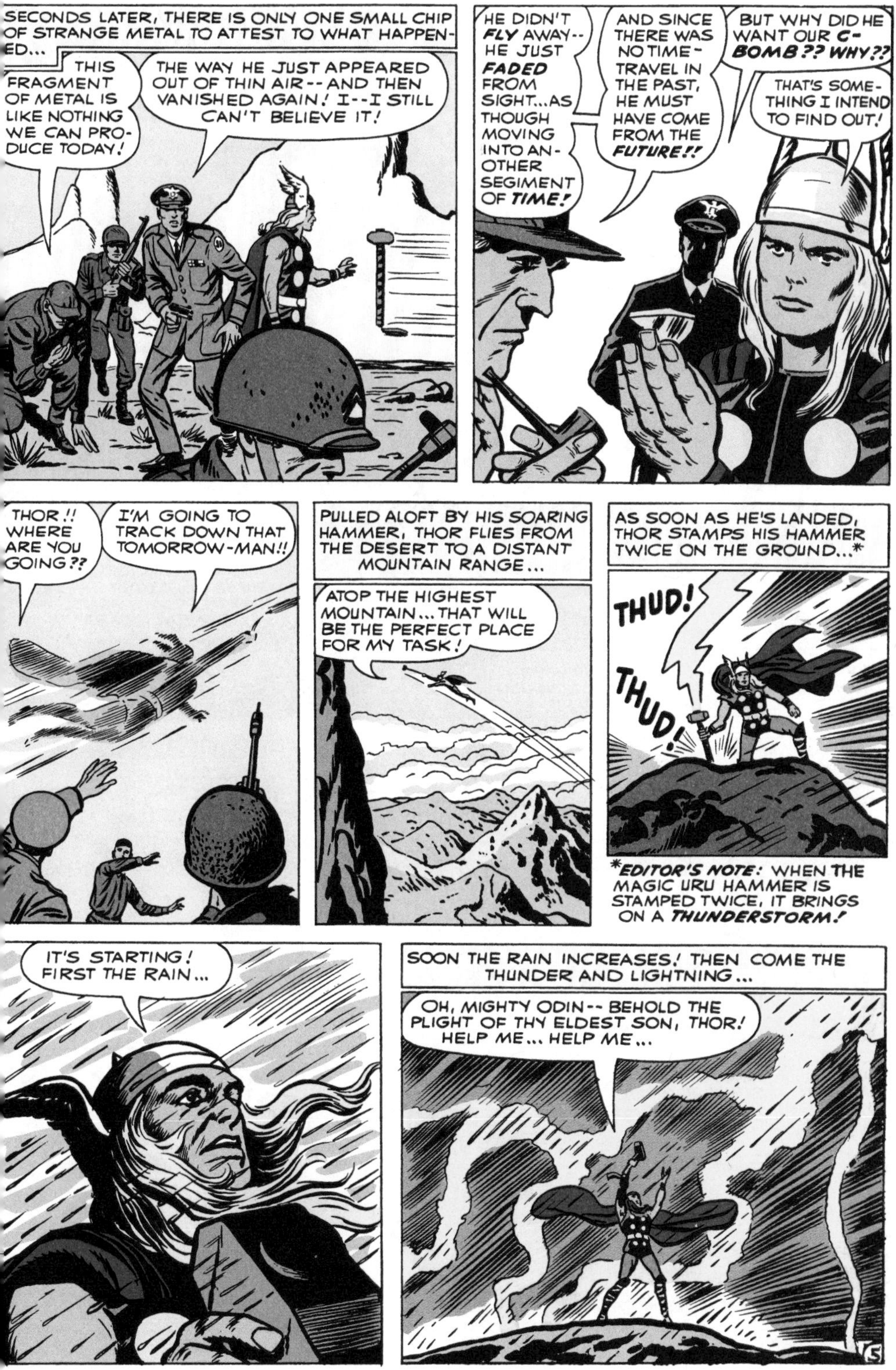

SECONDS LATER, THERE IS ONLY ONE SMALL CHIP OF STRANGE METAL TO ATTEST TO WHAT HAPPENED...
THIS FRAGMENT OF METAL IS LIKE NOTHING WE CAN PRODUCE TODAY!
THE WAY HE JUST APPEARED OUT OF THIN AIR--AND THEN VANISHED AGAIN! I--I STILL CAN'T BELIEVE IT!
HE DIDN'T FLY AWAY--HE JUST FADED FROM SIGHT...AS THOUGH MOVING INTO ANOTHER SEGIMENT OF TIME!
AND SINCE THERE WAS NO TIME-TRAVEL IN THE PAST, HE MUST HAVE COME FROM THE FUTURE!!
BUT WHY DID HE WANT OUR C-BOMB?? WHY??
THAT'S SOMETHING I INTEND TO FIND OUT!
THOR!! WHERE ARE YOU GOING??
I'M GOING TO TRACK DOWN THAT TOMORROW-MAN!!
PULLED ALOFT BY HIS SOARING HAMMER, THOR FLIES FROM THE DESERT TO A DISTANT MOUNTAIN RANGE...
ATOP THE HIGHEST MOUNTAIN...THAT WILL BE THE PERFECT PLACE FOR MY TASK!
AS SOON AS HE'S LANDED, THOR STAMPS HIS HAMMER TWICE ON THE GROUND...*
THUD!
THUD!
*EDITOR'S NOTE: WHEN THE MAGIC URU HAMMER IS STAMPED TWICE, IT BRINGS ON A THUNDERSTORM!
IT'S STARTING! FIRST THE RAIN...
SOON THE RAIN INCREASES! THEN COME THE THUNDER AND LIGHTNING...
OH, MIGHTY ODIN--BEHOLD THE PLIGHT OF THY ELDEST SON, THOR! HELP ME... HELP ME...

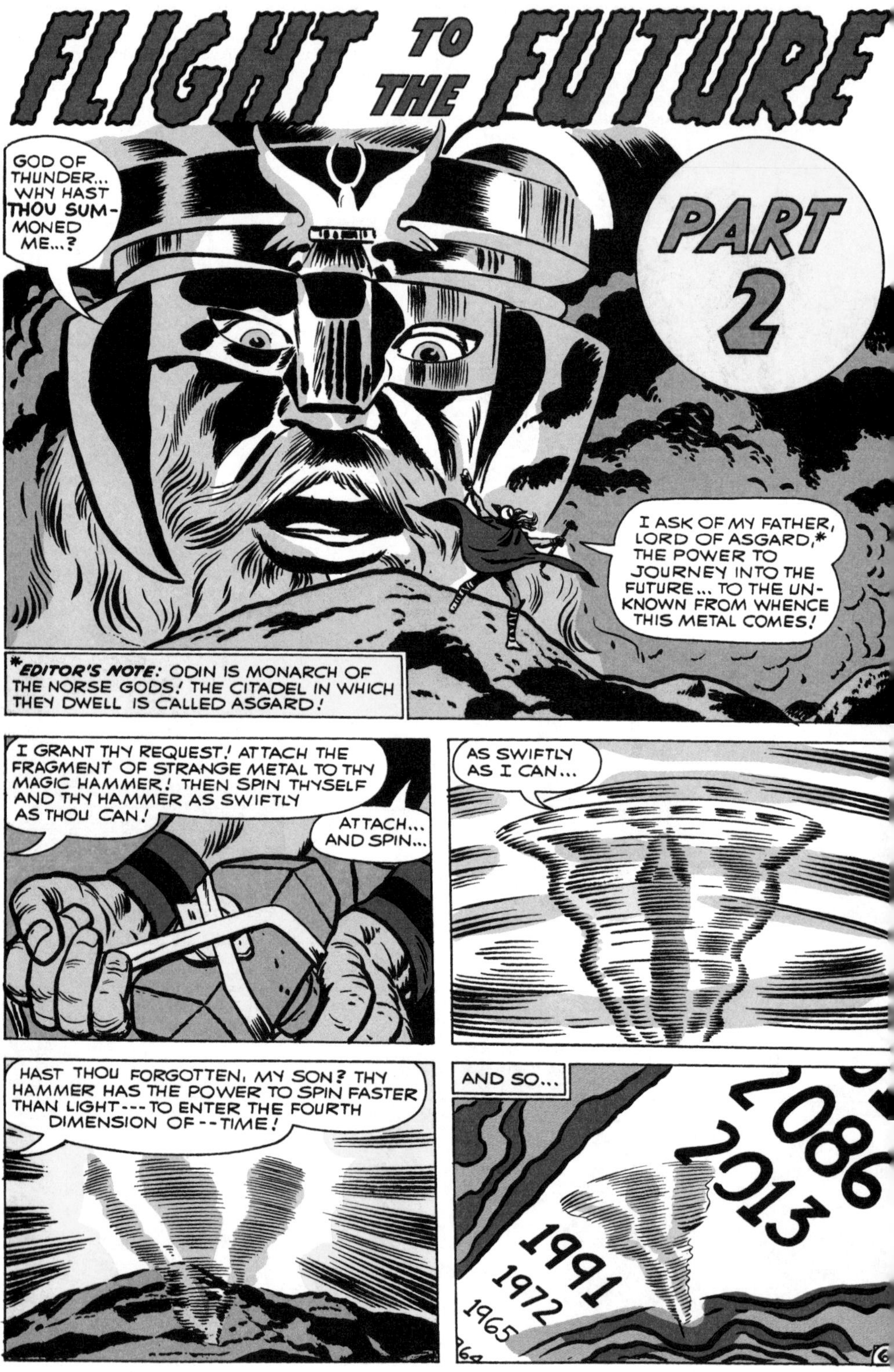
FLIGHT TO THE FUTURE
GOD OF THUNDER... WHY HAST THOU SUMMONED ME...?
PART 2
I ASK OF MY FATHER, LORD OF ASGARD,* THE POWER TO JOURNEY INTO THE FUTURE... TO THE UNKNOWN FROM WHENCE THIS METAL COMES!
*EDITOR'S NOTE: ODIN IS MONARCH OF THE NORSE GODS! THE CITADEL IN WHICH THEY DWELL IS CALLED ASGARD!
I GRANT THY REQUEST! ATTACH THE FRAGMENT OF STRANGE METAL TO THY MAGIC HAMMER! THEN SPIN THYSELF AND THY HAMMER AS SWIFTLY AS THOU CAN!
ATTACH... AND SPIN...
AS SWIFTLY AS I CAN...
HAST THOU FORGOTTEN, MY SON? THY HAMMER HAS THE POWER TO SPIN FASTER THAN LIGHT---TO ENTER THE FOURTH DIMENSION OF--TIME!
AND SO...
2086
2013
1991
1972
1965

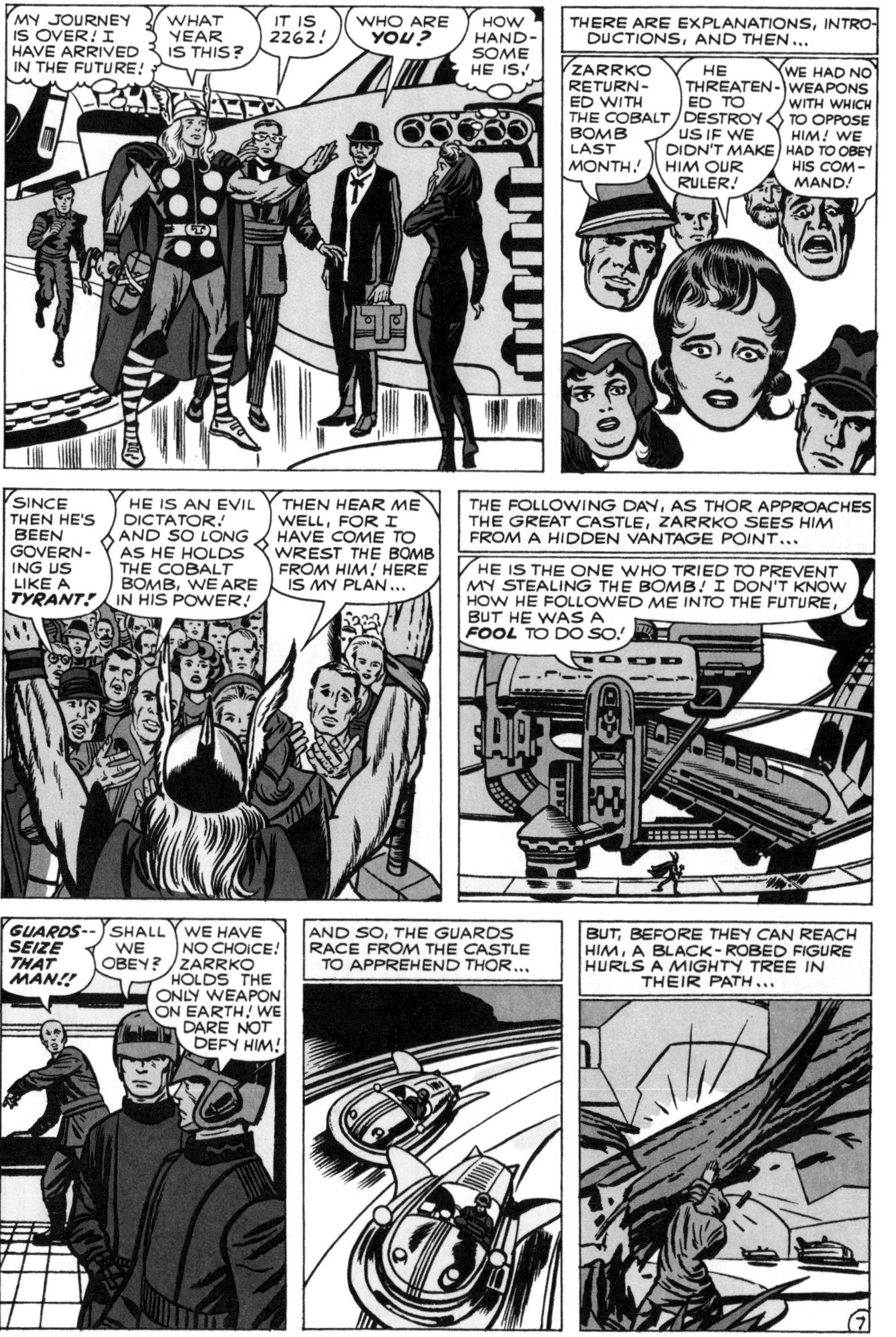
MY JOURNEY IS OVER! I HAVE ARRIVED IN THE FUTURE!
WHAT YEAR IS THIS?
IT IS 2262!
WHO ARE YOU?
HOW HANDSOME HE IS!
THERE ARE EXPLANATIONS, INTRODUCTIONS, AND THEN...
ZARRKO RETURNED WITH THE COBALT BOMB LAST MONTH!
HE THREATENED TO DESTROY US IF WE DIDN'T MAKE HIM OUR RULER!
WE HAD NO WEAPONS WITH WHICH TO OPPOSE HIM! WE HAD TO OBEY HIS COMMAND!
SINCE THEN HE'S BEEN GOVERNING US LIKE A TYRANT!
HE IS AN EVIL DICTATOR! AND SO LONG AS HE HOLDS THE COBALT BOMB, WE ARE IN HIS POWER!
THEN HEAR ME WELL, FOR I HAVE COME TO WREST THE BOMB FROM HIM! HERE IS MY PLAN...
THE FOLLOWING DAY, AS THOR APPROACHES THE GREAT CASTLE, ZARRKO SEES HIM FROM A HIDDEN VANTAGE POINT...
HE IS THE ONE WHO TRIED TO PREVENT MY STEALING THE BOMB! I DON'T KNOW HOW HE FOLLOWED ME INTO THE FUTURE, BUT HE WAS A FOOL TO DO SO!
GUARDS--SEIZE THAT MAN!!
SHALL WE OBEY?
WE HAVE NO CHOICE! ZARRKO HOLDS THE ONLY WEAPON ON EARTH! WE DARE NOT DEFY HIM!
AND SO, THE GUARDS RACE FROM THE CASTLE TO APPREHEND THOR...
BUT, BEFORE THEY CAN REACH HIM, A BLACK-ROBED FIGURE HURLS A MIGHTY TREE IN THEIR PATH...
7

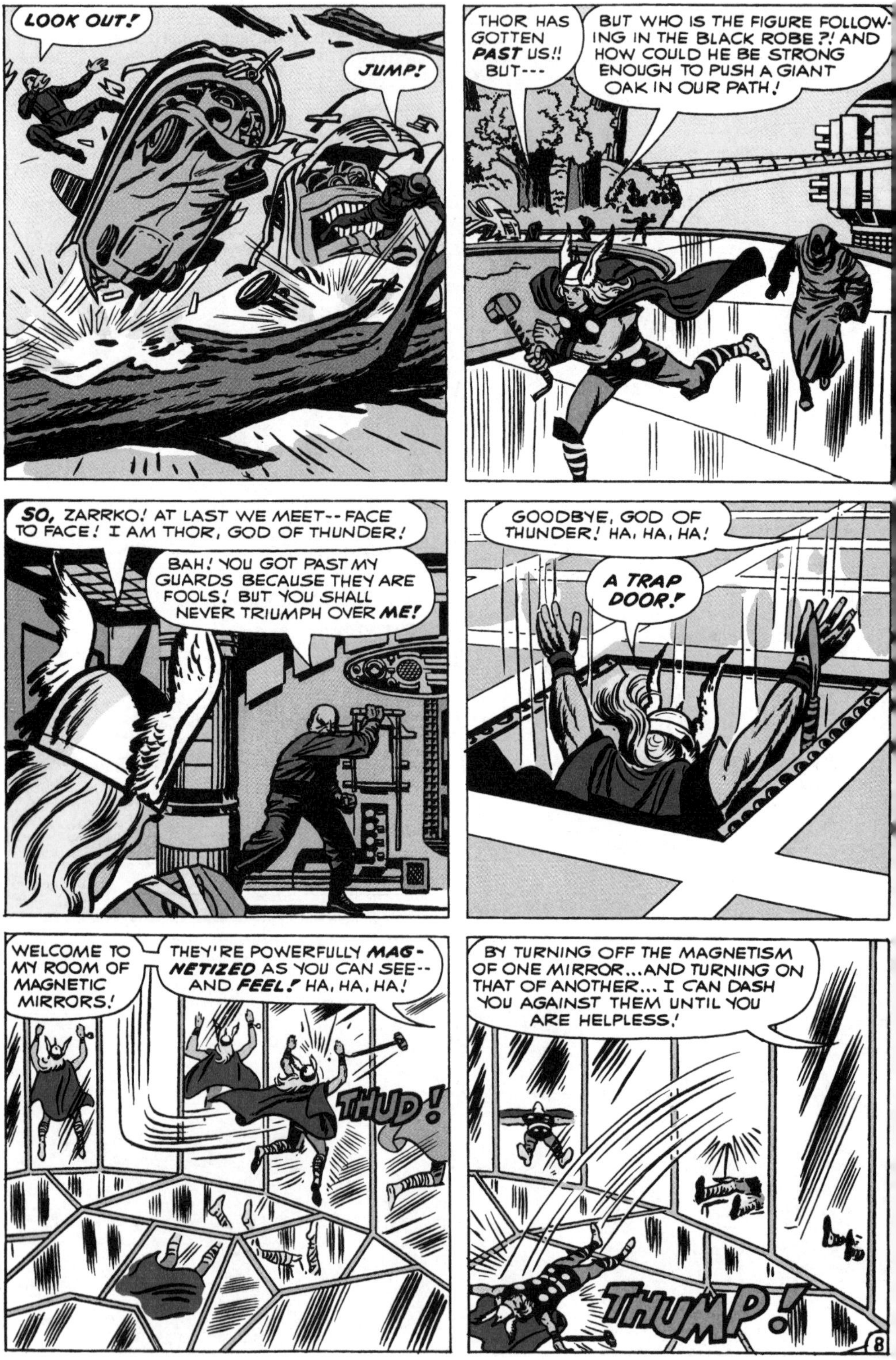
LOOK OUT!
JUMP!
THOR HAS GOTTEN PAST US!! BUT---
BUT WHO IS THE FIGURE FOLLOWING IN THE BLACK ROBE?! AND HOW COULD HE BE STRONG ENOUGH TO PUSH A GIANT OAK IN OUR PATH!
SO, ZARRKO! AT LAST WE MEET-- FACE TO FACE! I AM THOR, GOD OF THUNDER!
BAH! YOU GOT PAST MY GUARDS BECAUSE THEY ARE FOOLS! BUT YOU SHALL NEVER TRIUMPH OVER ME!
GOODBYE, GOD OF THUNDER! HA, HA, HA!
A TRAP DOOR!
WELCOME TO MY ROOM OF MAGNETIC MIRRORS!
THEY'RE POWERFULLY MAGNETIZED AS YOU CAN SEE-- AND FEEL! HA, HA, HA!
THUD!
BY TURNING OFF THE MAGNETISM OF ONE MIRROR...AND TURNING ON THAT OF ANOTHER... I CAN DASH YOU AGAINST THEM UNTIL YOU ARE HELPLESS!
THUMP!
8

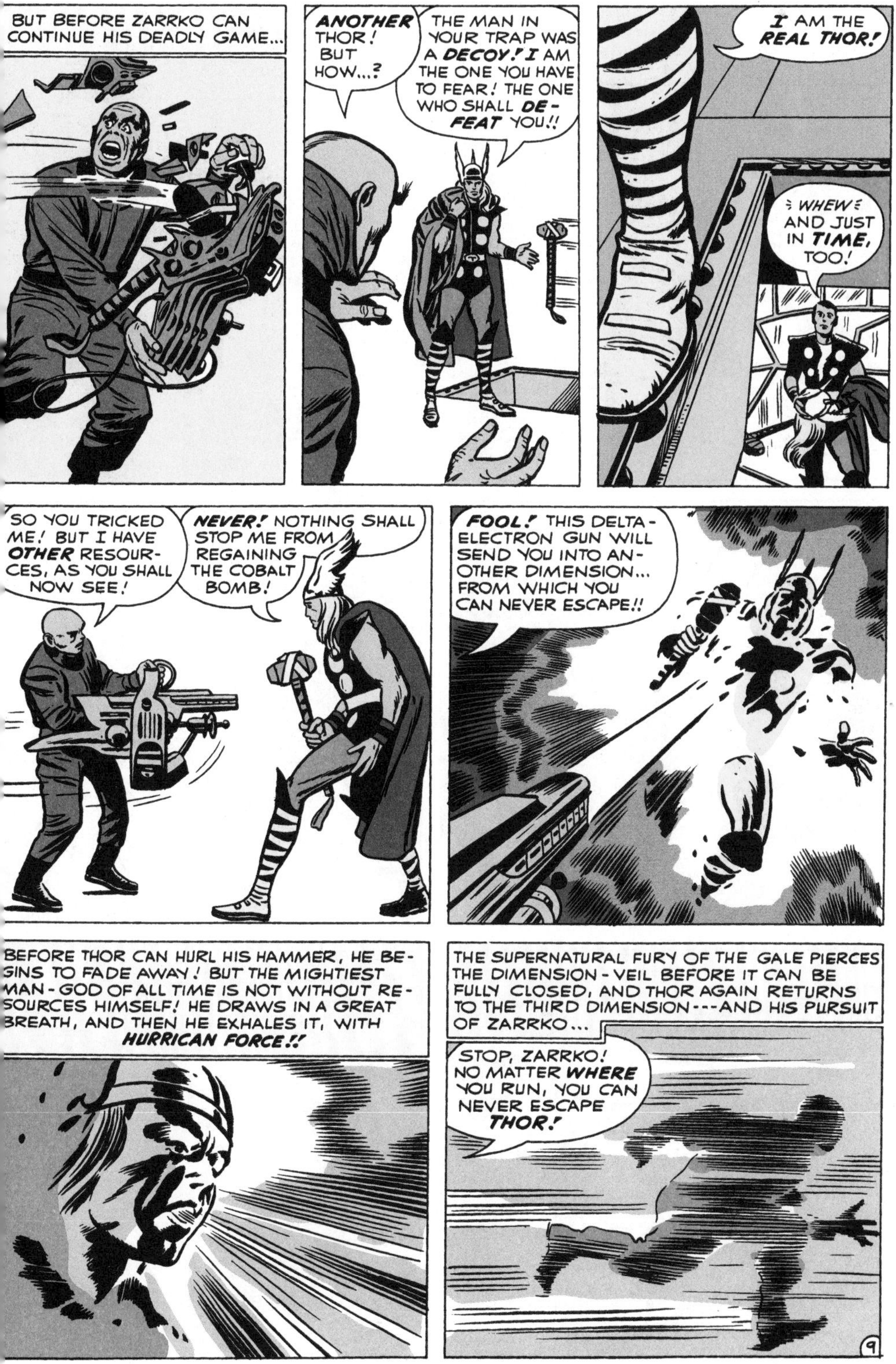
BUT BEFORE ZARRKO CAN CONTINUE HIS DEADLY GAME...
ANOTHER THOR! BUT HOW...?
THE MAN IN YOUR TRAP WAS A DECOY! I AM THE ONE YOU HAVE TO FEAR! THE ONE WHO SHALL DE-FEAT YOU!!
I AM THE REAL THOR!
WHEW AND JUST IN TIME, TOO!
SO YOU TRICKED ME! BUT I HAVE OTHER RESOURCES, AS YOU SHALL NOW SEE!
NEVER! NOTHING SHALL STOP ME FROM REGAINING THE COBALT BOMB!
FOOL! THIS DELTA-ELECTRON GUN WILL SEND YOU INTO ANOTHER DIMENSION... FROM WHICH YOU CAN NEVER ESCAPE!!
BEFORE THOR CAN HURL HIS HAMMER, HE BEGINS TO FADE AWAY! BUT THE MIGHTIEST MAN-GOD OF ALL TIME IS NOT WITHOUT RESOURCES HIMSELF! HE DRAWS IN A GREAT BREATH, AND THEN HE EXHALES IT, WITH HURRICAN FORCE!!
THE SUPERNATURAL FURY OF THE GALE PIERCES THE DIMENSION-VEIL BEFORE IT CAN BE FULLY CLOSED, AND THOR AGAIN RETURNS TO THE THIRD DIMENSION---AND HIS PURSUIT OF ZARRKO...
STOP, ZARRKO! NO MATTER WHERE YOU RUN, YOU CAN NEVER ESCAPE THOR!
9

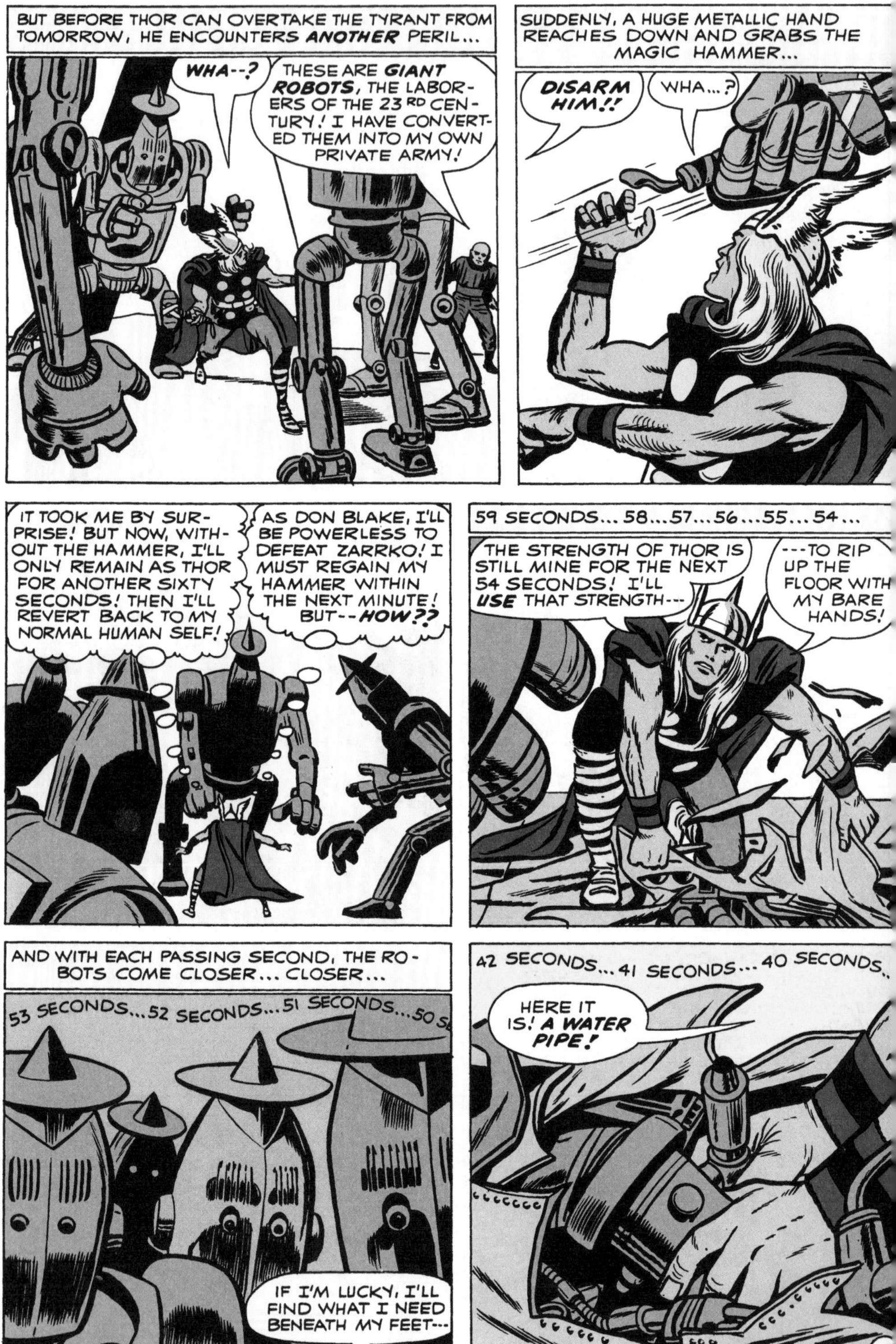
BUT BEFORE THOR CAN OVERTAKE THE TYRANT FROM TOMORROW, HE ENCOUNTERS ANOTHER PERIL...
WHA--?
THESE ARE GIANT ROBOTS, THE LABORERS OF THE 23RD CENTURY! I HAVE CONVERTED THEM INTO MY OWN PRIVATE ARMY!
SUDDENLY, A HUGE METALLIC HAND REACHES DOWN AND GRABS THE MAGIC HAMMER...
DISARM HIM!!
WHA...?
IT TOOK ME BY SURPRISE! BUT NOW, WITHOUT THE HAMMER, I'LL ONLY REMAIN AS THOR FOR ANOTHER SIXTY SECONDS! THEN I'LL REVERT BACK TO MY NORMAL HUMAN SELF!
AS DON BLAKE, I'LL BE POWERLESS TO DEFEAT ZARRKO! I MUST REGAIN MY HAMMER WITHIN THE NEXT MINUTE! BUT--HOW??
59 SECONDS... 58...57...56...55...54...
THE STRENGTH OF THOR IS STILL MINE FOR THE NEXT 54 SECONDS! I'LL USE THAT STRENGTH---
---TO RIP UP THE FLOOR WITH MY BARE HANDS!
AND WITH EACH PASSING SECOND, THE ROBOTS COME CLOSER... CLOSER...
53 SECONDS...52 SECONDS...51 SECONDS...50 S
IF I'M LUCKY, I'LL FIND WHAT I NEED BENEATH MY FEET---
42 SECONDS...41 SECONDS...40 SECONDS..
HERE IT IS! A WATER PIPE!
10

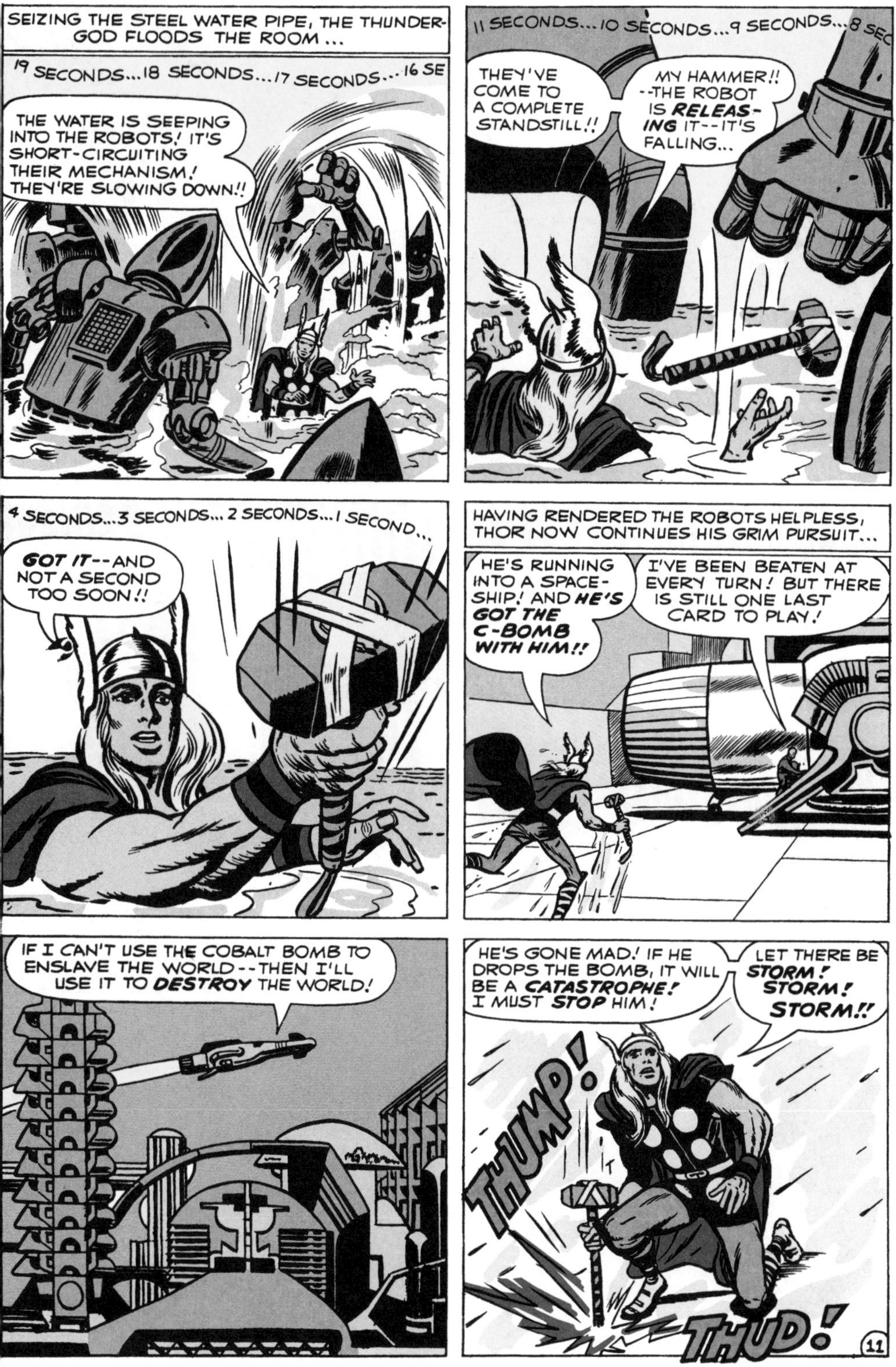
SEIZING THE STEEL WATER PIPE, THE THUNDER-GOD FLOODS THE ROOM ...
19 SECONDS...18 SECONDS...17 SECONDS...16 SE
THE WATER IS SEEPING INTO THE ROBOTS! IT'S SHORT-CIRCUITING THEIR MECHANISM! THEY'RE SLOWING DOWN!!
11 SECONDS...10 SECONDS...9 SECONDS...8 SEC
THEY'VE COME TO A COMPLETE STANDSTILL!!
MY HAMMER!! --THE ROBOT IS RELEASING IT--IT'S FALLING...
4 SECONDS...3 SECONDS...2 SECONDS...1 SECOND...
GOT IT--AND NOT A SECOND TOO SOON!!
HAVING RENDERED THE ROBOTS HELPLESS, THOR NOW CONTINUES HIS GRIM PURSUIT...
HE'S RUNNING INTO A SPACE-SHIP! AND HE'S GOT THE C-BOMB WITH HIM!!
I'VE BEEN BEATEN AT EVERY TURN! BUT THERE IS STILL ONE LAST CARD TO PLAY!
IF I CAN'T USE THE COBALT BOMB TO ENSLAVE THE WORLD--THEN I'LL USE IT TO DESTROY THE WORLD!
HE'S GONE MAD! IF HE DROPS THE BOMB, IT WILL BE A CATASTROPHE! I MUST STOP HIM!
LET THERE BE STORM! STORM! STORM!!
THUMP!
THUD!
11

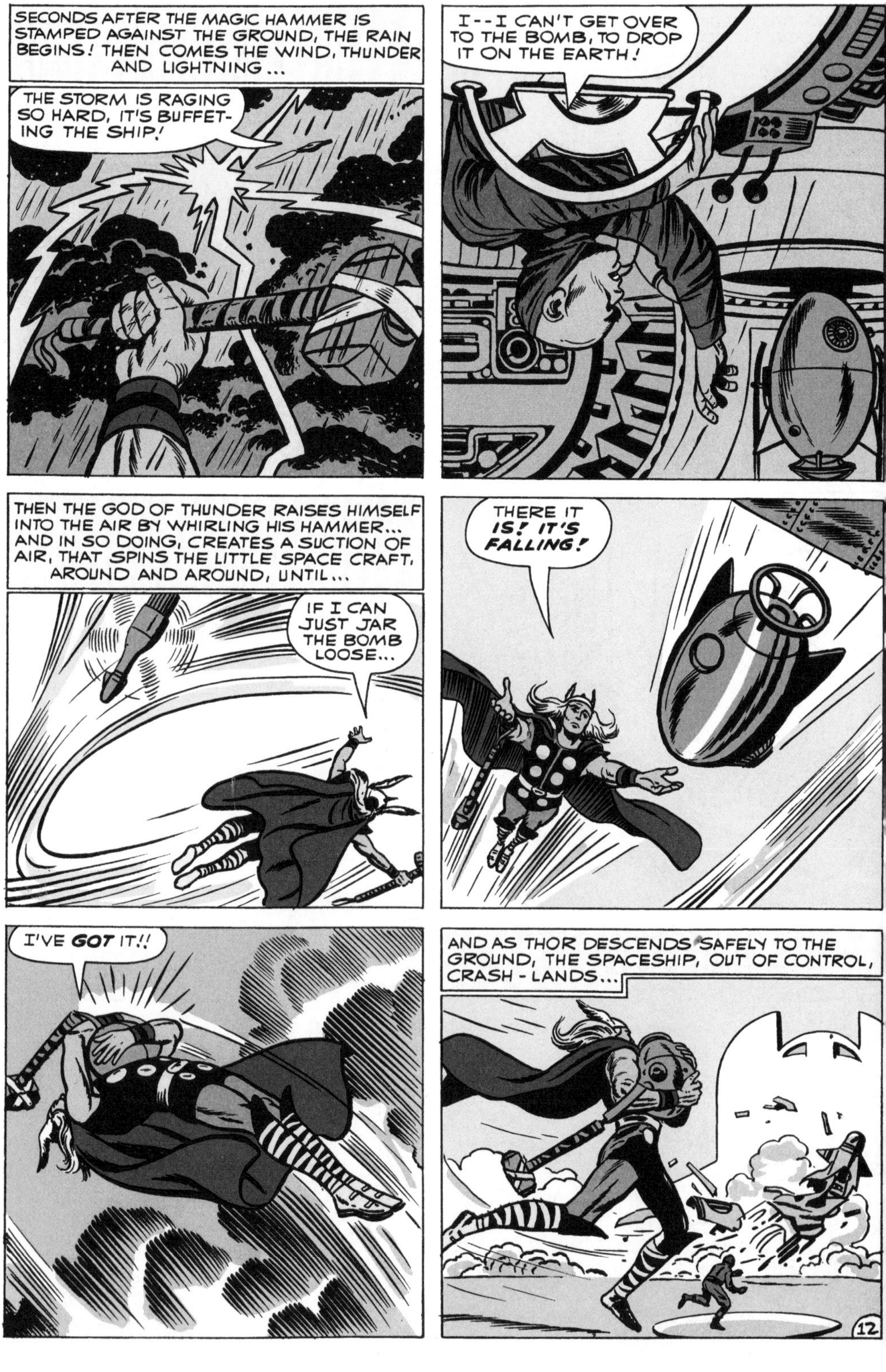
SECONDS AFTER THE MAGIC HAMMER IS STAMPED AGAINST THE GROUND, THE RAIN BEGINS! THEN COMES THE WIND, THUNDER AND LIGHTNING...
THE STORM IS RAGING SO HARD, IT'S BUFFETING THE SHIP!
I--I CAN'T GET OVER TO THE BOMB, TO DROP IT ON THE EARTH!
THEN THE GOD OF THUNDER RAISES HIMSELF INTO THE AIR BY WHIRLING HIS HAMMER... AND IN SO DOING, CREATES A SUCTION OF AIR, THAT SPINS THE LITTLE SPACE CRAFT, AROUND AND AROUND, UNTIL...
IF I CAN JUST JAR THE BOMB LOOSE...
THERE IT IS! IT'S FALLING!
I'VE GOT IT!!
AND AS THOR DESCENDS SAFELY TO THE GROUND, THE SPACESHIP, OUT OF CONTROL, CRASH-LANDS...
12

AND, THOUGH ZARRKO EMERGES FROM THE WRECKAGE STILL ALIVE...

WHO -- WHO AM I ?? WHAT AM I DOING HERE...??

WE'LL BE ABLE TO CURE HIS PHYSICAL INJURIES!

BUT HIS MEMORY WILL NEVER RETURN!

YOU DEFEATED A TYRANT! AND YOU SAVED OUR WORLD FROM DESTRUCTION!

WE SHALL BE FOREVER GRATEFUL!

LONG LIVE THE MIGHTY THOR!

NOW I MUST RETURN THE C-BOMB TO MY OWN TIME!

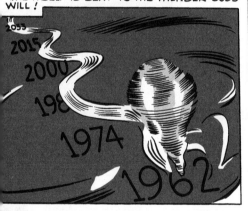

ONCE AGAIN THOR WHIRLS HIS LEGENDARY HAMMER AT UNIMAGINABLE SPEED, AS TIME ITSELF IS BENT TO THE THUNDER-GOD'S WILL!

2055
2015
2000
198
1974
1962

SOON THE YEAR IS 1962 AND THE PLACE IS THE NEW MEXICAN DESERT...

YOU HAVE YOUR BOMB BACK! LET US MENTION IT NO MORE! YOU WOULD NEVER BELIEVE MY TALE!

MAYBE NOT! BUT WE'D STILL LIKE TO KNOW WHERE IT WAS -- AND HOW YOU BROUGHT IT BACK!

FORGET IT, BOB! WE'VE GOT SOME WEAPONS TESTS TO PERFORM NOW!

A SHORT TIME LATER, AFTER THOR HAS TURNED BACK TO THE QUIET DR. DON BLAKE...

ANYTHING HAPPEN WHILE I WAS GONE, JANE?

ARE YOU KIDDING, DOCTOR? DON'T YOU READ THE PAPERS?!

THOR RESCUES C-BOMB
SURVIVES EXPLOSION

NO, JANE! NOTHING IN THE PAPERS INTERESTS ME... IT'S ALL TOO NERVE-WRACKING!

OH, IF ONLY I COULD WORK FOR THOR -- INSTEAD OF COLORLESS DR. BLAKE!

PRIV

I WONDER IF JANE WILL EVER SUSPECT THAT SOME OF US READ ABOUT THE NEWS...

...WHILE SOME OF US ARE TOO BUSY MAKING IT!

THE END

13

CHARACTER DESIGNS BY CHRIS SAMNEE

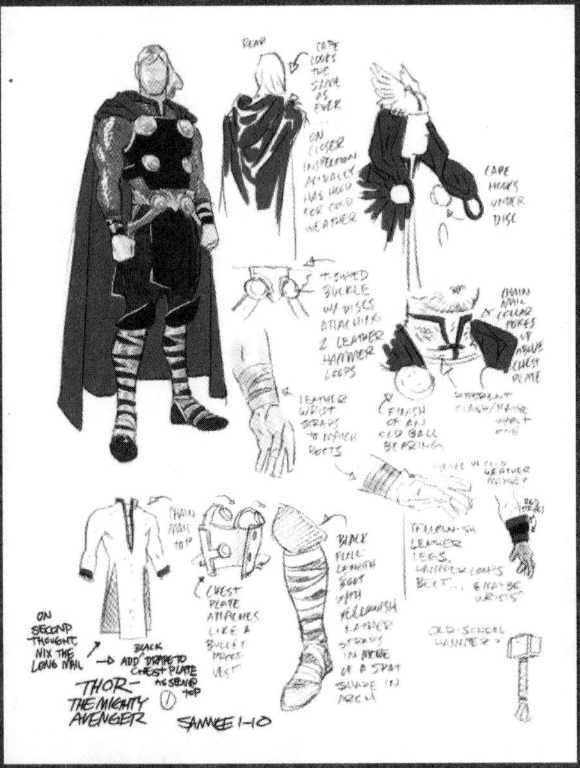
REAR
CAPE LOOKS THE SAME AS EVER ... ON CLOSER INSPECTION ACTUALLY HAS HOOD FOR COLD WEATHER
CAPE HOOKS UNDER DISC
T-SHAPED BUCKLE W/ DISCS ATTACHING 2 LEATHER HAMMER LOOPS
CHAIN MAIL COLLAR POKES UP ABOVE CHEST PLATE
LEATHER WRIST STRAPS TO MATCH BOOTS
FINISH OF AN OLD BALL BEARING
CHAIN MAIL TOP
CHEST PLATE ATTACHES LIKE A BULLET PROOF VEST
BLACK FULL LENGTH BOOT WITH YELLOWISH LEATHER STRAPS IN MORE OF A SPAT SHAPE IN ARCH
YELLOWISH LEATHER LEGS, HAMMER LOOPS BELT... & MAYBE WRISTS
OLD-SCHOOL HAMMER?
ON SECOND THOUGHT, NIX THE LONG MAIL
ADD BLACK DRAPE TO CHEST PLATE AS SEEN @ TOP
THOR- THE MIGHTY AVENGER
1
SAMNEE 1-10

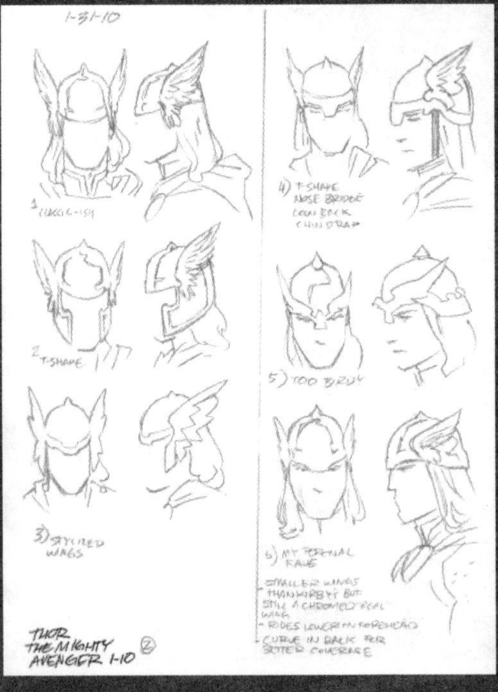
1-31-10
4) T-SHAPE NOSE BRIDGE LOW BACK CHIN STRAP
2 T-SHAPE
5) TOO BIRDY
3) STYLIZED WINGS
- RIDES LOWER ON FOREHEAD
- CURVE IN BACK FOR BETTER COVERAGE
THOR THE MIGHTY AVENGER 1-10
2

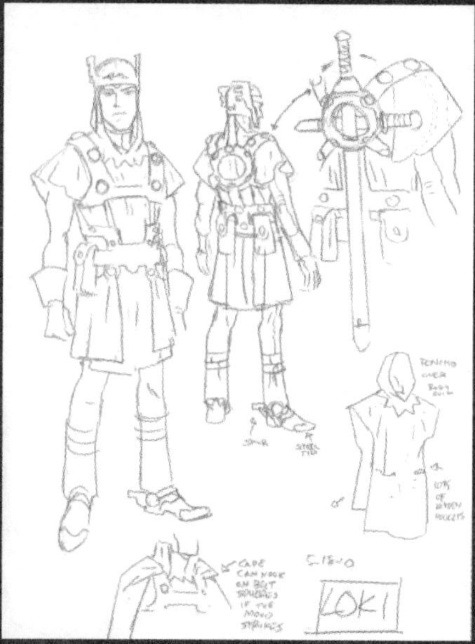
LOKI

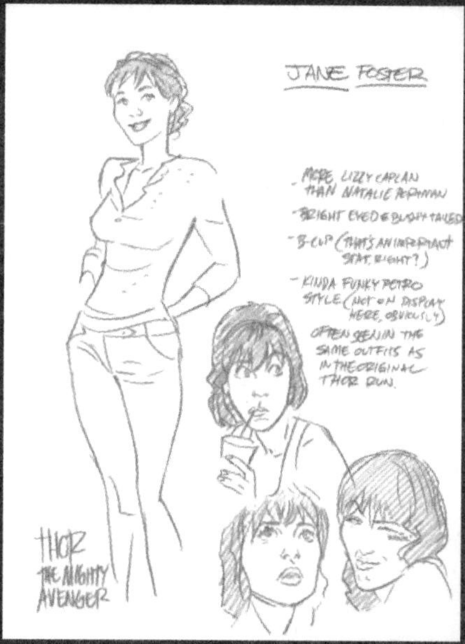
JANE FOSTER
- MORE LIZZY CAPLAN THAN NATALIE PORTMAN
- BRIGHT EYED & BUSHY TAILED
- B-CUP (THAT'S AN IMPORTANT STAT, RIGHT?)
- KINDA FUNKY PETRO STYLE (NOT ON DISPLAY HERE, OBVIOUSLY)
OFTEN SEEN IN THE SAME OUTFITS AS IN THE ORIGINAL THOR RUN.
THOR THE MIGHTY AVENGER

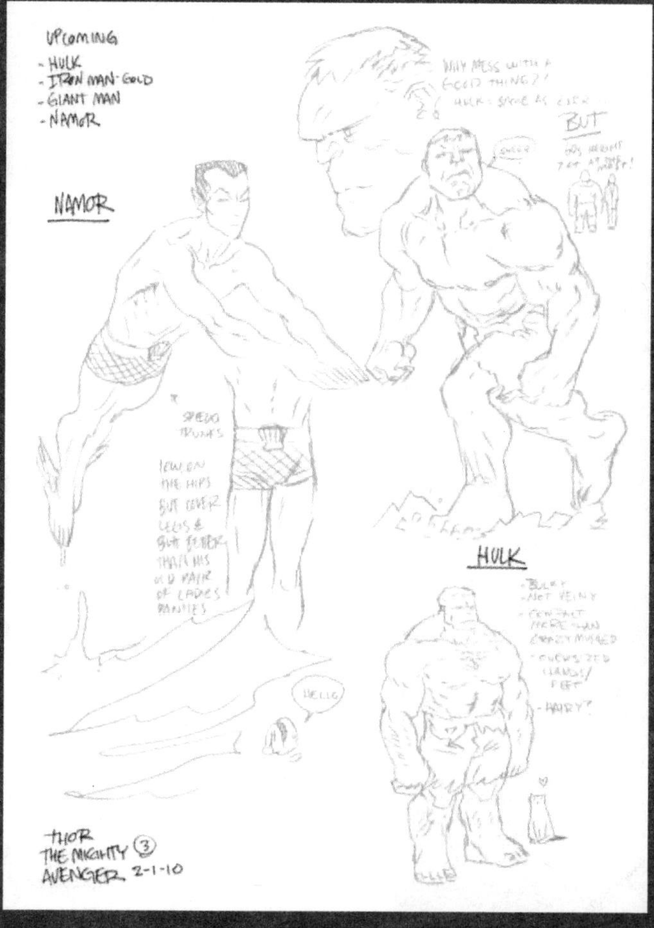
UPCOMING
- HULK
- IRON MAN - GOLD
- GIANT MAN
- NAMOR
NAMOR
WHY MESS WITH A GOOD THING?!
BUT
HELLO
HULK
- BULKY
- NOT VEINY
- HAIRY?
THOR THE MIGHTY 3 AVENGER 2-1-10

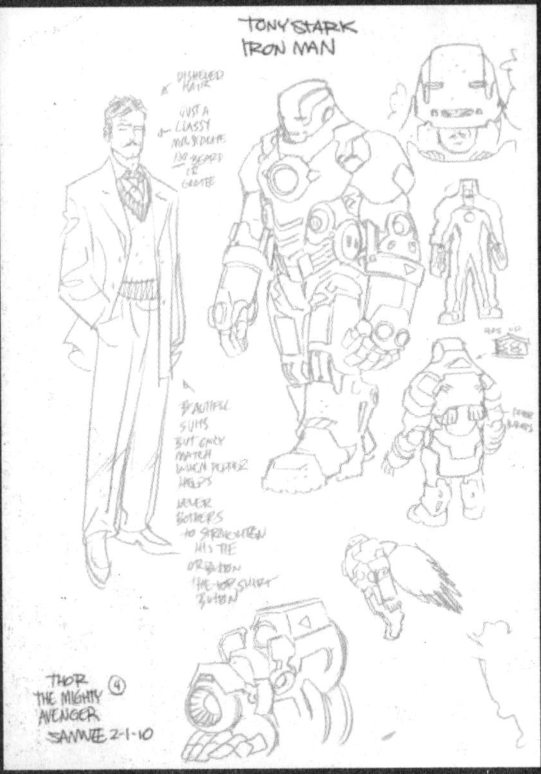
TONY STARK
IRON MAN
DISHEVELED HAIR
JUST A CLASSY
BEAUTIFUL SUITS BUT ONLY MATCH WHEN PEPPER HELPS
NEVER BOTHERS TO STRAIGHTEN HIS TIE
THOR THE MIGHTY AVENGER
4
SAMNEE 2-1-10

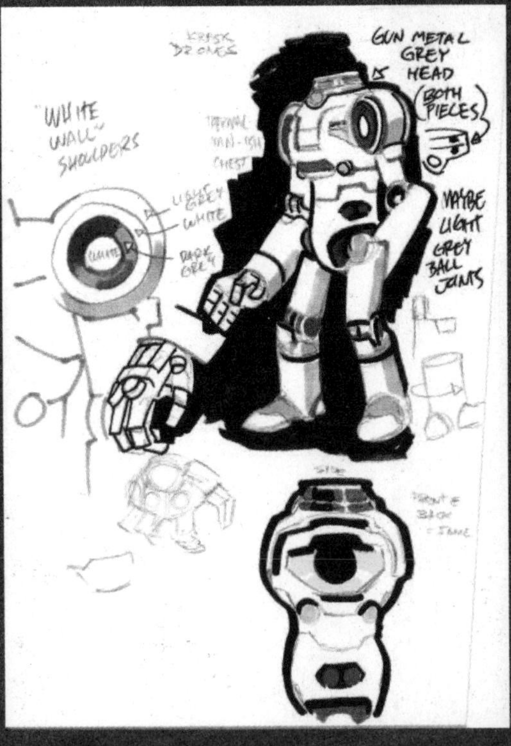
GUN METAL GREY HEAD
(BOTH PIECES)
"WHITE WALL" SHOULDERS
LIGHT GREY
WHITE
WHITE
DARK GREY
MAYBE LIGHT GREY BALL JOINTS